LAZARUS

He tried to cry out, to protest that they were making a travesty of a most important encyclical, but the only sound he could utter was Mu . . . Mu . . . until, for very shame, he fell silent, closed his eyes and waited for the verdict. Out of the darkness a voice commanded him: 'Open your eyes and read!'

When he obeyed he found himself a boy again, in a dusty classroom, staring at a blackboard upon which was written the word which had eluded him for so long, μετάνσια. A great sense of relief flooded through him. He cried out: 'You see, that's what I was trying to say – Metanoia, repentance, a change of heart, a new direction.' But no one answered. The room was empty. He was alone.

Then the door opened and he froze in terror at the vision that confronted him: an old, eagle-beaked man, with furrows of anger about his mouth and eyes black as volcanic glass. As the man moved towards him, silent and threatening, he screamed, but the sound would not come. It was as if a noose were knotted around his neck, cutting off air and life . . .

Morris West is the author of some twenty-odd bestselling novels. Among the best known are *The Devil's Advocate* and his Papal trilogy, *The Shoes of the Fisherman*, *The Clowns of God* and *Lazarus*. He has worked and travelled all over the world and now lives in Australia where he was born.

*Also by Morris West
and available in Mandarin*

The Ambassador
The Big Story
Children of the Sun
Daughter of Silence
Harlequin
McCreary Moves In
The Naked Country
The Navigator
Proteus
The Ringmaster
The Salamander
The Second Victory
The Shoes of the Fisherman
Summer of the Red Wolf
The Tower of Babel

MORRIS WEST

Lazarus

Mandarin

A Mandarin Paperback
LAZARUS

First published in Great Britain 1990
by William Heinemann Ltd
This Mandarin edition first published 1991
Reissued 1995
by Mandarin Paperbacks
an imprint of Reed International Books Ltd
Michelin House, 81 Fulham Road, London SW3 6RB
and Auckland, Melbourne, Singapore and Toronto

Copyright © Melaleuka Investments Pty Ltd 1990

A CIP catalogue record for this title
is available from the British Library
ISBN 0 7493 0495 2

Printed and bound in Great Britain
by Cox & Wyman Ltd, Reading, Berkshire

For Joy with love,
the best of the summer wine

'I've always wondered about Lazarus.
He had walked through the gates of death.
He had seen what was on the other side.
Did he want to return to life?
Did he thank Jesus for bringing him back?
What kind of man was he afterwards?
How did the world look to him?
How did he look to the world?'

Leo XIV Pont. Max.
Conversations

Book 1

Lazarus Aegrotus

'There was a man called Lazarus
of Bethany, who had fallen sick . . .
When Jesus arrived, he found Lazarus
had been four days in the grave.'

John xi: 1, 17

One

He was a high man and a hard one. His great beak and his jutting jaw and his dark obsidian eyes gave him the look of an old eagle, imperious and hostile. Yet, faced with the evidence of his own mortality, he felt, suddenly, small and ridiculous.

The surgeon, his junior by a quarter of a century, stood beside the desk, drew a sketch on a sheet of crested notepaper and explained it briskly.

'These are the two arteries on the left side of your heart. They are almost blocked with plaque, which is, in effect, the detritus from your blood stream. It builds up on the walls of the arteries, like scale on a water-pipe. The angiogram which we did yesterday shows that you have about five per cent of normal blood flow on the left side. That's the reason for the chest pains, the shortness of breath, the drowsiness and fatigue you have experienced lately. The next thing that will happen is this . . .' He sketched a dark globule with an arrow indicating the direction of its flow. 'A small blood clot travels along the artery. It lodges here, in the narrowed section. The artery is blocked. You have the classic heart attack. You die.'

'And the risk of that happening . . . ?'

'It's not a risk. It's an inevitable event. It can happen any day. Any night. Even now as we talk.' He gave a small, humourless laugh. 'To the pilgrims in St Peter's Square, you're Leo XIV, Vicar of Christ, Supreme Pontiff. To me, you're a walking time-bomb. The sooner I can defuse you, the better.'

5

'Are you sure you can?'

'At a purely clinical level, yes. We do a double bypass, replacing the blocked arteries with a vein taken from your leg. It's a simple plumbing job – the success rate is better than ninety per cent.'

'And how much life does that give me?'

'Five years. Ten. More perhaps. It depends on how you behave yourself after the operation.'

'And what precisely does that mean?' His Holiness was notoriously short-tempered. The surgeon remained calm and good-humoured.

'It means you've been damaging your body for years. You're at least fifteen kilos overweight. You eat enough for a peasant farmer. You've got gout. Your blood uric acid is abnormally high, but you still drink red wine and eat spices and high-purin foods. The only exercise you get is when you pace up and down reading your breviary. The rest of your life is spent at this desk or ambling through long rituals in clouds of incense, or being whisked around in automobiles and aircraft . . . Unless you make drastic changes in your lifestyle, all my skill will be wasted. *Osservatore Romano* will record that you died in the odour of sanctity. In fact, you'll have died of self-abuse.'

'You're impertinent, doctor!'

'I'm telling you a necessary truth. Unless you heed me, you'll be carried out of here in a box.'

There was a sudden anger in the hooded eyes. He looked like a predator ready to strike. Then, as swiftly as it had come, the anger died. His eyes became dull, his voice weary and querulous.

'You said a moment ago, "At a purely clinical level it's a simple plumbing job . . ." Does that imply certain reservations?'

'Reservations, no. Caveats, counsels for the patient, yes.'

'Will you explain them to me, please?'

'Very well. The risk factor first. I put it at ten per cent. I

6

hold to that. The nature of the risk? Sudden collapse, a stroke, a pericardial infection. It's like driving a car or stepping into an aircraft. You accept it and forget it. In your case, I imagine, you leave it to God to dispose the outcome.'

'Not quite.' A ghost of a smile twitched at the corners of the grim mouth. 'I have to leave certain directives. The first is that, if a collapse occurs, you terminate the procedure and let me die. The second is that if I am brain-damaged, I be not placed on any life-support system. Neither you nor I are obliged to the officious prolongation of a vegetable life. You will receive this directive in writing over my signature and seal. What next?'

'The sequelae – the consequences, short and long term, of the surgical procedures. It is very important that you understand them, think about them, talk about them freely. You must not – and I cannot emphasise this too strongly – try to cope with them by repression, by converting them into some kind of mystical, expiatory experience: a dark night of the soul, a stigma of the spirit . . .' He shrugged and grinned disarmingly. 'Somehow I don't think you're the kind of man who would do that. You might, on the other hand, be tempted to bear them in proud, dignified silence. That would be a grave mistake.'

The old man's answer was barbed.

'You have not yet told me what I am expected to bear.'

'I am not talking about pain. That is a controllable factor. You will be unconscious for at least forty-eight hours, perfused with potent anaesthetics. You will continue to be fed opiates and analgesics until the discomforts are within tolerable limits. However, you will suffer something else: a psychic trauma, a personality change whose dimensions still elude full explanation. You will be emotionally fragile – as prone to tears as to rage. You will be subject to depressions, sudden, black and sometimes suicidal. At one moment you will be as dependent as a child, seeking reassurance after a nightmare. The next

7

you will be angry and frustrated by your own impotence. Your short-term memory may be defective. Your tolerance of emotional stress will be greatly reduced. You will be strongly advised by the counsellors who will be working with you not to make any important decisions, emotional, intellectual or administrative, for at least three months . . . Most of these sequelae will pass. Some will remain, diminished but always present in your psychic life. The better your physical condition, the less will be your emotional handicap. So, after the first period of convalescence, you will be put on a rigid diet to lose fifteen or twenty kilograms. You will be required to do daily exercise on a graduated scale. And if you fail to do either of those things your psychic handicap will continue and your physical condition will deteriorate rapidly. In short, the whole exercise will be a painful futility. I'm sorry to make such a huge mouthful of this, but it is absolutely necessary that you understand it. Believe me, I do not exaggerate.'

'I believe you. I'd be a fool if I didn't.'

The old man seemed suddenly to withdraw into himself. His eyes became dull and expressionless as if a membrane had been drawn over them. The surgeon waited in silence until the words began to flow again.

'You raise, of course, the ultimate question: whether I shall be competent to resume the duties of my office.'

'True. And you will not be the only one to ask it. Your brethren in the Sacred College will have access to the same clinical information as I have just given you.'

For the first time, the grim mouth relaxed into a smile of genuine humour. The dull eyes lit up and the Vicar of Christ pronounced a private heresy.

'God is a practical joker, my friend. I've always known it.'

The surgeon waited for an explanation of the proposition. None came. Instead, the Pontiff asked: 'How long can I wait before the operation?'

'No time at all. I want you delivered to my clinic before midday tomorrow.'

'Why your clinic? Why not Gemelli or Salvator Mundi?'

'Because I work only with my own team in conditions I can guarantee. I control the post-operative and convalescent procedures. Your physician will tell you I'm the best in Italy. But once you put yourself in my care there's a contract in force. You do as you're told, or I wash my hands of you.'

'Before I commit to such a contract I'd like a second opinion.'

'You already have a second, and a third. Morrison from London, Haefliger from New York. Both have seen computer-enhanced images of the X-rays. They agree with my diagnosis and the surgical procedures. Morrison will fly in from London to assist at the operation.'

'And who, pray, authorised that little *démarche*?'

The surgeon shrugged and smiled.

'The Dean of the College of Cardinals. Your brother bishops thought they needed an insurance policy.'

'I don't doubt it!' The Pontiff gave a short, barking laugh. 'Some of them would be happy to see me dead; but they daren't risk losing another pontiff under suspicious circumstances!'

'Which brings me to my last counsel. I wish I could make it an order, but I cannot . . . Do not spend your convalescence at the Vatican or even at Castel Gandolfo. Take a month, at least, to be a private person. Lodge with friends or family; communicate only with your closest executives in Rome. Summer is coming. You will not be missed too much – believe me. All the faithful need to know is that you're alive and in office. One brief appearance and two communiqués should do the trick.'

'You presume, young man! This is my home. My household is the only family I have. Why should I not recuperate here?'

'Two reasons: first, the air in Rome is polluted beyond

belief. It will exacerbate any respiratory problems you may have after the surgery. The second is the more important: your own house, like it or not, will also be your battleground. Your competence will be on trial every day. Your every weakness will be gossiped abroad. You will know that. You will expect it. You will put yourself in a combat stance to defend yourself. Result? Stress, hypertension, anxiety; all the things we try to avoid after cardiac surgery. If that is presumption, I beg your pardon. Your Holiness has a reputation for obstinacy and brusqueness. My prime duty under the Hippocratic oath is to keep you from harm – *primum non nocere*. So I would rather be presumptuous than delinquent. But the decision is yours. Do we have a contract?'

'We do.'

'Good. I shall expect you at midday tomorrow. You will have a day and a half of preparation and premedication. You will meet and talk with the principal members of the team. We will operate on Wednesday morning at seven o'clock . . . Trust me, Holiness! Today you're in the shadow of death. A week from now you'll be like Lazarus walking out of the tomb and blinking in the sunlight.'

'I've always wondered about Lazarus.' The old man leaned back in his chair and smiled sardonically at the surgeon. 'He had walked through the gates of death. He had seen what was on the other side. Did he want to return to life? Did he thank Jesus for bringing him back? What kind of a man was he afterwards? How did the world look to him? How did he look to the world?'

'Maybe,' – the surgeon smiled and spread his hands in deprecation – 'maybe that should be Your Holiness's first discourse after his recovery!'

The brief dialogue had shocked him to the core of his being. Suddenly he was bereft of everything that had sustained him: *magisterium, auctoritas, potestas*; the office, the authority, the power to use them both. He was a man under sentence of death. Even the instrument of execution was specified: a small plug of clotted blood, sealing off the life-flow to his heart. Reprieve was offered; but he had to take it from the hands of an arrogant fellow, on his own confession a mere plumber, who presumed to lecture the Vicar of Christ because he was too fat, too self-indulgent and ate like a peasant farmer.

Why should he be ashamed? He *was* a peasant, born Ludovico Gadda, only child of share-croppers from the out-skirts of Mirandola, an antique principality near Ferrara. At twelve years old he was spending his mornings at school, his afternoons doing a man's work, herding the cattle and the goats, digging the vegetable plots, raking and piling the dung that would be used for fertiliser. One day his father dropped dead behind his plough. His mother sold out his share-cropper's rights, took service as housekeeper to a local landowner and set about educating her son to a better life.

Already his mathematics were sound and he could read any book that came his way, because Mama, who had once hoped to be a teacher, had sat with him by lamplight in the long, dark country winters and drummed into him the education she had never been able to use. Knowledge, she insisted, was the key to freedom and prosperity. Ignorance was a slave's brand on the forehead. She sent him first to the Salesians, old-fashioned pedagogues, who terrified him out of his pubescent lusts with tales of hell-fire and horrible plagues visited on the promiscuous. They crammed him with Latin and Greek and mathematics, a whole dictionary of dogmatic definitions and moral precepts, not to mention twenty centuries of the expurgated history of The Church Triumphal. They also inserted, like a bead in an oyster, the notion of 'vocation' – a special call to a special soul to a special life of service to God. From such a forcing-house of piety it was a short and easy step to the seminary as a candidate for the priesthood in the Archdiocese of Ferrara.

After the harsh country life to which he had been bred, the disciplines of the urban seminary and of the scholastic life were no burden at all. He was accustomed to a rhythmic existence. He was well fed, warmly clothed. His mother was protected and content. She made no secret of the fact that she much preferred the security of a son in the cloth to a gaggle of grandchildren in another woman's kitchen. Ambition made Ludovico a good scholar. He learned early that for a man who aspired to eminence in the Church the best qualifications were an orthodox theology, a solid grasp of canon law and an instant acceptance of every directive of authority – wise, foolish or merely expedient . . .

All the reports on him said the same thing. He was good clerical material. He was not profoundly spiritual, but he had, as his rector put it, '*animam naturaliter rectam*', a spirit of natural rectitude.

What he had practised in his own youth he rewarded in others as he rose from curate to monsignor, to suffragan bishop, to Secretary of the Congregation for the Doctrine of the Faith, first under the redoubtable Leone and then under the iron-fisted German Josef Lorenz, who had pushed him slowly but steadily upward until he became a candidate for the Sub-prefecture.

It was the Ukrainian pontiff, Kiril I, who had given him the appointment and the red hat that went with it. Kiril, who in the early years of his reign had been seen as an innovator and passionate reformer, had become latterly a compulsive traveller, totally immersed in his public role as Universal Pastor, rattling the Keys of Peter wherever he was permitted to make a landfall. But while he travelled, the cabals of the Curia took control of the administration of the Church, and its interior life, its involvement in the new dilemmas of human experience, languished for want of courageous interpreters.

Whenever the question of his successor arose, Ludovico

Gadda was counted among the *papabili* – a possible candidate for election. However, when Kiril died, on a flight from Rome to Buenos Aires, the man elected to succeed him was a Frenchman, Jean Marie Barette, who took the name of Gregory XVII.

This Gregory was a liberaliser, who saw little merit in the rigorist policies of surveillance, censorship and enforced silence which Cardinal Gadda had reinstituted at the Congregation for the Doctrine of the Faith. So he moved him sideways to be Prefect of the Congregation for the Bishops, knowing that the bishops were all grown-up fellows and perfectly able to take care of themselves.

But Ludovico Gadda, always the obedient servant of the system, performed ably and discreetly and managed to make a large number of friends in the most senior ranks of the episcopate. So, in that strange portentous time when Gregory XVII claimed to have had a private revelation of the Second Coming and to have received a call to preach it as one of the most ancient and enduring doctrines of Christianity, Gadda was able to procure his abdication by threat of a collegial vote to depose him on the grounds of mental incompetence.

He stage-managed the whole affair so adroitly that, in the hastily summoned conclave which followed, Cardinal Ludovico Gadda was elected Pope on the first ballot and took the name of Leo XIV. With so swift and massive a mandate, there was nothing now to restrain him. Within six weeks he had published his first encyclical, 'Obedient unto death . . .', a chill admonition to discipline, conformity, unquestioning submission to the dictates of papal authority within the Church.

The Press and a large section of the clergy and laity were stunned by its reactionary tone, its echoes of ancient thunders, its smell of old bonfires. The general inclination was to ignore it; but that was much harder than it sounded. Leo XIV had spent a lifetime learning how the machinery of the

Church worked and he manipulated every thread and cog like a thumbscrew to bring pressure on the recalcitrant, clergy and laity alike.

Like every bold general, he had calculated his losses in advance and, though to many they seemed appalling, he was ready to justify them by the end result: fewer clergy, smaller congregations, but all of them fired with redemptive and reforming zeal.

It was the post-Tridentine illusion. Rally the zealots, stiffen the waverers, purge out the objectors with bell, book and candle; in the end, the elect, aided by the Grace of God, would convert the backsliders by prayer and example. Instead, more and more decent folk carried on their decent lives in a silent schism of indifference to this hard-nosed pragmatist, who still believed that he could rule by fiat the consciences of a billion souls scattered across the spinning planet.

But Ludovico Gadda, the peasant from Mirandola, ran true to form. He had always believed that if you did right you were right – and if you did wrong in good conscience, it was up to God to take care of the consequences.

Now, at one stroke, he was robbed of these comforting certainties. He could die with the work unfinished. He could survive yet be in no condition to complete it.

To the devil with such melancholy thoughts! God would dispose matters in His own time and fashion. His servant would not, could not, sit here brooding. There was work to be done. Work and prayer were a single act. He had always sought solace in action, rather than in contemplation. He pressed the buzzer to summon his secretary and have him assemble the members of the Curia at five sharp in the Borgia chamber.

His allocution to the Curial Cardinals was almost good-humoured, but never less than precise.

'The Sala Stampa will be responsible for the announcement to the world press. The statement will be accurate in all particulars. The Pontiff is suffering from heart disease, a bypass operation is indicated. It will be undertaken at the International Clinic of Professor Sergio Salviati. The operation has a high statistical success rate. The prognosis is positive. The Pontiff will be grateful for the prayers of the faithful – even the prayers of his brethren in this assembly.

'Medical bulletins will be prepared at the clinic and sent by fax to the Sala Stampa for distribution. Our attitude to the press will be cordial and informative. Questions about negative possibilities will be answered frankly, with the assistance of the clinic.

'One question which will inevitably be raised – and which I am sure is in all your minds even as I speak – is whether or not I shall be competent, physically or mentally, to serve out the term of my pontificate. It is too early to judge that; but three months from now we should all know the truth. I wish only to affirm to you, as I have already done in writing to the Dean of the Sacred College, that, since we are now an embattled Church, I am the last man in the world who would wish her to be led by an incompetent general. My abdication is already written. I suggest only that it may be untimely and embarrassing to publish it at the moment.'

They laughed at that and gave him a round of applause. The tension that had been building all day was suddenly released. It seemed their country brother was not so stubborn after all. His next words cautioned them not to expect too easy a surrender of the Papal Seal.

'The surgeon recommends strongly that I absent myself from affairs of state and public ceremonial for about three months. Common sense dictates that I follow his advice and rusticate for a while away from either the Vatican or Castel Gandolfo . . . I have not yet decided where to go, or even whether to take so long a leave, but for however long or short a time I am absent, I am still the Pontiff, and I charge you all to pursue diligently the policies I have already determined with

15

you. There will be ample opportunity – no, daily necessity – for the exercise of your collegial discretion and authority, but the Chair of Peter is not vacant until I am dead or I have consented with you, my brethren, to step down from it . . . I reserve to myself the right to reverse any decisions made in my absence which do not conform to the policies we have laboured so hard to devise.'

There was an uneasy silence, broken at last by Cardinal Drexel, Dean of the Sacred College, eighty years old but still bright of eye and vigorous in argument.

'A point must be made here, Holiness. I make it because the rules disqualify a man of my age from voting in any future Papal election. Your Holiness reserves his right to reverse any decisions made by any member of the Curia, or by the Curia acting in concert, during his absence. None of us, I believe, has any problem with that. But the members of the Electoral College must equally reserve their right to decide upon Your Holiness's competence to continue in office. It would seem that the criteria applied to the abdication of His Holiness Gregory XVII might be mutually agreed, here and now, as guidelines. It was, after all, Your Holiness who drafted them as head of the Congregation for Bishops.'

There was a longer silence this time. Leo XIV sat hunched in his chair, staring at some point of focus in the centre of the floor.

Drexel was the last man in the world on whom he could vent his anger. He was too old, too wise, too versed in the subtleties of the canons. It was Drexel who had persuaded Jean Marie Barette to abdicate without a struggle or a scandal, and who still maintained contact with him in his secret existence abroad. It was Drexel who had censured so bluntly his own bid for election and yet, when it succeeded, had kissed hands and served as he had always done, asking no favours, condoning none of the mistakes of his new master. Drexel made no secret of his grief and anger at the new rigorism of Church government. Like Paul of old, he withstood the Pontiff to his face, claiming that he had already lapsed into gnostic error by trying to make a Kingdom of the Pure out of the tatterdemalion assembly of the errant children of God.

He stiffened the courage of other Papal Counsellors and was quite open in his intention to create a body of opposition opinion within the Curia – 'because,' as he put it bluntly to the Pontiff, 'Your Holiness acts sometimes like a country mule and we cannot truly tolerate that in this day and age.'

But, however bitterly he fought, he kept the battle private, as he had done in the case of Jean Marie Barette. More than most in Rome, he understood how ominous were the statistics of defection and he would not by word or gesture widen the gap between Pontiff and people. So finally, Leo the Bishop answered his brother bishop.

'As I remember, I produced a draft of the norms, which were then amended and agreed by the Sacred College before being submitted to the reigning Pontiff, who consented to their application even in his own case . . . So, there is no question, I too will submit myself to the same norms, if and when it is necessary to invoke them. Now, may we deal with other essential details . . .'

The details were legion: communications, security, protocols with the Republic of Italy while the Pope was resident outside Vatican territory, a schedule of those permitted access to the clinic while he was in intensive care and at each successive stage of convalescence . . .

Finally it was done. Then, to the surprise of the whole assembly, the Pontiff made the first apology they had ever heard from his lips.

'I had hoped to say Mass with you tonight. I cannot. I find that I am at the end of my strength. However, I cannot go without asking you all to hear my confession and to offer me your common absolution. I do not repent of what I have done in this office. I must repent of what I am – stubborn, blind, arrogant, swift to anger, slow to forgive. Touched by the corruption of power? Yes. A coward? That too, because I am very much afraid of what awaits me once I leave here. I lack compassion, because ever since I was a child I have been driven to thrust myself as far away as possible from the miseries of the human condition. And yet I cannot abjure what I believe, that a simple childlike obedience to the lessons of Our Lord and Saviour, as interpreted by the Holy See, is the only true road to salvation. If I err in this, believe me it is not for lack of goodwill, but from lack of light and understanding. So, in the presence of you all, I confess and repent and I ask our brother Drexel to absolve me in the name of God and of you all.'

He thrust himself awkwardly out of the great carved chair and knelt before them. Drexel approached and gave him the ritual absolution: *'Deinde ego te absolvo a peccatis tuis in nomine Patris et Filii et Spiritus Sancti . . .'*

'And for penance?' asked Leo the Pontiff.

'From us, none. You will have pain enough. We wish you the courage to endure it.' Drexel held out a hand to raise him to his feet and, in the midst of a winter silence, led him from the room.

As the Curial Cardinals dispersed in the glow of a Roman evening, MacAndrew, the Scotsman from Propaganda Fide, strolled out with Agostini, from the Secretariat of State. Together they provided an almost perfect metaphor for the nature of the Church. MacAndrew's Congregation was charged with the evangelisation of the nations, the propagation of the ancient faith among the unbelievers and the maintenance of missionary foundations. Agostini's job was to create and maintain the political relations that made such efforts possible.

MacAndrew said, in his dry, humorous fashion, 'Well now, that's something we haven't seen since seminary days! Public confession, with the Rector on his knees to the community. What did you make of it?'

Agostini, always the diplomat, shrugged eloquently and quoted from the Dies Irae: '*Timor mortis conturbat me!* He's scared. It's natural. He knows he can die under the knife. He knows he will die if he doesn't risk the operation.'

'I got the impression,'said MacAndrew deliberately, 'that he was casting up his accounts and finding a shortfall.'

'We all know there's a shortfall.' Agostini's tone was sombre. 'You at Propaganda Fide are in a position to know how catastrophic it is. Congregations are getting smaller, we're getting fewer candidates for the priesthood, the missions and religious life: the places where the faith is strongest seem to be those furthest from our jurisdiction or our influence! Maybe our lord and master is beginning to see that he is responsible for at least part of the mess.'

'We're all responsible.' MacAndrew was emphatic about it. 'You, me, the whole gilded gang of us. We're the Cardinals, the hinge men of the organisation. We're also bishops, vested in our own right with Apostolic authority. Yet look at us there today. Look at us any day! We're like feudal barons with their liege lord. Worse still, sometimes I think we're like a bunch of court eunuchs. We accept the pallium and the red hat and thereafter we take everything he hands out as if it were the voice of God from the holy of holies. We watch him trying to order back the waves of millennial events, silence by fiat the murmurs of troubled mankind. We listen to him preaching about sex as if he's spent his youth with the Manichees, like Augustine, and can't get the dirty notions out of his head. We know how he's silenced theologians and philosophers who are trying to make Christian redemption intelligible in our tooth and claw universe. But how many of us are prepared to tell him he just might be wrong, or needs new spectacles, or is looking at God's truth in a distorting mirror?'

'Would he listen if we did?'

'Probably not – but he'd have to treat with us as a body. All he has to do now is divide and conquer. He trades on that. So each of us has to find a separate way to deal with him. I can count 'em off for you – manipulation, evasion, flattery, the diplomacies of a kitchen cabinet . . . Drexel seems to be the only one ready to stand toe to toe with him and face him down.'

'Perhaps,' suggested Agostini mildly, 'perhaps Drexel has less to lose than the rest of us. He'd like nothing more than to retire completely and rusticate among his vines. Besides, so long as we are in office and in favour with the Pontiff, we can do some good. Out of it, we are impotent.'

'It's a fine piece of casuistry,' said MacAndrew gloomily, 'but it doesn't absolve us from our own delinquencies, does it? I wonder how I'd feel tonight if I were the one looking across the razor's edge to Judgement Day?'

'I'm a diplomat.' Agostini at his best had a small, vinegary humour. 'I am permitted – no, obliged – to heresies which in others are most damnable. I deal not with the perfect but with the possible, the relatively good or the acceptably evil. I'm not asked to provide doctrinal definitions, just pragmatic solutions: what is the best deal we can make between the Uniats and the Orthodox in Russia? How long can we hold our precarious position in Syria? How can I unpick the tangle with the Blue Christians in China? Our master understands that. He keeps the moralists away from my cabbage patch . . . But when you come down to it, he himself is an inquisitor born and bred. You know how close we've come several times to getting another Syllabus of Errors. You ask how you'd feel, or I. I can answer for myself. A mistaken servant perhaps. A time-server perhaps. But at least I'd be myself, without surprises. But Leo XIV is a man split clean down the middle. That confession we just heard. What did it say? My policies are dead right, even though I am as full of faults as a colander is full of holes. He'll be an absolutist to the end. He has to be, else he's nothing.'

'So what do we pray for?' MacAndrew was still in gallows humour. 'His speedy recovery or his happy death?'

'Whatever we pray for, we have to be prepared for what we get: Lazarus returning from the dead, confirmed in the beatific vision, or a corpse that we have to bury and a new candidate we have to find.'

'Who recommended Salviati?'

'Drexel. He gave him the highest praise.'

'Then whether our Lazarus lives or dies, Drexel will have a lot to answer for, won't he?'

Sergio Salviati's International Clinic was a splendid domain of parkland and pinewoods, perched high on the crater lip of Lake Nemi.

From the dawn of history it had been a sacred place, dedicated to Diana the Huntress, whose shrine in the dark woodland was served by a strange custodian called the King of the Woods. The king was a runaway slave, who was guaranteed his freedom provided he slew the custodian and took possession of the shrine. Each year, another assassin came, to attempt the ritual murder. Even Caligula, the crazed emperor, took part in the grisly game and sent one of his own young bondsmen to despatch the reigning king.

Later, much later, the Colonna family took over the place and turned it into a farm and a summer refuge from the foetid heat of Rome. Later they sold it to the Gaetani, who gave it the name it still bore, Villa Diana. During the Second World War the Germans used it as a command post and afterwards the Archbishop of Westminster bought it as a holiday house for the students and faculty of the English College. However, as vocations languished and maintenance costs climbed, it was sold again, this time to a consortium of Milanese and Torinese businessmen who were financing the foundation of a modern cardiology clinic under the direction of Sergio Salviati.

This place was ideal for the purpose. The sixteenth-century villa was refurbished as a residence for senior staff and professional visitors from abroad. The clinic itself, with its outbuildings and its auxiliary generating plant, was sited on the flat space of the original farm, where there was still enough land left to grow vegetables and fruit and provide pleasances and gardens where convalescent patients could take their exercise.

Backed by the biggest corporations in the Republic – Fiat, Pirelli, Montecatini, Italcimento, Snia Viscosa – Sergio Salviati was able to realise his life's ambition: a modern clinic with full training facilities, staffed by international talent, whose graduates were beginning to rejuvenate the archaic and cumbersome Italian hospital system.

At forty-three, Sergio Salviati was already the wonder child of Italian medicine and a peer to the best names in England, Europe and America. As a surgeon, he was passionless, precise and, in a crisis, steady as a rock. As a team leader and administrator, he was open and good-humoured, always ready to listen to a contrary opinion or an imaginative proposal. However, once the protocols were set he would accept neither slackness nor compromise. The International Clinic was run with the precision of an airliner and woe betide any staff member who fumbled an essential routine or failed to deliver smiling support and comfort to a patient.

When the Pontiff arrived, the motorcycle escort provided by the Republic peeled off at the gates of the Villa Diana, where a combined group of Italian Secret Service men and Vatican Vigilanza was already in place. Accompanied only by his valet and a domestic prelate, the Pontiff was greeted in the foyer by the administrator of the clinic and escorted immediately to his room, a bright, airy chamber that looked southward over the undulation of parklands and vineyards and hilltop towns that once had been fortified strongholds.

The valet unpacked his hospital clothing and laid out his breviary and the small Mass kit he had carried since his first day as a curate. The Pontiff signed the admission papers and the permission for the surgical procedures. The prelate handed over an envelope sealed with the papal arms, containing the personal instructions of the patient in the event of an unforeseen collapse or brain death. Then, prelate and valet were dismissed and His Holiness Leo XIV was left alone; a fat, ageing, eagle-beaked fellow in dressing-gown and slippers, waiting nervously for medical staff to attend him.

His first visitor was a woman dressed in hospital style: white coat over a tailored skirt and blouse, with a clipboard and set of notes to round out the image. He judged her to be in her early forties, married – if the wedding band were not a protective device – and, from her precise but academic Italian, probably Scandinavian. She greeted him with a smile and a handshake.

'Welcome to the Villa Diana, Your Holiness. I am Tove Lundberg, director of our counselling group.'

The Pontiff flinched at the familiar greeting, then smiled at the conceit of a young matron counselling the Vicar of Christ about anything. He ventured a small irony.

'And on what do you offer counsel, Signora Lundberg?'

She laughed, openly and happily, then sat down facing him.

'First, on how to adapt yourself to this new ambience. Second, how to cope with the aftermath of the surgery. Each patient has special needs. Each develops a special set of problems. When the problems reveal themselves, my staff and I are here to help.'

'I'm not sure I understand.'

'For instance, a young businessman is stricken with heart disease. He is terrified. He has a wife, young children. He

23

has debts which in normal circumstances he could easily have paid off. Now what? He is threatened at every point – in his finances, in his sex-life, in his self-esteem as a husband and father, his efficiency in the workforce . . . On the other hand, an elderly widow may be obsessed by the fear of becoming a burden to her family, ending up in a refuge for old people. The important thing is that each of these patients be able to talk out the fears and share the problems. That is where my work begins.'

'And you think I may have problems too?' He was still not finished with his joke.

'I am sure you will have. They may take just a little more time to surface but, yes, you will have them. Now, may we begin?'

'Please!'

'First item. The card on your door identifies you simply as Signor Ludovico Gadda.'

'I confess I had not noticed.'

'There is a reason, which I shall try to explain. After the operation, you will be taken first to the intensive care unit, where normally you will spend about forty-eight hours. After that, you will be transferred to a two-bedded room with another patient who is one or two days ahead of you in treatment. We have found that, at this critical stage, the elements of company, of mutual care, are vital. Later, as you begin to walk in the corridors, you will be sharing the experiences of recovery with men and women of all ages and conditions. Titles and honorifics are an impediment to this simple communication. So, we dispense with them. Does that trouble you?'

'Of course not. I was born to common folk. I have not altogether forgotten the language!'

'Next question. Who are your next of kin?'

'Both my father's and my mother's family are extinct. I was an only child. So my family is an adoptive one –

the Church, and specifically the Pontifical Family at the Vatican.'

'Do you have any close friends – what the Italians call friends of the heart?'

'May I ask the reason for the question?' He was suddenly wary and withdrawn. She was swift to calm him.

'Even for so exalted a man as you, there will be moments of deep emotional distress. You will feel, as you have never felt before, the need of companionship, consolation, a hand to hold, a voice of comfort. I should like to know whom to call to your side.'

The simple question underlined how solitary he really was and how much the climb to eminence had cost him. His seminary days had been spent under the old order, when the whole tenor of training was to detach the subject from worldly relationships. His mother's single-minded ambition had worked to the same end. Finally, it was like killing a nerve in a tooth. What was achieved was a permanent anaesthesia against passion and affection. Since he lacked the heart and the words to explain all that to Tove Lundberg, he told her simply: 'There is no one like that. No one at all. The nature of my office precludes it.'

'That's very sad.'

'I have never felt it so.'

'But if you should, I hope you will call me. I am trained in the sharing of grief.'

'I shall remember it. Thank you.' He was not joking now. He felt suddenly less a man than he would have wished to be. Tove Lundberg picked up the thread of her exposition.

'Everything we do here is designed to allay anxieties and help our patients to co-operate as calmly as possible in the healing process. It's not like the old days, when the Senior Surgeon and the Senior Physician stood next door to God and all the patient could do was bow his head and let them practise their magical skills on him . . .'

Once again, he might have embellished the commentary. That was the kind of Church he was trying to recreate: one in which the Supreme Pastor was the true Physician of Souls, the Surgeon-General lopping off diseased members. But Tove Lundberg was already ahead of him.

'Now, everything is explained to you. Your help is sought, because it is a necessary element in the therapy. Look at this . . .'

She handed him what looked like a comic book in which the process of open-heart surgery was described in a series of vivid little cartoons, each with a caption that a child could understand.

'You should read this at your leisure. If you have any questions, the surgeon or I will answer them. The notion of the book we have borrowed from the Americans. The title we invented for ourselves: A *light-hearted guide to heart surgery*. I think you will find it interesting.'

'I'm sure I shall.' He was less than convinced, but he had to be polite. 'What happens to me next?'

'Today and tomorrow, tests: blood samples, urinalysis, electrocardiogram, chest X-rays. At the end of it all you will be purged and then shaved from head to foot.' She laughed. 'You are, I see, a hairy man, so that will be a big job. Finally, you will be sent to sleep with a sedative. Next morning, very early, you will be given premedication and after that you won't know anything until it's all over.'

'It sounds very simple.'

'It is – for us. We've seen it all hundreds of times. We know that the failure rate is very, very low. But for you, for any patient, the waiting is the worst experience, the wondering if you're going to be the one statistical disaster. Of course, for a religious man like yourself it is probably very different. I cannot tell. I am – how do you say it in Italian? – a *miscredente*. Do you not teach that belief is a gift? Well, I am one of those who missed the prize-giving. Still, what one has never had, one does not regret – yes? In this connection, you should know that there is a chaplain service for all creeds. Roman Catholic, Orthodox, Anglican, Waldensian, Jewish and lately, by courtesy of the Egyptian Government, we have an Imam who will visit Muslim patients . . . I've never understood why we make so many quarrels about the same God! I am told that at one time such a diversity of religious service would have been impossible in Rome because the Vatican forbade it. Is that true?'

'Yes.' He himself had grave doubts about religious tolerance in modern society; but he would have blushed to reveal them to this woman.

Fortunately, she did not press the point but simply shrugged.

'Here at least there are no disputes. At the Villa Diana we try to please everyone. If you want the Catholic chaplain, just call your nurse and she'll arrange for him to visit you. If you want to meditate, there's a quiet room near the entrance. It's open to all faiths – very restful, very calm. If you want to say Mass in the morning, you can do it here or use the quiet room. No one will mind.'

'You're very thoughtful, Signora. I shall not bother to call the chaplain – I've already received the Last Rites. But that doesn't mean I'm not afraid. I am. The worst illness I've ever had in my life is gout. I was not prepared for this!'

'Now is the time to count your blessings.' There was a new note of authority in her tone. 'You are a very lucky man. You have millions of people to care about you and pray for you. You have no wife, no children, no dependents of any kind. So you have only to worry about yourself.'

'And the God to whom I must render account of my stewardship.'

'Are you afraid of Him?'

He searched her face for any hint of mockery, but found

none. Yet her question demanded an answer. It took him a few moments to frame it.

'It's not God I'm afraid of; it's what I may have to endure to reach Him.'

She looked at him for a long, silent moment and then admonished him gently.

'Let me reassure you. First, we are very skilful in the relief of pain. We see no point in unnecessary suffering. Second, your case was discussed in detail at the surgeon's conference last night. Everyone agrees the prognosisis excellent. As Dr Salviati put it, you're as tough as an old olive tree. You could last another decade or two!'

'That's comforting to know. And you, too, have a gift of comfort, Signora Lundberg. I'm glad that you came to see me.'

'And you will try to trust us all?'

Once again, he was wary and suspicious.

'Why should you think I would not?'

'Because you are a powerful man accustomed to command others and to control his own destiny. Here you cannot do that. You have to give up control and trust the people who are caring for you.'

'It seems I am already labelled as a difficult patient.'

'You are a very public man. The popular press has never been kind to you.'

'I know.' His smile had little humour in it. 'I'm the scourge of dissidents, the hammer of sinners. The cartoonists make a whole comic opera out of this ugly beak and this nut-cracker jaw!'

'I'm sure you're not half as menacing as they make you out to be.'

'Don't count on it, Signora! The older I get, the uglier I become. The only time I'll look into a mirror is when I'm shaving – so most days I let my valet do that for me.'

At that moment his lunch was delivered: a modest meal

of broth, pasta primavera and fresh fruit. He studied it with distaste. Tove Lundberg laughed and, to his surprise, quoted scripture.

"'Some devils are cast out only by prayer and fasting." Obesity is one of them.'

'I thought you told me you were an unbeliever.'

'I am; but my father was a Lutheran pastor in Aalund. So, I have a big repertoire of Bible quotations. Enjoy your meal. I'll see you tomorrow.'

When she had gone he pushed the food listlessly about the plates, then ate a pear and an apple and abandoned the rest of it. Tove Lundberg had troubled him strangely. All his conditioning – even his mother's obsessive devotion to his celibate career – had been towards alienation from women. As a priest, he had shielded himself from them behind the protective screen of the confessional and the protocols of clerical life. As bishop, he had become accustomed to their homage and he had been grievously shocked and brutally repressive when any strong-minded Mother Superior with modernist tendencies had challenged his edicts or his policies. As Pontiff he had become even more remote: the Congregation for Religious handled conventual affairs, while the Pontiff sedulously refused to open any discussions about the ordination of women or their right to a voice in the senior councils of the Church.

Yet, in less than an hour, Tove Lundberg – self-styled counsellor – had come closer to him than any other woman. She had brought him to the brink of a revelation which, so far, he had confided only to his most private diary:

'An ugly man sees an ugly world because his appearance excites derision and hostility. He cannot escape from the world, any more than he can escape from himself. So, he tries to remake it, to chisel angel-shapes out of the crude rock fused by the hand of the Almighty. By the time he understands that this is a presumption so vast that it is almost a blasphemy, it is too late . . . This is the nightmare which has begun to haunt me. I had been taught, and I had accepted with total conviction, that power – spiritual, temporal and financial – was the necessary instrument to reform the Church, the fulcrum and the lever to set the whole process in motion. I remembered my father's simple wisdom as he worked in his own smithy on the farm: "If I don't pump up the fire and swing the hammer, then the horses are never shod, the ploughshares are never made, the sods are never turned for the planting."

'I planned for power, I intrigued for it, I was patient for it. Finally, I achieved it. I was vigorous as Tubal Cain in his smithy. I pumped up the fire of zeal, I swung the hammer of discipline with a will. I ploughed the fields and planted the seed of the Gospel . . . But the harvests have been meagre. Year after year they have declined towards failure and famine. The people of God do not listen to me any more. My brother bishops wish me gone. I, too, am changed. The springs of hope and charity are drying up within me. I feel it. I know it. I pray for light, but I see none. I am sixty-eight years old. I am the most absolute monarch in the world. I bind and loose on earth and in heaven. Yet I find myself impotent and very close to despair. *Che vita sprecata*! What a waste of life . . .'

Two

The most complete and accurate report of those two days' proceedings in the Vatican was filed by Nicol Peters of the London *Times*. His official source was the press office of the Pontifical Commission for Social Communications. His unofficial informants ranged from Curial Cardinals to second and third-grade officials of the Congregations and junior clerks in the Private Archive.

They trusted him because he had never betrayed a confidence, never distorted a fact, nor stepped over the invisible line that divided the honest critic from the captious headline-hunter. His old mentor, George Faber, Dean of the Press Corps under the Ukrainian Pope Kiril I, had hammered the lessons into his skull: 'It's all summed up in one word, Nicki: *fiducia* – trustworthiness. It's not an Italian virtue, but, by God, they respect it when they see it. Never make a promise you can't keep, never break a promise you've made. This is an old, complicated and sometimes violent society. You don't want a man's death or even damage to his career on your conscience . . . Another thing. Rome is a small town. Scandal spreads like wildfire. The Vatican is a toy kingdom – one square mile of it, that's all – but its powerlines reach into every city on the planet. The report you file today will travel the world – and if it's a crappy piece of work, the crap will finally end back on your doorstep. First you have to make sure that your files are always up to date. The Roman Church has a billion adherents all round the world. You never know, but one day a minor bishop in exile may turn up as a cardinal *in petto!*'

Nicol Peters's files, stored on computer discs behind oak panelling in his study, were as jealously guarded as the Codices in the Vatican Library. They contained biographies of every senior prelate in the world and an updated analysis of each one's influence and importance in the affairs of the Roman Church. He had plotted their public journeys and the tortuous private paths they were following towards eminence or oblivion in the global organisation. His information about the financial affairs of the Vatican was uncomfortably accurate.

His wife Katrina had her own sources. She ran an elegant boutique on the Via Condotti and had a sharp ear for political and ecclesiastical gossip. She entertained constantly in their apartment – the top floor of a sixteenth-century palazzo in old Rome. The guest lists for her dinner parties were among the more exotic in the city. It was she who pointed out to her husband that, although the bulletin on the Pontiff's admission to hospital was unusually frank and optimistic, there was a distinct atmosphere of unease, both inside and outside the walls of Vatican City.

'Everybody's saying the same thing, Nicki. The odds are all in favour of his recovery; but there's grave doubt about how he's going to function afterwards. It's said that he's already consented to abdicate if he comes out handicapped; but everyone says that he'd have to be pushed pretty hard to make him go. Two abdications in a row would cause a hell of a scandal.'

'I doubt it, Kate. The Electoral College is already prepared for a short-notice conclave in case of the Pope's death or incapacity. The ground rules are in place. Gadda wrote them himself when he was a cardinal . . . But you're right. The whole place is on edge. Drexel talked to me this afternoon – off the record, not for attribution, the usual thing. He asked

32

what is the quickest way to break an actor's heart? Let him do Hamlet in an empty theatre. Then he gave me a neat little discourse on what he called the Age of Indifference and on the audience which has absented itself from the Church.'

'And how did he explain the absent audience?'

'He quoted St Paul. You know the text . . . "Though I speak with the tongues of men and angels and have not charity . . ." Then he added his own gloss: "In short, Nicki, the people turn away because they believe we no longer understand or share their concerns. They are not serfs to be disciplined. They are free people, our brothers and sisters; they need the hand's touch of compassion. When we elected this Pontiff we chose a law-and-order candidate, an old-fashioned papal imperialist to make us feel secure in a time of doubt and confusion. We didn't trust the people. We called in the gendarmerie. Well, we got what we voted for: a cast-iron man, absolutely inflexible. But we lost the people. We lost 'em, Nicki, in a vain attempt to restore the mediaeval notion of a papal monarchy, bolster that strange catch-all authority, the *magisterium*. The big gong booms, but people stop their ears. They don't want thunder. They want the saving voice that says, "Come to me, all ye who labour and are heavily burdened – and I will refresh you" I tell you, Kate, he was quite emotional about it. So was I. That's the piece I'm trying to write now.'

'But it still doesn't fully define this edginess we're talking about. Not everybody thinks the way Drexel does. Lots of Romans like the present Pontiff. They understand him. They feel a need for his kind.'

'Just as some of the old ones felt a need for Mussolini!'

'If you like, sure! It's the *Führerprinzip*, the illusion of the benevolent strongman, with the people marching behind him to death or glory. But without the people,

33

the leader is a straw man, with the stuffing spilled out of him.'

'That's it, by God!' Nicki Peters was suddenly excited. 'That's the theme I've been looking for. What happens to the Pontiff who alienates the Church? I don't mean just historically, though that's an essay in itself, a bloody and violent chronicle of pontiffs under siege, in exile, dogged by assassins. I'm talking about the man himself at the moment when he realises that he is a scarecrow, battered by the storms, with the crows pecking the straw out of his ears. Of course, if he doesn't realise it, there's no story; but if he does and if he's looking down the barrel of a shotgun as Leo XIV is today, then what happens? His whole internal life must be a shambles.'

'One way to find out, Nicki.'

'Oh, and what's that?'

'Ask his surgeon to dinner.'

'Would he come?'

'How many turn-downs have I had in ten years? I'll get him here; trust me'

'What do you know about him?'

'I'm told he's divorced, has no children, that he's Jewish and an ardent Zionist.'

'That's news! Are you sure it's true?'

'I heard it from a normally reliable source, the Principessa Borromini. Salviati is a Venetian name and apparently he was born into one of the old Sephardic families who traded out of the ghetto of Venice into the Adriatic dependencies of the Republic. There are Swiss and Friulan connections too, because Borromini met him first in St Moritz and he speaks Ladino and Venetian dialects as well as Italian. It's also said he's a Freemason, not one of the P2 brand, but old-fashioned square and compass style. If that's true, it's an interesting speculation as to who at the Vatican chose him and why. You know how stiff-necked and sensitive they are on the whole Zionist question, not to mention divorce and secret societies.'

Nicol Peters took his wife in his arms, kissed her soundly and waltzed her round the tiled pavement of the *salone*.

'Kate, sweet Kate! You never cease to amaze me. Divorced, Jewish, Zionist . . . what else?'

'Fanatically devoted to his job and – again, I quote my *principessa* – to one of his senior women at the clinic.'

'Do you have a name for her?'

'No. I'm sure I can get one quickly enough. But you're not going to write a scandal piece, are you?'

'On the contrary. I'm following Drexel's logic. Leo XIV has lost the people. Does he know it? If he does, what has it done to him? What will it do to him in the future? Why don't you see if you can set up a dinner for Salviati – and his girlfriend, whoever she is?'

'When?'

'As soon as you like; but I wouldn't make any calls or send out any invitations until we know the result of this operation. Even for Salviati, it's no small thing to have the life of the Vicar of Christ in your hands!'

It had been a day filled with minor humiliations. He had been pierced for blood samples, hooked up to a machine that spewed out his heart's history in scrawls and squiggles. He had been sounded, prodded, dressed in a backless gown and stood baretailed in front of an X-ray machine. All his questions had been answered in monosyllables that told him nothing.

As they wheeled him back to his room, he had a sudden, vivid recollection of those sessions at the Congregation for the Doctrine of the Faith, where a luckless divine from Notre-Dame or Tübingen or Amsterdam was quizzed obliquely on charges he had never heard, by men he had never met, and where his only defender was a cleric whose name was never revealed to him. As Sub-prefect and later Prefect of the Congregation, Ludovico Gadda had never admitted any need to change the procedures. The subject of the investigation, the central figure in the colloquy, was by definition less important than the subject of the discussion: the possible corruption of a truth, a morbidity of error which, being a disease, must be extirpated. Its old name was the Congregation of the Universal Inquisition, its later one the Holy Office and, last of all, the seemingly innocuous Doctrine of the Faith. But its competences were still the same, defined in the clearest terms: 'all questions that have regard to the doctrine of the faith and of the customs and usages of the faith, examination of new teachings, the promotion of studies and conferences about these same teachings, the reprobation of those which turn out to be contrary to the principles of the faith, the examination and eventually the condemnation of books; the Privilege of the Faith, judgment of crimes against the faith.'

Now he, the master of that ancient but still sinister machine, was himself under inquisition, by smiling nurses and blank-faced technicians and nodding note-takers. They were polite, as were the prelates of the Piazza del Sant'Ufficio. They were detached, impersonal. They cared not one whit for what he was or what he felt. They were interested only in the diseases that inhabited his carcass. They told him nothing of what they found. They were like his own inquisitors, dedicated to the Disciplina Arcani, the Discipline of the Secret, a cult of whispers and concealment.

By early evening he was frayed and ill-tempered. His supper pleased him no more than his luncheon. The walls of his room closed in on him like a monastic cell. He would have liked to walk out in the corridor with the other patients, but he was suddenly shy about his bulky body and the unfamiliar vestments of dressing-gown and pyjamas. Instead, he sat in a chair, picked up his breviary and began to read vespers and compline. The familiar cadences of the psalmody lulled him, as they always did, into a calm, not joyful, but close to the relief of tears which he could not remember to have shed since childhood.

> Create in me a clean heart O God
> And renew a right spirit within me
> Cast me not away from thy presence
> And take not thy holy spirit from me
> Restore unto me the joy of thy salvation . . .

The strophe hypnotised him. His eyes could not see past it. His lips refused to form the antistrophe . . .

Joy was the missed experience in his life. He had known happiness, satisfaction, triumph; but joy, that strange upswelling of delight, that tingling near-ecstasy in which every sense was like a fiddle-string, making music under the master's bow, joy had always eluded him. He had never had the chance to fall in love. He had deprived himself by a lifetime vow of the experience of bodily union with a woman. Even in his spiritual life, the agonies and exaltations of the mystics were beyond his reach. Catherine of Siena, Little Brother Francis, St John of the Cross, St Theresa of Avila, were alien to his mindset. The role models he chose were the great pragmatists, the orderers of events – Benedict, Ignatius of Loyola, Gregory the Great, Basil of Caesarea. His earliest spiritual director explained to him the degrees of meditative communion with God: the purgative, the illuminative, the unitive. Afterwards, he shook his head and patted his young disciple on the back and dismissed him: 'But for you, Ludovico my boy, it'll be the purgative way from beginning to end. Don't fret yourself about it. You're born to the plough. Just keep plodding, left right, left right, until God decides to lift you out of the furrow Himself. If He doesn't, be grateful still. The joy of illumination, the wonder of the mystical marriage with God, bring pain as well as ecstasy. You can't have one without the other . . .' It was strange that now, at sixty-eight,

he felt suddenly so deprived and cheated. The remainder of
the psalm echoed his sadness:

Uphold me with the presence of thy spirit
For thou desirest not sacrifice, else I would give it thee.
Thou hast no delight in burnt offerings
The Godly sacrifice is a troubled spirit
A broken and contrite heart thou wilt not despise . . .

He had just finished the last prayer when Salviati walked
in with a lean, shambling fellow in his late fifties, whom he
introduced as Mr James Morrison of the Royal College of
Surgeons in London. Morrison had a rumpled, comfortable
look about him and a humorous, faintly mocking twinkle in
his brown eyes. To the Pontiff's surprise, he spoke passable
Italian. He explained with a grin.

'I have what you might call Italian connections. One of
my ancestors led a train-band of Scots mercenaries in the
service of Pius II. The Morrisons, who now call themselves
Morrissone, manufacture expensive shoes in Varese.'

Leo XIV gave a short, barking laugh and shrugged off the
joke with a Latin tag: 'Tempora mutantur . . . times change,
and we with them. Thank you for coming, Mr Morrison.
May I ask your opinion on my case?'

'It differs not at all from that offered by Dr Salviati. In fact,
I have to say I have nothing new to offer. I am expensive and
redundant.'

'On the contrary, James, you're my insurance policy –
medical and political.'

Morrison picked up the little comic book from the bedside
table and asked: 'Have you read this, Holiness?'

'Yes. I can't say I found it amusing.'

Morrison laughed. 'I agree. It's a good try; but heart disease
is not exactly a laughing matter. Is there anything you'd like
to ask me?'

'How long will I be in hospital?'

'That's up to Dr Salviati. The average time is about two weeks.'

'And after that?'

'Six to eight weeks of convalescence while the bones in your ribcage knit. We have to cut the sternum, you see, then stitch it back with wire. There's quite a bit of discomfort attached to that part of the convalescence, but it's still pretty controllable. Also it takes time to recover from the anaesthetic. The physical and psychic traumas are great, but the procedures, thank God, are almost fail-safe. How do you feel in yourself?'

'Afraid.'

'That's normal. What else?'

'Troubled.'

'By what in particular?'

'Things done, things undone.'

'That's normal too.'

'Your counsellor came to see me this afternoon.' This to Salviati.

'Tove Lundberg? I know. I read her first report this evening.'

'Report?'

Salviati laughed. 'Why are you shocked? Tove Lundberg is a highly trained professional. She holds doctorates in Behavioural Sciences and Psychiatric Medicine. Her information is vital in our post-operative care.'

'And what does she say about me?'

Salviati considered the question for a moment and then delivered a cool, judicial answer.

'She points to two problems. The first is that a man like yourself, vested with enormous authority, resigns himself with difficulty to the dependence of illness. That's not new. We have had Arab princes in here whose tribal power is as absolute as yours. They have exactly the same problem. But they do not repress it. They rage, they protest, they make scenes. *Bene!* We can deal with that. But you, the report tells me – and my own contacts with you confirm it – have a second problem. You will repress, hold back, brood in silence, because this is both your training in clerical discipline and your notion of the comportment of the Supreme Pontiff of the Roman Church. You will also, consciously or unconsciously, react against ministration by women. This will not help your recovery, but rather delay it. To use a figure of speech, you are not made of spring steel, forged and tempered and flexible. You are iron, cast in a mould. You are strong, yes; but you are not supple. You are rigid, vulnerable to shocks. But,' he shrugged and spread his hands in a dismissive gesture, 'we are used to that too. We shall cope with you.'

'Why,' asked Leo the Pontiff flatly, 'why should you care? You fix the plumbing. You pack your tools. You turn to another job.'

James Morrison gave a pawky Scots smile and said: 'Never tangle with the Church, Sergio! They've been playing the dialectic game for centuries!'

'I know,' said Salviati tartly. 'Ever since Isidore wrote his first forgeries and Gratian turned them neatly into a Code!' To the Pontiff he gave a softer answer. 'Why do I care? Because I'm more than a plumber. I'm a healer. After the operation, another job begins. We have not only to retrain you to cope with what has happened. We have to educate you to ensure it doesn't happen again. We also hope to learn from your case lessons we can apply to others. This is a research and teaching institution. You, too, can learn much here, about yourself and about other people.'

At that moment, Salviati's beeper sounded, a series of sharp, fast signals. He frowned and turned to Morrison.

'We have an emergency. Cardiac arrest. Come with me, James. Excuse us, Holiness!'

They were gone in an instant, leaving the Pontiff with one more ironic comment on his own impotence and irrelevance in the life and death situations of common folk.

It was this irony which had troubled him more and more in the last months, as he tried first to explain away and then to comprehend the growing rift between himself and the Christian Assembly. The reasons were various and complex; but most had to do with the spread of popular education and the speed and potency of modern communications: press, radio, television and satellite dissemination of information.

History was no longer the domain of scholars, ferreting in dusty libraries. It was relived every day, in fiction or in documentary form on television screens. It was invoked in panel discussions as a paradigm of the present, a warning for the future. It stirred in the dark pools of tribal memory, raising old ghosts and the stink of ancient battlefields.

It was no longer possible to rewrite history – the facts showed through the overwritten fiction. It was not possible to plaster over the graffiti scratched into ancient stone. The plaster flaked off or fell away under the tapping hammers of the archaeologists.

He himself had written two encyclicals: the one on abortion, the other on in vitro fertilisation. In each, the words were his own; in each, he had insisted with absolute sincerity and unaccustomed eloquence on the sanctity and the value of human life. Even as he was writing them, the prancing demons of the past mocked his noble rhetoric.

Innocent III had claimed sovereign dominion of life and death over all Christians. He had decreed that the mere refusal to take an oath was a crime worthy of death. Innocent IV had prescribed the use of torture by his inquisitors. Benedict XI had declared the inquisitors who used it absolved from blame and penalty ... . What respect for life was there in the madness of the witchcraft trials, the carnage of the Crusades against the Cathars, the persecution of the Jews down the centuries? The massacres of Montsegur and Constantinople were still remembered, like Belsen and Auschwitz. The unpaid debts were still on the books, piling up interest.

It was no longer enough to say baldly that these horrors belonged to other times, were committed by primitive or barbarous men. The acts were ordered under the same *magisterium* which he exercised. They were justified by the same logic in which he himself had been schooled. He could not establish his own probity without admitting that the logic was flawed, that the men who preceded him had been in error.

But Roman policy had long since determined that no Pope should recant or attempt to explain the mistakes of his predecessors. Silence was prescribed as the safest remedy – silence, secrecy and the incredible tolerance of believers whose need of faith was greater than their disgust for its faithless ministers. But their tolerance was wearing thin and their faith was sorely tried by the garbles and glosses of its official interpreters. For them, the only time of salvation was now.

The only hope of easement was a grand illusion; a universal amnesty, a single cleansing act of repentance, universally acknowledged. But if the man who called himself the Vicar of Christ could not contemplate a public penitence, who else would dare dream it?

Decades ago, the good Pope John had acknowledged the errors and tyrannies of the past. He had called a great Council, to open the minds of the People of God and let the wind of the Spirit blow through the assembly. For a brief while there was a surge of hope and charity, a message of peace for warring nations. Then the hope waned, and the charity cooled, and Ludovico Gadda came to power on the wave of mistrust and fear that followed. He saw himself at first as the stabiliser, the great restorer, the man who would bring unity back into a community wearied and divided by a chase after novelties.

But it had not turned out so. In the privacy of his own conscience, at this moment of close encounter with Brother Death, he had to admit defeat and default. If he could not close the widening breach between Pontiff and people, then he had not merely wasted his life, but laid waste the City of God.

He looked at his watch. It was still only eight-thirty. Desiring to be spared the humiliation of his illness, he had declined all visitors on this first night in the clinic. Now, he regretted it. He needed company, as a thirsting man needed water. For Ludovico Gadda, called Leo XIV, Bishop of Rome, Patriarch of the West, Successor to the Prince of the Apostles, it promised to be a long, restless night.

At eighty years of age, Anton Cardinal Drexel had two secrets which he guarded jealously. The first was his correspondence with Jean Marie Barette, formerly Pope Gregory XVII, now living in a secret Alpine retreat in southern Germany. The second was the pleasure of his old age, a small villa estate in the Alban Hills, some fifteen minutes' drive from the Vilia Diana.

He had bought it many years before from Valerio Cardinal Rinaldi, who had been Camerlengo at the time of the election of Kiril I. The purchase had been pure indulgence. Valerio Rinaldi had been a papal prince in the old mode – a scholar, a humanist, a sceptic, a man of much kindness and humour. Drexel, recently made a cardinal and translated to Rome, had envied both his lifestyle and the skill with which he navigated the shoals and over-falls of Curial life. Rinaldi had made a generous deal with him and he entered with zest and skill into his existence as an elderly anonymous gentleman retired to the country.

Then, an extraordinary thing happened. At seventy years of age, Anton Cardinal Drexel, Dean of the Sacred College, Cardinal Bishop of Ostia, fell hopelessly in love.

The manner of it was very simple. One warm spring day, dressed in country clothes, checked shirt, corded trousers and hobnailed boots, he walked the five kilometres into Frascati to discuss the sale of his wine to a local *cantina*. The orchard trees were in flower, the new grass was ankle high, the first young tendrils were greening on the vines. In spite of his years, he felt supple and limber and ready to walk as far as the road would take him.

He had always loved the old town, with its baroque cathedral, its crumbling palace and the dark, cavernous wine shops in the back alleys. Once upon a time it had been the episcopal seat of His Serene Highness, Henry Benedict Mary Clement, Cardinal Duke of York, last of the Stuarts, who had once proclaimed himself Henry IX of England. Now it was a prosperous tourist resort, filled with a weekend horror of motor vehicles and petrol fumes. But in the cobbled lanes the charm of the past still lingered, and the old-fashioned courtesies of country folk.

Drexel's destination was a deep cave hewn into the tufa rock, where great tuns of ancient oak lined the walls and the serious drinkers and buyers sat at long refectory tables, with dusty bottles and plates of green olives set in front of them. The padrone, who knew Drexel only as *il Tedesco* – the German – haggled a while over the price and the delivery, then agreed to accept a sample consignment and opened a bottle of his best vintage to seal the bargain.

After a few moments, the padrone left him to attend to another customer. Drexel sat relaxed in the half-light, watching the small passage of people on the sunlit pavement outside the entrance. Suddenly, he felt a tug at his trouser leg and heard a strange gurgling sound, like water swirling down a pipe. When he looked down he saw a cascade of blonde curls, an angelic little girl-face and a flurry of spidery legs and arms that seemed to have no co-ordinated connection with the tiny body. The voice was out of control too, but the mouth seemed to be trying to form sequential sounds. 'Ma-no-no, ma-no-no . . .'

Drexel lifted the child on to the table, so that she sat facing him. Her tiny marmoset hands, soft as silk, groped at his face and hair. Drexel talked to her soothingly.

'Hullo, little one! What's your name? Do you live around here? Where is your mama?'

But all he got was the agonised twisting of the mouth and the sound gurgling out of the tiny gullet. 'Ma-no-no, ma-no-no.' Yet she was not afraid. Her eyes smiled at him and there was, or seemed to be, a light of intelligence in them. The padrone came back. He knew the child by sight. He had seen her before, sometimes with a mother, sometimes with a nurse. They came to Frascati for shopping. They didn't belong in town, but maybe to one of the villas in the near countryside. He had no name for them, but the mother seemed to be foreign. She was a *bionda*, like this one. He shook his head sadly.

'Poor little mite. You have to think God must be dozing when he makes mistakes like this one.'

'Do you think you're a mistake, little one?' Drexel stroked the blonde curls. 'I'm sure you know angel talk. I don't. What are you trying to tell me?'

'I've got fifteen grandchildren,' the padrone told him. 'Not a runt among 'em. A man can be lucky. What about you?'

Drexel smiled and shook his head.

'No children. No grandchildren.'

'That's hard, for a wife especially. A woman always needs someone to cluck over.'

'No wife,' said Drexel.

'Well then!' The padrone seemed embarrassed. 'Maybe you're the lucky one. Families keep you poor – and when you're dead they pick you bare like vultures. Would you like me to call the police and let them know we've got this one?'

'I could perhaps take her outside and look for the mother.'

'Not a good idea!' The padrone was very firm about it. 'Once you leave here with her, you're suspect. Abduction, abuse. That's the times we live in. Not our folk here, but the *forestieri*, the outsiders. You could have a hell of a time proving different. Best you sit there and let me call the cops.'

'Do you have something for her to eat or drink – an *aranciata*, a biscuit perhaps? Do you like sweet things, little one?'

The tiny soft hands groped at his face and she said, 'Ma-no-no, ma-no-no . . .'

The padrone produced a saucer of sweet biscuits and a glass of *aransoda*. The child slopped over the drink, but Drexel steadied her and wiped her lips with his handkerchief. He helped her to manipulate the biscuit into her mouth. A woman's voice spoke behind him.

'I'm her mother. I hope she hasn't been too much trouble to you.'

'No trouble at all. We're getting along famously. What's her name?'

'Britte.'

'She seems to be trying to tell me something. It sounds like Ma, no, no.'

The woman laughed.

'That's as close as she can get to Nonno. She thinks you look like her grandfather. Come to think of it, you do . . . He's tall and white-haired like you.'

'Aren't you worried about her being lost?'

'She wasn't lost. I was just across the street in the *salumeria*. I saw her come in here. I knew she would come to no harm. The Italians care for children.'

The child scrabbled awkwardly for another biscuit. Drexel fed it to her. He asked: 'What's the matter with her?'

'Cerebral diplegia. It's due to a defect of the nerve cells in the central cortex of the brain.'

'Is there any cure?'

'In her case, there's hope of improvement, but no cure. We

46

work very hard with her to establish muscular co-ordination and adequate speech. Fortunately, she's one of the special ones.'

'Special?'

'In spite of the lack of muscular co-ordination and the almost incoherent speech, she has a very high intelligence. Some victims verge on idiocy. Britte could turn out to be a genius. We just have to find ways to break into this – this prison.'

'I'm being very rude,' said Anton Drexel. 'Won't you sit down and take a glass of wine with me? Britte hasn't finished her drink or her biscuits. My name is Anton Drexel.'

'I'm Tove Lundberg . . .'

And that was the beginning of the love affair between an elderly Cardinal of the Curia and a six-year-old girl-child, a victim of cerebral palsy. His enchantment was instant, his commitment total. He invited the mother and child to lunch with him at his favourite trattoria. Tove Lundberg drove him home, where he introduced the child to the married couple who cared for him, and the gardener and the cellar master who made his wines. He announced that he had been officially adopted as her *nonno* and that henceforth she would be visiting every weekend.

If they were surprised they gave no sign. His Eminence could be very formidable when he chose – and besides, in the old hill towns discretion about the doings of the clergy and the gentry was a long ingrained tradition. The child would be welcome; the signora also, whenever His Eminence decided to invite them.

Afterwards, on the *belvedere*, looking out over the fall of the land towards the hazy cupolas of Rome, confidences were exchanged while the child limped happily among the flowerbeds. Tove Lundberg was unmarried; her partner's love had not been strong enough to bear the tragedy of a maimed love-child. The break-up of the union was somehow less tragic than the damage to her own self-image and self-esteem as a woman. So, she had fought shy of new attachments and devoted herself to her career and to the care and education of the girl. Her medical training had helped. Salviati had been more than supportive. He had offered to marry her; but she was not ready yet, perhaps she would never be. One day at a time was enough . . . As for His Eminence, she would not have taken him for a sentimentalist or an impulsive man. What in fact did he have in mind when he proposed himself as a surrogate grandfather? A shade less eloquently than was his wont, Anton Cardinal Drexel explained his folly . . .

'According to some of the most ancient protocols in the western world, I am a prince – a prince of the Holy Roman Catholic and Apostolic Church. I am the most senior member of the College of Cardinals, Prefect of a Congregation, member of Secretariats and Commissions – the perfect and perfected ecclesiastical bureaucrat. At seventy-five I shall offer my resignation to the Holy Father. He will accept it, but ask me to continue working, *sine die*, so that the Church may have the benefit of my experience. But the older I get, the more I feel that I shall leave this planet the way a snowflake disappears, without a trace, without a single permanent imprint to mark my passing. What little love I have left is withering inside me like a walnut in the shell. I should like to spend the last of it on this child. Why? God knows! She took possession of me. She asked me to be her *nonno*. Every child should have two grandfathers. So far she has only one.' He laughed at his own earnestness. 'In another age, I'd have kept mistresses and bred my own children and called them, for decency, nephews and nieces. I would have enriched them out of the coffers of the Church and made sure my sons became bishops and my daughters married nobly. I can't do that for Britte, but I can get her whatever training and therapy she needs. I can give her time and love.'

'I wonder,' Tove Lundberg was suddenly withdrawn and

thoughtful, 'I wonder if you will understand what I am about to say.'

'I can try.'

'What Britte needs is the company of her peers, children who are handicapped but of high intelligence. She needs the inspiration of loving and enlightened teachers. The institute which she attends now is run by Italian nuns. They are good, they are devoted, but they have the Latin view of institutional life. They dispense charity and care by routine, old-fashioned routine . . . That works for children who are mentally handicapped and who tend to be docile and responsive. But for those like Britte, imprisoned intelligences, it is far, far from enough. I don't have the time or the money, but what I would love to see started is a group, what the Italians call a *colonia*, properly staffed with trained people from Europe and America, supported by parent groups, subsidised if possible by the State and the Church.' She broke off and made a little shrugging gesture of self-mockery. 'I know it's impossible, but it would be one way to getting yourself a late-life family.'

'For that,' said Anton Drexel, 'one needs more life than I have at my disposal. However, if God has endowed me with a granddaughter, He will hardly deny me the grace to perform my duties towards her. Let's walk awhile. I'll show you what we have here, the vineyards, the farmland. Then you will choose the room where you and Britte will stay whenever you visit . . . A colonia, eh? A colony of new intelligences to grace this battered planet! I'm sure I can't afford it, but the idea is wonderful!'

And that, whenever he looked backwards, was the day he identified as the beginning of his career as a surrogate grandfather to Britte Lundberg and sixteen other girls and boys who, year by year, had taken over his villa, most of his income, and the happiest corner of his life – from which small, secret standing place he now proposed to launch the most foolhardy venture of his career.

Three

It was ten o'clock when the night nurse came in to settle the Pontiff and give him a sedative. It was nearly one in the morning before he lapsed into an uneasy sleep, haunted by a serial dream.

. . . He was at his desk in the Vatican surrounded by expectant dignitaries, the highest in the Church: patriarchs, archbishops, of every rite and nationality – Byzantine, Melchite, Italo-Greek, Malakanese, Ruthenians, Copts, Bulgars and Chaldeans. He was writing a document which he intended to read aloud to them, seeking their approval and endorsement. Suddenly, he seemed to lose control of his fingers. The pen slipped from his grasp. His secretary picked it up and handed it back to him; but now it was a goose-quill, too light to handle, which dribbled ink and moved scratchily on the paper.

For some reason, he was writing in Greek instead of Latin, because he was anxious to impress on the Byzantines that he was open to their spirit and understanding of their needs. Suddenly he blocked on a word. All he could remember was the first letter – μ. The Patriarch of Antioch reproved him gently: 'It is always safer to use a translator who has the language as a mother tongue.' The Pontiff nodded a reluctant agreement, but continued to grope for the word among the cobwebs that seemed to have invaded his mind.

Next, still holding the paper, he found himself walking across St Peter's Square to the Via del Sant'Ufficio. It seemed important that he confer with the Consultors to the Congregation for the Doctrine of the Faith for an explanation of the mysterious letter. They were vigilant guardians of the ancient truth, who would first rise to salute the Vicar of Christ and then enlighten him with their wisdom.

They did nothing of the kind. When he entered the *aula* where the Consultors were assembled, they sat like mutes, while the Prefect pointed to a stool where he must sit, isolated under their hostile scrutiny. The paper was taken from his hand and passed around the assembly. As each one read it, he clucked and shook his head and mouthed the sound 'Mu', so that soon the room was full of the bourdon as it were of swarming bees: Mu . . . Mu . . . Mu . . .

He tried to cry out, to protest that they were making a travesty of a most important encyclical, but the only sound he could utter was Mu . . . Mu . . . until, for very shame, he fell silent, closed his eyes and waited for their verdict. Out of the darkness a voice commanded him: 'Open your eyes and read!'

When he obeyed, he found himself a boy again, in a dusty classroom, staring at a blackboard upon which was written the word which had eluded him for so long, μετάνοια. A great sense of relief flooded through him. He cried out: 'You see, that's what I was trying to say – Metanoia, repentance, a change of heart, a new direction.' But no one answered. The room was empty. He was alone.

Then the door opened and he froze in terror at the vision that confronted him: an old, eagle-beaked man, with furrows of anger about his mouth and eyes black as volcanic glass. As the man moved towards him, silent and threatening, he screamed, but the sound would not come. It was as if a noose were knotted around his neck, cutting off air and life . . .

The night nurse and a young male orderly helped him to get up. While the orderly remade his tangled bed, the nurse

51

walked him into the bathroom, peeled off his sodden pyjamas, sponged the sweat from his body, then brought him clean night clothes and a cool drink. When he thanked her and apologised for putting her to trouble, she laughed.

'The first night in hospital is always a bad one. You're full of fears that have to be dreamed out because you can't put them into words. The sedatives get you to sleep, but they can disturb the normal rhythms of rest and dreaming . . . You're better now. Your pulse rate's steadying down. Why don't you read for a little while? You'll probably doze off again . . .'

'What time is it, please?'

'Three in the morning.'

'Then it's bad luck, isn't it?'

'Bad luck? I don't understand.'

Leo the Pontiff gave a small, unsteady laugh.

'Around Mirandola – that's where I come from – the peasants say that the dreams we have after midnight are the ones that come true.'

'Do you believe that?'

'Of course not. I was joking. It's an old wives' tale.'

But even as he said it, he knew it was an evasion. What he had dreamed was more than half the truth and what was not yet true might well be prophecy.

He could not read. He could not sleep. He felt too arid and empty to pray. So, wakeful in the dim light of the night lamp, he gave himself up to contemplation of his very uncertain future.

The word which he had been chasing through his dreams had become very important in his latter-day thinking. It expressed accurately what he desired to convey to the Church – a penitence for the mistakes of the past, a change for the better, a future openness to the needs of the faithful and to the designs of the Almighty. But the change had to be wrought in himself first of all and he could find no sure ground on which to stand while he made it.

The whole bent of his mind, the whole thrust of his education, all the transactions of his career, had been to conserve and not to change. No matter that so many historical claims made by the Church were based on forgery and fabrication; no matter that so much canonical legislation was unjust, intrusive and hopelessly loaded against the individual and in favour of the institution; no matter that so much dubious teaching was presented from the pulpit as official doctrine on the flimsiest foundation of scripture or tradition; no matter that the reforms envisaged in the decisions of a great Council were still unrealised four decades later . . . no matter, no matter! Just so the history remained obscure, the canons unchallenged, the dubious teaching unquestioned, then each generation would make, as it always had, its own accommodation with the paradox. It was better that the unbelievers should be cast out, the sceptics silenced and the disobedient censured, than that any rent should appear in the seamless robe of Roman unity.

In this frame of reference, theologians and philosophers were a dangerous luxury, biblical scholars a tendentious nuisance, still seeking to establish an historic Jesus instead of offering Jesus Christ yesterday, today and the same for ever. As for the faithful, they were at the best of times a wayward family, easily seduced by passion or by novelty.

This attitude of magisterial expediency dated far back through the centuries to an epoch when the faithful were illiterate and uncritical and the dispensation of faith, along with the exercise of power, were the prerogatives only of the literate, the clerics who were the natural custodians of knowledge and authority. As for the aberrant ones, the speculators, the too-bold theorists, they were easily dealt with. Error had no right to exist. The errant would repent or be burned.

In the twentieth century, however, in post-revolutionary, post-conciliar societies, these attitudes had no place. They were at worst an unacceptable tyranny, at best a class snobbery that clerics, high or low, could ill-afford to practise. The faithful, up to their necks in the problems of modern living, had the need and the right and the duty to reason with their pastors, and no less a right and a duty to hold them accountable for their exercise of the *magisterium*, because if magistracy were an autarchic exercise beyond appeal, then at one stride they were back to secret denunciations, witch-hunts, *autos-da-fé* and automatic excommunications. The faithful would not take that any more. They were Children of God, free agents co-operating with His divine plan. If this liberty were abridged, they would refuse the abridgement and absent themselves from the assembly to await a more propitious time or a more charitable shepherd.

In the small half-light of the hospital room, whose silence was broken only by the distant sound of a patient's call-buzzer, Leo the Pontiff saw it all clearly. No matter how bitterly he regretted his own defaults, he saw no easy way to mend them. He lacked the one essential talent which the good Pope John and Jean Marie Barette had both possessed: a sense of humour, a readiness to laugh at themselves and the egregious follies of mankind. There was not one photograph in existence of Leo XIV laughing. Even his rare smile was more like a grimace than an expression of pleasure.

Yet, in all truth, only part of the blame attached to him. The sheer size and mass of the institution created an inertia like that of a black hole in the galaxies. Enormous energy was sucked into it. The energy that emerged was constantly diminishing. The old Curial cliché 'We think in centuries and plan for eternity' had turned into a doom-saying.

The great tree of the Gospel parable, in which all the birds of the air could nest, was dying back from the tips of its spreading branches. The trunk was still solid, the great mass of foliage seemed intact; but at the outer edges there were dead twigs and sere leaves, and the nourishment from the taproot flowed more and more sluggishly.

The slow curse of centralism was working in the Church, as it had worked in every empire since Alexander's. The British had succumbed to it, the Russians and the Americans were the latest to be forced into divestment of their territories and spheres of influence. The symptoms of malaise were always the same; disaffection in the outer marches, disenchantment with bureaucracy, alienation and indifference on the part of the people and, on the part of government, a growing impulse towards reaction and repression.

In religious terms, the numen of the papacy was fading, as its aura of mystery was dissipated by constant exposure on television and in the Press. Government by fiat brought small joy to folk in crisis, who yearned for compassion and for understanding of the God abiding among them. They did not reject the pastoral office. They paid ritual homage to the man who held it, but they asked how he mediated for them in the double mystery of the creative Godhead and confused humanity. For Leo the Pontiff the question was personal and immediate; but it was still unanswered when sleep claimed him again. This time, mercifully, he did not dream at all. He woke at first light to find Salviati standing beside the bed, with the night nurse a pace behind him. Salviati was counting his pulse rate.

'Nurse tells me you had a rough night.'

'I was having nightmares. However, I've just had a couple of hours' good rest. How is your patient?'

'Which patient are you talking about?'

'The cardiac arrest. You and Mr Morrison went off in a great hurry last night.'

'Oh, that one . . .' Salviati shook his head. 'We lost her. She'd already had two heart attacks before they brought her to see me. Her case was always a long shot. Sad though; she leaves a husband and two young children . . . If I've got the story right, the husband's one of your people.'

'Mine?'

'A priest, one of the Roman clergy. Apparently he fell in love, got the girl pregnant and walked out of the ministry to marry her. He's spent the last five years trying to have his position regularised by the Vatican – which, they tell me, isn't as easy as it used to be.'

'That's true,' said Leo the Pontiff. 'It isn't easy. Disciplines have been tightened.'

'Well, it's beyond mending now. The girl's dead. He's got two kids to care for. If he's wise, he'll try to find 'em a stepmother. So the situation repeats itself; yes?'

'If you'd give me his name, I could perhaps . . .'

'I wouldn't recommend it.' Salviati was studiously offhand. 'I'm a Jew, so I don't understand how you Christians reason about these things; but the boy's very bitter and your intervention may be unwelcome.'

'I'd still like to have his name.'

'Your life is complicated enough. As from tomorrow, you begin a minimalist existence. So start now to be grateful – and let the Almighty run His own world. Open your pyjamas, please. I want to listen to your chest. Give me deep breaths now.' After a few minutes of auscultation, he seemed to be satisfied. 'You'll do! It's going to be a beautiful day. You should take a little stroll in the garden, get some clean air into your lungs. Don't forget to tell the nurse when you're going. You can't get lost, but we like to know where all our patients are.'

'I'll take your advice. Thank you . . . I'd still like to have that young man's name.'

'You're feeling guilty about him.' It was more an accusation than a question.

'Yes.'

'Why?'

'You gave the reason yourself. He's one of mine. He broke the law. I set the penalties he incurred. When he wanted to come back, the way was barred to him by rules I made . . .

I'd like to be reconciled with him, help him, too, if he'll permit me.'

'Tove Lundberg will give you his name and address. But not today, not until I say you're ready to occupy yourself with affairs other than your own survival. Do I make myself clear?'

'Abundantly,' said Leo the Pontiff. 'I wish my mind were half as clear as yours.'

To which Sergio Salviati answered with a proverb: "Every wolf must die in his own skin."

'If you want to swap proverbs,' said Leo the Pontiff, 'I'll give you one from my home place: "It's a hard winter when one wolf eats another."'

For a moment Salviati seemed to withdraw into some dark recess of himself; then he laughed, a deep happy rumbling that went on for a longtime. Finally, he dabbed at his streaming eyes and turned to the night nurse.

'You're witnessing history, my girl! Write it down and tell it to your grandchildren. Here's a Jew from Venice disputing with the Pope of Rome in his own city.'

'Write this down also . . .' The Pontiff laughed as he said it. 'The Pope is listening very carefully, because this time the Jew is the one with the knife in his hands! He can kill me or cure me!'

'There's a proverb for that, too,' said Sergio Salviati. '"You've got a wolf by the ears. You can't hang on and you can't let go . . ."'

On that fine spring morning there were other folk, too, who found themselves hanging on to a wolf's ears. The Secretariat of State was swamped with enquiries from all quarters of the globe, from legates and nuncios and metropolitan archbishops, from cardinals and patriarchs, from diplomats and intelligence agencies of one colour or another. The burden of their questions was always the same: how serious was the

Pontiff's illness; what were the odds on his recovery; what would happen if . . . ?

The Secretariat, under Matteo Cardinal Agostini, normally conducted its business with an air of Olympian detachment. Its officials were a select tribe of polyglots who maintained diplomatic – and undiplomatic – relations with every region under the sun, from Zaire to Tananarive, from Seoul to St Andrews, from Ecuador to Alexandria of the Copts. Their communications were the most modern and the most ancient: satellites, safe-hand couriers, whispers at fashionable gatherings. They had a passion for secrecy and a talent for casuistry and discretion.

How could they be otherwise, since their competence, defined by Apostolic Constitution, was the widest of any organisation in the Church: 'to help from close at hand (*da vicino*) the Supreme Pontiff, both in the care of the Universal Church and in his relations with the dicasteries of the Roman Curia.' The which, as cynics pointed out, put the job of managing the Curia on a par with the care of a billion human souls!

The word dicastery had its own Byzantine coloration. It signified a tribunal, a court and, by extension, a ministry or department. It suggested a complicated protocol, an intricate web of interests, an ancient subtlety in the conduct of affairs. So when the diplomats of the Secretariat of State dealt with their secular peers or with the Dicasts of the Sacred Congregations, they were required to be quick on their feet, nimble of tongue and very, very wide awake.

Their replies to the questions that poured into their offices were bland, but not too bland. They were, after all, dealers in the marts of power. They were, for the moment, the spokesmen for the Holy See. They must make it clear that Rome was never taken by surprise. What the Holy Ghost did not reveal they supplied from their own refined intelligence services.

Yes, the medical bulletins on His Holiness could and should be taken at face value. The Holy Father had decreed an open information policy. No, the Electoral College had not been summoned, nor would it be until the Camerlengo declared that the throne of Peter was vacant. In fact, the Secretariat was actively discouraging visits to Rome by cardinals and archbishops from abroad. The Holy Father understood and commended their desire to offer support and loyalty but, frankly, he would prefer them to be about God's business in their own vineyards.

Questions about the future competence of the Pontiff were dealt with curtly. They were inopportune and unfruitful. Common decency demanded that public speculation on this delicate matter be discouraged.

Time elements? The doctors advised a period of three months' convalescence before the Pontiff resumed his normal schedules. In fact, this pointed to his return after the usual summer vacation, perhaps a month or so later than Ferragosto . . . Most certainly, Excellency! His Holiness will be informed of your call. He will no doubt wish to acknowledge it in person after his recovery. Meanwhile, our compliments to Your Excellency and his family . . .

All of which was sound enough, but hardly sufficient for the hinge-men of the Church, the Papal Princes who would have to decide upon the competence of the living pope or the successor to a dead one. In the context of the third millennium, total secrecy was an impossibility and the leisure for informed decision was an antique luxury. They had to be prepared at every moment. Their groupings had to be stable, their alliances tested, the terms of their bargainings and the price-tags on their votes had to be agreed in advance. So, there was a great mass of traffic – by telephone, by fax, by safe-hand courier – which bypassed Rome altogether. Chicago talked to Buenos Aires, Seoul talked to Westminster, Bangkok talked to Sydney. Some of the talk was blunt and pragmatic:

'Are we agreed . . . ?'; 'Can we afford . . . ?' Some of it was in *sfumature*, hints and nuances and careful allusions which could be disclaimed or reinterpreted with any shift of events.

The question which required the greatest delicacy in discussion was the one whose answer was the least evident: How far could an ailing pontiff be trusted to direct the affairs of a global community in crisis?

Tradition, established by long-dead papal dynasts, determined that a pontiff served until he dropped. History, on the other hand, proved beyond all doubt that one who outlived his usefulness became a liability to the community of the faithful – an instant liability, because in the modern world time telescoped itself, because act and consequence were immediately conjoined. There was sound argument for a term of service fixed by canonical statute, as it was in the case of cardinals and other prelates; but the man who raised the argument might well find his own career suddenly ended.

However, the subject was touched in an early morning telephone conversation between Anton Drexel and his old friend Manfred Cardinal Kaltenborn, Archbishop of Rio de Janeiro. Each was German-born, the one in Brasilia, the other in the Rhineland. They spoke in their mother tongue and their conversation was cryptic and good-humoured. They were old friends and sturdy campaigners who knew how to spell all the words in the book.

'Can we talk freely, Anton?'

'Never quite as freely as we'd like.' Drexel had a healthy respect for satellite technology and the possibilities of espionage. 'But let me give you some background. Our friend is already in care. I have it on the best authority that the odds are all in favour of recovery.'

'To full competence?'

'Yes; but in my view that will not be the issue.'

'What then?'

'It seems to have escaped most of our colleagues that our friend is undergoing a *Gewissenskrise,* a crisis of conscience. He has tried to reform the Church. Instead, he has created a wasteland. He sees no way to make it fruitful again. He has few confidants, no emotional supports, and a spiritual life based wholly on orthopraxis . . . right conduct, according to his limited lights. He will not risk beyond that, or reason beyond it either. So he is desperately lonely and afraid.'

'How have the others missed this? They're all intelligent observers.'

'Most are afraid of him. They spend their lives either avoiding or managing him. I'm too old to care. He knows that. He doesn't try to intimidate me.'

'So what will he do?'

'He will break or he will change. If he breaks, my guess is that he will simply surrender his hold on the office and possibly on life itself. If he is to change, he will need the experience of a charity he has never known in his life.'

'We can't endow him with that. It's something we have to pray for.'

'I'm proposing to work on it as well. I'm inviting him to spend part of his convalescence at my villa. It's only a stone's throw from Castel Gandolfo and an hour's drive from the Vatican . . . He's a farmer's son, he might appreciate a change to country manners. He can also meet my little tribe and see how they handle their lives.'

There was a brief silence and then His Eminence from Rio de Janeiro murmured a warning.

'Some of our colleagues might not understand your intentions, Anton. They mistrust kingmakers and grey eminences.'

'Then they will say so.' Anton Drexel's tone was testy. 'And His Holiness will decide for himself. Charity may bend that stubborn will of his. Opposition will only stiffen it.'

'So, let's go one step further, Anton. Our master has his second Pentecost – tongues of fire, an infusion of the Spirit, a rush of charity like the flush of spring. What next? What does he do about it? How does he retreat from the trenches he's dug for himself – for us all? You know the way it works in Rome. Never explain, never make excuses. Never appear to hurry a decision.'

'I've talked about this at length with his physician, who is as concerned as I, though for other reasons. He's a Jew. He lost relatives in the Holocaust and the Black Sabbath in Rome . . . For him, this is a moment of extraordinary irony. He holds the life of the Roman Pontiff in his hands. You see the implications?'

'Some at least I see very clearly. But how does he answer my question? What does the Holy Father do – afterwards?'

'Salviati is emphatic that the Pontiff can do nothing unless we help him. I agree. I know his family history. Subsistence farming. A father dead too early. A mother determined to lift her son and herself off the dung heap. The best, if not the only, solution was the Church. It's a sad, sterile story. The one thing he has never experienced is the human family, the quarrels, the kisses, the fairytales around the fire.'

'You and I, my dear Anton, are hardly experts in that area.'

'You underrate me, my friend,' Anton Drexel laughed. 'I have a very large adoptive progeny, sixteen boys and girls. And they all live under my roof.'

'Don't teach your grandmother to suck eggs, Anton! I've got a million homeless kids in the *favelas* here! If you're ever short, I can always send you some replacements.'

'Send me your prayers instead. I'm not half as confident as I sound in this affair.'

'It seems to me you're juggling with a man's soul – and quite possibly with his sanity. You're also playing very dangerous politics. You could be accused of making a puppet out of a sick man. Why are you doing it, old friend?'

It was the question Drexel had dreaded, but he had to answer it.

'You know I correspond with Jean Marie Barette?'

'I do. Where is he now?'

'Still in Germany, in that little mountain commune I told you about; but he manages to be very well informed about what's going on in the big world. It was he who encouraged me in this work with the children . . . You know Jean Marie; he can make jokes like a Parisian music-hall comedian and the next moment he is discoursing deep mysteries. About a month ago he wrote me a very strange letter. Part of it was pure prophecy. He told me that the Holy Father would soon be forced to make a dangerous voyage and that I was the one marked to support him on the journey. Soon afterwards the Pontiff's disease was diagnosed; the papal physician named Salviati as the best heart surgeon in Italy – and the mother of my favourite *Enkelin* is a counsellor at his clinic. So a whole pattern of related events began to form itself around me. Does that answer your question?'

'You've left out something, Anton.'

'What?'

'Why do you care so much about a man you've disliked for so long?'

'You're being rough with me, Manfred.'

'Answer my question. Why do you care so much?'

'Because I'm past eighty. I am perhaps closer to judgement even than our Pontiff. I have been given many of the sweets of life. If I don't share them now, they will be like Dead Sea fruit – dust and ashes in my mouth!'

Nicol Peters sat under a pergola of vines on his terrace, sipped coffee, ate fresh pastry and watched the roof-dwellers of old Rome wake to the warm spring morning.

There was the fat fellow with striped pyjamas gaping open at the crotch, whose first care was to take the cover off his canary cage and coax the birds into a morning chorus, with trills and cadenzas of his own. There was the housewife in curlers and carpet slippers, watering her azaleas. On the next terrace, a heavy-hipped girl in a black leotard laboured through fifteen minutes of aerobic exercises to the tinny tunes of a tape machine. Over by the Torre Argentina a pair of lovers thrust open their shutters and then, as if seeing each other for the first time, embraced passionately and tumbled back into bed for a public mating.

Their nearest audience was a skinny bachelor with a towel for a loincloth, who did his own laundry and hung out every morning the shirt, the jockey shorts, the cotton vest and socks which he had just washed under the shower. This done, he lit a cigarette, watched the love-making of his neighbours and went inside to reappear a few minutes later with coffee and a morning paper . . . Above them, the first swifts dipped and wheeled around the campaniles and through the forest of antennae and satellite discs, while shadowy figures passed and repassed by open doors and casements to a growing cacophony of music, radio announcements and a rumour of traffic from the alleys below.

These folk were the theme upon which Nicol Peters was building the text for his weekly column, 'A View From My Terrace'. He stacked the scattered pages, picked up a pencil and began his editing.

' . . . The Romans have a proprietary interest in the Pope. They own him. He is their elected Bishop. His domains are all on Roman soil. They cannot be exported, but they may in some future crisis be expropriated. There is not a single Roman citizen who will not freely admit that most of his personal income depends directly or indirectly upon the Pontiff. Who else brings the tourists and the pilgrims and the art lovers and the romantics, young and old, to clog the airport and pack the hotels and pump tourist and export currency into the city?

'The fact that they need him, however, does not compel the Romans to love him. Some do. Some don't. Most accept him with a shrug and an expressive "Boh!", a monosyllable which defies translation but conveys a wholly Roman sentiment: "Popes come, Popes go. We acclaim them. We bury them. You must not expect us to tremble at every proclamation and every anathema they utter.

'"That's our way, you see. Foreigners never understand it. We make horrendous laws, load them with terrible penalties – and then water them all down with *tolleranza* and casuistry! . . .

'"It has nothing to do with faith and only a little to do with morals. It has to do with *arrangiarsi*, the art of getting along, of managing oneself in a contradictory world. If the cogs of creation slip, that has to be due to defects in the original workmanship. So, God can't be too hard on his creatures who live on a defective planet.

'"The Pope will tell you Christian marriages are made in heaven. They are made to last a lifetime. We're good Catholics, we have no quarrel with that. But Beppi and Lucia next door come close to murder every night, and keep us all awake. Is that Christian? Is that a marriage? Does it have the seal of heaven stamped on it? We beg leave to doubt the proposition. The sooner they break up, the sooner we'll all get some sleep; but, for pity's sake, don't stop 'em finding new mates; otherwise our lives will be disrupted again by a randy bull and a heifer in heat . . ."

'Clearly, there is no way your average Roman wants to argue this with the Pope. After all, a Pope sleeps alone and loves everybody in the Lord, so he is ill-equipped to deal with such matters. So your Roman listens politely to what he has to say, makes his own arrangements and turns up faithfully in church for marriages, christenings, funerals and first communions.

'So far, so good – for the Romans! They have no need or desire to change their capital interest in the Pope. But what about the rest of Christendom – not to mention the millions outside the pale? Their attitude is exactly the reverse. They are happy to accept the Pope – or anyone else for that matter – as a champion of good conduct, just dealing, stable family relationships, social responsibility. It's his theology which now becomes the root problem. Who, they ask, determines that the Pope sees all creation plain as day, the moment after he is elected? Who gives him the prescriptive right to create, by simple proclamation, a doctrine like the Assumption of the Virgin or to declare that it is a crime most damnable for a husband and wife to control their own breeding cycle with a pill or a condom?

'The questions, it seems to this writer, are legitimate and they deserve open discussion and answers more frank than those which have yet been given. They need something else, too – a compassion in the respondent, an openness to history and to argument, a respect for the honest doubts and reservations of his questioners. I have been unable to find the source of the following quotation, but I have no hesitation in adopting it as my own sentiment: "There will be no hope of reform in the Roman Catholic Church, there will be no restoration of confidence between the faithful and the hierarchy, unless and until a reigning pontiff is prepared to admit and abjure the errors of his predecessors . . ."'

They were strong words, the strongest Nicol Peters had written in a long time. Given the subject and the circumstances, an ailing pontiff under threat of death, they might even be considered a gross breach of etiquette. The longer he practised his craft, the more conscious he became of the dynamic of language, of speech and writing as events in themselves. The simplest and most obvious proposition, stated in the most elementary language, could so mutate itself in the mind of the reader that it could express the opposite of what the writer had intended. What he wrote as evidence for the defence could hang the man he was defending.

Nicol Peters's credit and credibility as a commentator on the Vatican depended upon his ability to render the most complex argument into clear prose for the hurried reader. The clarity of the prose depended upon a precise understanding of the matter at issue. In this case, it was a highly delicate one. It had to do with the Roman view of orthodoxy (right doctrine) and orthopraxis (right practice), the nature of the pontiff's right to prescribe either – and his duty to recant any error that might creep into the prescription.

This was the problem which still split Christendom like an apple, and which the old-fashioned absolutism of Leo XIV had only exacerbated. It would not be solved as the Romans solved it, by cynical indifference. It would not go away like a wart or heal itself like a razor nick. It would grow and fester like a cancer, sapping the inner life of the Church, reducing it to invalidism and indifference.

Which raised quite other questions for Nicol Peters, doyen of the press corps, confidant of cardinals, comfortable in his elegant Roman domain: 'Why should I care so much? I'm not even a Catholic, for God's sake! Why should I sweat blood over every shade of clerical opinion, while the hierarchs themselves sit content inside the ramparts of Vatican City and watch the decline and fall of the Roman Church?'

To which his wife Katrina, arrived with fresh coffee and her good morning smile, delivered the perfect answer: 'Glum today, are we? Morning sex doesn't agree with you? Brighten up, lover boy. Spring is here. The shop's making money. And I've just had a fascinating phone call about Salviati and his girlfriend and, of all people, your friend Drexel.'

Four

Precisely at ten that same morning, Monsignor Malachy O'Rahilly, senior private secretary to the Pontiff, waited on his master at the clinic.

His presence was a radiant one: round, glowing face, blue eyes of limpid innocence, a joyful smile, six languages tripping off his tongue with a beautiful blarneying brogue to sweeten them all. His Holiness, a cross-tempered man, depended upon his good humour and even more on his Celtic talent for smelling the winds of intrigue, which in the Curial enclaves blew hot and cold and every which way in the same moment.

Monsignor O'Rahilly's loyalties were absolute. They pointed always to magnetic north, the dwelling-place of power. Statistically, papal secretaries outlived their masters; the wise ones made sure that they had post-mortem insurance always in place. Of course, all insurance required the payment of premiums: a discreet recommendation, a file brought to the Pontiff's attention, a name dropped at the right moment. The currency might vary; but the principle was ironclad and backed by biblical mandate: make friends of the mammon of iniquity, so that when you fail (or when your patron dies, which is the same thing) they may receive you into their houses!

This morning the Monsignor was serving his alternate master, the Cardinal Secretary of State, who had admonished him firmly: 'No business, Monsignore, absolutely none! Tomorrow he goes under the knife and there'll be nothing, absolutely nothing, he can do about anything!'

To the Pontiff, Malachy explained with voluble good humour: 'I'm under pain of instant exile if I raise your blood pressure by a single point. I'm to tell you from Their Eminences of the Curia that everything's being handled according to your instructions and that prayers and good wishes are pouring in like water from the Fons Bandusiae . . . There's even a love note from the Kremlin and one from the Patriarch Dimitri in Moscow. Chairman Tang has sent a polite note from Beijing and the Secretariat is making a full list of all the other communications . . . Cardinal Agostini said he'll be in to see you just before lunch. Once again, it's strictly no business, as the doctor has most firmly ordered. But if there are any personal things you'd like me to take care of . . .'

'There's only one.' Monsignor Malachy O'Rahilly was instantly at the ready – notebook open, pen poised in his chubby fist. 'A young woman died here last night. She leaves a husband and two young children. Her husband is a priest of the Roman diocese who broke his vows and contracted a civil marriage. I am told he made a number of applications to us to laicise him and to regularise the union. The applications were all refused. I want you to get me full details of the case and copies of all the documents on the file . . .'

'Be sure, I'll get on to it right away. Does Your Holiness have a name to give me?'

'Not yet. I'm waiting to speak to the counsellor here.'

'No matter. I'll dig it out somehow . . . Not that you'll be able to give it much attention for a week or two . . .'

'Nevertheless, you will treat the matter as most urgent.'

'May one ask the reason for your interest in this case, Holiness?'

'Two children and a grieving husband, my dear Malachy . . . and a text that keeps running through my head: "The bruised reed he will not break, the smoking flax he will not extinguish."'

'First, in a messy affair like this, I'll have to find out who's got the papers – Doctrine of the Faith, the Congregation for Clerics, the Apostolic Penitentiary, the Rota. None of them will be happy about an intervention by Your Holiness.'

'They're not asked to be happy. Tell them this is a matter of personal concern to me. I want the documents in my hands as soon as I'm fit to read them.'

'Now that,' Monsignor O'Rahilly looked very dubious, 'that's going to be the nub of a lot of arguments. Who will say when Your Holiness is ready – and for what? This is a big operation for a man past middle age and it needs a longish convalescence . . . You've done a pretty effective job of concentrating power in your own hands. Now the *grossi pezzi* in the Curia will be working to claw it back. I can keep you informed, but I can't stage a pitched battle with the Prefect of a Roman Congregation.'

'Are you saying you have trouble already?'

'Trouble? That's not a word I'd dare breathe to Your Holiness, especially at a time like this. I'm simply pointing out that the members of your household will be rather isolated during your absence. Authorities greater than ours will be brought into play. So we need a clear direction from the Chair of Peter.'

'You already have it!' The Pontiff was suddenly his old self again, frowning and emphatic. 'My reserved business and my private documents remain private. In other matters, you will represent what you know to be my views. If contrary orders are given by any member of the Curia, you will request a direction in writing before you comply. If you have a big problem, go to Cardinal Drexel and put the matter to him. Is that clear?'

'It's clear,' said Monsignor O'Rahilly, 'but a little surprising. I'd always felt there was a certain tension between Drexel and Your Holiness.'

'There was. There is. We are very different beings. But

Drexel has two great virtues: he has overpassed ambition and he has a sense of humour rare in the Germans. I disagree with him often; but I trust him, always. You can, too.'

'That's good to know.'

'But there's also a warning, Malachy. Don't try any of your Irish tricks on him. I'm Italian, I understand – most of the time – how your mind works. Drexel's very direct: one-two-three. Work that way with him.'

Monsignor O'Rahilly smiled and bowed his head under the admonition. The Pontiff was right. The Irish and the Italians understood each other very well. After all, the great St Patrick himself was a Roman born; but once the Celts were converted it was they who exported learning and civility to Europe while the Empire was tumbling into ruins. Besides, there was much shared experience between the son of a peat-digger from Connemara and a man who had shovelled dung on a share-farm in Mirandola. All of which gave Malachy O'Rahilly a certain freedom to advise his high master.

'With the greatest respect, Holiness . . .' He made a careful actor's pause.

'Say it, Malachy! Say it plain, without the compliments! What's on your mind?'

'The report on the finances of the Church. It will land on your desk at the end of this month. That's definitely not a matter I can refer to Cardinal Drexel.'

'There's no reason why you should. I can study the document while I'm convalescing.'

'Four years' work by fifteen prelates and laymen? With every bishop in the world looking over your shoulder? And all the faithful asking themselves whether they will or they won't be donating to Peter's Pence and Propaganda Fide next year? Don't delude yourself, Holiness. Better you shouldn't open the report than that you should botch the handling of it.'

'I'm perfectly capable of –'

'You're not. You won't be for some time. And I'd be a bad

servant if I didn't say so! Think of all the hard-nosed fellows who've been working four years on that document. Think of all the messes they've uncovered – and the ones they'll have tried their damndest to bury . . . And you'll be just recovering from a massive surgical invasion. No way you can do a proper job of study.'

'And who else is going to do it for me, Malachy? You?'

'Listen to me Holiness, please!' He was pleading now, earnestly. 'I remember the day, and the hour, when you swore by all the saints in the calendar that you'd clean up the *covo di ladri* who were running the Institute for Religious Works and all its banking agencies. You were so angry that I thought you'd swell up and burst. You said: "These bankers think they're impressing me with their money jargon. Instead, they're insulting me! They're like fairground jugglers, pumping wine out of their elbows, picking coins out of children's ears! I'm a farmer's son. My mother kept all our spare cash in a jam-jar. She taught me that if you spend more than you earn, you're bankrupt – and if you lie down in the pigpen you'll get dirty. I'll never be canonised, because I'm too bad-tempered and stiff-necked, but I promise you, Malachy, I'll be one pope they never call a crook or a friend of crooks – and if I find another financial rogue wearing the purple I'll have it off his back before he goes to bed!" Do you remember all that?'

'I do.'

'Then you have to admit that this report will be your first and last chance to make good on the promise. You can't, you daren't, try to study it while your mind is skewed by anaesthetics or clouded by depressions. Salviati gave you clear warning. You must heed him. Don't forget either that you promised to call a Special Synod to consider the report. Before you confront your brother bishops you'll have to be figure-perfect and fact-perfect on the document.'

'What do you suggest I do with it meanwhile?'

'Receive it. Keep it *in petto*. Lock it in your private safe.

Gag all discussion. Let it be known that it's any man's career if he breaks silence before you speak. If you don't, the Curia will pre-empt you, and when you come to make your statement there'll be mantraps and spring-guns at every corner.'

'Then answer me this, Malachy. Suppose that I don't survive the surgery. What will happen then?'

Monsignor O'Rahilly had the answer on the tip of his fluent tongue.

'It's elementary. The Camerlengo will take possession of it, as he'll take possession of the Ring, the Seal, your will and all your personal chattels. If past history is any guide – and if my mother's second sight is still working – sometime between burying you and installing your successor, they'll lose the document, shove it in the archive, drown it deeper than the Titanic.'

'And why would they do that?'

'Because they're convinced you made a mistake in ordering the study in the first place. I thought so myself – though it wasn't my place to say it. Look! The most profound mystery in this Holy, Roman and Universal Church isn't the Trinity, or the Incarnation, or the Immaculate Conception. It's the fact that we're mired up to our necks in money. We're the biggest banking house in the world. We take in money, we lend it out, we invest it in stocks and bonds. We're part of the world community of money-folk. But money makes its own rules, as it makes its own geniuses and its own rogues – of whom we have our fair share, in the cloth or out of it. The Curia expected you to understand that because they saw you swallowing a whole lot of other indigestible facts about the place and the office. But in this matter, you didn't. For some reason you gagged on it; but they still make the valid point that if you want to have your budget balanced and your staff maintained and the whole huge fabric of the Church kept in running order, then you have to stay in the banking business. If you're in it, you play by the rules and try to embarrass your colleagues as little as possible! There's much sense in that – if not a whole lot of religion . . . And now that I've recited my little piece, how would Your Holiness like my head – on a silver dish or impaled on a pike by the Swiss Guard?'

For the first time, Leo the Pontiff smiled, and the smile turned into his strange barking laugh.

'It's a shrewd head, Malachy. I can ill afford to lose it at this time. As to your future, I'm sure you've realised that I may not be the one who determines it.'

'I've thought about that, too,' said Malachy O'Rahilly. 'I'm not sure I'd want to stay in the Vatican – presuming I were even asked. They do say that service with one pontiff is as much as the human frame can stand.'

'And with Ludovico Gadda it's already too much! Is that what you're telling me, Malachy?'

Malachy O'Rahilly gave him a small, sidelong grin and a shrug of deprecation.

'It hasn't always been easy; but for a big country boy like me there'd have been no fun sparring with a lightweight – no fun at all. I was told I mustn't stay too long. So if there's nothing else I can do for Your Holiness, I'll be on my way.'

'You have our leave, Malachy. And you won't forget that other matter, will you?'

'I'll be on to it this very day. God smile on Your Holiness. I'll be offering my Mass for you in the morning . . .'

'Go with God, Malachy.'

Leo the Pontiff closed his eyes and lay back on the pillows. He felt strangely bereft, a piece of human flotsam bobbing helplessly in a vast and empty ocean.

On his way out of the clinic, Malachy O'Rahilly stopped at the reception desk, gave the girl his most winning Irish smile and asked: 'The young lady who died here last night . . .'

'The Signora de Rosa?'

'The same. I'm most anxious to get in touch with her husband. Do you have an address for him?'

'As a matter of fact, Monsignore, he's here now, talking with the Signora Lundberg. The undertakers have just removed his wife's body. She's being buried in Pistoia. If you'd care to wait . . . I'm sure he won't be very long.'

O'Rahilly was trapped. He could not leave without making a fool of himself, yet the last thing he needed was a confrontation with a grieving and aggrieved husband. In that same instant, bells rang loudly in his head. De Rosa, Lorenzo, from Pistoia in Tuscany, his own contemporary at the Gregorian University. He'd been a handsome devil, bursting with brains and passion and charm and so much unconscious arrogance that friends and masters alike swore that one day he would turn into a Cardinal or an heresiarch.

Instead, here he was, caught up in a shabby little matrimonial tragedy which did no credit to himself or to the Church – and from which not even the Pope could take him now. Not for the first time, Malachy O'Rahilly thanked his stars for a good Irish Jansenist education which assured that, though the drink might snare him one day, no woman ever would.

Then, like a walking corpse, Lorenzo de Rosa stepped into the foyer. His skin, pale and transparent, was drawn drumtight over the bones of his classic face. His eyes were dull, his lips bloodless. He moved like a sleepwalker. O'Rahilly would have let him pass without a word, but the receptionist sprang the trap on him.

'Signor de Rosa, there's a gentleman to see you.'

Puzzled and disoriented, de Rosa stopped dead in his tracks. O'Rahilly stood up and offered his hand.

'Lorenzo? Remember me? Malachy O'Rahilly from the Greg. I happened to be visiting someone here and I heard the news of your sad loss. I'm sorry, truly sorry.'

His hand flapped uselessly in front of him like an autumn leaf. He let it fall to his side. There was a long, hostile silence. The dull eyes surveyed him from head to toe like a specimen of noxious matter. The bloodless lips opened and a flat, mechanical voice answered him.

'Yes, I remember you, O'Rahilly. I wish I had never known you or any other of your kind. You're cheats and hypocrites, all of you, and the god you peddle is the cruellest cheat of all. As I remember, you became a papal secretary, yes? Then tell your master from me I can't wait to spit on his grave!'

The next moment he was gone, a dark, spectral figure out of some ancient folk-tale. Malachy O'Rahilly shivered in the sudden winter of the man's rage and despair. From somewhere in the far distance, he heard the receptionist's voice, soothing and solicitous.

'You mustn't be upset, Monsignore. The poor man's had a terrible blow; his wife was such a sweet woman. They were devoted to each other and to the children.'

'I'm sure they were,' said Malachy O'Rahilly. 'It's all very sad.'

He was tempted to go back and tell the Pontiff what had happened. Then he asked himself the classic question: *cui bono*? What good could possibly come of it? All the harm had been done centuries ago, when the law had been set above simple charity and suffering souls were counted as necessary casualties in the unending crusade again the follies of human flesh.

The rest of the Pontiff's day was a slow processional towards the merciful darkness they had promised him. He strolled alone in the garden, fragrant with the first blossom trees, the smell of mown grass and fresh-turned earth. He sat on the marble lip of the fountain which the gardener told him was the site of the ancient shrine of Diana, where the new king of the woods cleansed himself after the ritual murder. He climbed the slope to the verge of the estate to peer down into the inky depths of Lake Nemi; but when he got there, he was breathless and dizzy and there was the familiar constriction in his chest. He leaned against a pine-bole until the pain passed and he had wind enough to walk himself back to the safety of his room, where the Secretary of State was waiting for him.

Agostini's performance was, as always, impeccably rehearsed. He brought only good news: the solicitous good wishes of Royalty and of Heads of State, the prayerful greetings of members of the Sacred College and the senior hierarchy . . . the replies he had drafted for the Pontiff's approval. Everything else was working to the norms that His Holiness had approved. He declined absolutely to engage in any discussion of business or statecraft.

There was, however, one important matter. If His Holiness wished to spend part of his convalescence outside Vatican territory, in the Republic of Italy, no objection would be raised, provided that adequate security could be maintained, and the Vatican was prepared to meet the cost of a State security contingent. The only caveats were that the Republic retained its right to approve the location, and that provincial and *comune* authorities be consulted in advance on problems of traffic and public assembly.

The Secretary of State understood very well that His Holiness would not wish to make a decision until after the operation, but at least the options were open. The Pontiff thanked him. Agostini asked: 'Are there any personal commissions I can execute for Your Holiness?'

'None, thank you, Matteo. I am comfortable here. I have accepted that the future is out of my hands. I stand in a quiet place – but a solitary one, too.'

'One wishes it were possible to share the experience, make the solitude a little more bearable.'

'It is not, my friend; but one does not come to solitude wholly unprepared. It is almost as if there were a mechanism in the mind, in the body, which prepares us for this moment. May I tell you something? As a young priest, I used to preach

77

very ardently about the consolations of the last sacraments, the confession, the anointing, the viaticum . . . They seemed to have a special meaning for me because my father, whom I loved very dearly, had died without them. He had simply dropped dead in the furrows behind his plough. In a way, I suppose I resented that. He was a good man, who deserved better. I felt that he had been deprived of something he had truly earned . . .'

Agostini waited in silence. It was the first time he had seen the Pontiff in this mood of elegy.

'As you know, before I came in here, I had my chaplain give me the last rites. I don't know what I expected – a sense of relief, of excitement perhaps, like standing on a railway station with all one's baggage packed, waiting to board a train for some exotic place . . . It wasn't like that at all. It was – how can I explain it? – a propriety only, a thing well done but somehow redundant. Whatever had subsisted between myself and the Almighty was as it had been, complete and final. I was held, as I had always been, in the palm of His hand. I could leap out of it if I chose; but so long as I wanted to stay, I was there. I was, I am. I have to accept that it is enough. Do I embarrass you, Matteo?'

'No. But you surprise me a little.'

'Why?'

'Perhaps because Your Holiness is not usually so eloquent about his own emotions.'

'Or as sensitive to those of other people?'

Matteo Agostini smiled and shook his head.

'I'm your Secretary of State, not your confessor.'

'So, you don't have to judge me; but you can afford to indulge me a moment longer. Ask yourself how much of what we do in Rome, how much of what we prescribe and legislate, is truly relevant in the secret life of each human soul. We've been trying for centuries to persuade ourselves and the faithful that our writ runs right up to the gates of heaven and down to the portcullis of hell. They don't believe us. At bottom, we don't believe ourselves. Do I shock you?'

'Nothing shocks a diplomat, Holiness. You know that. But I would wish you happier thoughts.'

'So, Matteo! Each man comes, in the end, to his own special agony. This is mine: to know how much I have failed as a man and a pastor; not to know whether I shall survive to repair the damage. Go home now. Write to your premiers and presidents and kings. Send them our thanks and our Apostolic Benediction. And spare a thought for Ludovico Gadda, who must soon begin his night watch in Gethsemane.'

The night watch, however, was preceded by a series of small humiliations.

The anaesthetist came to explain the procedures, to allay his patient's fears about the pain he might expect, and then to read him a lecture about the regimen he should follow afterwards to reduce his weight, increase his exercise, keep his lungs free of fluid.

Then came the barber, a voluble Neapolitan, who shaved him, clean as an egg, from throat to crotch and laughingly promised him all sorts of exquisite discomforts when the hairs started to grow again. The barber was followed by a nurse who shoved a suppository into his rectum and warned him that he would purge rapidly and frequently for an hour or two, and that afterwards he might ingest fluids only – and nothing at all after midnight.

It was thus that Anton Drexel found him, empty of dignity, empty of belly and sour of temper, when he came to pay him the last permitted visit of the day. Drexel was carrying a leather briefcase and his greeting was brisk and direct as always.

'I can see you've had a bad day, Holiness.'

'I've had better. I'm told they put me to sleep with a pill tonight. I'll be glad of it.'

'If you like, I'll give you communion and read compline with you before I go.'

'Thank you. You're a thoughtful man, Anton. I wonder why it's taken me so long to appreciate you.'

Anton Drexel laughed.

'We're a pair of hard-heads. It takes time to beat sense into us . . . Let me move this bed-lamp a little. I have something to show you.' He opened his briefcase and brought out a large photographic album, bound in tooled leather, which he laid in the Pontiff's lap.

'What is this?'

'Look at it first. I'll explain later.'

Drexel busied himself laying out on the bed-table a linen cloth, a pyx, a small silver flask and a cup. Beside them, he laid his breviary. By the time he had finished the Pontiff was halfway through the volume of photographs. He was obviously intrigued.

'What is this place? Where is it?'

'It's a villa, fifteen minutes away from here. It used to belong to Valerio Rinaldi. You must have known him. He served under your predecessor, Pope Kiril. His family were old nobility, quite wealthy I believe.'

'I knew him, but never well. The place looks charming.'

'It's more than that. It's prosperous and profitable – farm-land, vineyards and vegetable gardens.'

'Who owns it now?'

'I do.' Drexel could not resist a small theatrical flourish. 'And I have the honour to invite Your Holiness to spend his convalescence there. That's the guest villa you're looking at now. There's room for a resident servant if you choose to use your own valet. Otherwise my staff will be delighted to serve you. We have a resident therapist and dietician. The big building is occupied by my family and the people who look after them . . .'

'I can see it's a very large family.' The Pontiff's tone was dry. 'I'm sure Your Eminence will explain it to me in due course. I hope he will also explain how a member of my Curia can afford an establishment like this.'

'That part is easy.' Drexel was obviously enjoying himself. 'Rinaldi sold me the place on a low deposit and a long mortgage which was financed by the Institute for Religious Works at standard rates. There was also a proviso, that on my death the title should pass from me to a recognised work of charity. With a little good luck and good management I was able to meet the mortgage payments out of the farm revenues and my own stipend as a prelate . . . I knew it was a luxury – but I knew I could not endure to live in Rome without a place to which I could retreat, be myself. Besides,' he made a small joke, 'as Your Holiness knows, we Germans have a long tradition of Prince Bishops! I liked the way Rinaldi lived. I admired his old-fashioned style. I was self-indulgent enough to want to emulate it. And I did, with no spiritual merit but great human satisfaction – until I decided to found this family of mine.'

'Which so far you have managed to keep secret from us all! Explain, Eminence! Explain!'

Drexel explained, eloquently and at length, and Leo the Pontiff was jealous of the joy in his voice, his eyes, his every gesture, as he told the history of his encounter in Frascati with the child Britte and how she had adopted him as her grandfather. She was sixteen years old now, he announced proudly, a talented artist who painted with a brush held between her teeth, and whose pictures were sold by a very prestigious gallery in Via Margutta.

The others? Tove Lundberg had introduced some parents of diplegic children. They had recommended others. Anton Drexel had begged money from richer colleagues in the United States and Latin America and Europe. He had improved the quality of his wine and his farm produce and doubled the income of his land. Salviati had introduced him to specialists in cerebral dysfunction and to a small cadre of money-men who helped to pay his teaching and nursing staff . . .

'So, although we've lived pretty much hand to mouth for ten years, we're educating artists and mathematicians and designers of computer programmes – but most of all we've given these children a chance to be truly human, to show forth the Divine image in which, despite their grievous afflictions, they were truly made . . . It is their invitation as much as mine, Holiness, that you should come and begin to mend yourself with us. You don't have to decide now. Just think about it. One thing I can promise you: it's a very happy family.'

The Pontiff's reaction was strange. For an instant he seemed very close to tears, then his face hardened into that familiar, implacable predator's mask. His tone was harsh, accusatory and pitilessly formal.

'It seems to us, Eminence, that, however worthy this enterprise, you have paid us small compliment by concealing it for so long. We deprecate, as you know, any and all aspects of luxury in the lives of our brother bishops. But all this aside, it seems you have been guilty of certain presumptions touching our office as Vicar of Christ. We are not so ill informed or so deaf to palace gossip as people sometimes believe. We are aware, for instance, that Dr Salviati is Jewish by race and Zionist in sympathy; that his trusted counsellor, the Signora Lundberg, is an unwed mother, and that there is talk of a liaison between them. Since neither is of our Faith, their private morals are no concern of ours. But that you should have formed this . . . this quite fictional relationship with her child and, by inference, with her, that you should have concealed it for so long and then attempted to draw us into it, for however good a reason . . . This we find quite intolerable and highly dangerous to us and to our office.'

Anton Drexel had heard, in his time, some classic tirades from Leo XIV, but this one topped them all. All the man's fears, frustrations and angers had been poured into it, all the buried rages of the ploughboy who had climbed and clawed his way up to be a prince. Now, having vented it in such fury, he waited, tense and hostile, for the counter attack. Instead, Drexel replied with calm formality.

'Your Holiness makes it clear that I have a case to answer. Now is not the time to do it. Let me say only that if I have offended Your Holiness I am deeply sorry. I was offering what I believed to be a kindness and a service. But we should not part like this, in anger. Can we not pray together, like brothers?'

The Pontiff said nothing, but reached for his spectacles and his breviary. Drexel opened his book and recited the opening versicle: '*Munda cor meum* . . . Cleanse my heart, O Lord, that my lips may announce your praises . . .' Soon the rhythm of the ancient psalms took hold of them, soothing them like waves on a friendly sea. After a while the Pontiff's taut face began to relax, and the hostility died out of his dark eyes. When he read the words 'Yea, though I walk in the valley of death, His rod and His staff shall comfort me . . .' his voice faltered and he began to weep quietly. It was Drexel now who carried the burden of the recitation, while his hand closed over that of his master and held it in a firm and comforting grip.

When the last Amen had been spoken, Drexel put a stole around his neck and gave the Pontiff communion, then sat silently while he made his thanksgiving. No words but prayers had been spoken between them for nearly forty minutes. Drexel began repacking his briefcase. Then, as protocol prescribed, he begged leave to go.

'Please!'It was a poignant appeal from a high, proud man. 'Please stay awhile! I'm sorry for what I said. You understand me better than anyone else. You always have. That's why I fight you. You will not leave me any illusions.'

'Do you know why?' Drexel was gentle with him, but he would not yield an inch.

'I would like to hear it from you.'

'Because we cannot afford illusions any more. The people of God cry out for the bread of life. We are feeding them stones.'

'And you think I have been doing that?'

'Ask yourself the question, Holiness.'

'I have – every day, every night for months now. I am asking it tonight, before they wheel me out and freeze me and split me like a carcase of beef and put my life into syncope . . . I know things must change and I must be the catalyst of change. But how, Anton? I am only what I am. I cannot crawl back into my mother's womb and be born again.'

'I am told,' said Drexel slowly, 'by those who have undergone this operation, that it's the nearest one can come to being reborn. Salviati and Tove Lundberg tell me the same thing. It's a new lease on life – and, perforce, a new kind of life. So the question for me, the question for the Church, is what use you're going to make of the new gift.'

'And you have a prescription for me, Anton!'

'No. You already know the prescription. It's repeated over and over again in Scripture. "My little children, love one another . . . Above all, have a constant mutual charity among yourselves . . ." The question is how you will interpret the revelation, how you will respond to it in the future.'

'How have I done so until now?'

'The old Roman way! Legislation, admonition, fiat! We are the custodians of truth, the censors of morals, the only authentic interpreters of revelation. We are the binders and the loosers, the heralds of good tidings. Make straight the way of the Lord! Prepare the paths before Him!'

'And you don't agree with that?'

'No. I don't. I have been fifty-five years a priest in the Roman rite. I was trained in the system and to the system. I kept my priestly vows and I lived according to the canons. I have served four pontiffs – two as a member of the Sacred

College. Your Holiness will bear witness that though I disagreed often and openly, I bowed always in obedience to the *magisterium*!'

'You did, Anton, and I respected you for it. But now you say we have failed, that I have failed.'

'All the evidence says we have.'

'But why?'

'Because you and I, all of us, Curia and hierarchy alike, are the nearly perfect products of our Roman system. We never fought it. We marched with it every step of the way. We cauterised our emotions, hardened our hearts, made ourselves eunuchs for the love of God! – how I've come to hate that phrase! – and somewhere along the way, very early I think, we lost the simple art of loving. If you come to think about it, we're very selfish people, we bachelor priests. We're the true biblical Pharisees. We bind heavy and insupportable burdens on men's backs and we ourselves lift no finger to ease them! So, the people turn away; not to strange gods, as we like to think; not to orgies and self-indulgence that they can't afford; but in search of simplicities which we, the custodians, censors and governors, have obscured from them. They want care and compassion and love and a hand to lead them out of the maze. Does yours? Does mine? I think not. But if an honest, open, brave man sat in the chair of Peter and thought first, last and always of the people, there might be a chance. There just might be!'

'But I am not that man?'

'Today, you are not. But afterwards, given a new lease on life and the grace to use it aright, who knows but that one day Your Holiness may write the great message for which the people hunger and thirst: the message of love, compassion, forgiveness. It's a call that needs to be sounded loud and clear as Roland's horn at Roncesvalles . . .' He broke off, suddenly aware of his own fervour. 'In any case, that's the reason for my invitation to spend part of your healing time with my family. You will see love in action every day. You will see people giving it, taking it, growing in the warmth of it. I can promise it will be spent on you, too, and one day you will be rich enough to return it . . . You need this time; you need this experience. I see what this office does to you – to any man! It dries the sap out of you, withers you up like a raisin in the sun. Now is your chance of renewal. Take it! Be, for once, generous with Ludovico Gadda who has been a long time away from his home-place!'

'I ask myself,' said the Pontiff wryly, 'why I did not make you Preacher to the Pontifical Household.'
Drexel laughed.

'Your Holiness knows very well why. You would have sent me to the stake within a week.' The next moment he was back to formality. 'It is long past my bedtime. If Your Holiness will give me leave to go?'

'You have our leave.'

'Once again, I beg forgiveness for my presumption. I hope there is peace between us at last.'

'There is peace, Anton. God knows, there is no time left for quarrels and banalities. I am grateful for your counsel. Perhaps I will come to stay with you; but as you well know, there are other considerations: protocols, palace rivalries, old memories of bad times in our history. I cannot ignore these things or override them rashly. However, once I'm through the tunnel, I'll think about it. Now go home, Anton! Go home to your family and give them my blessing!'

In the last private time left to him before the arrival of the night nurse, Leo XIV wrote what he knew might be the final entry in his diary. Even if there were to be other entries, they would be written by another Leo, a reconstructed man who had been disconnected from his life source and then set working again like a mechanical toy. So there was a certain brutal urgency in the record.

'I behaved like a country clod. I abused a man who wished me nothing but good. Why? In simple truth, I always have been jealous of Anton Drexel. At eighty, he is much healthier, happier and wiser than I have ever been. To become what I am, Supreme Pastor of the Universal Church, I have worked like a brute every day of my life. Drexel, on the other hand, is a self-indulgent man whose style and talent have brought him, almost without effort, to eminence in the Church.

'In Renaissance times, they would certainly have made him Pope. Like my namesake, Leo X, he would have set out to enjoy the experience. Whatever his imperfections as a cleric, he is the most perfect diplomat. He will always tell the truth, because it is his master, not himself, who must bear the consequences. He will argue a position in the strongest terms; but in the end he will bow to the decision of authority. Rome is a very comfortable and rewarding place for such a man.

'However, tonight it was clear that he was offering me a share in a loving experience which had transformed his life and turned even his self-indulgence to good account. I did not have the courage to tell him how much I envied the intimacy and immediacy of his love for his adopted children, while whatever love I have is diffused and diluted out of existence over a human multitude.

'Nonetheless, I felt that he was still trying to manipulate me, to regulate, however indirectly, what might remain of my life and authority as Supreme Pontiff. Even that I could tolerate, because I need him. My problem is that he has the luxury of being mistaken without too grave a consequence. I am bound by every protocol, aware of every risk. I am power personified, but power inert and in stasis.

'The cold facts are these. My policies have been

proven wrong. Change, radical change, is necessary
in the governance of the Church at every level. But
even if I survive, how can I make the change? It was
I who created the climate of rigorism and repression.
It was I who recruited the zealots to impose my will.
The moment I begin to hint a change, they will rally
to circumvent me, by clogging my communications,
confusing me with scenarios of scandal and schism,
misrepresenting my views and directives.

'I cannot fight that battle alone. Already I have
been warned that I shall be vulnerable for some time,
emotionally fragile, subject to sudden threatening
depressions. If I am already a casualty, how can I mount
a campaign which may well turn into a civil war?

'It is an enormous risk; but if I am not fit to take it,
then I am not fit to govern. I shall have to consider the
question of abdication – and that, too, is fraught with
other risks for the Church.

'Even as I write these words, I am caught up in
a memory of my schooldays. My history master was
trying to explain to us the Pax Romana, the period
of calm and prosperity throughout the Empire under
Augustus. He explained it thus: "So long as the legions
were on the march, so long as the roads they trod were
maintained and extended, the peace would last, trade
would flourish, the Empire would endure. But the day
they pitched the last camp, threw up the last earthworks
and palisades and retired behind them as garrison troops,
the Pax Romana was finished, the Empire was finished,
the barbarians were on the move towards the heart of
Rome."

'As I sit here now, writing these lines to distract myself
from tomorrow, I imagine that last commander of that
last *castra* on the outer marches. I see him making his
night rounds, checking the guard-posts, while beyond the

ditch and the palisades and the cleared ground, men in animal masks made their war dance and invoked the old baleful gods of woodland, water and fire.

'There was no retreat for him. There is no retreat for me. I hear the night nurse trundling her little trolley down the corridor. She will come to me last of all. She will check my vital signs, pulse, temperature, blood pressure. She will ask whether I have passed water and whether my bowels have moved. Then, please God, she will give me a pill that will send me to sleep until dawn. Strange, is it not, that I who have always been a restless man, should now court so sedulously that sleep which is the brother of death. Or perhaps not so strange, perhaps this is the last mysterious mercy, that God makes us ready for death before death is quite ready for us.

'It is time to finish now, put down the pen and lock away the book. Sufficient unto the day is the evil thereof. More than sufficient are the fears and angers and the shame I feel for Ludovico Gadda, the ugly man who lives inside my skin . . . Forgive him his trespasses, O Lord, as he forgives those who have trespassed against him. Lead him not into trial he cannot endure and deliver him from evil – Amen.'

Five

When he returned to his lodgings in Vatican City, Monsignor Malachy O'Rahilly telephoned his colleague, Monsignor Matthew Neylan of the Secretariat of State. Matt Neylan was a tall, handsome fellow, dark as a gypsy, with a crooked, satiric grin and a loose athlete's stride that made women look twice at him and then give him one more glance to fix him in their memories and wonder what he'd look like out of uniform. His title was Segretario di Nunziature di prima classe, which, however awkwardly it translated into English, put him about number twenty in the pecking order. It also gave him access to a great deal of information on a wide range of diplomatic matters. O'Rahilly saluted him with the full brogue and blarney.

'Matt, me fine boyo! Malachy! I have a question for you.'

'Then spit it out, Mal. Don't let it fester in your mouth!'

'If I were to ask you, very politely, whether you'd dine with me tonight, what would you say?'

'Well now, that would depend.'

'On what?'

'On where we'd eat and who was paying – and what quid I'd be asked for O'Rahilly's quo!'

'A three-in-one answer, boyo. We eat at Romolo's, I pick up the check, and you give me a piece of advice.'

'Whose car do we take?'

'We walk! It's ten minutes for a one-legged man!'

'I'm on my way already. Meet you at the Porta Angelica – oh, and bring cash; they don't like credit cards.'

'That's my careful friend!'

Da Romolo, near the Porta Settimiana, had once been the house of *la Fornarina*, mistress and model to the painter Raphael. However unreliable the legend, the food was good, the wine honest and the service – in age-old Roman style – agreeably impertinent and slapdash. In winter one ate inside, warmed by a fire of olive wood in the old baker's oven. In spring and summer one dined outside under a canopy of vines. Sometimes a guitarist came, singing folk songs in Neapolitan and Romanaccio. Always there were lovers, old, young and in-between. The clergy came too, in or out of uniform, because they were as much a fixture in the Roman scene as the lovers and the wandering musicians and the jostling purse-snatchers in the alleys of Trastevere.

In true Roman style, O'Rahilly kept his question until after the pasta and the first litre of wine.

'Tell me now, Matt, do you remember a fellow called Lorenzo de Rosa at the Greg?'

'I do. Handsome as Lucifer. Had a phenomenal memory. He could recite pages of Dante at a stretch! As I remember, he was laicised a few years ago.'

'He wasn't. He skipped the formalities and got himself married under the civil code.'

'Well, at least he had sense enough to cut clean!'

'He didn't. That was his problem. He's been trying to tidy the whole mess. Naturally enough, nobody's been very co-operative.'

'So?'

'So last night his wife died in the Salviati clinic, leaving him with two young children.'

'That's tough.'

'Tougher than you know, Matt. I was at the clinic tonight to see our lord and master. De Rosa was just coming out. We spoke. The poor devil's near crazed with grief. He said – and I quote: "I can't wait to spit on your master's grave!"'

'Well. I've heard the same thought expressed by others – more civilly, of course.'

'It's not a laughing matter, Matt.'

'And did I say it was? What's bothering you, Mal?'

'I can't make up my mind whether he's a threat to the Holy Father or not. If he is, then I've got to do something about it.'

'Like what?'

'Call our security people. Have them make contact with the Carabinieri and arrange some surveillance on de Rosa.'

'They won't only put him under surveillance, Mal. They'll roast him on a spit, just to frighten him off. That's pretty rough for a man with two kids and a wife hardly cold in the ground.'

'That's why I'm asking your opinion, Matt. What should I do?'

'Let's be legal first of all. He uttered a malediction, not a menace. It was a word spoken in private to a priest. So he didn't commit a crime; but if it suited them, the security boys could make it look like one at the drop of a hat. More than that, your report and their embellishments would go on his dossier – and they'd be there till doomsday. All the other circumstances of his life would be read in the light of that single denunciation. That's the way the system is designed. It's a hell of a burden to lay on an innocent man!'

'I know. I know. But take the worst scenario: the man is really a nut-case, bent on vengeance for an injustice done to him and to the woman he loved. One summer day he goes to a public audience in St Peter's Square and shoots the Pope. How will I feel then?'

'I don't know,' said Matt Neylan innocently. 'How has the Man been treating you lately?'

Malachy O'Rahilly laughed.

'Not so well that I'd give him a good-conduct medal. Not

so badly that I'd want to see him bumped off. You'd have to agree there's that risk.'

'I don't have to agree anything of the kind. You met de Rosa. I didn't. Besides, if you wanted to eliminate every possible threat to your Sacred Person, you'd have to make pre-emptive arrests up and down the peninsula. Personally, I'd be inclined to ignore the whole thing.'

'I'm the man's secretary, for God's sake! I've got a certain special duty to him.'

'Wait a minute! There may be a simple way to handle this, with no extra grief to anyone. Let me think it through while you order another bottle of wine. Make it a decent red this time. This house Frascati is so thin you could keep goldfish in it.'

While Malachy O'Rahilly went through his little fandango over the wine, Matt Neylan sponged up the last sauce from his pasta and then delivered his verdict.

'There's a fellow who works for our security people here in Vatican City. His name is Baldassare Cotta. He owes me a favour because I recommended his son for a clerk's job in the Post Office. He used to be an investigator for the Guardia di Finanza and I know he moonlights for a private detective agency in town. I could ask him to check out de Rosa and give me a report. It would cost you round about a hundred thousand lire. Can you touch the petty cash for that much?'

'Wouldn't he do it for love?'

'He would, but then he'd have the arm on me for another favour. Come on, Mal! How much is the Bishop of Rome worth?'

'It depends on where you're sitting,' said Malachy O'Rahilly with a grin. 'But it's a good idea. I'll underwrite it from somewhere. You're a good man, Matt. They'll make you a bishop yet.'

'I won't be around that long, Mal.'

Malachy O'Rahilly gave him a swift, appraising look.

'I do believe you're serious.'

'Dead serious.'

'What are you trying to tell me?'

'I'm thinking of giving the game away, just walking out, like our friend de Rosa.'

'To get married?'

'Hell no! Just to get out! I'm the wrong man in the wrong place, Mal. I've known it for a long time. It's only lately I've put together enough courage to admit it!'

'Matt, tell me honestly, is there a woman in it?'

'It might be easier if there were – but no. And it isn't the other thing either.'

'Do you want to talk about it?'

'After the steak, if you don't mind. I don't want to choke in the middle of my own valediction.'

'You're taking this very lightly.'

'I've had a long time to think about it, Mal. I'm very calm. I know exactly what Luther meant when he said, "Here I stand, I can do no other". All I'm trying to figure is how to make the move with as little upset as possible . . . Here's the steak now, and the wine. Let's enjoy 'em. There'll be plenty of time to talk afterwards.'

The Florentine steak was tender. The wine was soft and full-bodied and for a man facing a drastic change in his life and his career, Matt Neylan was singularly relaxed. Malachy O'Rahilly was forced to contain his own curiosity until the meat dishes had been cleared away and the waiter had consented to leave them in peace to consider dessert. Even then, Neylan took a roundabout route to deliver the news.

'Where to begin? That's a problem in itself, you see. Now, it's all so simple and matter-of-fact that I can hardly believe the agonies I put myself through. You and I, Mal, had the same career, chapter and verse: school with the Brothers in Dublin, seminary at Maynooth, then Rome and the Greg. We paced it out together: Philosophy, Biblical Studies, Theology – Dogmatic, Moral and Pastoral – Latin, Greek, Hebrew and Exegetics and History. We could put together a thesis, defend it, turn it inside out like a dirty sock and make it into heresy for the next debate in the Aula. Rome was right for us, we were right for Rome. We were the bright boys, Mal. We came from the most orthodox Catholic country in the world. We just had to run up the ladder, and we did, you to the Papal Household, me to the Secretariat of State, attaché first class . . . The only thing we missed was the thing that we swore brought us into the priesthood in the first place: pastoral service, the care of the people, Mal! We didn't do any of that worth a tinker's curse! We became career clerics, old-time court *abbés* from the monarchies of Europe. I'm not a priest, Mal. I'm a goddam diplomat – a good one, too, who could hold his own in any embassy in the world – but I could have been that anyway, without forswearing women and marriage and family life.'

'So now we come to it!' said Malachy O'Rahilly. 'I knew we would, sooner or later. You're lonely, you're tired of a solitary bed, bored with bachelor company. No discredit in that, boyo. It comes with the territory. You're riding through the badlands just now!'

'Wrong, Mal! Wrong, wrong. Rome's the easiest place in the world to come to terms with the flesh and the devil. You know damn well you can sleep two in a bed here for twenty years, with nobody any the wiser! The point – the real, needle-sharp point, old friend – is that I'm not a believer any more.'

'Would you call that one back to me, please?' O'Rahilly was very quiet. 'I want to be sure I've heard aright.'

'You heard me, Mal.' Neylan was calm as a lecturer at the blackboard. 'Whatever it is that makes for faith – the grace, the gift, the disposition, the need – I don't have it. It's gone. And the strange thing is I'm not troubled at all. I'm not like poor Lorenzo de Rosa, fighting for justice inside a community to which he's still bound, heart and soul, then despairing because he doesn't get it. I don't belong in the community because I don't believe any longer in the ideas and the dogmas that underpin it . . .'

'But you're still part of it, Matt.'

'By courtesy only. My courtesy!' Matt Neylan shrugged. 'I'm doing everyone a favour by not making a scandal, carrying on the job until I can arrange a tidy exit. Which will probably take the form of a quiet chat with Cardinal Agostini early next week, a very polite note of resignation and presto! I'm gone like a snowflake.'

'But they won't let you go like that, Matt. You know the whole rigmarole: voluntary suspension *a sacris*, application for a dispensation . . .'

'It doesn't apply.' Matt Neylan explained patiently. 'The rigmarole only works when you believe in it. What have they got to bind me with except moral sanctions? And those don't apply, because I don't subscribe any longer to the codex. They don't have the Inquisition any more. The Papal States don't exist. The Vatican *sbirri* can't come and arrest me at midnight. So, I leave in my own time and in my own way.'

'You'll go gladly, by the sound of it.' O'Rahilly's tone was sour.

'No, Mal. There's a sadness in it – a misty, grey kind of sadness. I've lost or mislaid a large part of my life. They say that an amputee can be haunted by the ghost of a missing limb; but the haunting stops after a while.'

'What will you do for a living?'

'Oh, that's easy. My mother died last year. She left me a smallholding in County Cork. And last week, on the strength of my experience of Vatican diplomacy, I signed a two-book contract with a New York publisher for better money than I've ever dreamed of. So I have no financial worries, and the chance to enjoy my life.'

'And no conscience problems either?'

'The only problem I've got, Mal — and it's too early to know how I'll adjust to it — is how I'll cope with living in neutral gear, without the creed and the codex.'

'You may find it harder than you think.'

'It's hard already.' Matt Neylan grinned at him across the table. 'Right now! Between thee and me! You're inside the Communion of Saints. I'm outside it. You're a believer. I'm a *miscredente*, an infidel. We look the same, because we wear the uniform of a pair of ship's officers on the Barque of Peter. But you're still carrying the pilot. I've dropped him and I'm steering my own ship; which is a lonely and perilous thing to do in shoal waters.'

'Where are you thinking of living afterwards? The Vatican won't want you hanging around Rome. They can make things quite uncomfortable if they want, as you well know.'

'The thought hadn't entered my mind, Mal. I'll go first to Ireland to settle the legacy and see that the property's well managed. Then I'll take myself round the world to see how it looks to a simple tourist with a fresh mind. Wherever I end up, I hope we can still be friends. If we can't, I'll understand.'

'Of course we'll be friends, man! And to prove it, I'll let you buy me a very large brandy — which, after this shock, I damn well need!'

'I'll join you — and if it makes you any happier, I'll get you the report on de Rosa for nothing!'

'That's big of you, boyo. I'll see you get credit for it on judgement day!'

For Sergio Salviati, Italian born, a Jew by ancestry and tradition, a Zionist by conviction, surgeon extraordinary to a Roman Pontiff, judgement day had already arrived. A personage, sacred to a billion people on the planet, was committed to his custody and care. Instantly, before a scalpel had been lifted, the sacred personage was under threat – a threat as deadly as any infarct or aneurysm.

It was conveyed by Menachem Avriel, Israeli Ambassador to the Republic, who delivered it over dinner in Salviati's house.

'Late this afternoon our intelligence people informed me that an attempt may be made to assassinate the Pontiff while he is at the clinic.'

Salviati weighed the information for a moment and then shrugged.

'It was always on the cards, I suppose. How good is the information?'

'Grade A-plus, first hand from a Mossad man working undercover in an Iranian group, the Sword of Islam. He says they're offering a contract – fifty thousand dollars up front, fifty thousand when the job is done. He doesn't know yet what takers they've had.'

'Do the Italians know about this – and the Vatican?'

'Both were informed at six this evening.'

'Their answers?'

'Thank you – and we'll take appropriate action.'

'They'd better.' Salviati was terse. 'It's out of my hands now. I start scrubbing with the team at six in the morning. I can't cope with anything else.'

'Our best judgement – that is to say, Mossad's best judgement – is that any action will be taken during the convalescent period and that the attempt will be made from inside – by tampering with drugs, medications or life-support systems.'

'I've got nearly a hundred staff at the clinic. They've got eight, ten languages between them. I can't guarantee that one of them isn't an agent in place. Damn it, I know at least three are agents in place for Mossad!'

Menachem Avriel laughed.

'Now you can be glad you let me put 'em there! At least they know the routines and can direct the people we're sending in tomorrow.'

'And who, pray, will they be?'

'Oh, didn't you know? The Agenzia Diplomatica got a call late this afternoon for two extra wardsmaids, two electrical maintenance technicians and two male orderlies. They'll be reporting for duty at six in the morning. Issachar Rubin will be in charge. You won't have to worry about a thing – and Mossad will pick up the bill. You can concentrate on your distinguished patient. What's the prognosis, by the way?'

'Good. Very good, in fact. The man's obese and out of condition, but as a boy he was farm-fed and farm-worked. He's also got a will of iron. That helps him now.'

'I wonder if it will help us?'

'To what?'

'Vatican recognition for the State of Israel.'

'You're joking!' Salviati was suddenly tense and irritable. 'That's been a dead duck from day one! No way will they back Israel against the Arab world! No matter what they say officially, by tradition we're Christ-killers, accursed of God. We have no right to a homeland, because we cast out the Messiah and we in our turn were cast out! Nothing's changed, believe me. We did better under the Roman Empire than under the popes. It was they who put the yellow star on us, centuries before Hitler. During the war, they buried six million dead in the Great Silence. If Israel were dismembered again, they'd be there, scrabbling for the title-deeds to their Holy Places.'

'And yet you, my dear Sergio, are going to endow this man with a new lease of life! Why you? Why not remit him to his own?'

'You know why, my friend! I want him in my debt. I want him to owe me his life. Every time he looks at a Jew I want him to remember that he owes his survival to one and his salvation to another.' Suddenly aware of his own vehemence, he grinned and spread his hands in a gesture of surrender. 'Menachem, my friend, I'm sorry. I'm always edgy the night before a big operation.'

'Do you have to spend it alone?'

'Never, if I can help it. Tove Lundberg will come over later. She'll spend the night and drive me to the clinic in the morning. She's good for me – the best thing in my life!'

'So when are you going to marry her?'

'I'd do it tomorrow, if she'd have me.'

'What's the problem?'

'Children. She doesn't want any more. She's made sure she can't have them. She says it's unfair to ask a man to wear that, even if he's willing.'

'She's wise!' The Ambassador was suddenly very quiet. 'You're lucky to get a good woman on such easy terms. But if you're thinking of marriage and a family . . .'

'I know! I know! Your Leah will find me a nice bright Jewish girl, and you'll both send us off to Israel for the honeymoon. Forget it!'

'I'll move it up in the calendar, but I won't forget it. Where's Tove now?'

'She's entertaining James Morrison, our visiting surgeon.'

'Question: does she know about the Agenzia Diplomatica, and your other connections?'

'She knows my sympathies are with Israel. She knows the people you send me to be entertained. For the rest, she doesn't ask questions and I don't volunteer answers.'

'Good! The Agenzia is very important to us, as you know. It's one of the best ideas I've had in my life . . .'

Menachem Avriel spoke no more than the truth. Long before his first diplomatic appointment, when he was still a field agent for Mossad, he had proposed the notion of a chain of employment agencies, one in each diplomatic capital, which could offer casual labour – cooks, waiters, chambermaids, nannies, nurses, chauffeurs – to diplomats on station and business families serving overseas terms. Every applicant for listing on the agency's books was screened, bonded and paid the highest rate the traffic would bear. Local employment regulations were meticulously observed. Taxes were paid. Records were accurate. The clientele expanded by recommendation. Israeli agents, male and female, were filtered into the lists and Mossad had eyes and ears at every diplomatic party and business entertainment. Sergio Salviati himself kept places open on his roster for casual staff from the Agenzia, and if he ever had misgivings about the double role he was playing, he buried it under an avalanche of bitter folk-memories: the decrees of mediaeval popes that foreshadowed the Nuremberg laws of Hitler in 1935, the infamies of ghetto existence, the Black Sabbath of 1943, the massacre of the Ardeatine Caves.

There were moments when he felt that he could be riven asunder by the forces thrusting out from the centre of himself – the monomania that made him a great surgeon and a medical reformer, the fierce attachment of every Latin to his *paese*, his home-place, the tug of ten thousand years of tribal tradition, the nostalgia of psalmodies that had become the voice of his own secret heart: 'If I forget thee, O Jerusalem, let my right hand forget its cunning.'

'I should be going,' said Menachem Avriel. 'You need an early night. Thanks for the dinner.'

'Thank you for the warning.'

'Try not to let it worry you.'

'It won't. I work with life in my hands and death looking over my shoulder. I can't afford any distractions.'

'Time was,' said Menachem Avriel drily, 'when a Jew was forbidden to give medical aid to a Christian – and a Christian doctor had to convert the Jew before he could offer treatment.'

It was then, for the first time, that Sergio Salviati revealed the torment that was tearing him apart.

'We've learned well, haven't we, Menachem? Israel has come of age. We've got our own ghettoes now, our own inquisition, our own brutalities; and our own special scapegoats, the Palestinians! That's the worst thing the *goyim* have done to us. They've taught us to corrupt ourselves!'

In her own apartment on the other side of the courtyard, Tove Lundberg was explaining Salviati to his English colleague.

'He is like a kaleidoscope, changing every moment. He is so various that it seems he is twenty men, and you wonder how you can cope with so many – or even how he copes with himself. Then suddenly he is clear and simple as water. That is how you will see him tomorrow morning in the theatre. He will be absolutely controlled. He will not say an unnecessary word, or make a redundant gesture. I have heard the nurses say they have never seen anyone so careful with human tissue. He handles it like gossamer.'

'He has respect.' James Morrison savoured the last of his wine. 'That's the mark of a great healer. It shows. And how's his touch for other things?'

'Careful always. Very gentle most of the time. But there are lots of angers in him that I wish he could spare himself. I never understood until I came to Italy how deep is the prejudice against Jews – even against the native born with long ancestries in the land. Sergio told me that he decided very early that the best way for him to cope with it was by studying its roots and causes. He can talk for hours on the subject. He quotes passages from Doctors of the Church, from papal encyclicals and decretals, from archival documents. It's a sad and sorry tale, especially when you think that the ghetto here in Rome was abolished and the Jewish people enfranchised by royal decree only in 1870.

'In spite of soothing noises and half-hearted verbal amends, the Vatican has never repudiated its anti-semitic stance. It has never recognised the right and title of the Jewish people to a traditional homeland . . . These things trouble Sergio. They help him, too, because they drive him to excellence, to make himself a kind of banner-bearer for his people . . . Yet the other part of him is a Renaissance man, seeing all, trying desperately to understand and pardon all.'

'You love him very much, don't you?'

'Yes.'

'So . . . ?'

'So sometimes I think I love him too well for my own good. One thing I'm sure of, marriage would be the wrong move for both of us.'

'Because he's Jewish and you're not?'

'No. It's because . . .' She hesitated a long time over the words as if testing each one for the load it must bear. 'It's because I've arrived at my own standing place. I know who I am, where I am, what I need, what I can have. Sergio is still travelling, still searching, because he will go much further and stand much higher than I could even dream. A moment will come when he will need someone else. I'll be excess baggage . . . I want to make that moment as simple as possible, for him and for me.'

'I wonder . . .' James Morrison poured himself another glass of wine. 'I wonder if you really know how much you mean to him?'

'I do, believe me. But there are limits to what I can provide. I've spent so much love and care on Britte, there is so much more that I shall have to spend, that there's none left for another child. I haven't grudged any of it; but my capital is used up . . . I am almost at the end of my breeding time – so that special part of my passion for a man is gone. I'm a good lover and Sergio needs that because, as you well know, James, surgeons spend so much of their lives thinking about other people's bodies, they sometimes forget the one beside them in bed. On top of all that, I'm a Dane. Marriage

103

Italian style or Jewish style isn't for me. Does that answer your question?'

'It does, thank you. It also raises another one. How do you read our distinguished patient?'

'I rather like him. I didn't at first. I saw every objectionable feature that sixty years of clerical education, professional celibacy and bachelor selfishness can produce in a man – not to mention the greed for power that seems to afflict some elderly bachelors. He's ugly, he's cross-grained, he can be quite rude. But as we talked I caught glimpses of someone else, a man who might have been. You will laugh at this, I know, but I was reminded of the old fairy story of the Beauty and the Beast . . . remember? If only the Princess could summon up courage to kiss the Beast, he would turn into a handsome prince.'

James Morrison threw back his head and laughed happily.

'I love it! You didn't try, did you?'

'Of course not. But tonight, on my way home, I called in to see him. It was a few minutes after nine. They had just given him the sedatives to settle him for the night. He was drowsy and relaxed but he recognised me. There was a lock of hair hanging down into his eyes. Without thinking, I brushed it away. He took my hand and held it for the briefest of moments. Then he said, so simply I almost wept: "My mother used to do that. She used to pretend it was my guardian angel, brushing me with her wings."'

'Is that what he said, "*her* wings"?'

'Yes. Suddenly I saw a little, lonely boy with a girl-angel for a ghostly playmate. Sad, isn't it?'

'But for that one small moment, joyful. You're quite a woman, Tove Lundberg, quite a woman! Now, I'm going to bed, before I make a fool of myself.'

In the Apostolic Palace in Vatican City, the lights burned late. The Cardinal Secretary of State had summoned into conference the senior officials of his Secretariat and those of the Council for the Public Affairs of the Church. These two bodies between them dealt with all the external relations of Vatican City State and, at the same time, held together the complex and sometimes conflicting interests within the body of the Church. In the daily conduct of Curial affairs they were a kitchen cabinet; tonight, with the safety of the Pontiff at stake, they were a very cool and quite ruthless council of war.

Agostini, the Secretary of State, summed up the situation.

'I accept the Israeli information as authentic. I accept, with considerable relief, that Mossad undercover agents will be working with normal staff around the intensive care unit and, later, on the ward occupied by His Holiness. This is an irregular and unofficial intervention, so we can take no formal notice of it. We rely upon the forces of the Republic of Italy – especially the Nucleo Centrale Anti-Terrorismo, who are at this moment reinforcing the perimeter protection of the clinic and will be placing plainclothes guards at strategic points within the building itself. This is about as much as we can do for the physical security of the Pontiff during his illness. However, a hurried check this evening with our diplomatic contacts indicates that things may not be quite so simple as they seem. Our colleague Anwar El Hachem has something to say on the Arab-Israeli aspect of the matter.'

El Hachem, a Maronite from Lebanon, delivered his report.

'Sword of Islam is a small splinter group of Iranians from Lebanon, operating in Rome itself. They are not associated with the mainstream of Palestinian opinion, but are known to be able to touch large funds. Even as we speak, Italian security agents are pulling some of them in for questioning. Embassy representatives of Saudi Arabia and the North African republics, as well as the Emirates, disclaim all knowledge of the threat and offer full co-operation against what they see as a free-booting operation which can only do them harm. One or two of them raised the question as to whether the Israelis were setting up the whole thing as a provocative gesture. But I found little support for this view.'

'Thank you, Anwar.' The Secretary continued. 'Is there any doubt at all that the contract offer of $100,000 was made by Sword of Islam?'

'None at all. But the man who made it is now in hiding.'

'The Americans know nothing.' Agostini hurried through the list. 'The Russians disclaim all knowledge but are happy to exchange news if they get any. The French are referring back to Paris. What about the British?'

The British were the territory of the Right Reverend Hunterson, titular Archbishop of Sirte, a senior Vatican servant for many years. His report was brief but specific.

'The British Embassy said tut-tut how distressing, promised to look into it and came back about nine with the same information as Anwar, that Sword of Islam is a shop-front title for an Iranian-backed group out of Lebanon. They do have money in the quantities suggested. They do finance hostage-taking and murder. In this instance, His Holiness presents a prominent target-of-opportunity.'

'Which he wouldn't be,' said the Substitute Secretary tartly, 'if we'd gone to Salvator Mundi or Gemelli. We have only ourselves to blame for exposing him to a hostile environment.'

'It's not the ground that's hostile.' Agostini was testy. 'It's the terrorists. I doubt we could provide as good security elsewhere. But it does raise one important issue. His Holiness talked of spending his convalescence outside Vatican territory, in a private villa perhaps. I don't think we can permit that.'

'Can we stop it?' This from a German member of the Council. 'Our master does not take kindly to opposition.'

'I'm sure,' said the Secretary of State, 'the Republic has very good reason not to want him killed on its own soil. His Holiness, Italian born, has very good reason not to embarrass the Republic. Leave that discussion to me.'

'How soon can we get him home?'

'If all goes well, ten to fourteen days.'

'Let's make it ten. We could move a team of nursing sisters into Castel Gandolfo. I could talk to the Mother General of the Little Company of Mary. She could even fly in some of her best people from abroad.'

'As I remember,' said Archbishop Hunterson, 'most nursing orders are hard put to service the hospitals they have. Most now depend on lay staff. Quite frankly, I don't understand the hurry. So long as security can be maintained, I'd leave him at the Villa Diana.'

'The Curia proposes,' said Agostini, with tart humour, 'but the Pontiff disposes – even from his sickbed! Let me see what notions I can plant in his head while he's still amenable.'

It was at this precise moment in the discussion that Monsignor Malachy O'Rahilly presented himself, in response to a beeper summons from the central communications office. He was flustered and breathless and slightly – only slightly – befuddled from the white wine and the red and the strong brandies he had taken to help him through Matt Neylan's defection from the Faith.

Neylan, too, was summoned because he was a first-class Secretary of Nunziatures and his work was to edit the news and spread it around his bailiwick. They bowed to the assembled prelates, took their seats in silence and listened respectfully while Agostini first admonished them to secrecy and then walked them through the outline of threats and remedies.

Monsignor Matt Neylan had no comment to make. His functions were predetermined. His punctual performance was taken for granted.

O'Rahilly, on the other hand, with drink taken, was inclined to be voluble. As a personal assistant to the Pontiff and the bearer of a Papal commission as to the conduct of his office, his address to Agostini tended to be more emphatic than discreet.

'I already have a list of those to be given access to His Holiness at the clinic. In the circumstances, should they not be supplied with a special card of admission? After all, the security people cannot be expected to recognise faces, and a soutane or a Roman collar readily disguises a terrorist. I could have the entire set printed and distributed within half a day.'

'A good idea, Monsignore.' Agostini nodded approval. 'If you will put the matter in hand with the printers first thing in the morning. My office will be responsible for distribution – against signatures always.'

'It will be done, Eminence.' Wildly elated by the commendation – rare and precious in Curial circles – O'Rahilly decided to push his luck a little further. 'I talked with His Holiness earlier this evening and he asked me to make special enquiries into the case of one Lorenzo de Rosa, formerly a priest of this diocese whose wife – that is to say, under the civil code – died in the Salviati clinic yesterday. Apparently de Rosa had made repeated but unsuccessful bids to be laicised canonically and have his marriage validated, but . . .'

'Monsignore!' The Secretary of State was cool. 'It would seem this matter is neither relevant to our present concerns nor opportune in the context . . .'

'Oh, but it is, Eminence!'

O'Rahilly with the bit between his teeth would have put a Derby runner to shame. In the midst of a frozen silence, he described to the assembly his personal encounter with de Rosa and his later discussion with Monsignor Matt Neylan as to whether or not the threat should be taken seriously.

'. . . Matt Neylan here was of the opinion, which I shared, that the poor fellow was simply overwhelmed with grief and that to expose him to interrogation and harassment by security forces would be a great and unnecessary cruelty. However, after what we've just heard, I have to ask myself – and to ask Your Eminences – whether certain precautions, at least, should not be taken.'

'They most certainly should!' The Substitute Secretary was in no doubt about it. His name was Mikhaelovic and he was a Jugoslav already preconditioned to security procedures. 'The safety of the Holy Father is of paramount concern.'

'That is, at best, a dubious proposition.' Matt Neylan was suddenly a hostile presence in the small assembly. 'With great respect, I submit that to badger and bedevil this grieving man with police inquiries would be an unconscionable cruelty. The Holy Father himself is concerned that, even before his bereavement, de Rosa may have received less than Christian justice and charity. Besides, what Monsignor O'Rahilly has omitted to mention is that I have already instituted a private inquiry into de Rosa's circumstances.'

'And by so doing have exceeded your authority.' Cardinal Mikhaelovic did not take kindly to correction. 'The very least precaution we can take is to denounce this man to the security people. They are the experts. We are not.'

'My point precisely, Eminence.' Neylan was studiously formal. 'The anti-terrorist troops are not bound by the normal rules of police procedure. Accidents happen during their interrogations. People have their limbs broken. They fall out of windows. I would remind you also that there are two young children involved.'

'Illegitimate offspring of a renegade priest!'

'Oh, for Christ's sweet sake! What kind of a priest are you?'

The blasphemy shocked them all. Agostini's rebuke was icy.

'You forget yourself, Monsignore. You have made your case. We shall give it careful consideration. I shall see you in my office at ten tomorrow morning. You are excused.'

'But Your Eminence is not excused – none of you is excused – the duty of common compassion! I bid Your Excellencies good night!'

He bowed himself out of the meeting and hurried back to his small apartment in the Palace of the Mint. He was blazing with anger: at Mal O'Rahilly who couldn't keep his big Irish gob shut, but had to make a great fellow of himself with a bunch of elderly eminences and excellencies; at the eminences and excellencies themselves, because they symbolised everything that, year by year, had alienated him from the Church and made a mockery of the charity which was radical to its existence.

They were mandarins, all of them, old-fashioned imperial *Kuan*, who wore bright clothes and buttoned headgear, and had their own esoteric language and disdained all argument with the common herd. They were not pastors, ardent in the care of souls. They were not apostles, zealous for the spread of the godspell. They were officials, administrators, committee men, as privileged and protected as any of their counterparts in Whitehall, in Moscow, or the Quai d'Orsay.

To them a man like Lorenzo de Rosa was a non-person, excommunicated, committed with a shrug to the Divine Mercy, but excluded for ever from any compassionate intervention by the human Assembly – unless it were earned by penitential humiliation and a winter vigil at Canossa. He knew exactly what would happen to de Rosa. They would delate him to the Security Services. A quartet of heavies would pick him up at his apartment, take him down town, hand the children to a police matron for custody, then bounce him off the walls for two or three hours. After that they would make him sign a deposition he would be too groggy to read. It would all be quite impersonal. They wouldn't mean any real harm. It was standard procedure, to get the facts quickly before a bomb went off, and to discourage any counteraction from an innocent suspect – but then, under the old inquisitorial system, no one was innocent until proven so in court.

And what of himself, Matt Neylan? The quiet exit he had planned for himself was impossible now. The unsayable had been said. There was no way to recall the words – and all because Mal O'Rahilly couldn't hold his liquor and had to go trailing his coat-tails at a crisis conference of the biggest big shots in the Holy Roman Church! But wasn't that the way of it, the whole conditioning process that produced a perfect Roman clerical clone? The trigger-words in the formula had never changed since Trent – hierarchy and obedience. The effect they produced on simple priest or lordly bishop was always the same. They stood with eyes downcast, tugging their forelocks, as if listening to thunders from the Mountain of Revelation.

Well, tonight was one time too many for Matt Neylan. Tomorrow he would pack and go, without regret, without a by-your-leave. The day after, they would name him a renegade like de Rosa and strike his name out of the book of the Elect and commit him with something just short of contempt to the God who made him.

He reached for the Rome telephone directory and ran his finger down the list of folk called de Rosa. There were six entries with the initial L. He began dialling them in sequence, trusting that a mention of the Salviati clinic would bring forth an identifying response. He hoped the man would be sane enough to accept a warning from a one-time colleague. It would be nice to set Brother Fox well on his way to a safe earth, before the hounds began baying in his tracks.

Over the compound of Salviati's house, the new summer moon rode high in a sea of stars. In the shadows of the garden a nightingale began to sing. The light and the music made an antique magic in the vaulted chamber where Salviati slept and Tove Lundberg, propped on her elbow, hovered over him like a protecting goddess.

Their loving had followed their familiar pattern: a long, tender prelude, a sudden transition to play, a swift leap to the high plateau of passion, a series of fierce orgasms, a languid recall of fading pleasures, then Sergio's sudden lapse into sleep, his classic features youthful and unlined against the pillow, the muscles of his shoulders and breast frozen into marble in the moonglow. Tove Lundberg always lay wakeful afterwards, wondering that so wild a storm could be followed by so magical a calm.

Of herself she had no clear image; but the role she was expected to play on these crisis nights was one she knew by heart. She was the servant of his body, the perfect hetaera, pouring herself out on him, asking nothing but to serve him. The why of it for him was buried deep in his unconscious and she had no desire to lug it out into the light. Sergio Salviati was the perennial alien. He had become a prince by conquest. He needed the spoils to attest his victories – the gold, the jewels, the slave girls, and the respect of the mighty in the land.

The why for her was different, and she could confront it without shame. As mother, she had delivered defective offspring; she had no wish to repeat the experience. As lover, she delivered perfect pleasure and while time might diminish her charm or her capacities as a bed-mate, it could only increase her stature and influence as a professional comrade. Best of all was Sergio's own acknowledgement: 'You are the one wholly calm place in my life. You are like a deep pool in the middle of a forest and every time I come to you I am refreshed and renewed. But you never ask me for anything. Why?'

'Because,' she told him, 'I need nothing but what I have: work I can do well, a place where my Britte can grow to be an independent and talented woman, a man I trust and admire and love.'

'How much do you love me, Tove Lundberg?'

'As much as you want, Sergio Salviati. As much as you will let me.'

'Why don't you ask how much I love you?'

'Because I know already . . .'

'Do you know that I am always afraid?'

'Yes.'

'Of what I am afraid?'

'That one day, at some bad moment, the healing magic will fail you, you will misread the signs, lose the master touch. But it will not happen. I promise you.'

'Are you never afraid?'

'Only in a special way.'

'What way?'

'I am afraid of needing anything so much that someone could hurt me by taking it away.'

And, she might have added, she came of old Nordic seafaring stock, whose women waited on windswept dunes and cared not whether their men were drunk, sober or scarred from brawling, just so that, one more time, they had escaped the grey widow-maker.

In the small, dark hours before the false dawn, Leo the Pontiff began rolling his head from side to side on the pillow and muttering restlessly. His gullet was thick with mucus and his brow clammy with night-sweat. The night nurse shifted him in the bed, sponged his face and moistened his lips with water. He responded drowsily.

'Thank you. I'm sorry to be a trouble. I was having a bad dream.'

'You're out of it now. Close your eyes and go back to sleep.'

For a brief, confused moment he was tempted to tell her the dream, but he dared not. It had risen like a new moon from the darkest places of childhood memory; and it shed a pitiless light upon a hidden hollow in his adult conscience.

At school there was a boy, older and bigger, who bullied him continually. One day he confronted his tormentor and asked why he did such cruel things. The answer still echoed in his memory: 'Because you're standing in my light; you're taking away my sun.' How could he, he asked, since he was so much smaller and younger. To which the bully answered: 'Even a mushroom throws a shadow. If it falls on my boot, I kick it to pieces.'

It was a rough but lasting lesson in the usances of power. A man who stood against the sun became a dark shadow, faceless and threatening. Yet the shadow was surrounded by light, like a halo or the corona of an eclipse. So the shadow-man assumed the numen of a sacred person. To challenge him was a sacrilege, a most damnable crime.

So, in the last hours before they drugged him and wheeled him off to the operating theatre, Ludovico Gadda, Leo XIV, Vicar of Christ, Supreme Pastor of the Universal Church, understood how, in learning from the bully, he had himself been tipped into tyranny.

In defiance of biblical injunction, of historic custom, of discontent among clergy and faithful, he had appointed as senior archbishops, in Europe and the Americas, men of his own choosing, hard-line conservators, stubborn defenders of bastions long overpassed, deaf and blind to every plea for change. They were called the Pope's men, the praetorian guard in the Army of the Elect. They were the echoes of his own voice, drowning out the murmurs of discontented clerics, of the faceless crowd outside the sanctuaries.

It had been a harsh encounter and a heady victory. Even as he remembered it, his face hardened into the old raptor look. Dissenting clerics had been silenced by a double threat: suspension from their functions and the appointment of a special apostolic administrator. As for the people, when their shepherds were silenced they, too, were struck dumb. They had no voice in the assembly. Their only free utterance was outside it, among the heretics and the infidel.

It was the childhood nightmare which shamed Leo the Pontiff into admitting the harm he had done. It was the shadow of the surgeon's knife which reminded him that he might never have the chance to repair it. As the first cocks crowed from the farmlands of the Villa Diana, he closed his eyes, turned his face to the wall and made his last desperate prayer.

'If my presence hides the light of Yours, O God, remove me! Strike me out of the book of the living. But if you leave me here, give me, I beg You, eyes to see, and heart to feel, the lonely terrors of your children!'

Book 2

Lazarus Redivivus

'He cried out in a loud voice:
"Lazarus, come here, to me!" Whereupon
the dead man came out, his hands and feet
tied with strips of linen, his
face covered with a veil. Jesus said:
"Untie him. Let him go free."'

John xi: 43, 44

Six

About the same hour on the same morning, Monsignor Matt Neylan finally made telephone contact with Lorenzo de Rosa, one-time priest of the Roman diocese, excommunicated, newly widowed, the father of two small children. Neylan explained himself curtly.

'There's a terrorist threat to the Pontiff, who is at this moment a patient in the International Clinic. You're a suspect, because you sounded off yesterday to Malachy O'Rahilly. So you're bound to get a visit from the anti-terrorist squad. My suggestion would be to get out of town as quickly as you can.'

'And why should you care?'

'God knows. Maybe a visit from the Squadristi sounds like one grief too many.'

'There's nothing they can do to us now. But thank you for calling. Goodbye.'

Matt Neylan stood like a ninny with the dead receiver in his hand. Then a dark thought took hold of him and sent him racing for his car and careering like a madman through the morning traffic towards EUR.

De Rosa's house was a modest but well-kept villa in a cul-de-sac near the Via del Giorgione. There was a car in the driveway and the garden gate was unlocked. The front door was open, too. Neylan called a greeting, but there was no answer. He went inside. The ground floor was deserted. Upstairs in the nursery, two little girls lay still and waxen-faced in their beds. Neylan called to them softly. They did not answer. He touched their cheeks. They were cold and lifeless. Across the hall, in the big matrimonial bed, Lorenzo de Rosa lay beside the body of his wife, who was dressed as if for a bridal night. De Rosa's face was distorted in the last rictus of dying. There was a small cake of foam about his lips.

Matt Neylan, new to unbelief, found himself murmuring a prayer for all their sad souls. Then the prayer exploded into a blasphemy against all the hypocrisy and folly that lay at the root of the tragedy. He debated, for the briefest moment, about calling the police; decided against it, then walked out of the house into the deserted street. The only witness to his departure was a stray cat. The only person to hear of his encounter was the Cardinal Secretary of State, to whom he exposed, in the same speech, his discovery of the tragedy and his decision to leave the Church.

Agostini, the lifetime diplomat, took the news calmly. With Neylan, there was no ground of argument. As an unbeliever he belonged henceforth to another order of being. The situation with the police was even easier to arrange. Both parties had a common interest. His Eminence explained it simply.

'You were wise to leave the scene. Otherwise everybody would have been swamped with depositions and interrogations. We have advised the police of your presence in the house and your discovery of the bodies. They will accept your visit as a pastoral call, subject to confessional secrecy. They will not involve you in any further questioning.'

'Which, of course, leaves everything very tidy.'

'Spare me the ironies, Monsignore!' His Eminence was suddenly angry. 'I am just as unhappy about this sad affair as you are. The whole thing was bungled from the start. I have no taste for zealots and bigots, no matter how high they sit in the Sacred College; but I have to work with them, with as much tolerance and charity as I can muster. You can afford your anger. You have chosen to withdraw from the community of the faithful and dispense yourself from its obligations. I don't blame you. I understand what has brought you to this decision.'

'It's hardly a decision, Eminence. It's a new state of being. I am no longer a believer. My identity has changed. I have no place in any Christian assembly. So I'm separating myself as discreetly as possible. I'll move out of my office today. My apartment is on a private lease, not a Vatican one, so that's no problem. I have an Irish passport, so I'll hand you back my Vatican documents. That should leave everything tidy.'

'For our purposes,' – Agostini was studiously good-humoured – 'we'll formally suspend you from the exercise of priestly functions and proceed immediately to have you laicised.'

'With respect, Eminence, these procedures are a matter of indifference to me.'

'But I, my friend, am not indifferent to you. I have seen this coming for along time. It was like watching a classic rose mutate slowly into hedgerow stock. The beautiful bloom is gone, but the plant is still vigorously alive. I reproved you last night; but I understood your anger and admired your courage. I must say that in that moment you looked very like a Christian to me!'

'I'm curious,' said Matt Neylan.

'About what?'

'We both know the Holy Father has asked for a special report on the de Rosa affair.'

'So?'

'My question: how will he react to the news of their deaths – by murder and suicide?'

'We have no intention of telling him the news – until he is strong enough to receive it.'

'And then what? How will he react? Will he repent his original harshness? How will he judge de Rosa – and himself? Will he amend the legislation in the canons, or mitigate its penalties?'

'What you're really asking,' – Agostini permitted himself

a small, wintry smile – 'is a perennial question. Does the Church change when a pope changes his mind or his heart? In my experience, it doesn't. The inertia is too great. The whole system is geared against swift movement. Besides— and this is the nub of the matter – the Church is so centralised now that every tremor is magnified to earthquake scale. The simplest act of official tolerance can be turned into a scandal. The most innocent speculation by the most orthodox theologian on the mysteries of the Faith sets off a heresy hunt.' Agostini's humour turned suddenly rueful. 'Living at this altitude in this place is like being perched on the edge of the San Andreas fault. So the answer to your question: every public utterance of the Pontiff is ritually controlled. In his private life he may dress in sackcloth, powder himself with ashes, mourn like Job on his dunghill; but who will know about it? The Church has its own *omerta*', its rule of silence, every whit as binding as that of the Mafia.'

'And what would happen . . .' Matt Neylan laughed as he put the question. 'What would happen if I decided to breach the wall of silence?'

'Nothing.' Agostini dismissed the thought with a gesture. 'Nothing at all! What authority could you invoke? You'd be called an apostate, a renegade priest. In the Church you'd be prayed for and ignored. Outside it you'd carry another stigma: a fool who let himself be gulled for half a lifetime before he quit.'

'A warning, Eminence?'

'A counsel only. I am told you are seeking to make a new career as an author. You will not, I am sure, damage it by peddling scandals, or betraying professional secrets.'

'I am flattered by your confidence,' said Matt Neylan.

'We shall all remember you as a discreet and loyal colleague. We shall pray for your well-being.'

'Thank you – and goodbye, Eminence.'

So, simply and curtly, a lifetime was ended, a whole identity shucked off like a reptile's skin. He passed by the Apostolic Palace to say goodbye to Malachy O'Rahilly, but was told he was waiting at the clinic until the result of the Pontiff's surgery was known.

So, because he needed at least one stepping stone between his old life and a new one, because he needed at least one weapon against the pitiless rectitude of Vatican bureaucracy, he telephoned Nicol Peters and begged to be offered a cup of coffee.

'It's my lucky day.' Nicol Peters slipped a new cassette into the tape-recorder. 'Two big stories and you've given me the inside running on both of them. I'm in your debt, Matt.'

'You owe me nothing.' Neylan was emphatic. 'I believe the de Rosa business is a scandal that should be aired . . . you can do that. I can't – at least not until I've established a new identity and authority. Which, by the way, is a problem you have to face. If I'm revealed as your informant, your story will be discredited. Drop-outs like me can be an embarrassment.'

Nicol Peters shrugged off the warning.

'We agreed the ground rules. Trust me to play by them.'

'I do.'

'So let's go back. The assassination threat is the number one story, though I'm not sure how I can use it if it jeopardises the life of an undercover agent. Anyway, that's my problem, not yours. Let's look at the sequence of events. Mossad gets the news from an agent in place. The Israelis pass the news to the Vatican and to the Italian authorities. Those two set up a joint security operation inside and outside Salviati's clinic. The Israeli's can't participate openly; but obviously they're in it up to their necks.'

'Obviously.'

'So far the Pontiff knows nothing of all this?'

'Nothing. The news came in early yesterday evening. The meeting which I attended did not take place until very late. The countdown to the Pontiff's surgery had already begun. There was no point in disturbing him with the news.'

'I accept that. Now let's speculate a little further. An assassin is identified before an attempt is made on the Pope's life. Who deals with him – or perhaps with her, as the case may be?'

Matt Neylan poured himself more coffee and gave a slightly parodied exposition of the argument.

'The Vatican position would be defined very simply. I've written enough position papers to give it to you verbatim. Their sole concern is the safety of the Sacred Person of His Holiness. They leave the criminal to be dealt with by the Republic. Simple! Clean hands! No imbroglios with the Muslim world. The position of the Republic of Italy is somewhat different. They have the right, the power, the sovereign authority to deal with criminals and terrorists. Do they want to? Hell no! That means more terror – hijacks, hostages, kidnappings to bring the criminals out of custody. Conclusion: though they'd never admit it, they'd love Mossad to handle the business quickly and neatly and have the body buried by sunrise. You want me to prove it? No way. You want me to swear that's what I heard in the Apostolic Palace – no way either! It wasn't said. It would never be said!'

'Me thinks,' said Nicol Peters amiably, 'me thinks the lady hath protested enough! I've got enough to frame the story and prise the rest of it out of other sources. Now let's talk about de Rosa. Here again, the sequence is clear. De Rosa quits the priesthood, beds down with a girl without benefit of clergy, has two children by her. They are happy. They want to regularise their union – a situation not without precedent, not at all impossible under the canons . . .'

'But quite contrary to present policy, which is to make things as tough as possible for offenders and damp down hopes of lenient solutions.'

'Check. Now tragedy strikes. The woman dies, still unreconciled, in spite of her wish to be so. The despairing husband stages a macabre family reunion, kills his children with an overdose of sleeping pills and himself with cyanide – all this while under suspicion as a possible assassin of the same Pope who had denied him canonical relief.'

'A caveat here! Until I called de Rosa in the small hours of this morning he didn't know he was a suspect. He couldn't have.'

'Could your news have precipitated his decision to kill his children and himself?'

'It could have. I doubt it did. The fact that he had brought his wife's body back to the house seems to indicate that he had already decided on some kind of ceremonial exit . . . But what do I know? The whole thing is a madness – all because a bunch of clerical bureaucrats refused legitimate relief in a human situation. Let me tell you something, Nico! This is one story I want His Holiness to read, no matter what it does to his sacred blood pressure!'

'Do you really think it will matter a damn what he thinks or says about it?'

'It could. He could change a lot of lives overnight if he had the will and the courage. He could bring back compassion and clemency into what, believe me, has become a rigorist institution.'

'Do you really believe that, Matt? I've lived in this town longer than you have and I don't believe it for a minute. In the Roman Catholic Church, the whole system – the hierarchy, the education of the clergy, the Curial administration, the Electoral College – is designed to perpetuate the status quo and eliminate along the way any and every aberrant element. The man you get at the top is the nearest you can come to the Manchurian Candidate, the perfectly conditioned representative of the majority interest of the Electoral College itself.'

'It's a good argument,' said Matt Neylan with a grin. 'I'm a conditioned man myself. I know how deeply the imprint goes, how potent the trigger-words become. But, by the same token, Nico, I'm the flaw in the argument too. I've lost all the conditioning. I've become another person. I know that change is possible for good or ill – and the two most potent instruments of change are power and pain.'

Nicol Peters gave him a long, searching look and then said gently: 'It seems I've missed something, my friend. Would you be patient enough to tell me what it is?'

'It's nothing much, Nico. And yet, in a way, it's everything. It's why I feel so angry about what happened to de Rosa. Agostini put it very bluntly this morning. I'm labelled now – I'm an apostate, a renegade, a defector, a fool. But that isn't the nature of my experience at all. I've lost something, a capacity, a faculty – as one can lose sexual potency or the gift of sight. I am changed, irrevocably. I am back at the first day of creation, when earth was still an empty waste and darkness hung over the deep . . . Who knows? There may be wonders still to come but I do not expect them. I live in the here and now. What I see is what is. What I know is what I have experienced and – most terrifying of all, Nico! – what will be is a totally random matter. That makes the world a very bleak place, Nico. So bleak that even fear can hardly survive in it.'

Nicol Peters waited a long moment before he offered a dry comment.

'At least you're at the beginning of a new world, not at the end of it. And it's not all that new either. It's the same place lots of us inhabit who have never been conditioned or gifted with the massive certainties of Christianity. We have to make do with what we get – the fleeting light, the passing storm, enough love to temper the tears of things, the rare glimpse of reason in a mad world. So don't be too dismayed, matey! It's a big club you've joined – and even Christians believe that God was a founding member!'

While the Pontiff, cold and cyanosed, festooned with tubes and electrodes, was being settled in the Intensive Care Unit, Sergio Salviati took coffee with James Morrison and wrote his first communiqué to the Vatican.

'His Holiness, Pope Leo XIV, today underwent elective bypass surgery, following a short history of angina pectoris. The operation, in which three saphenous vein grafts were inserted into the coronary circulation, was performed at the International Clinic under the direction of Professor Sergio Salviati, assisted by Mr James Morrison of the London College of Surgeons, with the Papal Physician, Professor Carlo Massenzio, in attendance. The procedures were successfully completed in two hours and fifty minutes. His Holiness is now in the Intensive Care Unit, in a stable and satisfactory condition. Professor Salviati and the attending physician anticipate an uncomplicated convalescence and are optimistic about the long-term prognosis.'

He signed the document with a flourish and handed it to his secretary.

'Please send two facsimile copies to the Vatican, the first to the Secretary of State personally, the second to the Sala Stampa. Then type the following text which our switchboard operators will use verbatim to respond to all inquiries about the Pontiff. Text begins: "The operation on His Holiness has been successfully completed. His Holiness is still in Intensive Care. For further details, apply to the Sala Stampa, Vatican City, which will issue all future bulletins."'

'Anything else, Professor?'

'Yes. Please ask the Chief of Hospital Staff and the two senior security officers to meet me here in thirty minutes. That's all for the moment.'

When the secretary had left, James Morrison offered enthusiastic praise.

'Full marks, Sergio! You've built a great team. I've never worked with a better one.'

'My thanks to you, James. I was grateful to have you with me. This was a rough one for me.'

'The old buzzard should be grateful he fell into your hands!'

Salviati threw back his head and laughed.

'He is an old buzzard, isn't he? That great beak, those hooded, hostile eyes. But he's a tough bird. There's probably another decade in him after this.'

'It's a moot point, of course, whether the world or the Church will thank you for that.'

'True, James! Very true! But at least we've honoured the Hippocratic oath.'

'I wonder if he'll offer you a Vatican decoration.'

'To a Jew? I very much doubt it. I wouldn't accept it. I couldn't. Anyway, it's much too early to talk about success, let alone rewards. We still have to keep him alive until the end of his convalescence.'

'Are you that worried about the assassination threat?'

'You're damn right I'm worried! No one goes in or out of the Intensive Care Unit without an identity check. No drugs are dispensed to this patient except from sealed bottles by nominated personnel. Even the goddamned scrub women are searched, and the garbage collectors!'

'But I notice you and Tove still drive back and forth to the clinic without a bodyguard. Is that wise?'

'We're not the target.'

'You could be a secondary one.'

'James, if I thought about all the dangers of this job, I'd

lock myself in a padded cell . . . To change the subject, what are your plans now?'

'I'll take a leisurely run up north to see my Italian relatives, then I'll head back to London.'

'How do you want to be paid?'

'Swiss francs in Zurich, if that's possible.'

'Since the money will come from the Vatican, everything is possible. When will you leave?'

'Two days, three maybe. The British Ambassador has bidden me to dinner. He'd like to make some capital out of my presence – for which I don't blame him, because I'll be eating my own tax money. But before I leave I'd like to entertain you and Tove. You pick the place. I'll pick up the bill.'

'It's a date. Do you want to stroll along with me and take a quick look at our patient? He should be settled by now. And that Irish monsignor, his secretary, insists on a personal word . . .'

Monsignor Malachy O'Rahilly was tired and low-spirited. The fine glow of liquor and righteousness which had sustained him at the Secretariat meeting had subsided into the grey ashes of remorse. He had driven to the clinic just as the Pontiff was being wheeled in for surgery and he had spent three long hours wandering the grounds under the vigilant eyes of armed men.

Even before Salviati's communiqué had been issued, he had telephoned the Secretary of State to tell him that the operation had been successful. His Eminence had returned the compliment with a brief summary of the de Rosa affair and an admonition that none of the newspaper reports – which were bound to be lurid – should be communicated to His Holiness until he was well on the road to recovery. O'Rahilly read the order as a reproof for his indiscretions, and wished there were someone like Matt Neylan to whom he could make a fraternal confession.

So, when he stood by the Pontiff's bedside with Salviati and Morrison, he felt flustered and uncomfortable. His first remark was a banality.

'The poor man looks so . . . so vulnerable.'

Morrison reassured him cheerfully.

'He's in great shape. The whole procedure was a copy-book exercise. There's nothing to be done now except monitor the screen and change his drips. He won't be halfway lucid for another day and a half. If I were you, I'd go home and let Professor Salviati's people look after him.'

'You're right, of course.' O'Rahilly still felt the need to patch up his dignity. 'I wondered if I should walk through the security arrangements with you, Professor Salviati; just so I can reassure the Secretary of State and the Curia.'

'Not possible, Monsignore!' Salviati was curt. 'Security is not your business, or mine. We should leave it to the professionals!'

'I thought only that . . .'

'Enough, please! We are all tired. I don't tell you how to write the Pope's letters. Don't tell me how to run my clinic. Please, Monsignore! Please!'

'I'm sorry.' Malachy O'Rahilly was chastened but not silenced. 'I had a bad night, too. I'm sure the security is first class. I couldn't move twenty yards in the garden without looking down a gun-barrel. When may His Holiness have visitors?'

'Any time. But he won't begin to make sense for at least thirty-six hours. Even then, his attention span will be limited and his emotions barely under control. Just warn your people not to expect too much and to keep their visits short.'

'Be sure I'll do that. There's just one thing you should know . . .'

'Yes?'

And that was all the prompting Malachy O'Rahilly needed to blurt out the story of de Rosa's suicide, the murder of his children and the macabre obsequies he had prepared in his house.

Morrison and Salviati heard him out in silence; then Salviati led the way out of the Intensive Care Unit and into the corridor. He was deeply shocked, but his comment was studiously restrained.

'What can I say? It's a tragic mess and a sad waste of human lives.'

'We are anxious,' – Malachy O'Rahilly was happy to have the spotlight again – 'we are most anxious that His Holiness should be spared this news, at least until he is strong enough to cope with it.'

Salviati dismissed the notion with a shrug.

'I'm sure he won't hear it from our staff, Monsignore.'

To which James Morrison added a tart reminder.

'And he's not going to be able to hold, let alone focus on, a newspaper for days yet.'

'So you should look to your own gossips, Monsignore.' Salviati was already on the move towards the elevators. 'You must excuse us now. We've had a busy morning; and it isn't over yet.'

Anton Drexel, too, was having a busy morning; but a much more relaxing one. He had risen early, made his morning meditation, said Mass in the tiny villa chapel with his cellar master for acolyte and those of his household and the colonia who wished to attend. He had breakfasted on coffee and home-baked rolls and honey from his own hives. Now, dressed in workman's clothes, with a big straw hat on his white head and a basket on his arm, he was making the rounds of the garden plots, cutting fresh artichokes, pulling lettuce and radishes, picking red tomatoes and white peaches and the big yellow persimmons that the local folk called 'kaki'.

His companion was a skinny, shambling boy with a hydrocephalic skull, who knelt among the bean rows, clutching a tape-recorder into which from time to time he murmured some runic words of his own. Later, Drexel knew, the sounds would be transcribed into the written record of a Mendelian experiment on the hybridisation of *fave*, the broad beans which flourished in the friable soil of the foothills. The boy, Tonino, was only in his fifteenth year, but already, under the tutelage of a botanist from the University of Rome, he was deep into the principles of plant genetics.

Verbal communication with Tonino was difficult, as it was with many of the children in the colonia, but Drexel had developed a technique of patient listening and a language of smiles and gestures and approving caresses, which somehow seemed to suffice these small, maimed geniuses whose intellectual reach, he knew, was light years further than his own.

As he went about the simple, satisfying landsman's tasks, Drexel pondered the paradoxes, human and divine, which presented themselves to him every precious day of his Indian summer. He saw himself very clearly as a hinge-man of a Church in crisis, a man whose time was running out, who must soon stand for judgement on what he had done and left undone.

His prime talent had always been that of a navigator. He knew that you couldn't sail into the eye of the wind or buck the seas head-on. You had to haul off and tack, take the big waves on the shoulder, run for shelter sometimes and always be content to arrive in God's time.

He had always refused to involve himself in the battles of the theologians, being content to accept life as a mystery, and Revelation as a torch-light by which to explore it.

For him, faith was the gift that made mystery acceptable, while hope made it endurable and love brought joy even in the cloud of unknowing. He had no belief at all in the efficacy of *Romanita'*, the ancient Roman habit of prescribing a juridical solution to every human dilemma, and then stamping every solution with a sacred character under the seal of the *magisterium*.

His method of dealing with *Romanita'* – and of salving his own conscience – had always been the same. He made his protest, plainly but in strictest protocol, he pleaded his cause without passion, then submitted in silence to the verdict of the Pontiff or the curial majority. Had he been challenged to justify such conformity – and not even the Pontiff wanted a head-on collision with Anton Drexel! – he would have answered with reasonable truth that open conflict would avail nothing for him or for the Church, and that while he was happy to resign and become a country curate, he saw no virtue in abdication, and even less in rebellion. In his official life he followed the motto of Gregory the Great: *'Omnia videre, multa dissumulare, pauca corrigere.'* See all, keep a lot to yourself and correct a few things!

But in his private, intimate life at the villa, with the children, their parents and teachers, he no longer had the luxury or the protection of protocol and obedience. In a very special sense, he was the patriarch of the family, the shepherd of the tiny flock, to whom everyone looked for guidance and decision. He could no longer gloss over the patent facts of a tooth and claw creation, and the random nature of human tragedy. He could no longer signify personal assent to the prohibition of artificial birth control, or affirm that every marriage formally contracted in the Church was, of its nature, Christian, made in heaven, and therefore indissoluble. He was no longer prepared to pronounce a final ethical judgement on the duty of a surgeon faced with a monster birth, or the conscience of a woman desperate to terminate a pregnancy in order to prevent one. He was angered when theologians and philosophers were silenced or censured for their attempts to enlarge the understanding of the Church. He fought a long war of attrition against the secrecies and injustices of the inquisitorial system, which still survived in the Congregation for the Doctrine of the Faith. He found himself insisting more and more upon the liberty of enlightened conscience and the constant need of every human creature for compassion, charity and forgiveness.

It was to this that he sought to persuade his friends in the senior hierarchy and ultimately the Pontiff, if and when he came to spend time with the children in the colonia. It was for this that he offered his daily Mass and his nightly prayers. It was for this that he sought to prepare mind and spirit by his musings in the summer garden. Even his harvest of the summer fruits made a text for his discourse to the children and their teachers, gathered on the lawn for morning coffee.

'You see, there is an order even in what presents itself to us as cataclysm. Lake Nemi up there was once an active volcano. This land was once covered with ash and pumice and black lava. Now it is sweet and fertile. We did not see the change happen. If we had seen it, we would not have understood what was happening. We would have tried to explain the phenomenon by myths and symbols . . . Even now, with all our knowledge of the past, we still find it hard to disentangle the historical facts from the myths, because the myths themselves are a part of history . . . This is why we must never be afraid to speculate – and never, never be afraid of those who urge us to contemplate the seemingly impossible, to examine ancient formulae for new meanings. Believe me, we are more readily betrayed by our certainties than by our doubts and curiosities. I believe that half the heresies and schisms would never have happened if Christians had been willing to listen to each other in patience and charity, and not tried to turn the Divine mysteries into geometric theorems which could be taught with compass and set-squares . . . Listen now, my friends, to what the Fathers of Vatican Council II have said about our dangerous certainties: "If the influence of events or of the times has led to deficiencies in conduct, in Church discipline, or even in the formulation of doctrine (which must be carefully distinguished from the deposit of faith itself) these should be appropriately rectified at the proper moment."   But what am I truly trying to say with all these words? I am an old man. I hold to the old Apostolic faith. Jesus is the Lord, the Son of the Living God. He took flesh. He suffered and died for our salvation and on the third day God raised him up again. Everything I see in this garden is a symbol of that birth and death and resurrection . . . Every truth that has ever been taught within the Church flows from it. Every evil that has ever been done in the Church has been a contradiction of that saving event . . . So do not ask me to judge you, my children, my family. Just permit me to love you, as God loves us all . . .'

The talk ended as informally as it had begun. Drexel moved over to the big trestle table, where one of the women offered him coffee and a sweet biscuit. It was then that he became aware of Tove Lundberg standing a few paces away with James Morrison in attendance. Tove Lundberg presented him to Drexel. Morrison paid him a sober compliment.

'I've been deaf to sermons for a good many years, Eminence. That one moved me deeply.'

Tove Lundberg explained their presence.

'Sergio wanted you to know personally that the surgery was successful . . . And I thought James should see what you are doing here for Britte and the others.'

'That was kind.' Drexel felt as if a great load had been

137

lifted from his shoulders. 'I presume, Mr Morrison, that means there were no unforeseen consequences – stroke, brain damage, that sort of thing?'

'None that we can see or foresee at this moment.'

'Thank God! And you clever gentlemen, too!'

'We did, however, get some sad news.' Tove Lundberg told him of the de Rosa affair as reported by Monsignor O'Rahilly. Drexel was suddenly grim.

'Shocking! Absolutely disgraceful that a tragedy like this could be permitted to happen! I shall take it up with the dicasteries concerned and with the Holy Father when he is sufficiently recovered.' He turned to James Morrison. 'Bureaucrats are the accursed of God, Mr Morrison. They record everything and understand nothing. They invent a spurious mathematic by which every human factor is reduced to zero . . .' To Tove Lundberg he said more calmly: 'I imagine Professor Salviati was very upset.'

'More than he would confess, even to me. He hates the waste of human beings. Besides, the clinic is like an armed camp just now and that's a reminder of another kind of waste.'

'Come!' said Anton Drexel abruptly. 'Let's be grateful for a while. I'll walk you round the villa and the vineyards – and after that, Mr Morrison, you shall taste some of the best wine that's been grown in these parts for a long time. I call it Fontamore, and it drinks better than Frascati. I'm very proud of it . . .'

Sergio Salviati's conference with the security men lasted nearly an hour. It dealt, for the most part, with the details of personnel control: a roll-call of each oncoming shift, a check of hospital identity cards against personal documents like passports and drivers' licences, access to drug cabinets and surgical instruments, routes and times by which certain key people might enter sensitive areas, the mobile surveillance of strategic points inside and outside the building. So far, it was agreed, all staff within the compound had been accounted for and were about their normal business. Visitors could be dealt with without too much fuss. Tradesmen would be met by armed guards and the goods they delivered screened and hand searched before they passed into the storerooms. So far, so good. The security men assured the Professor that he could sleep as soundly and as safely as if he were in the crypt of St Peter's itself.

His next caller was less comforting: a lean, sallow, cold-eyed fellow in the white jacket of a male nurse. He was one of the Mossad men in permanent residence at the clinic, an elusive figure whom everybody recognised, who was on hand for every emergency, yet whose name never appeared on any regular roster. His first words were cryptic:

'Grants and scholarships.'

'What about them?'

'You give a certain number to non-Italians. How are they allotted?'

'On the basis of merit and recommendation. We accept only candidates with full nursing certificates from their countries of origin and references from their consulates or embassies in Rome. We offer them two years of specialised training in cardiac theatre and post-operative practice. The scholarships are advertised in the consulates and in professional journals in Tunisia, Saudi Arabia, Trucial Oman, Israel, Kenya and Malta. We supply board, lodging, uniforms, training and health care. The candidates or the country which sponsors them must come up with the rest. It works pretty well. We get staff eager to learn, the sponsoring countries get trained personnel capable of passing on their education. End of story . . .'

'Are any security checks made on applicants?'

'You know there are. They have to apply for visas and

student sojourn permits. The Italians run their own vetting system. Your people do any unofficial check for me. So there shouldn't be any surprises.'

'There shouldn't be; but this time we've got a nasty one. Recognise her?'

He tossed on the desk a small, passport-size photograph of a young woman. Salviati knew her instantly.

'Miriam Latif. She's been here a year now. She comes from Lebanon. She's working in the haematology unit. And she's damned good. What the hell could you possibly have on her?'

'She has a boyfriend.'

'Most girls do – and Miriam's a very pretty one.'

'The boyfriend is one Omar Asnan, designated a merchant from Tehran. He trades in tobacco, hides, spot oil and pharmaceutical opium. He also disposes of large quantities of ready cash and has a string of girlfriends, some of them even prettier than Miriam Latif. He is also a known paymaster of the Sword of Islam group.'

'So?'

'So the least we can say is that he has a friend, an ally, a possible assassin, in place in the clinic . . . And if you think of it, the haematology unit is a very useful place to have her.'

Sergio Salviati shook his head.

'I don't buy it. The girl's been here for twelve months. The Pontiff's operation was decided only a few days ago. The assassination threat is a matter that arose in response to the opportunity.'

'And why,' asked the Mossad man patiently, 'why else do you have people in place, under deep cover, as sleepers – except to take advantage of unforeseen opportunities? Why the hell do you think I'm here? Think of all the famous or politically important people who pass through the clinic. This is a stage simply waiting for a drama to happen . . .

And Miriam Latif could be the leading lady in a tragedy.'

'So what are you going to do about her?'

'Watch her. Put one of our magic rings around her, so that she can't even go to the toilet unless we know about it. There's not much time. How long before your patient is discharged?'

'Barring complications, ten days, fourteen at the outside.'

'So, don't you see, they have to move fast. But now that we're alerted, we can move faster.'

'Do the Italians know this?'

'No. And we don't intend to tell 'em. We'll do whatever is necessary. One thing you have to remember. If the girl fails to show up for work, I want you to make a big song and dance about it – question the staff, inform the police, call her embassy, all that!'

'And I don't ask why you want it done like that?'

'Exactly,' said the Mossad man. 'You are a very wise monkey, who hears no evil, sees no evil, speaks no evil.'

'But you could be wrong about Miriam Latif.'

'We hope we are, Professor. None of us wants to have blood on the sidewalk! None of us wants reprisal for a lost agent.'

Sergio Salviati felt himself suddenly drowning in the black waters of fear and self-loathing. Here he was, a healer, netted like a tunny in a labyrinthine trap, waiting helplessly for murder to happen. The message he had been given was clear as daylight. In the game of terror, the slaughter was serial; you kill mine, I kill yours. Now there was a new twist to the sport – make the killing but put the blame on someone else: a hit-and-run motorist, a vengeful lover, an addict in search of a fix. And so long as the blood didn't splash on his own doorstep, Sergio Salviati would be silent lest even worse things should befall.

Then, because it was nearly midday, he walked to the Intensive Care Unit to take a look at the cause of all his problems, Leo XIV, Pontifex Maximus. All the signs said that he was doing well; his breathing was regular, the atrial fibrillations were within normal limits, his kidneys were functioning and his body temperature was rising slowly. Salviati smiled sourly and made a silent apostrophe to his patient: 'You are a terrible old man! I give you life and what do you give to me? Nothing but grief and death . . . Morrison was right. You're a bird of ill-omen . . . Yet – God help me! – I'm still committed to keeping you alive!'

Seven

The first drugged confusions were over: the long unstable
hours when he drifted between sleep and waking, the half-seen
procession of Vatican visitors murmuring solicitous courtesies,
the broken nights when his thorax hurt abominably and he
had to ring for the nurse to move him in the bed and
give him a pill to ease him back into sleep. But neither
the confusions nor the pain could mask the wonder of
the prime event: he had been taken apart like a watch
and put together again; he had survived. It was exactly
as Salviati had promised. He was like Lazarus stepping
out of the tomb to stand, blinking and uncertain, in the
sunlight.

Now, every day was a new gift, every unsteady step a new
adventure, every word spoken a fresh experience of human
contact. At moments the newness was so poignant that he
felt like a boy again, waking to that first flush of spring when
all the blossom trees in Mirandola seemed to burst into flame
at once. He wanted to share the experience with everyone:
the staff, Malachy O'Rahilly, the cardinals who came like
courtiers to kiss hands and congratulate him.

The strange thing was that when he tried to express to
Salviati both the wonder and his gratitude for it, his words
seemed suddenly arid and inadequate. Salviati was courteous
and encouraging; but when he had gone, Leo the Pontiff felt
that a most important event had slipped past him, never to be
celebrated again.

This sense of loss plunged him, without warning, into

a black depression and a prolonged fit of weeping which shamed him into a deeper gloom. Then Tove Lundberg appeared and sat by his bedside to hold his hand and coax him out of the dark valley and on to the sunlit slopes again. He did not withdraw from her touch but surrendered to it gratefully, knowing, however vaguely, that he needed every possible handhold to anchor him to sanity. She used her own handkerchief to wipe away his tears and chided him gently:

'You must not be ashamed. This is the way it goes with everybody – high elation, then despair, a huge swing of the pendulum. You have just been subjected to an enormous invasion. Salviati says that the body weeps for what has been done to it. He says something else, too. We all believe we are immortal and invulnerable. Then something happens and the illusion of immortality is shattered for ever. We weep then for our lost illusions. Even so, the tears are part of the healing process. So let them flow . . . My father used to remind us that Jesus wept for love and for loss, just like the rest of us . . .'

'I know that. Why, then, am I so unprepared and inadequate?'

'Because . . .' Tove Lundberg pieced out her answer with great care, 'because to this moment you have always been able to dictate the terms of your life. In all the world there is no one who sits higher or more securely, because you are elected for life and no one can gainsay you. All your titles affirm, beyond question, that you are the man in control. Your whole character urges you to hold that control.'

'I suppose so.'

'You know so. But now you are no longer master of yourself or of events. When my father was in his last illness he used to quote us a passage from the Gospel of John. It is, I believe, part of Christ's Commission to Peter . . . How does it go? "When you were young, you used to buckle on your belt and go wherever you wanted . . ."'

Leo the Pontiff gave her the rest of the text as if it were a response in choir.

'"But when you are old, you will hold out your hands and another will gird you and lead you where you do not want to go . . ." For a man like me, that's a hard lesson to learn.'

'How can you teach it, if you haven't learnt it?'

A ghost of a smile twitched at the corners of his bloodless lips. He said softly: 'Now there's a change! The Pope is taught sound doctrine by a heretic – and a woman at that!'

'You'd probably be a whole lot wiser if you listened to both the heretics and the women!' Her laugh took the sting out of the reproof. 'I must go now. I have three more patients to see before lunch. Tomorrow, we'll walk in the garden. We'll take a wheelchair so that you can rest when you feel tired.'

'I'd like that. Thank you.'

As a parting gesture she sprinkled cologne on a facecloth and dabbed it on his forehead and his cheeks. The gesture moved him to an unfamiliar emotion. The only woman who had ever soothed him like that was his mother. Tove Lundberg ran her fingertips over his cheek.

'You're stubbled as a wheat field. I'll send someone in to give you a shave. We can't have the Pope looking scrubby for all his important visitors.'

'Please, before you go . . .'

'Yes?'

'The day I came in a woman died here. The name escapes me, but her husband used to be a priest. I asked my secretary to make enquiries about him and his family. So far he hasn't given me any information. Can you help me?'

'I'll try.' The tiny hesitation seemed to escape him. 'There are certain rules about confidentiality; but I'll see what I can do. Until tomorrow then.'

'Until tomorrow. And thank you, signora.'

'Please, would Your Holiness do me a favour?'

'Anything in my power.'

'Then call me simply Tove. I am not married, though I do have a child. So I am hardly a signorina either.'

'Why,' he asked her gently, 'why have you found it necessary to tell me this?'

'Because if I do not, others will. If I am to help you, you must be able to trust me and not be scandalised by what I am or do.'

'I am grateful to you. And I already know who and what you are from Cardinal Drexel.'

'Of course! I should have remembered. Britte calls him Nonno Anton even now. He is very important in both our lives.'

'As you are in mine at this moment.' He took her hands in his own and held them for a long moment, then he reached up and signed a cross on her forehead with his thumb.

'Peter's blessing for Tove Lundberg. It is not any different from your father's.'

'Thank you.' She hesitated a moment and then posed the diffident question. 'Some day you must explain to me why the Roman Church will not permit its priests to marry. My father was a good man and a good pastor. My mother was his helpmeet in the Church and with the people . . . Why should a priest be forbidden to marry, to love like other men . . . ?'

'That's a big question,' said Leo the Pontiff. 'Bigger than I could possibly answer now. But certainly we can talk about it another time . . . For the present, just let me tell you I am glad and grateful for what you are doing for me. I need this help in a way you may never understand. I shall pray for your well-being and that of your daughter . . . Now, please send me the barber and have nurse bring me fresh pyjamas. A scrubby Pope indeed! Intolerable!'

The small tenderness she had shown him, and the rush of emotion it had produced in him, lent all the more emphasis to her question about celibate clergy and his own unanswered enquiry about Lorenzo de Rosa. This cluster of small incidents was simply a micro-image of problems which had bedevilled him for a long time and had plagued the Church for more than fifteen hundred years.

The discipline of enforced clerical celibacy in the Roman communion had proved at best questionable, at worst a creeping disaster for the community of the faithful. The attempt to equate celibacy, the unmarried state, with chastity, the avoidance of unlawful sexual intercourse, was doomed to failure and productive of a whole crop of ills, not least an official hypocrisy and a harvest of tragedies among the clergy themselves. Forbidden to marry, some found relief in secret liaisons, others in homosexual practice or, more commonly, in alcohol. Not infrequently, a promising career ended in mental breakdown.

In the mid-sixties, after the Second Vatican Council, discipline had been relaxed to permit those in distress to quit the priesthood and marry validly. There had been a sudden rush for dispensations. Tens of thousands left the ministry. New vocations slowed to a trickle. The sad truth had been revealed, that this was no happy band of brothers, joyful in the service of the Lord, but a lonely ministry of lonely men facing an old age lonelier yet.

Thenceforward every attempt to drown the problem in a flood of pious rhetoric had failed miserably. His own rigorist policy – 'few but good, and for none an easy exit' – had seemed at first to succeed, with a small crop of Spartan zealots coming up each year for ordination. But even he, Leo XIV, Hammer of God, had to admit in his secret heart that the remedy was a placebo. It looked good, tasted good, but did nothing for the health of the Mystical Body. There were too few shepherds for the vast flock. The zealots – in whom he recognised his younger self – were out of touch with reality. The threadbare theology that backed a face-saving legislation was no excuse for depriving the people of the saving word.

What he could or should do about it was another matter entirely. He had – at least to this moment – no intention of going down in history as the first Pope in a thousand years to legalise a married clergy. Whatever the morals of such a move, the economics of it opened a new chapter of horrors. Meantime, the personal tragedies proliferated; the faithful gave tolerance and affection to their pastors, young and old, and made their own provisions to keep the sacred fire of the Word alive. There was nothing he could do but wait and pray for light in his own puzzled mind, and strength for his still shaky limbs.

The barber came, a new one this time, sallow and saturnine, wielding an old-fashioned cut-throat razor, who shaved him clean as a billiard ball and uttered no more than a dozen words in the process. A nurse brought him fresh pyjamas and then walked him to the shower and helped him scrub himself, because his chest and back still hurt. He was no longer humiliated or even displeased by his dependence; but he was beginning at least to make a comparison between his own circumstance and that of any ageing cleric, forced to depend upon the ministrations of women, from whom he had been exiled by decree all his life. Finally, shaved, dressed and lighter in spirit, he walked back to his room, seated himself in his chair and waited for visitors to arrive.

The first, as usual, was Monsignor Malachy O'Rahilly, who brought with him a roster of those who had applied to call on His Holiness to pay respect and to keep themselves and their business under Pontifical notice. They had always recognised in him an old-fashioned Italian traditionalist and this was the old-fashioned way of papal business: protocol, propriety, compliment and courtesy.

With his master restored to him, Malachy O'Rahilly was himself renewed, bubbling with busy good humour.

'And are they treating you well, Holiness? Is there anything you need? Any delicacy to tempt your fancy? I'll have it here for you in an hour. You know that.'

'I know it, Malachy. Thank you. But there's nothing I need. Who's on your list for today?'

'Four people only. I'm holding the numbers down because once they see that bright look in your eye they'll all be wanting to talk business – and that's *verboten!* First on the list is the Secretary of State. He has to see you. Then there's Cardinal Clemens from the Congregation for the Doctrine of the Faith. He's still jumping up and down about the Tübingen Petition. There's more and more discussion in the Press and on television. His Eminence wants your consent to take immediate disciplinary action against the theologians who signed the document . . . You know his arguments, it's a direct challenge to Papal authority, it calls in question your own right to appoint bishops to local churches . . .'

'I know the arguments.' The familiar predator look transformed him instantly into an adversary. 'I told Clemens very plainly that we should take time to reflect before we answer. We need light, not heat, in this matter. Very well. I'll see him at four-thirty. Fifteen minutes. No longer. If he runs on, you come in and get rid of him. Who's next?'

'Cardinal Frantisek, Congregation for the Bishops. That's a courtesy call on behalf of the hierarchy. It will be brief. His Eminence is a model of tact.'

'Would we had more like him, Malachy! Five-fifteen?'

'Finally, Cardinal Drexel. He's spending the day in Rome; he asks if he may call on you between seven and eight, on his way home. I'm to telephone his office if you agree.'

'Tell him I'll be delighted to see him.'

'And that's all, Holiness. It doesn't mean I haven't been busy. It means that the Secretary of State will have my head if I submit you to even a hint of harassment.'

149

'I'll tell him myself you're a model chamberlain, Malachy. Now, you had some enquiries to make for me about the young woman who died the night I came here. The one who was married to a priest of the Roman diocese.'

Now Malachy O'Rahilly was caught between a very large rock and a very thorny place. The Pontiff demanded information. The Secretary of State had promised to boil him in oil if he divulged it. True always to his nature, Malachy O'Rahilly decided that if he wanted to stay in his job, he must cleave to the Bishop of Rome and not to his adjutants in the Curia. So, he told the truth; but this time at least he told it penny-plain, making no mention of the newspaper cuttings in his briefcase, no reference to the security meeting in the Apostolic Palace or Matt Neylan's passionate intervention on behalf of de Rosa.

When he ended his story, the Pontiff was silent a long time. He sat bolt-upright in his chair, his hands clamped to the arm-rests, his eyes closed, his mouth a pale razor-slash across his chalk-white face. Finally, he spoke. The words issued in a harsh, strained whisper, simple and final as the deaths that prompted them.

'I have done a terrible thing. May God forgive me. May He forgive us all.'

Then he began to sob convulsively, so that his whole body was racked with the pain and the grief. Malachy O'Rahilly, the perfect secretary, stood mute with embarrassment, unable to raise hand or voice to comfort him. So he tiptoed out of the room and signalled a passing nurse to tell her that her patient was in distress.

'Explanations please, Professor.' The Mossad man, humourless and laconic as always, pushed a clipboard across Salviati's desk. 'I know most of it, but I want to check it off with you.'

'Go ahead.'

'That's a specimen of the chart which is hung at the foot of every patient's bed, right?'

'Right.'

'Where are the charts produced?'

'On our own copier in the clinic.'

'Now would you read the column headings, please?'

'Time. Temperature. Pulse. Blood pressure. Treatment administered. Drugs administered. Nurse's observations. Physician's observations. Treatment ordered. Drugs ordered. Signature.'

'Now take a look at the chart in front of you. Look at yesterday's date. How many signatures are there?'

'Three.'

'Can you identify them?'

'Yes. Carla Belisario, Giovanna Lanzi, Domenico Falcone.'

'Functions?'

'Day nurse, night nurse, physician on duty.'

'Now look at the notations. How many different handwritings are there?'

'Six.'

'How do you explain that?'

'Simple. The nurses who sign are responsible for the patient. Each has several patients. Temperature, pulse and blood pressure are taken by juniors. Dosages are administered by pharmacy personnel, treatment may be given, for example, by a physiotherapist. The system is essentially simple. The physician prescribes, the nurse supervises, the others work under direction and supervision . . . Now perhaps you can tell me what you're looking for.'

'Loopholes,' said the Mossad man. 'How to murder a Pope in a Jewish clinic and get away with it.'

'And have you found one yet?'

'I'm not sure. Look again at that chart. Is there any mention of haematology?'

'Right at the beginning, in the pre-operative stage of this patient. There's an order for a whole series of blood tests.'

'Explain exactly how they would be done – in respect of the patient.'

'The test is ordered on the chart. The office on this floor calls haematology and puts in the order. They send someone to take blood samples, which are taken back to the laboratory for testing.'

'That someone who takes the samples. What equipment does he have? How does he proceed?'

'It's generally a she,' said Salviati with a grin. 'She has a small tray on which there is alcohol, cotton wool swabs, some small adhesive patches, stoppered phials with the patient's name and room number written on the labels and a sterile hypodermic needle in a sealed plastic packet. She may carry a small rubber strap to constrict circulation and pump up the vein. That's the lot.'

'How does she proceed?'

'She identifies the vein in the crook of the arm, swabs the spot with alcohol, inserts the needle, draws the blood and transfers it to the phial. She staunches the puncture with cotton wool, then seals it with an adhesive patch. It's all over in a couple of minutes.'

'Nobody else in the room during the procedure?'

'Not usually. Why should there be?'

'Exactly. That's the loophole, isn't it? The girl is alone with the patient. She is carrying a lethal weapon.'

'Which is what, precisely?'

'An empty syringe, with which blood can be extracted from a vein, or a lethal bubble of air pumped into it!'

'That's something I hadn't thought of. But there's a big hurdle she has to jump first. Our distinguished patient has had all his blood tests. Who's going to write the order for new tests on his chart? Who's going to call up haematology?'

'That's the second loophole,' said the Mossad man. 'Under your very thorough system, Professor, the clipboards are brought to the office at the end of each day shift and night shift. They are hung on numbered hooks and the charge sister inspects each one before completing the diary of her tour of duty. Anyone can pass by and make a notation. I've seen it done. The girl who took the patient's temperature forgot to write down the pulse rate or the blood pressure. You know it happens, and how it happens. How many times has a nurse had to ask you whether or no a dosage is to be continued?'

Salvati rejected the whole idea out of hand.

'I don't believe it – not a single damned word! You're synthesising a fiction; how a murder might happen! You're pulling an assassin out of thin air. This girl is one of my people. I'm not going to let you frame her like this.'

The Mossad man was unmoved. He announced flatly:

'I haven't finished yet, Professor. I want you to listen to something.' He laid on the desk a small pocket recorder and plugged in an earpiece which he handed to Salviati. 'We've had Miriam Latif bugged for days now – her room, her laboratory jacket, the lining of her pocket-book. She always uses a public phone, so she has to carry *gettoni*. The pocket-book goes with her everywhere. What you will hear is a series of brief conversations with Omar Asnan, the boyfriend. They're in Farsi, so you'll have to take my word for their meaning.'

Salviati listened for a few minutes then, exasperated by his inability to follow the dialogue, took out the earpiece and handed it back.

'Translation, please.'

'The first conversation was from a bar in the village. She says yes, the arrangement is possible. Asnan asks how soon. She says a few days yet. He asks why. She says because of the logic.. He asks what she means by logic. She says she can't tell him now. She'll try to explain at the next call . . . The explanation comes a little later in the tape. She explains that no one is allowed access to the man without passing through the security screen. She points out it wouldn't be logical to have a blood test ordered in the middle of convalescence. It would be more normal just before the patient was due to be discharged. Asnan says it's running things very fine. He'll have to think of back-up arrangements. Her answer to that clinches matters as far as we're concerned. She says: "Be careful. The place is crawling with vermin and I haven't identified all of them yet." There's more, but that's the core of it.'

'There's no possible doubt that she's the assassin?'

'None.'

'What happens now?'

'You don't ask. We don't tell.'

'Would it help – it's a long shot and I'd hate to do it – would it help if I transferred the patient to Gemelli or Salvator Mundi?'

'Would it be good for the patient?' The Mossad man seemed willing to consider the idea.

'Well, it wouldn't be the best, but he'd survive it.'

'What's the point then, Professor? So far as Miriam Latif is concerned it would make no difference at all. She's identified as a killer. The Vatican doesn't want her. Because she hasn't committed a crime yet, the Italians wouldn't do more than deport her back to Lebanon. We certainly don't want her running around loose in our theatre of operations. The conclusion's obvious enough, isn't it?'

'Why,' asked Sergio Salviati bitterly, 'why the hell did you have to tell me?'

'It's the nature of things,' said the Mossad man calmly. 'You're family. This is your home place, we're protecting you and all who abide here. Besides, what's to fret about? You're a doctor. Even your most successful cases end up with the undertaker!'

Then he was gone, a sinister, bloodless ghost haunting the corridors of an underworld that ordinary folk hardly believed to exist. Now he, Sergio Salviati, was a denizen of that underworld, caught in the toils of its conspiracies like a wasp in a spider web. Now he, the healer, would be made a silent party to murder; yet if he did not consent to silence, more and bloodier murders might be done. As an Italian, he had no illusions about the underside of life in the Republic; as a Jew and a Zionist, he understood how bitter and brutal was the struggle for survival in the Fertile Crescent.

Willy-nilly, he had been for a long time a player in the game. His clinic was a listening post and a refuge for sleepers in the intelligence trade. He himself, like it or not, was playing a political role; he could not, on the same stage, play the innocent dupe. Come to think of it, if the person of the Pope were directly threatened would the Vatican security men hold fire? He knew they would not. Sergio Salviati was not asked to pull a trigger, only to be silent while the professionals went about their normal business. The fact that their target was a woman had no weight in the case. The female was as lethal an instrument as the male. Besides, if any blood splashed on Sergio Salviati's hands, he could always get rid of it when he scrubbed up for surgery. There at least and at last he had to be clean . . .

In the midst of that wintry meditation, a courier brought the invitation for Tove Lundberg and himself to dine with Mr & Mrs Nicol Peters at the Palazzo Lanfranco.

The Secretary of State had a tidy mind and a subtle one. He hated a clutter of trifles on his agenda; he insisted always that they be disposed of before addressing himself to major issues. So, on his afternoon visit to the clinic he spoke first with Salviati, who assured him that the Pontiff was making a normal and satisfactory recovery and that he could probably be discharged in five or six days. He also talked briefly to the Italian and Vatican officials in charge of security, careful always to avoid any questions which might suggest that His Eminence knew more than his prayers. Then he presented himself to the Pontiff and walked with him to a sheltered spot in the garden, while an attendant waited at a discreet distance with the wheelchair. His Holiness came brusquely to the nub of the matter.

'I am ill, my friend; but I am not blind. Look around you! This place is like an armed camp. Inside I am hedged and picketed wherever I move. What is going on?'

'There have been threats, Holiness – terrorist threats against your life.'

'By whom?'

'An extremist Arab group, calling itself the Sword of Islam. The information is high-grade intelligence.'

'I still don't believe it. The Arabs know our policies favour Islam over Israel. What have they to gain by killing me?'

'The circumstances are special, Holiness. You are a patient in a clinic run by a prominent Zionist.'

'Who still treats many Arab patients.'

'All the more reason to teach everyone a lesson. But however twisted the logic, the threat is real. Money is on the table – big money.'

'I'll be out of here in a few days – less than a week probably.'

'Which brings me to my next point, Holiness. Most of us in the Curia are strongly against your proposal to lodge with Anton Drexel. It means a new and very expensive security operation, possible danger to the children and – let me say it frankly – the last thing in the world you want: jealousies within the Sacred College itself.'

'God give me strength! What are they! A bunch of schoolgirls?'

'No, Holiness. They are all grown men, who understand the politics of power – and not all of them are friends of Anton Drexel. Please, Holiness, I beg you to consider this carefully. When you go from here, go straight back to Castel Gandolfo. You will have the best of care, as you know. From there, you can visit Drexel and his little tribe whenever you choose . . .'

The Pontiff was silent for a long moment, watching Agostini with hostile, unblinking eyes. Finally, he challenged him: 'There's more, isn't there? I want to hear it, now.'

He did not expect evasion. He did not get it. Agostini set down the core of the argument.

'All of us are aware, Holiness, of your concern at the divisions and dissensions in the community of the faithful. Those of us who are close to you have sensed for some time that you are going through a period of . . . well, of doubt and reassessment of the policies you have pursued so vigorously during your pontificate. That state of uncertainty has been increased by your illness. There are those – and let me hasten to say I am not one of them – who believe that the same illness, the sense of urgency it provokes, may cause Your Holiness to take precipitate action which, instead of doing good for the Church, may damage it further. Here is my point: if changes for the better are to take place, you will need all the help you can get from the Curia and the senior hierarchy of the National Churches. You're one man in the world who knows how the system works and how it can be used to frustrate the most determined or the most subtle of Pontiffs . . . You trust Drexel. So do I. But he is a man in the evening of his years; he is a German; he is too impatient of our Roman follies. He is, in my view, a handicap to your plans; and if you were to put that to him, I believe he would agree with you.'

'Have you yourself put it to him, Matteo?'

'No.'

'And where do you stand on the question of policy?'

'Where I always stand. I'm a diplomat. I deal in possibles. I'm always afraid of hasty decisions.'

'Drexel is coming to visit me this evening. I owe him the courtesy of a discussion before I decide anything.'

'Of course . . . There is one other matter on which I need a personal authority from Your Holiness, otherwise it will be floating around the Congregations for months. We've lost one of our best men from the Secretariat this week, Monsignor Matt Neylan.'

'Lost him? What does that mean, precisely?'

'He's left us.'

'A woman?'

'No. In a way, I wish it were. He came to tell me that he is no longer a believer.'

'That's sad news. Very sad.'

'From our point of view, he has conducted himself with singular propriety. It's tidier to laicise him without fuss.'

'Do it, and do it quickly.'

'Thank you, Holiness.'

'I will tell you a secret, Matteo.' The Pontiff suddenly seemed to have withdrawn into a private world. 'I have often wondered what it would be like to wake up one morning and find that one no longer had the faith one had professed for a lifetime. One would know it all, as one might know a matter of law or a chemical equation or a piece of history; but it would no longer have any relevance . . . What is the phrase in *Macbeth*? "It is a tale, told by an idiot, full of sound and fury, signifying nothing." In the old days, you know, we'd have turned away from a man like that, treated him like a leper, as if the loss were his own fault. How does anyone know that? Faith is a gift. The gift may be withdrawn, as the gifts of sight or hearing may be taken away. It could as easily happen to you or me. I trust you were kind to him. I know you would never be less than courteous.'

'I'm afraid he wasn't very happy with me, Holiness.'

'Oh, why not?'

The question took them by a single stride to the story of

the final Vatican involvement in the fate of Lorenzo de Rosa and his family. This time, however, it seemed that the Pontiff had no more emotion left to spend. What he uttered was a lament for lost hopes.

'We're losing too many, Matteo. They are not happy in the family of the faithful. There is no joy in our house, because there is too little love. And it is we the elders, who are to blame.'

Once each week, at an unscheduled hour, Sergio Salviati made what he called the 'white-glove round' of the clinic. He had borrowed the phrase from an elderly relative who used to extol the spacious days of sea travel under the British flag, when the Captain, accompanied by the Commodore and the Engineering Officer, donned white gloves and inspected the vessel stem to stern. The white gloves showed every trace of dust or grime and protected the soft hands of authority.

Sergio Salviati did not wear white gloves but his Chief Of Staff carried a clipboard and a xeroxed plan of the institution on which every shortcoming was noted for immediate remedy. It was a very un-Latin procedure; but Salviati had too much at stake in patronage and professional reputation to trust to the shifting standards of a polyglot staff. He checked everything: toolsheds, linen stocks, pharmacy, pathology, files and records, surgical waste disposal, kitchen, bathrooms. He even took micro-samples from the air-conditioning ducts, which in the hot Roman summer might house dangerous bacteria.

The inspections were always made in the late afternoon, when his stint in the operating theatre was over and his ward rounds were all complete. At this hour, too, the staff were more relaxed and open. They were coming up to the end of the day and were vulnerable to criticism and well pleased by a word of praise. It was a few moments after five on this same ominous day when he came to the Haematology

Department, where blood and sera were stored and analyses made of samples brought in from the wards.

Normally there were three people on duty in the laboratory. This time there were only two. Salviati wanted to know why. He was told that Miriam Latif had asked for the afternoon off to attend to some personal business. She was expected back on duty the next day. The arrangement had been cleared with the Chief of Staff's office. People within departments covered for each other as a matter of course.

Back in his own office, Salviati summoned the Mossad man and quizzed him about the girl's absence. The Mossad man shook his head sadly.

'For an intelligent fellow, Professor, you're a very slow learner. Your own staff have told you all you need to know. Best of all, they have told you the truth. The girl was called away on personal business. She made the excuse in person. Leave it at that!'

'And the threat to our patient?'

'Her absence has removed it. Her presence would restore it. We wait and watch, as always. For tonight at least you can sleep soundly.'

'And tomorrow?'

'Forget tomorrow!' The Mossad man was impatient and abrupt. 'You, Professor, must make a decision today – now, this moment!'

'About what?'

'The role you want to play: the reputable healer going about his reputable business in a wicked world, or the meddler who can't keep his nose out of other people's business. We can accommodate you, either way. But if you're in, you're in up to the neck and you play by our rules. Do I make myself clear?'

'Either way,' said Salviati, 'it seems I'm being manipulated.'

'Of course you are!' The Mossad man gave him a vinegary

smile. 'But there's one big distinction: as Professor Salviati you are manipulated in innocence and ignorance. The other way, you do as you're told, eyes open, mouth shut. If we want you to lie, you lie. If we want you to kill, you kill – the Hippocratic oath notwithstanding. Can you wear that, my friend?'

'No. I can't.'

'End of argument,' said the Mossad man. 'You'll enjoy your dinner tonight and sleep a lot more soundly.'

But you don't sleep,' Tove Lundberg chided him tenderly. 'You don't even enjoy making love; because you're not innocent, you're not ignorant, and the guilt gnaws at you all the time.'

They were sitting over cocktails on the terrace of Salviati's house, looking out at a sky full of stars, misted and blurred by the emanations of Rome: river fog, traffic fumes, dust and the exhalations of a city slowly choking itself to death. He had not wanted to share the story with her, because the mere knowledge of it put her at a certain risk. However, concealment put him at greater hazard, because it clouded his judgement, robbed him of that detachment upon which his patients' lives depended. Tove Lundberg summed up her argument.

'The problem is, my love, you know too little and want too much.'

'I know Miriam Latif is going to be killed – if she's not dead already.'

'You don't know it. You're surmising. You can't possibly be sure she's even missing until tomorrow.'

'Then what do I do?'

'What would you do if it were another person altogether?'

'I would I hear it much later than everyone else. The Chief of Staff's office would already have inquired into her absence. If she didn't show up in a reasonable time, they'd ask me to authorise a replacement. I would probably advise them to contact the police and immigration officials, because the clinic has sponsored the girl's entry and guaranteed her employment. After that, it's out of our hands.'

'Which is no more or no less than your Mossad man told you at the beginning.'

'But don't you see . . . ?'

'No! I don't. I can't see one step beyond the routine you have just outlined. Whom else are you going to tell? The Pope? He knows about the threat to his life. He knows about the security measures. He consents, tacitly at least, to anything that may happen as a result of those measures. If the girl is a terrorist, she herself has already accepted all the risks of the job for which she has been trained.'

'But that's just the point.' Salviati was suddenly angry. 'All the evidence against her is circumstantial. Some of it is negative, in the sense that no other more likely candidate has shown up on the Mossad lists. So she's being condemned and executed without a trial.'

'Maybe!'

'All right. Maybe!'

'Again, what can you do about it, when the Italian Government abdicates its legal authority in favour of direct action by the Israelis? That's what's happening, isn't it?'

'And the Vatican sits pat on the protocol of the Concordat. The Pope's bodyguards may protect him by force of arms if necessary; but the Vatican may not intervene in the administration of justice in the Republic.'

'So why go on beating your head against your own Wailing Wall?'

'Because I'm not sure any more who I am or where my loyalties lie. The Pope's my patient. Italy is my country. The Israelis are my people.'

'Listen, my love!' Tove Lundberg reached across the table and imprisoned his hands in her own. 'I will not take this kind of talk from you. Remember what you told me when I first came to work for you. "Cardiac surgery is a risk business. It depends on free choice, an acceptance of known odds, clearly stated between surgeon and patient. There can be no trading back if an unknown factor tips the odds the wrong way!" So, it seems to me you're in the same position in the case of Miriam Latif. The odds are she's a trained assassin, nominated to kill the Pope. A choice has been made: to stop her without attracting reprisals. In this case, however, the choice was made by others. Your identity is not challenged; rather, it is confirmed. You are a healer. You have no place on the killing ground. Stay away from it!'

Sergio Salviati disengaged himself from her handclasp and thrust himself up from the table. His tone was rasping and angry.

'So! It's happened at last! It always does in Rome! My loyal counsellor has become a Jesuit. She should do very well with His Holiness.'

Tove Lundberg sat a long while in silence, then, with an odd, distant formality, she answered him.

'A long time ago, my dear, you and I made a bargain. We could not share our histories or our traditions. We would not try. We would love each other as much as we could, for as long as we could, and when the loving was over we would stay friends always. You know I have neither taste nor talent for cruelty games. I know you play them sometimes, when you are frustrated and afraid, but I have always believed you had too much respect to force me into them . . . So, I'm going home now. When we meet in the morning I hope we can forget this ugly moment.'

The next instant she was gone, a blurred figure hurrying through the twilight towards her car. Sergio Salviati raised neither hand nor voice to stay her. He stood like a stone man, clamped to the crumbling balustrade, lonelier and more desolate than he had ever felt in his life. The valiant of Zion had rejected him with contempt. A woman of the *goyim* had probed with an unerring finger towards the hollow place in his heart. Each had acknowledged him as a healer. Both had challenged him to the impossible, to mend his damaged self.

That night, the Pontiff sat late with Anton Drexel. After the emotional storms of the day he felt a need for the calm, quiet discourse which Drexel dispensed. His answer to the objections raised against a papal sojourn at the colonia was typical of the man.

'If it raises problems, then forget the idea. It was intended as a therapy, not as a stress factor. Besides, Your Holiness needs allies and not adversaries. When all the brouhaha has died down and the risks of attack on your person have diminished, as they always do, then you can visit the children. You can invite them to visit you . . .'

'And what of your own plans for me, Anton? My education to new views and policies?'

Drexel laughed, a man at ease with himself and his master.

'My plans depend on the working of the Spirit, Holiness. Alone, I could not bend you a millimetre. Besides, your Secretary of State is right – as he is most of the time. I am too old and still too much the *Ausländer,* to be a true power-broker among the Curia. That is how Your Holiness won the battle over Jean Marie Barette. You assembled the Latins against the Germans and the Anglo-Saxons. I would never attempt the same strategy twice.'

Now it was the Pontiff's turn to laugh – a painful business with little amusement at the end of it.

'So what is your strategy, Anton? And what do you hope to win from me or through me?'

'What I believe you hope for yourself – a revival in the Assembly of the Faithful, a change in the attitudes which dictate the laws which are the greatest obstacle to charity.'

'Easy to say, my friend. A lifetime's work to accomplish – and I have learned how short and fragile life can be.'

'If you are thinking of serial solutions – picking off problems one by one like ducks in a shooting gallery – then of course you are right. Each issue sets off a new debate, new quarrels and casuistries. Finally, weariness sets in and the kind of creeping despair that has afflicted us since the Second Vatican Council. The fire of hope that John XXIII kindled has died to grey ashes. The conservatives – yourself, Holiness, not least among them – had a whole series of pyrrhic victories and the faithful were the losers every time.'

'Now tell me your remedy, Anton.'

'One word, Holiness – decentralise.'

'I hear you. I'm not sure I understand you.'

'Then I'll try to make it plainer. What we need is not reform, but liberation, an act of manumission from the shackles which have bound us since Trent. Give back to the local churches the autonomy which is theirs by apostolic right. Begin to dismantle this creaking edifice of the Curia, with its tyrannies and secrecies and sinecures for mediocre or ambitious prelates. Open the way to free consultation with your brother bishops . . . Affirm in the clearest terms the principle of collegiality and your determination to make it work . . . One document would start it – a single encyclical written by yourself, not constructed by a committee of theologians and diplomats and then emasculated by the Latinists and bled white of meaning by conservative commentary . . .'

'You're asking me to write a blueprint for revolution.'

'As I remember, Holiness, the Sermon on the mount was a revolutionary manifesto.'

'Revolutions should be made by young men.'

'The old ones write the documents, the young translate them into action. But first they have to break out of the prison in which they are kept now. Give them liberty to think and speak. Give them your confidence and a charge to use the liberty. Perhaps then we will not have so many casualties, like de Rosa and Matthew Neylan.'

'You're a stubborn man, Anton.'

'I'm older than you are, Holiness. I have even less time.'

'I promise you I'll think about what you've said.'

'Think about this too, Holiness. As we stand now in the Church, the centuries-old fight for papal supremacy is won – and the penalties of that victory are costing us dearly. All power is vested in one man, yourself; but you can only exercise it through the complicated oligarchy of the Curia. At this moment, you are almost impotent. You will remain so for months yet. Meantime, the men whom you appointed to positions of power are ready to range themselves in opposition to any new policies. That's a fact. Agostini has already given you the same warning. Is that a healthy state of affairs? Is that the true image of the Church of which Christ is the head and all we are members?'

'No, it is not.' Leo the Pontiff was weary now. 'But there is not a single thing either of us can do about it at the moment except think and pray. Go home, Anton! Go home to your family and your vineyards. You should be picking and crushing very soon, yes?'

'Very soon. Two weeks, my man tells me.'

'Perhaps I could come for that. I haven't been to a *vendemmia* since I was a child.'

'You'll be very welcome.' Drexel bent to kiss the Ring of the Fisherman. 'And a papal blessing might do wonders for the wine of Fontamore.'

Long after Drexel had gone, long after the night nurse had settled him for sleep, Leo XIV, successor of the Prince of the Apostles, lay awake listening to the night noises, trying to decipher his destiny in the shadows cast by the night light.

The argument which Drexel had put to him had a certain grand simplicity on the one hand and, on the other, a very subtle distinction between authority and power.

The concept of papal power had been given its most rigid and extreme definition by Boniface VIII in the fourteenth century and Pius V in the sixteenth. Boniface had declared *tout court* that 'because of the need for salvation, every human creature is subject to the Roman Pontiff'.

Pius V had elaborated the proposition with breathtaking presumption. Leo XIV, his modern successor, inheritor of his rigid will and irascible temper, could recite the words by rote: 'He who reigns in heaven, to whom is given all power in heaven and on earth, gave the one Holy Catholic and Apostolic Church, out of which there is no salvation, to be governed, in the fullness of authority, to one man only, that is to say, to Peter, the Prince of the Apostles and to his successor, the Roman Pontiff. This one ruler He established as prince over all nations and kingdoms, to root up, destroy, dissipate, scatter, plant and build . . .'

This was the ultimate and most flagrant claim of an imperial papacy, discredited long since by history and by common sense; but the echoes of it still lingered in the Vatican corridors. Power was still the ultimate human prize and here resided the power to move nearly a billion people, by the ultimate sanction – *timor mortis*, the fear of death and its mysterious aftermath.

Drexel's proposal was therefore an abdication of positions held for centuries, surrendered piecemeal and then only under extreme duress. It involved not an imperial concept, but a much more primitive and radical one, that the Church was one because it possessed one faith, one baptism and one Lord, Jesus Christ, in whom all were united as branches to a living vine. It involved not power, but authority – authority founded upon free consent, free conscience, an act of faith freely made. Those who were vested with authority must use it with respect and for service. They must not pervert authority to an instrument of power. To use it rightly, they must not only delegate it, but acknowledge freely the source from which it was delegated to them and the conditions of its use. It was one of the ironies of a celibate hierarchy that when you deprived a man of one satisfaction you sharpened his appetite for others, and power was a very spicy taste in the mouth.

Even if he agreed with Drexel's plan – and he had many reservations about it, as he had about Drexel himself – the obstacles to its accomplishment were enormous. That very afternoon his quarter-hour interview with Clemens of the Congregation for the Doctrine of the Faith had gone on for nearly forty minutes. Clemens had insisted very firmly that his Congregation was the watchdog guarding the Deposit of Faith – and if it were forbidden to bark, let alone bite, then why bother to have it? If His Holiness wanted to respond directly to the protestors of Tübingen, that was his right, of course. But a word from the Pontiff was not easily recalled, nor should it be gainsaid, as it might be, by these intransigent clerics.

It was the power game again and even he, the Pontiff, depleted of strength was not exempt from it. What chance had a rural bishop, ten thousand miles from Rome, delated from some act or utterance by the local Apostolic Nuncio? Drexel could fight, because he was Clemens's peer, older and wiser in the game. Yet this very Olympian detachment made him, in some degree, a suspect advocate.

On the other hand, a man who called himself Vicar of Christ was given, perforce, a place in history. His words and acts were cited as precedents down the centuries and their consequences weighed in the balance on his own judgement day. So, it was hardly surprising that the dreams that haunted his pillow that night were a strange kaleidoscope of scenes from the Michelangelo frescoes and of men, masked and armed, stalking their quarry through a pine wood.

Eight

Outside the enclave of the International Clinic, between the hours of five and ten, a series of trivial events took place.

A woman made a phone call and left a message; another woman boarded an aircraft which two hours later arrived at its scheduled destination. A crate, labelled diplomatic documents, was loaded on to another aircraft for another destination. In a villa on the Appia Antica a man waited for a call which never came. Then he summoned his chauffeur and had himself driven to a nightclub near the Via Veneto. At Fiumicino airport, a clerk in the office of Middle East Airlines made a photocopy of a ticket coupon, put the copy in his pocket and, on his way home, delivered it to the doorman of an apartment block. The whole cycle of small events was reported to the duty officer at the Israeli Embassy in Rome. Before he left for the clinic in the morning, the Mossad man was informed of their meaning.

The telephone call to the clinic was made at seven p.m. from the foyer of the airport. The voice was distorted and almost drowned by background noise, but the switchboard operator at the clinic claimed to have understood the message and to have logged it accurately. Miriam Latif would not be reporting for work in the morning as she had promised. Her mother was very ill. She was taking the night flight to Beirut on Middle Eastern Airlines. If she did not return, her due salary should be paid to her account in the Banco di Roma. She regretted the inconvenience but hoped that Professor Salviati would understand.

At seven-thirty a woman, veiled in traditional style, checked in at the Middle East Airlines counter. She had a ticket to Beirut and a Lebanese passport in the name of Miriam Latif. She carried only hand baggage. Since she was leaving the Republic and not entering it, the frontier police did not require her to unveil. Three hours later the same woman disembarked at Beirut airport, presented a passport in another name and disappeared.

The crate labelled diplomatic documents was loaded on to the El Al evening flight to Tel Aviv. Inside it lay Miriam Latif, heavily drugged, wrapped in thermal blankets and ventilated by air-holes and an oxygen tank on slow release. When she arrived in Tel Aviv she was raced to the infirmary of a Mossad detention centre and registered with a number and coding that indicated special and prolonged debriefing.

In the nightclub near the Veneto, Omar Asnan, the merchant from Tehran, ordered champagne for his usual girl and stuffed a 50,000 lire note into her cleavage. The message folded in the note was delivered ten minutes later to two men drinking coffee in one of the curtained alcoves. The delivery was noted by the cigarette girl, an Israeli agent who spoke French, Italian and Arabic.

Her report completed the operation. Miriam Latif the assassin had been eliminated from the game. Mossad was in possession of a valuable hostage and a source of vital intelligence. Omar Asnan and his cohorts of the Sword of Islam were still ignorant of what had happened. All they knew was that Miriam Latif had failed to keep a rendezvous. It would take them at least twenty-four hours to put together a feasible outline of events. There was only a slim chance that they could organise another assassination attempt during the limited time of the Pontiff's convalescence.

The only problem left was to reassure Salviati and rehearse him in his testimony. The Mossad man did it with his usual brevity.

'Your switchboard operator copied the message from Miriam Latif?'

'Yes. I have it here.'

'Is she usually accurate and reliable?'

'All our operators have to be. They deal with medical matters – life and death.'

'What are you doing with the girl's clothes, her personal effects?'

'I've asked her room-mate to list and pack them. We'll hold them in store pending word from Miriam herself.'

'Then that's the lot,' said the Mossad man. 'Except, I thought you should see this to set your tender conscience at rest.'

He handed Salviati the photostat of the ticket coupon made out in the name of Miriam Latif. Salviati scanned it quickly and handed it back.

'You haven't seen it, of course,' said the Mossad man.

'I'm a wise monkey,' said Sergio Salviati sourly. 'Deaf, dumb and blind.'

The Mossad man, however, was not blind. He saw very clearly the new options for violence opened up by the disappearance of Miriam Latif. The operation against the Pontiff was blown sky-high, as Latif herself had warned it might be: 'the place is crawling with vermin'. Nevertheless, money had been paid – big money – and the rules of the killing game were very explicit: we pay, you deliver. So, someone owed the Sword of Islam a lot of money. He had to hand back the cash or a body in lieu.

There was more than money involved. There was honour, esteem, the authority of the movement over its followers. If the rules were not enforced, if the promised victim were not delivered, the followers would drift away to another allegiance.

Finally – and this was perhaps the bitterest blow of all to the professionals – once the abduction of Miriam Latif had been established, the terrorist group would disperse and all the labour of penetrating it, all the risks taken to keep an agent in place within it, would be lost overnight.

Which left the Mossad man some delicate decisions. How much should he tell the Italians? What kind of warning, if any, should he give the Vatican folk – and whether Sergio Salviati himself needed, or was worth, protection? On balance it seemed wise to keep the safety nets around him. It would be a long time before Mossad could develop a cover as deep, as useful and as authentic as the International Clinic.

In a quiet angle of the garden, sheltered from the breeze by an ancient wall and from the sun by a canopy of vines, Leo the Pontiff sat at a table of weathered stone and wrote the diary of his seventh day in hospital.

He felt much stronger now. He stood straighter, walked further. The mood-swings were less violent, though he was still easily moved to tears or to doleful anxieties. Each day a therapist worked on his back and shoulders and, although his cloven ribcage still hurt, he was beginning to sit and lie more comfortably. The one thing that bothered him more than all else was the knowledge that he was under close surveillance at every hour of the day and night. Even so, he did not speak about it, for fear of seeming crotchety and querulous.

It was Salviati himself who raised the question with him when he came to share morning coffee with his patient. The Pontiff expressed pleasure at the unusual concession. Salviati shrugged and laughed.

'I had no operations today. I thought you could use some company. These fellows . . .' His gesture took in three marksmen who encircled the area. 'These fellows aren't very talkative, are they?'

'Not very. Do you really think I need them?'

'My opinion wasn't asked,' said Salviati. 'Nor, I imagine, was yours. Odd, when you come to think of it. You're the

Pope. I run this place. But it seems there's always a moment when the Palace Guard takes over. Anyway, you won't be here much longer. I'm discharging you very soon.'

'When?'

'Three days from now. Saturday.'

'That's wonderful news.'

'But you'll have to stick to the regimen – diet and exercise.'

'I will, believe me.'

'Have you decided where you'll be staying?'

'I had hoped it would be at Cardinal Drexel's villa; but my Curia doesn't approve.'

'May I ask why?'

'They tell me it would require a new and expensive security operation.'

'I would doubt that. I've visited the place several times with Tove Lundberg. It would probably be very easy to seal off. The perimeter wall is clearly visible from the villa itself.'

'That, of course, isn't the only reason. The Vatican is a court, as André Gide once observed. And courtiers are jealous as children of their precedence and privileges.'

'I thought Churchmen were above such worldly matters.'

Salviati's grin took the malice out of the gibe. The Pontiff laughed.

'The habit, my friend, does not make the monk.'

'And since when has the Pope been reading Rabelais?'

'Would you believe, my friend, I have never read him. My reading list was rather restricted.'

'You profited well from it.'

'I've learned more in the last week than I have in half a lifetime – and that's the truth, *senza complimenti*! I am deeply in your debt and I owe much to the wisdom and the gentleness of your counsellor.'

'She's very good. I'm lucky to have her.'

'Obviously you are very fond of each other.'

'We've been close for a long time.'

'No thought of marriage?'

'We've discussed it. We agree it wouldn't work for either of us . . . But let's talk about you for a moment. It's clear you're going back into the stress situation of your own household. I had hoped to defer that until you were stronger . . . You are doing very well indeed; but you must be aware that the sense of well-being is relative. Today is better than yesterday, tomorrow you will feel stronger still, but the energy is quickly spent and you are still dependent on the ministrations of our staff. With your permission, I'd like to talk to Cardinal Agostini about this. Frankly, I believe your well-being is more important than the jealousies of your Curial Cardinals. Why not override them and follow my advice?'

'I could. I would rather not.'

'Then let me be your advocate. At least no one can accuse me of self-interest. My clinical opinion has to carry some weight. I'd like to talk to Cardinal Agostini.'

'Then do so.'

'I will.'

'I want you to know, my friend, how grateful I am for your skill and your care of me.'

Salviati grinned like an embarrassed schoolboy.

'I did tell you I was a very good plumber.'

'You are much more than that. I see all the dedication which has gone into this place and which still holds it together. Afterwards, I should like to discuss some permanent contribution to your work – an endowment perhaps, some special equipment. You will tell me.'

'You can endow me now.' Salviati was direct and forceful. 'Tove Lundberg and I are putting together a series of psychic profiles on post-operative cardiac patients. In all our patients we note symptoms of radical psychic change. We need to understand that better. In your counselling sessions with Tove, you have described that change with various metaphors:

a snake sloughing off its old skin, a graft on an orchard tree that produces a different fruit, Lazarus walking out of the tomb, a new man in a new world . . .'

'That's the best description I have found so far. Of course I know that I did not die, but . . .'

'You came close enough,' said Salviati drily. 'I wouldn't argue a heartbeat or two. But here's my question. You came to this situation better equipped than most. You had a clear faith, a whole well-packed baggage of philosophy, theology and moral practice . . . How much of that baggage have you left behind? How much have you brought back?'

'I don't know yet.' The words came slowly as if he were weighing each one. 'Certainly not all the baggage has survived the journey and what I have brought back is much, much less than I had at the beginning. For the rest, it's too early to know or to say . . . Later, perhaps, I may be able to tell you more.'

'The answer will be important to us all. You have only to look around this garden to know that the fanatics are taking over the world.'

'Part of the baggage I still carry,' said Leo the Pontiff, 'is a set of instructions for survival. It was written by a Jew, Saul of Tarsus . . . "Now there remain these things: faith, hope and charity. And the greatest of these is charity." I haven't always used them very well myself; but I'm learning.'

Sergio Salviati looked at him for a long moment and then a slow smile softened the saturnine lines of his face.

'Perhaps I did a better job than I thought.'

'I for one will never underrate you,' said Leo the Pontiff. 'Go with God.'

He watched Salviati striding swiftly through the garden. He saw the guards salute him as he passed. Then he opened his diary and began again the task of explaining his new self to his old one.

'In my argument with Cardinal Clemens yesterday, he made much of the dangers of "the new theology", the rejection by certain Catholic scholars of what he called "the classic norms of orthodox teaching". I know what he means. I understand his suspicion of novelty, his concern that new concepts of traditional doctrines are being proposed to students in seminaries and universities before they have been proven by argument and experience against the Deposit of Faith, of which Clemens and I are appointed guardians and I am the final arbiter and interpreter.

'There! I have written it! It stares at me from the page . . . "I am the final arbiter and interpreter." Am I? What makes me so? Election by a college of my peers? A private colloquy with the Holy Ghost, of which I personally have no record or recollection? Would I even as Pope presume to pit myself in argument against any philosopher, or theologian, or biblical scholar from the great universities? I know I could not. I should make a fool of myself; because I could only appeal to those "classic norms" and their traditional expression, in which I was drilled so thoroughly in another age. I was not elected for my intellectual attainments or the stretch of my intuition in spiritual matters. I am no Irenaeus, no Origen, no Aquinas. I am and always have been a man of the organisation. I know it inside out, how to service it, how to keep it running. But now the organisation is outmoded and I am not inventive enough to remodel it. I am as deficient in social physics as I am in philosophy and theology. So I am forced to admit that my arbitrations and interpretations are those of others, and that all I contribute to them is the Seal of Peter.

'So, next question: what is the real authority of

those upon whose judgement I rely? Why have I chosen them above others more forward-looking, more understanding of the language, temper and symbolism of our times? The answer is that I have been afraid, as so many in this office have been afraid, to let the wind of the Spirit blow freely through the House of God. We have been garrison men, holding the ramparts of a crumbling citadel, afraid to sally out and confront the world which bypasses us on the pilgrim road.

'When I first left home to go to seminary, I was surprised to find that the commerce of the world was not carried on in the Emilian dialect of my home-place. The first step in my education was to learn the language of a larger world, the customs of a less rustic society. However, in the government of the Church which calls itself universal I have tried to anchor it to the language and the concepts of centuries past, as though in some magical fashion antiquity guaranteed security and relevance.

'Our blessed Lord used the language and the metaphors of a rural people, but his message was universal. It embraced all creatures, as the sea embraces all the denizens of the deep. I have tried to reduce it to a static compendium, to stifle speculation about its myriad meanings.

'I begin, slowly, to understand what one of my more outspoken critics meant when he wrote: "This pontiff is like a scientist trying to run the third millennium on a textbook of Newtonian physics. The cosmos has not changed, but our understanding of how it works is greater and different . . . To that extent we have all penetrated a little more deeply into the mystery of the Godhead. Just so, in the confusions and threats of the modern world, the pedagogy of the past is not enough for us. We need a teacher who will discourse with us in terms of the world in which we are involved."

'When I first read those lines I was outraged. I felt that the writer, a layman, was uttering an arrogant insult. Now I see it differently. I am being asked to explore boldly the mysteries of a new time, by the light of ancient truth, confident that the light will not fail . . .'

A shadow fell across the page and he looked up to see Tove Lundberg standing a pace or two away. He gave her a smile of welcome and invited her to join him at the table. As he did so, a spinal spasm hit him and he winced at the pain. Tove Lundberg moved behind him and began to massage his neck and shoulders.

'When you write your posture is wrong. So when you straighten up you get a pinch and go into spasm . . . Try to hold yourself erect.'

'My old master used to scold me for the same thing. He said I looked as though I were trying to crawl into the paper like a bookworm.'

'But you listen only now, because it hurts!'

'True, my dear Tove. True!'

'There now, does that feel better?'

'Much better, thank you. Can I offer you some mineral water?'

'You can offer me some advice.'

'Willingly.'

'Do you extend the seal of confession to unbelievers?'

'They have a specially strong seal. What's troubling you?'

'Sergio and I have quarrelled.'

'I'm sorry to hear that. Is it serious?'

'I'm afraid it is. We haven't been able to exchange anything but cold courtesies since it happened. It's something that goes to the root of our relationship. Neither of us is prepared to surrender our position.'

'And what precisely are your positions?'

'First, we've been lovers a long time. You probably know that.'

'I guessed it.'

'But you don't approve, of course?'

'I cannot read your private consciences.'

'We've talked often about marriage. Sergio wants it, I don't.'

'Why not?'

'My reasons are very clear to me. I'm not prepared to risk another child. I don't believe I should condemn my man – any man – to a childless marriage. Britte is completing her education at the colonia; but at a certain moment she will have to leave it and I will have to provide a home and care for her. I do not want to contemplate lodging her in an institution. She is much too intelligent for that. So that's another burden I'm not prepared to lay on a husband. As a lover, I feel the contract is more equal, if more temporary . . .'

'And Sergio Salviati? How does he feel about all this?'

'He accepts it. I think he's even relieved, because he has problems of his own, which go deeper than mine but are less easy to define. First, he's a Jew – and you, of all people, must know what it means to be a Jew, even now, in this country. Second, he's a passionate Zionist, who often feels frustrated and demeaned because he's here making money and reputation, while his people are fighting for survival in Israel. At the same time, his position involves him in all sorts of compromises. You're one of them. You're the reigning Pontiff, but you still refuse to recognise the State of Israel. The Arab sheikhs he treats here are another compromise – and the fact that this place is also an undercover post for Mossad agents working in Italy. There's nothing too secret about that. The Italians know it and profit by it. The Arabs know it and feel safe against their own factions. But all of it tears Sergio apart and when he's upset and frustrated a streak of cruelty comes out, which I find unbearable. That's what caused our argument.'

'You still haven't told me what the argument was about.'

'Are we still under the seal?'

'We are.'

'The argument was about you.'

'All the more reason to tell me.'

'You don't know this; but the person who was named to assassinate you was a woman, an Iranian agent who was actually employed in this clinic. Mossad agents identified her, kidnapped her and . . . well, nobody's quite certain what happened after that. The Vatican was not involved because of jurisdictional reasons. The Italians were happy to let the Israelis handle it because they didn't want reprisals. Sergio felt very guilty, because the girl was one of his employees; he knew and liked her. He felt that the evidence against her was highly circumstantial. Even so, he could not intervene in what happened. I tried to comfort him by saying that even you had to play a passive role. You accepted armed guards, which meant that you accepted that they might kill someone to protect you. Sergio wasn't happy with that either. He said . . . it doesn't matter what he said. It was just very painful and, somehow, final.'

'Say the words!'

'He said: "It's happened at last. It always does in Rome. My loyal counsellor has become a Jesuit. She should do very well with the Pope."'

She was near to tears. The Pontiff reached across the table and imprisoned her hands in his own. With careful gentleness he told her: 'Don't be, too hard on your man. Guilt is a bitter medicine to swallow: I've been sitting here trying to digest a lifetime of it . . . As for cruelty, I remember that when I was a small boy, my dog had his leg broken in a rabbit snare. When

I tried to release him he bit my hand. My father explained to me that an animal in pain will snap at anyone. What other response is left to it? Your man must be hurting very badly.'

'And what about me? Don't you think I'm hurting too?'

'I know you are; but you will always heal more quickly. You have learned to look outside yourself, to your daughter, your patients. Every time your Sergio goes into the operating theatre, he is engaged in a private duel with death. When he comes out, he finds that all the fears he has left outside the door lie in wait for him.'

'What are you telling me to do?'

'Kiss your man and make up. Be kind to each other. There is too little love in the world. We should not waste a drop of it . . . Now, could you spare the time to walk me down to the pine wood?'

She gave him her arm and they walked slowly down the paved walk to the shelter of the pines. The guards, vigilant and edgy, fanned out to encircle them. Monsignor Malachy O'Rahilly, who had just arrived for his morning visit, was tempted to follow them. Then, watching them together, animated but relaxed, like father and daughter, he thought better of it and sat down at the stone table to await his master's return.

Katrina Peters's dinner party was staged on the terrace of the Palazzo Lanfranco, with the rooftops of old Rome for backdrop and a pergola of vines for canopy. Her waiters were hand-picked from the best agency. Her cook was borrowed from Adela Sandberg, who reported Italian fashion for the glossiest of New York fashion magazines. Her guests were chosen to indulge her own taste for exotic encounters and her husband's talent for making a commentator's capital out of them.

To confront Sergio Salviati and Tove Lundberg she had chosen the Soviet Ambassador and his wife. The Ambassador was reputed to be a formidable Arabist who had spent five years in Damascus. His wife was a concert pianist of high reputation. For a partner to Matt Neylan – who, according to Nicol, had more than earned his place at table – she had invited the latest arrival at the American Academy, an attractive thirty-year-old who had just produced a highly praised thesis on the status of women in the mystery religions. To these she added Adela Sandberg for colourful gossip, Menachem Avriel because his wife was away in Israel and he enjoyed Adela Sandberg. Then, for good measure, she added Pierre Labandie, who drew satirical cartoons for *Le Canard Enchainé,* and Lola Martinelli, who had made rich marriages and profitable divorces into a serial art-form. The fact that she was a lawyer in her own right added a certain patina to the product.

The ceremonies opened with champagne and a *pavane* around the terrace to admire the view, identify the cupolas and turrets, black against the skyline. During this prelude, Katrina Peters moved lightly but warily among her guests, bridging awkward gaps in the talk, explaining one guest to another, plagued always by those banes of Roman intercourse, the limp handshake, the muttered introductions, the almost furtive confessions of identity and profession.

This time she was lucky. Matt Neylan, trained to diplomacy, was easy and talkative. The Russian was hearty and opinionated. They took care of Tove Lundberg and the lady of the mysteries, each of whom was an agreeable and easy talker.

Nicol Peters took the opportunity for a first quick exchange with Salviati and Menachem Avriel on the terrorist threat.

'I hear you've got almost an armed camp out there in Castelli.'

'We're protected.' Salviati tried to evade the discussion. 'We have to be in any case, threat or no threat.'

'The threat is real.' Avriel was an old hand at managing the Press. 'The group has been identified.'

'Off the record, I understand Mossad had already penetrated the group?'

'No comment,' said Avriel.

'I still can't understand the political thinking behind it. The relations between Islam and the Vatican are at least stable. What's to gain by assassinating the Pontiff?'

'A statement.' Menachem Avriel gestured emphatically. 'Israel is a plague carrier. Any contact or compromise means death.'

'But why not knock off Salviati here? He owns the place. He's a known Zionist.'

'Counterproductive. Sergio treats a lot of wealthy Arabs. He's the first and best clinic between Karachi and London . . . Why lose his services? Why make enemies of the money men in Islam?'

'It's feasible; but I feel there's something missing in the logic.'

Menachem Avriel laughed.

'Haven't you learned yet that there's always a term or two missing in Farsi logic? You start off with a set of clear propositions, on flat and open ground, then – hey presto! – you're winging with the bats on Magic Mountain!'

'I'm not sure I like our own logic any better,' said Sergio Salviati.

'Who cares about logic?' Adela Sandberg swept in to take control of the small conclave. 'Love comes in; logic goes out the window! Kiss me, Menachem! You may kiss me, too, Sergio Salviati!'

At the far end of the terrace, the Soviet Ambassador was deep in conversation with Tove Lundberg.

'You work with this Pope . . . what is he like? How does he react with you?'

'I have to say he is, even now, a very formidable man. Sometimes I think of him as an old olive tree, gnarled and twisted, still putting out leaves and fruit . . . But inside the tree is a vulnerable, loving man trying to claw his way out before it is too late. With me he is very humble, very grateful for the simplest service. But,' – she smiled and shrugged – 'it is like playing with a drowsy lion. I have the feeling that if he woke in a bad temper he would eat me in one gulp!'

'I am told there have been threats against his life.'

'That's true. The clinic is under guard day and night.'

'That troubles him?'

'He is troubled for the staff, for the other patients, but for himself not at all.'

'You have to understand something, Excellency.' Matt Neylan, with the lady of the mysteries on his arm, drifted into their talk. 'This man, Leo XIV, is an archetype, a throwback. He refuses all dialogue with today's world.'

'I don't agree,' Tove Lundberg challenged him brusquely. 'I'm not even a believer, in spite of the fact that my father was a Lutheran pastor. But I see the man every day for post-operative counselling. I find him open, self-questioning, always preoccupied by the question of change within the Church.'

'I believe you.' Matt Neylan was bland as honey. 'But do you have any Latin about you?'

'A little,' said Tove Lundberg.

'My husband is a very good Latin scholar,' said the pianist. 'He is fluent in ten languages.'

'Then he'll have no difficulty with this little proverb: *Lupus languebat, monachus tunc esse volebat; sed cum convaluit, lupus ut ante fuit.*'

The Ambassador laughed and rendered the proverb in heavily accented English.

'When the wolf was sick he wanted to be a monk. When he recovered he was still a wolf . . . And you are saying, Mr Neylan, this is what will happen to your Pope?'

'I'll lay long odds on it.'

'Pardon?'

'I'm sure, almost a hundred per cent sure, he'll revert to exactly what he was.'

'Five thousand lire says you're wrong,' said Tove Lundberg. Matt Neylan grinned.

'You've got a bet, ma'am! And if you win I'll throw in the best dinner in this city.'

'It's hard to find a really first-class restaurant nowadays.' Katrina Peters slipped quietly into the group.

'It's a damned sight harder to find a first-class man!' said Lola Martinelli.

'Don't give up yet, Lola,' said Katrina Peters. 'Matt Neylan here has just come onto the market – mint-new and beautifully trained!'

'I got him first,' said the lady of the mysteries. 'And we're in the same business!'

They sat, the round dozen of them, at a round table laid with Florentine linen, Venetian glass, Buccellati silver and porcelain from the house of Ginori. Nicol Peters offered a toast of welcome: 'This house is your house. Whatever is said here tonight is spoken between friends, in trust and confidence. *Salute!*'

Then the food was offered and the talk began to circulate, more loudly and more freely as the evening went on. Nicol Peters watched and listened and picked up the scraps of dialogue that later would fit into the mosaic of his column, 'A View From My Terrace'. This was the heart of his work. This was what they paid him for. Any fool could report the news: that the Pope washed feet on Maundy Thursday, that Cardinal Clemens had censured another German theologian. But it took a bright and free-ranging fellow like Nicol Peters to read the Richter scales and say bravely that an earthquake would happen on Friday.

The man from Moscow was both industrious and entertaining. He was concentrating his attention on Matt Neylan who, launched auspiciously into the world of fashionable women, was dispensing lavish doses of Irish charm.

'So I'd like your opinion, Mr Neylan . . . What role do you see for Russian Orthodoxy in the policies of the next decade?'

'Outside Russia,' said Matt Neylan judiciously, 'in the Christian communities of the West, it has to create a role for itself, in theological, philosophical, socio-political debate. That's not going to be easy. Its intellectual life has been in stasis since the Great Schism in the eleventh century. Politically, you people have held it captive since the revolution . . . In spite of that, it still remains closest to the spirit of the early Eastern fathers. It has much to offer the West. For you, it may well be the strongest buffer you have against the expansion of Islam within the Soviet Union itself . . . I'm sure I don't have to tell you the statistical extent of that expansion.'

'And you dealt with these matters at the Secretariat of State?'

'Not personally. Not directly. The *peritus* in this area is Monsignor Vlasov, whom you may have met . . .'

'I have not, but I should like to do so.'

'Under other circumstances I should have offered to arrange a contact. Now, as you see, I am no longer a member of the club.'

'Do you regret that?'

'What's to regret?' The lady of the mysteries patted Neylan's hand approvingly. 'Don't they say the late vintage makes the sweetest wine!'

Over the dessert, Nicol Peters turned suddenly to Menachem Avriel and said, apropos of nothing at all: 'I'm still worried about the logic.'

'And . . . ?'

'I think I've got the missing proposition.'

'Which is?'

186

'Double-think, double-shuffle. What you called "winging with the bats on Magic Mountain".'

'Spell it for me slowly, Nico.'

'It's a fair assumption – though you can't admit it – that Mossad had penetrated the Sword of Islam.'

'And what follows from that?'

'A possible scenario. The group puts out a phoney plan. The Vatican, the Republic, Mossad, all make dispositions to deal with it. Maybe they're even handed a phoney assassin who is arrested or killed. Then they don't need the Pope or Salviati. They've got what they really want – a *casus belli*, a reason to stage any public coup they want, from kidnap to hijacking an airliner. It's a thought, isn't it?'

'A damned uncomfortable one,' said Sergio Salviati.

Menachem Avriel shrugged off the notion. He was, after all, a diplomat skilled in social lying. Nicol Peters let the subject drop and addressed himself to the brandy. He was after all a newsman, who understood that truth lay often at the bottom of the pool and you had to stir up the mud to reach it.

When they rose from table, he drew Sergio Salviati away from the others for a private interrogation.

'I'd like to make this as simple as I can. I get the daily bulletins on the Pope's progress. Anything you can add to them without a breach of ethics?'

'Not too much. He's making very good progress. His mental faculties are unimpaired – which I guess is what you're driving at.'

'Will he be able to function fully in office?'

'If he follows the regimen, yes. He will probably function better than in the immediate past.'

'Differently? I caught the tag end of the talk between Tove and Matt Neylan.'

'You can't quote me on this.'

'I won't.'

'Tove is right. The man is greatly changed. I believe he will continue so.'

'Could you call it a "conversion" in the religious sense?'

'That's a matter of semantics. I prefer to limit myself to a clinical vocabulary . . . Now could I ask you a question?'

'Go ahead.'

'Your scenario of the phoney assassin; do you believe it?'

'I think it's very feasible.'

'Suppose,' said Salviati carefully, 'just suppose the assassin had already been identified.'

'And taken out?'

'Suppose that, too, if you want.'

'Anything else I could suppose?'

'That there had been no reaction from the Sword of Islam.'

Nicol Peters pursed his lips and then let out a long, low whistle of surprise.

'In that case, then I would say, fasten your seat belts. You could be in for a very bumpy ride! Let me know what really happens, won't you?'

'You'll probably know it before I do,' said Sergio Salviati. 'The way my life runs, I never get time to read the morning papers!'

After that it was playtime. As the night mist rolled in from the Tiber, they moved into the *salone*. Matt Neylan sat down at the piano and sang Neapolitan songs in a smooth Irish tenor. Thus encouraged, the Ambassador's wife sat down and unleashed a whole torrent of music – Chopin, Liszt, Tchaikovsky. Even Katrina Peters, most critical of hostesses, had to agree that the evening had been a success. Nicol Peters was preoccupied. Every instinct told him that something was about to break. He could not for the life of him define what it was.

Nine

Omar Asnan's villa on the Old Appian Way had cost him a
mint of money. Situated on the most expensive stretch of the
ancient road, between the tomb of Cecilia Metella and the
crossroad to Tor Carbone, it was a hotchpotch of constructions
that dated from Roman times to the twentieth century.

A high blank wall, topped with broken glass, hid it from
the road and from the open fields of the *campagna* behind
it. The garden with its swimming-pool and tubs of flowering
plants was shaded by tall cypresses and spreading pines. It was
also patrolled at night by an armed watchman and a pair of
Dobermanns.

One special feature of the house was a square watch-
tower, built around a chimney, from which it was possible
to survey the Appia Antica in both directions, watch the
shepherds grazing their herds in the *campagna* and look
clear across the rooftops of other villas to the apartment
blocks of EUR.

The second feature, an unexpected bonus for Omar Asnan,
was the cellar, vaulted and bricked in reticulated stone, which
dated back to the same period as the nearby Circus of
Maxentius. There was nothing unusual about the cellar
itself, but a loose slab in the floor had revealed a set
of ten steps that led to a tunnel. The tunnel, dug into
the friable tufa rock, ran fifty metres across the *campagna*
and opened into a large, circular chamber lined with great
earthenware pots which had once been used to store grain.
The air was foul, but the place was bone dry, and it was the

simplest thing in the world to install a ventilating system with intake and outlet hidden in the garden shrubbery.

So, Omar Asnan – thanks to Allah, the just and the merciful! – had found himself endowed with a storeroom for special merchandise like guns, grenades and drugs, a conference room hidden from prying eyes, and a safe house to hold friends or enemies. It was here that he met with his four most trusted lieutenants to discuss the disappearance of Miriam Latif from the International Clinic.

They sat on cushions set about a carpet, two on either side, with Omar Asnan presiding. He was a small, dark man, put together as neatly as a manikin, with eloquent hands and a ready smile. His speech was brisk and businesslike.

'This is what we have been able to confirm in twenty-four hours. At three in the afternoon I myself called Miriam at the clinic to set up a meeting here. She agreed. She said she could easily arrange the time off at the end of the day. She would drive into Rome to do some shopping and see me on the way back.'

He turned to the man on his right.

'You remember all this, Khalid. You were here with me.'

'I remember.'

'We arranged to have dinner here, in the villa. She never arrived.'

'Clearly she was –'

'Please!' Asnan raised a warning hand. 'Please, let us discuss what we know, not what we think we know. Miriam never arrived here. Round about ten p.m. I drove into the club to pass the word, that probably our operation was blown. You all got that message, yes?'

There was a murmur of assent.

'Now let me tell you what I have since established, through our various contacts in the police and at the airport. Miriam's car was found in the long-term parking bay at Fiumicino. The hospital claims – and I have seen the message taken down by the switchboard operator – that Miriam called from the airport at seven p.m. to say that her mother was very ill and she was leaving immediately for Beirut on Middle East Airlines. I personally have checked with our friends in the airline office. A woman calling herself Miriam Latif did buy a ticket, did present a Lebanese passport, did check on to the aircraft. The only problem is that this woman was veiled in traditional style. Miriam Latif never wore a veil . . . More than that, I have confirmed with Beirut that no one presented Miriam Latif's passport or a landing card with her name on it. Miriam herself made no contact with her parents, who are both in excellent health . . . So, my friends, what are we to conclude?'

The man who called himself Khalid answered for everyone.

'I think it is obvious. She must have been under surveillance. She was intercepted and abducted on the way into Rome. Someone else drove her car to the airport and booked out in her name to Beirut.'

'Why go to all that trouble?'

'To delay what we have now begun – the search for her.'

'Is she alive or dead?'

'My guess is that she's alive.'

'Reason?'

'Why go through all the charade at the airport? Much simpler to kill her and dump the body.'

'Next question: who is holding her?'

'Mossad, without a doubt.'

'Why?'

'Interrogation. They know we exist. They must have had some word of our plans; otherwise why would there be that large concentration of forces at the clinic?'

'How would they know?'

'They would know because they were told.'

'You are saying there is a traitor among us?'

'Yes.'

'Precisely,' said Omar Asnan. 'And to unmask that traitor it was necessary to sacrifice Miriam Latif. I regret that very much.'

There was dead silence in the chamber. The four men looked at each other and then at Omar Asnan, who sat calm and benign, enjoying their discomfiture. Then he reached into his breast pocket and brought out a pen and a small leather-covered notebook. He opened the notebook and took up again the thread of his discourse.

'You know how we are organised. We here are five. Below us are groups of three. Each group is self-contained. Each person within it has contact with only one person from another group. Thus treachery cannot spread easily. Only we five knew about Miriam Latif and our plans for her. Only one of you knew that I had summoned her here.' In a gesture almost playful, he held the lip of the pen against Khalid's temple. 'Only you, Khalid, friend of my heart!'

He pressed the clip of the pen. There was a small, sharp sound and Khalid slumped to the floor. A thin trickle of blood and fluid oozed from the hole in his head. Omar Asnan said curtly: 'Pick him up. Put him in the big jar, the glazed one with the lid. Seal the lid with cement. Then spray this place. Already, it stinks of Jew! We'll meet upstairs when you've finished.'

In his office at the clinic, Sergio Salviati was conferring with Cardinal Matteo Agostini, Secretary of State. After a late night and a piece of simple surgery that went suddenly and dangerously wrong, his patience was wearing thin.

'Understand me, Eminence. I am talking in clinical terms about the welfare of my patient. He has said he will abide by your judgement . . . I know you have other concerns, but these are not my affair.'

'His Holiness does not need my consent to do anything.'

'He wants your approval, your support against possible critics.'

'Is that a clinical matter?'

'Yes it is!' Salviati was curt. 'At this stage of cardiac recovery, everything is a clinical matter – every unnecessary stress, every shock or anxiety. If you don't believe me, I can show you how those things read on a monitor screen.'

'I believe you, Professor.' Agostini was totally at ease. 'So I shall make immediate arrangements for the transfer of His Holiness to Cardinal Drexel's villa. The security there will be our affair. I take it you will still be able to provide adequate medical supervision?'

'His own physician should supervise him on a day to day basis. I am close by for ready reference. I shall, in any case, see him at the end of the month. Tove Lundberg is a constant visitor to the villa. However, I would suggest you employ a good physiotherapist to supervise His Holiness in daily exercise. I can recommend such a one.'

'Thank you. Now I have questions of my own. Is His Holiness fit to resume his normal duties?'

'He will be, after an adequate convalescence.'

'How long is that?'

'Eight weeks for the ribcage to heal. Six months at least of graduated activity. Remember, he is not a young man. But since he is not engaged in heavy physical work – yes, he can certainly function quite well. There are, however, a couple of caveats: no long ceremonies, Masses in St Peter's, carrying the cross around the Coliseum, that sort of thing. I know you have to have him on stage from time to time, but get him on and off as quickly as possible. Second caution: no long-haul air travel for at least six months.'

'We'll do what we can to manage him,'said Agostini. 'Next question: his mind? Will he be . . . stable? God knows, he's never been an easy man to deal with and we do know that he is emotionally fragile at this moment.'

'Fragile, yes. But he understands the condition and deals with it. Tove Lundberg is full of admiration for him. She has volunteered to stay close to the case for as long as she is needed.'

'My last questions then. Is he changed? How is he changed? And how permanently?'

'Certainly he is changed. In the old days the patient underwent the "experience of the God" – the *metanoia* which was the crisis point of the therapy. The experience, however it was engineered, certainly involved terror, trauma and the shock of survival. Your man has been through all that . . . It sounds perhaps overdramatised, but . . .'

'I see the drama,' said Agostini quietly. 'I wonder how it will go in public performance.'

'There, I'm afraid, I can't help you.' Salviati laughed and spread his hands in a gesture of helplessness. 'I'm only the plumber. Prophecy is the Church's business.'

'So, Anton, for better or for worse, you have me as house guest.'

'I can't tell you how happy I am, Holiness.'

They were seated in his favourite corner of the garden, under the pergola of vines, sipping iced lemonade which Tove Lundberg had sent out to them. Drexel was flushed with pleasure. The Pontiff seemed to have certain misgivings.

'Hold a moment, my friend! It's not only me. There's a whole retinue. Security men, valet, physiotherapist, visitors I can't refuse. Are you sure you can cope with all this?'

'Absolutely sure. You will be lodged in the villetta, the small villa at the lower boundary of the estate. It's comfortable and private, with its own garden and orchard. Also it is easy to protect. The security men have looked at it and they see no problems. There are quarters for your valet. Your own suite has a *salone*, study and dining-room. You will have my cook. I'm bringing her up from Rome.'

'Anton, I really believe you are enjoying all this fuss.'

'Of course I am! Do you realise that the first and last Pope to visit my villa was Clement VIII, Ippolito Aldobrandini, in 1600? His nephew Piero built that big palazzo in Frascati . . . But imagine what a papal visit must have been in those days – with carriage drivers, outriders, grooms, men at arms, courtiers and their women . . .' He laughed. 'Given more time, I'm sure we could have arranged at least some pageantry for you.'

'To the devil with pageants.' The Pontiff rejected the notion with a gesture. 'I am coming because I want to be a country-man again. I want to shed my white cassock and put on work clothes and busy myself with simple things like rust on the tomatoes and whether the lettuces are hearting properly. I won't need a secretary, because I don't propose to open a book or a letter, though I would like to listen to some good music.'

'And so you shall. I'll have a player installed and some tapes and discs sent down for you.'

'And I want to talk, Anton. I want us to talk like friends, looking back on a lifetime, but looking forward, too, to the world the children will inherit. I want to share your family, though I confess that scares me somewhat. I am not sure I have the skill or the energy to cope with them.'

'Please! Don't worry about that. You don't have to cope with anything. You won't have to learn anything, except how to manage yourself. You will arrive. I'll introduce you. They'll welcome you. You give them your blessing. All that is five minutes, no more. Then you forget about them . . . You will find, as I did, that they are all very intelligent creatures, anxious to be about their own affairs. When they are ready to approach you they will and they will establish the communication much more quickly than you ever could. All they need is your smile and your touch to reassure them. Remember that. Touch is very important. They are sensitive to any sign of revulsion or even of timidity. They are not timid themselves. They are brave and strong and highly intelligent.'

'And they have a Nonno who loves them.'

'That too, I suppose. But they give more than they get.'

'I have a confession to make to you, Anton. Suddenly I am afraid of leaving this place. I am protected here against pain and discomfort. I am counselled like a novice. I know that if something goes wrong, Salviati will know exactly what to do about it . . . you understand?'

'I think so.' Drexel seemed to dredge up the words from deep inside himself. 'I lie awake at night and wonder how Brother Death will come for me. I pray that he will arrange the meeting decently, without mess or fuss. But if he chooses otherwise – Boh! – to whom do I turn? The children can't help. The women sleep far away from my quarters . . . So, yes! I know how you feel. It's the solitude of the aged and the ailing. But since we have been given more than most, we should bear it with more grace.'

'I am reproved,' said Leo the Pontiff with wry humour. 'Next time I will find myself a more complaisant confessor.'

'No one is better placed to do so,' Drexel rounded off the joke.

'Now I need some advice.' The Pontiff laid on the table two small packages wrapped in tissue. 'These are gifts from me to Salviati and to Tove Lundberg. I'd like to have your opinion of them. I thought a lot about Salviati. He's a brilliant, haunted man. I wanted something that would give him a moment of joy.' He unwrapped the first package to reveal, laid on a bed of silk in a velvet box, an old silver *mezuzah*. 'My clever secretary O'Rahilly chose this for me. It dates from the sixteenth century and is said to have been brought back from Jerusalem. The provenance is there, written in Hebrew. Do you think it will please him?'

'I'm sure it will.'

'And for Tove Lundberg, this.' He brought out a disc of beaten gold, incised with runic letters and hung on a golden chain. 'This, O'Rahilly tells me, came originally from Istanbul, and is attributed to the first Vikings who found their way down the river systems of Russia into Turkey.'

'O'Rahilly has very good taste – and obviously a good knowledge of antiquities.'

'For that he depends on the Sub-prefect of the Vatican Museum, who is also an Irishman! I am told they drink together on occasion.'

'I am told,' said Drexel, 'that he may drink too much and too often. In your present situation, that could be more dangerous for Your Holiness than for him.'

'He's a good man, a kind man. He is a very good secretary.'

'But not necessarily a discreet one. You may have to ask yourself whether you can afford him.'

'Or whether in fact there is anyone I can afford. Is that what you are telling me, Anton?'

'To be blunt, Holiness, yes. We are all dispensable – even you. And that is my point. When you are restored, as you will be, when you begin the battle to rebuild the city of God, you will have less to fear from your enemies than from the slothful and indifferent who will never fight you but will wait, comfortable and happy, until you are dead.'

'And how do I deal with that, dear Eminence?'

'Like any good countryman, Holiness. You plough the furrow and cast the seed – and wait for God to provide the harvest!'

The departure of the Pontiff from the clinic was a much more ceremonious affair than his arrival. This time there were three limousines; one for the Pontiff, another for the Secretary of State, a third for the prelates of the Papal Household. The men of the Vigilanza had their own fast cars, at front and rear and on the flanks of the motorcade. The Polizia Stradale provided a motorcycle escort. Barricades had been erected along the route from the clinic to Drexel's villa and sharpshooters were located at danger points along the winding road.

The Pontiff's farewells to Salviati and to Tove Lundberg had been made in the privacy of his room. His gifts had pleased them both. Salviati had told him that he would save the *mezuzah* for the house he planned to build on the site of an old farmhouse he had just bought near Albano. Tove Lundberg bent her head and asked that he himself invest her with the runic talisman. When he had done so, he joined hands with both of them and said his farewells.

'I have never in my life felt so poor as I do now. I have not even the words to thank you. The best I can do is leave you God's own gift: peace on your houses. *Shalom!*'

'*Shalom aleichem*,' said Sergio Salviati.

'You aren't rid of me yet,' said Tove Lundberg. 'I have to introduce you to my daughter.'

Then she settled him in the wheelchair and pushed him along the corridor and out into the driveway, where the staff were assembled to bid him goodbye.

As the motorcade swept through the gates and out on to the open road, he felt a sudden stifling rush of emotion. This was truly resurrection day. Lazarus was out of the tomb, freed of his grave-clothes and moving among the living who were strung out along the roadside, waving flags and flowers and leafy twigs torn from the hedgerows. The cry they raised was always the same: '*Eviva il papa*', 'Long live the Pope'. And the Pope devoutly hoped their wish might come true.

Because of the risk which everyone knew, the police escort set a fast pace for the motorcade and the drivers were forced to slew sharply round the bends of the hillside. The sharp motions put a strain on the Pontiff's back and chest muscles, so that by the time they reached Drexel's villa, he was sweating with pain and nausea. As he was helped from the limousine he whispered to his driver: 'Don't go. Stay with me. Steady me.'

The driver stood with him, holding his arm while he breathed in deep gulps of mountain air and focused his eyes on the serried ranks of orchard trees and vines and the tall cypresses marching like pike men along the contours of the hills. Drexel, tactful as always, hung back until he was ready, then led him on a quick circuit of the women of the colonia, mothers and teachers and therapists.

Then the children were brought to him, a strange shambling procession, some in wheelchairs, some walking, others supported on sticks or crutches. For a moment he felt as though his unstable emotions would betray him; but he managed to contain them and, in a display of tenderness that amazed even Drexel, he embraced each one, touching their cheeks, kissing them, letting them lead him as they wished from one to the other. The last one of all was presented by Drexel himself.

'And this is Britte. She wants me to tell you she'd like to paint your portrait.'

'Tell her, tell her . . .'

His voice faltered. He could not bear the sight of that beautiful child-woman face perched on the spidery body.

'Tell her yourself.' Drexel's voice steadied him like a military command. 'She understands everything.'

'I will sit for you every day, Britte, my dear. And when the picture is done I will take it to the Vatican and hang it in my study.'

Then he reached out and drew her to him, wishing he had the faith to command the miracle that would make her whole and beautiful.

On the terraces of the Palazzo Lanfranco, Nicol and Katrina

Peters were taking coffee. Nicol was sorting through the facsimile messages which had accumulated overnight on his machine.

'The Pope's being discharged from hospital this morning. His condition is satisfactory. His convalescence will be supervised by the papal physician . . . we know all that . . . Here's something odd. It comes from the Arab newsagency. Reuters and Associated Press have picked it up. It's captioned: "Mysterious Disappearance. Muslim girl feared abducted. Miriam Latif, an attractive twenty-four-year-old laboratory technician is employed at Professor Salviati's clinic in Castelli, where the reigning Pope, Leo XIV, is a patient. On Tuesday last she asked for an afternoon's leave to go shopping in Rome and then keep a dinner engagement with a friend.

'"She did not keep the dinner date. At seven in the evening the clinic received a telephone call, supposedly from Miriam Latif. She said she was at Fiumicino airport and was leaving immediately for Beirut because her mother was seriously ill.

'"Police enquiries have confirmed that a woman using Miriam Latif's name did buy a ticket to Beirut on Middle East Airlines and the same woman, heavily veiled in traditional fashion, presented Miriam Latif's passport and boarded the aircraft. Arrived in Beirut, the woman used another passport to go through customs and immigration and then disappeared. Miriam Latif's parents, who live in Byblos, north of Beirut, were contacted. Both are in perfect health. They know nothing of their daughter's movements and have not heard from her.

'"Late today, airport police discovered Miriam Latif's car in the long-term parking lot at Fiumicino. Forensic tests are being conducted on the vehicle. The Director of the clinic, Professor Sergio Salviati, describes Miriam as a highly competent and valued member of his staff. He says that all members of staff take occasional short absences for shopping and personal visits to Rome. No objection is raised, provided permission is obtained and a substitute is in place. Miriam's room-mate and her friends on the staff describe her as cheerful and conscientious. Asked whether Miriam Latif had any political affiliations, Dr Salviati said he knew of none and that in any case Miriam Latif had been vetted by Italian authorities before she was permitted to take up appointment under the training scheme run by the International Clinic.

"'Miriam's current boyfriend, Mr Omar Asnan, with whom she was to dine on the night of her disappearance, is deeply distressed and admits frankly that he entertains fears for her safety. Mr Asnan is an Iranian national who runs a prosperous import-export business between Italy and the Middle East . . ."

'And that,' said Nicol Peters, 'tells me exactly what I wanted to know.'

'Do you think you could explain it to me?'

'At the party, Salviati was dancing on eggshells, with "suppose this . . . suppose that". It's all here! We knew the Pope was under threat of assassination. The Sword of Islam obviously had a plant in the clinic – Miriam Latif. Mossad removed her, alive or dead – who knows? Now the Sword of Islam are beginning the "mystery and martyr" process.'

'And what good does that do them?'

'It covers their present activities and prepares a climate for whatever reprisals they're planning. And, believe me, there will be reprisals!'

'So what are you going to do about it?'

'The usual. Talk around: to the Italians, the Israelis, Salviati, the Vatican, all the Muslim Ambassadors, including the Iranians. Also I'll try this Mr Omar Asnan, the grieving lover.'

'You be careful, lover boy!'

'Am I not always? Is there any more coffee?'

Katrina Peters poured the coffee and then began her own recital of affairs, which she claimed were much more important than the politics of terror and theology. As he grew older and wiser in the ways of a very old city, Nicol Peters was inclined to agree with her.

'The Russians ask us to dine at the Embassy on the 25th. She wants me to help her choose an autumn and winter wardrobe for Rome. There's a nice little profit already! Salviati wrote a very warm note. He enjoyed himself. Tove Lundberg sent a piece of Danish porcelain, which was sweet and unexpected. I like that woman!'

'That's a rare compliment from you!' Nicol Peters grinned at her over his coffee cup.

'However, I'm not so sure that I like Micheline Mangos-O'Hara!'

'And who might that be?'

'Our lady of the mysteries, from the American Academy. I can't believe the name either. It seems her mother was Greek, her father Irish.'

'Like Lafcadio Hearn?'

'And who, pray, is he?'

'A journalist, like me, but he lived in a more spacious age. He married a Japanese. Forget it. What about Mangos-O'Hara?'

'She's giving a lecture on the mystery religions. We're invited.'

'Decline!'

'I have. But she also says that Matt Neylan is the most interesting male she's met in years. His note says he found her great fun and he might well invite her to move in with him for the rest of her stay in Rome!'

'That's rushing the fences, I'd say; but he does have a lot of time to make up.' Nicol's thoughts were elsewhere. 'He also called me. The Russians are wooing him, obviously because of his Vatican background. He's bidden to lunch at the Embassy and the Ambassador has floated the idea of a trip to Moscow to meet members of the Orthodox hierarchy. Matt is not all that keen. He says he's had a bellyful of the God-business and wants a good long swallow of the wine of life! Which means he's likely to get a bellyful of reality. He's got a lot to learn.'

'And there'll be a lot of women dying to teach him.'

'Why not? He's intelligent. He's fun. He really can sing – and even after all those years in the cloth he's not a tenor castrato.'

'Lola Martinelli's got her eye on him.'

'How do you know that?'

'She called to ask whether I thought Matt would be interested in a job as her private secretary. I told her to ask the man himself.'

'And?'

'And she did and he said in his best and sweetest brogue: "Dear lady, I'm a gentlemen of independent means, so I don't need the money. I have many talents, but I'd make a lousy secretary. But if there's anything else on offer I'd be happy to discuss it with you over dinner at a convenient time and place."'

'Well, if it's not true, it's at least *ben trovato*. It sounds like Matt. What did Lola say?'

'She told him to go to hell. Then she rang me and told me he was just another of those ex-priests who get too big for their boots.'

'Good for her!'

'That's what I thought; but let's keep Matt on the guest list. He can always sing for his supper.'

'True, my love. True. Now I'd better settle down and work out a line of attack on this Miriam Latif story.'

The first persons to greet the Pontiff in his new lodging were his valet, Pietro, and an apple-cheeked young woman wearing the blue veil of the Little Company of Mary. She had a broad smile and a no-nonsense humour and she introduced herself as Sister Pauline.

'His Eminence brought me up from Rome to look after you. I come from Australia, which explains my bad Italian. The first thing you're going to do is get into bed and rest for a couple of hours. You're pale and clammy and your pulse is racing with all this excitement . . . Pietro here can help you undress. I'll be back to settle you and give you some medication . . . His Eminence said you might be difficult; but you won't be, will you? I've got an infallible cure for difficult patients. I just start talking and keep talking . . .'

'I surrender.' He raised a weak hand in protest. 'You can stop talking now. I'm ready for bed.'

Ten minutes later he was settled, with the smell of fresh linen about him, listening to the shrilling of the cicadas in the garden outside. The last sound he heard was Sister Pauline explaining to Pietro.

'Sure I can handle him! He's a pussycat. Our old parish priest would have eaten him for breakfast. He was a holy terror, that one!'

When he woke it was late afternoon. He felt calm and relaxed, eager to explore this small corner of a world from which he had been excluded for so many years. On the table beside his bed was a small silver bell. When he rang it, Pietro appeared, with towels, dressing-gown, slippers – and orders from on high.

'Sister says I'm to shave you, help you to shower and dress, then take you for a stroll. They've started harvesting the grapes. His Eminence is down in the vineyards. He suggests you might like to walk down and watch.'

'Let's do that, Pietro.' Suddenly he was eager as a schoolboy. 'And Monsignor O'Rahilly told me you've brought civilian clothes for me.'

'I have, Holiness.' He looked faintly dubious. 'I know they fit, because I gave the Monsignore the measurements. The style he chose himself.' He laid the clothes out on the bed for his master's inspection – cotton slacks, open-necked shirt, loafers and sporty-looking pullover. The Pontiff hesitated for a moment and then surrendered with a laugh.

'Who's to know, Pietro! If there's any scandal we'll blame His Eminence.'

'Wait until you see how he dresses, Holiness. He looks like any old peasant.'

'Perhaps that's what we should do, Pietro: turn all our princes into peasants — myself included.'

When he stepped into the open air and stood looking down over the fall of the rich land, he was suddenly aware how much of his life had been spent in cloisters and chapter rooms and corridors that smelt of carbolic and beeswax and chapels that reeked of old incense. Worse still was to think how much precious time he had wasted on paperwork and arguments worn threadbare by centuries of sterile debate. In Vatican City and in Castel Gandolfo he was a prisoner, let out for ceremonial occasions and so-called missionary journeys, where every move was plotted for him and every word written in advance . . .

Suddenly here he was, on a hillside in Castelli, watching the grape pickers moving up and down the vine-rows, tossing the fruit into baskets, emptying the baskets into the cart hitched to the yellow tractor that would haul them off to the crushing vats. Everyone was out there: the villa staff, the farm hands, teachers, therapists, Sister Pauline. Even the children were busy with whatever task they could perform. Those in wheelchairs trundled them between the vines. Those on crutches leaned against the upright stakes and picked within arm's stretch. Only Britte was not picking. She sat, perched — or was it laced? — precariously on a stool, with an easel and paintbox, sketching with a brush clamped between her teeth.

The scene was so lively, so full of human detail, that the Pontiff stood for a long while contemplating the simple wonder of it — and the bleak futility of much of his own existence. This was where the people of God were to be found. This was how they were to be found, doing everyday things to the rhythms of a workaday world.

He, Leo XIV, Bishop of Rome, once called Ludovico Gadda, what did he do? Well, he ruled the Church, which meant that most days he sat at his desk and received people, read papers, wrote papers, took part in occasional pageantry, made a speech every Sunday in St Peter's Square – which everybody heard but nobody understood, because the echo and the feedback across St Peter's Square made the whole thing ridiculous . . . As well, therefore, not to waste a moment of this beautiful, this specially vintaged, day . . .

With Pietro supporting him on the steps of the terraces, he walked slowly down to mingle with the pickers. They saluted him as he passed, but did not pause in their tasks. This was serious business, there was money at the end of it. One of the men offered him a swig of wine. He took the bottle, tilted it to his mouth and drank, gratefully. He wiped his mouth with the back of his hand and passed back the bottle with a word of thanks. The man grinned and settled back to work.

Finally, at the end of the third row, they came upon Drexel, sitting at the wheel of a tractor waiting to move as soon as the cart was filled with grapes. He stepped down to greet the Pontiff.

'You're looking better, Holiness.'

'I should be, Anton. I had a wonderful rest this afternoon. And thank you for providing me with a nurse.'

Drexel laughed.

'I've known Sister Pauline since she came to Rome. She's a real character. She's even tamed me! When I first visited the community she asked me what a Cardinal Protector was supposed to do. I told her: to protect the interests of the Congregation. She looked me straight in the eye and told me in that horrible Italian of hers: "Well, for a start, here's a whole list of things in which we're not getting protection

– and here's another list where the protection we're getting is quite inadequate!" She was right, too. We've been good friends ever since.'

'What can I do to help here?'

'For the moment, nothing. Just look around and relax. You could ride with me on the tractor, but it might shake you up too much. Pietro, why don't you take His Holiness into the orchard and pick some fruit for dinner. We eat country-style tonight – and another thing! You have to meet Rosa. She's got a pocketful of medals she wants you to bless – and our dinner depends on how well you do it!'

On the way back he faltered a little and Pietro scolded him.

'Please, Holiness! This is not an Olympic race. You do not have to prove you are an athlete. You never were. You never will be. So take it easy. *Piano, piano!* One step at a time.'

They halted for a while to watch Britte at work on her canvas. She was totally absorbed, as if the contorted physics of the operation permitted no break in her concentration. Yet the picture that was growing under the brush was one of quite extraordinary vigour and colour. With the brush clamped between her teeth and her head bobbing between the palette and the canvas, she looked like some grotesque bird, suddenly invaded by the spirit of a master painter. Pietro, only half aware of what he was saying, uttered the poignant plea.

'Why? Why does this have to happen? Sometimes I wonder if God gets overworked and goes crazy for a while. How else could he commit such cruelty?'

At another time in another place, Leo the Pontiff would have felt obliged to reprove him for blasphemy, or at least to read him a homily on the mysterious ways of the Almighty. This time he simply shook his head sadly.

'I don't know, Pietro. Why is an old donkey like myself allowed to survive and this one condemned to imprisonment and early death?'

'Is that what you will say to them on Sunday?'

Leo the Pontiff turned swiftly to face him.

'What do you mean?'

'Nothing, Holiness – except that on Sunday the folk here are expecting you to say a short Mass for them and give them a little sermon. A few words only, of course – His Eminence was very clear about that.'

And there it was, neatly dressed up as the courtesy of the house – the first test of the new man, Lazarus *redivivus*. It was the simplest and most traditional of Christian customs: the visiting bishop presided at the Eucharistic table, spoke the homily, affirmed the unity of all the scattered brethren in the bond of common faith. As a custom he could not evade it; as a courtesy he could not refuse it.

But Pietro's question pinned him more tightly yet. All his audience, women, therapists and children alike, were faced with the same paradox. All looked to him – the infallible interpreter of revealed truth! – to explain the paradox and make it acceptable and fruitful in their lives.

Why, Holiness? Why, why, why? We live in faith and hope, we are the givers of love. Why is this torment visited upon us and upon our children? And how dare you and your celibate presbyters ask us to breed again at random or live lonely and unsolaced in the name of this God who does indeed play a cruel dice game with his creatures?

'So tell me, Pietro,' the Pontiff asked the question with rare humility. 'What do you think I should say to them?'

'Tell them the truth, Holiness, just as you have told it to me. Tell them you don't know, you can't know. Tell them that sometimes God gives them more light and understanding than he gives to you, and they must follow the light in peaceful conscience.'

The which, Leo the Pontiff was forced to agree, was a very polite way of saying that not even a Pope is a hero to his valet.

Mr Omar Asnan received his guest in the garden of his villa on the Appia Antica. He offered coffee and sweetmeats and free access to all the information at his disposal.

'You must understand first, Mr Peters, that Miriam Latif is a friend, a very dear friend. I am deeply troubled by what has happened. I have consented to speak with you because I believe the matter must be made known as quickly and widely as possible.'

'You do not, I take it, question Dr Salviati's account of her disappearance.'

'No, I do not. As far as it goes, his account is accurate.'

'Do you suggest he knows more than he is telling?'

'Of course! He was – and is – in a very difficult position. He is a Jew, treating the Pope who, like every public man, is deemed to be constantly under threat. Salviati has mixed staff: Christians, Muslims, Jews, from all round the Mediterranean basin. I admire his policy. Let me say that plainly. I think it is enlightened and useful. However, in an atmosphere of threat and crisis such as we had while the Pontiff was in residence, staff members themselves were under a certain threat – at least to their privacy.'

'How so, Mr Asnan?'

'Well, it is a fact, is it not, that the clinic was heavily guarded by Vatican, Italian – and, I believe, Israeli – security men!'

'Do you know that, Mr Asnan? Israeli agents are not officially permitted to work in Italy. Even the Vatican Vigilanza works under very restrictive protocols.'

'Nevertheless, Mr Peters, you and I know, as a matter of pure logic, that Israeli agents were involved.'

'Are you saying they were involved in the abduction of Miriam Latif?'

'Without a doubt.'

'But why? Professor Salviati speaks of her in the highest

terms. So far as he knows, she has no political connections.'

'So far as I know also, she has none; but she has been on occasion extremely indiscreet in speech. Her brother was killed in an Israeli raid on Sidon. She has never forgotten or forgiven that.'

'And yet she accepted a subsidy to work and be trained at a Jewish hospital.'

'I urged her to do it. I told her she could look at it in two ways – as a healing act or as part payment of a blood-debt. She chose to regard it as the latter.'

'So it's possible she could have been identified – rightly or wrongly – by the Israelis as an agent for the Sword of Islam?'

'That is what I am saying, yes.'

'Where do you think she is now?'

'I hope she is still in this country. If she is not, the position may become very complicated, very dangerous.'

'Can you explain that, Mr Asnan?'

'It is, I fear, quite simple. If Miriam Latif is not returned, violence will follow. None of us wants to see it happen – I least of all, because I live a quiet life here. I enjoy good business and personal relations with Italians. I do not want those relations spoiled. But, my dear Mr Peters, I do not control events.'

'I don't either,' said Nicol Peters.

'But you can and do influence them, by what you publish, even by the information you transmit between your sources. I know that you will go from here and then use what I have said to elicit a comment from someone else. I don't object to that. I have nothing to hide. You may do some good . . . But remember the most important thing I have said – trouble is brewing!'

'I'll remember,' said Nicol Peters. 'One final question, Mr Asnan. What is your own connection with the Sword of Islam? Obviously you know it exists.'

Omar Asnan shrugged off the question with a smile.

'I know it exists. I have no connection with it at all, Mr Peters. Like Miriam Latif, like so many of my countrymen, I am expatriate. I try to live comfortably under the laws of the country which has received me. I do not believe in terrorism – and may I remind you the only act of terror that has been committed is the abduction of Miriam Latif. It is not impossible that the whole Sword of Islam story was a fiction cooked up by the Israelis. Have you thought of that?'

'I'm sure someone has,' said Nicol Peters cheerfully. 'I'm still the neutral observer, like yourself.'

'Don't mistake me, Mr Peters. I have only said that I try to live within the law. In fact, I am outraged by what has happened to Miriam Latif and I care not who knows it.'

And that, Nicol Peters recorded, was about as close as one could get to a declaration of war, and it was a sentiment reiterated in all his interviews with Muslim sources around Rome. The Italians understood the sentiment and, for the record at least, expressed sympathy with it. They were bending over backwards to maintain friendly relations all round the Mediterranean rim. The Pope was problem enough – but at least they had been dealing with popes for centuries. The imams and the ayatollahs were another kettle of fish altogether.

The Israelis, however, were much more pragmatic. Menachem Avriel listened to the account of his other interviews and then introduced him to a lean, soldierly fellow with a cool eye and a thin smile and Mossad written all over him. His name – at least for the purpose of the exercise – was Aharon ben Shaul. He had a proposal.

'I'm going to give you some facts, Mr Peters. Most of them you can't print; but it's background you'd never come by otherwise. Then I'm going to make a projection about what may happen very soon. After that, I'm going to ask your advice as a long-time resident with good connections in this city. Deal?'

'Deal.'

'First item. Omar Asnan runs the Sword of Islam group in Rome.'

'I rather thought he might.'

'Miriam Latif is an agent of that group. She is in our hands in Israel. We have no present intention of releasing her. She cost us too much to surrender her now.'

'I don't understand that.'

'We had a man inside the Sword of Islam. He was very close to Omar Asnan. When we decided to pick up Miriam Latif we blew his cover. Asnan killed him, in the cellar of his villa.'

'How can you be sure of that?'

'Because we have it on record. Our man was wearing a bug in the collar button of his shirt. He had also planted two others, one in the garden and another in the *salone* of the villa. So we have fragments of later conversations between Omar Asnan and other members of the group. The purport of those conversations is twofold: the assassination of the Pope has been upgraded from a target of opportunity to a target of honour. He is now the Great Shaitan who must be brought down by the Sons of the Prophet, and a woman hostage will be taken to trade off against Miriam Latif. That hostage has been named.'

'Who is she?'

'Tove Lundberg, Salviati's mistress!'

'God Almighty! Do they know about this?'

'Not yet. We've got them both covered and we don't believe Asnan is ready to make his move yet.'

'How can you know that?'

'Because there's a fragment on our tape which suggests that Asnan will try to use local muscle to steal the girl – Calabresi or Sicilians probably. Also he knows we're on to him, so he's more concerned to cover his own back at this moment.'

'Can't you do anything about him?'

'Of course we can. We're trying to do it at the least possible cost in terms of reprisals. We know he's committed murder, we know where the body is. But if the Italians charge him for the murder of an Israeli agent, they'll make themselves and us very unpopular when the vendetta begins.'

'And what about the new threat to the Pope?'

'The Secretary of State will have the evidence in his hands today.'

'And where do I fit in to all this?'

'In everything I have told you, the one thing you can't print is Omar Asnan's name. The rest we'll give you – transcripts of the tapes, circumstantial details, everything. We'd like you to file the story as quickly as you can.'

'And what does that buy you?'

'Action. The Vatican pressures the Italians. The Italians have to move against Asnan and his group. You reinforce them with the old battle-cry – no negotiation under terror!'

'And Miriam Latif?'

'She's ours as long as she's useful.'

'Salviati?'

'He's the safest of all. Nobody wants him dead, not even Asnan.'

'Tove Lundberg? She's got a handicapped child.'

'We know that. It's a complication. For a while at least we have to get her off the scene. She just has to disappear . . .'

On Saturday afternoon, while the pickers were still at work and the crushers were pouring out the first murky liquor, there was a crisis conference in the garden of the villetta. Present were the Pontiff himself, the Secretary of State, Drexel, Monsignor O'Rahilly and the chief of the Vatican Vigilanza. The Secretary of State read the reports he had received from the Israelis and from the Italians. The Pontiff sat bolt upright in his chair, his jaw and beak clamped together in the old predator look. He spoke with harsh finality: 'There is no doubt in my mind. I cannot indulge myself in a vacation which puts others at risk. I shall stay here tonight, say Mass as I promised for the children and the parents of the colonia. After that, I shall go to Castel Gandolfo and remain there until the end of the summer vacation . . . I am sorry, Anton. You have been put to so much trouble, and I am more disappointed than I can say.'

Drexel made a gesture of resignation.

'Perhaps another time, Holiness.'

'Perhaps. Now, gentlemen!' The aura of command enveloped him. He seemed to grow stronger before their eyes. 'The Pope retires behind the ramparts. He leaves behind a woman who, because of her service with him, is now endangered, not only in her own person, but in that of her child. I take it this danger has not been overstated?'

The question was addressed in the first instance to the Secretary of State.

'In my view, it has not, Holiness.'

The Vigilanza man confirmed the verdict.

'The threat is very real, Holiness.'

The Pontiff put another question: 'Is it not possible for the Italian authorities, with the resources and skills which we know they have, to guarantee protection for this woman and her child?'

'No, Holiness, it is not. In fact, it is not possible for any police force to do so.'

'Is it not possible for them to terminate the threat by summary action; for example, by the arrest and detention of the known conspirators?'

'It might be, given an adequate will on the part of the Italian government; but that government itself is severely handicapped by its vulnerability to terrorist methods. Even if the law is suspended to permit or tolerate unorthodox intervention, the consequences are not always controllable, as we have seen in the present case.'

'Thank you. A question for you, Anton. Has Tove Lundberg been informed of this threat?'

'Yes. She telephoned today to ask my advice on what to do about Britte.'

'Where is she now?'

'At the clinic, working as usual.'

'Would you ring and ask her to call in here, before she goes home?'

Drexel hesitated for a moment and then left the room. Monsignor O'Rahilly began a tentative intervention.

'May I suggest, Holiness . . .'

'No, you may not, Malachy!'

'As Your Holiness wishes.'

The Pontiff was beginning to sweat. He mopped his face with a handkerchief. O'Rahilly handed him a glass of water. When Drexel came back, he was accompanied by Sister Pauline. She went straight to the Pontiff, felt his pulse and announced firmly: 'This meeting is over. I want my patient in bed.'

'It will take only a moment, Sister.' He turned to the others and said simply: 'For what has happened I am responsible, at least in part. The risk is real for Tove Lundberg and her child. The protection that can be offered is minimal. Until the threat is removed or greatly reduced, I want them both to come and live within the confines of Vatican City.' He turned to the Secretary of State. 'Our good sisters can make room for them and see that they are comfortable.' Then he addressed himself to Drexel. 'You are the Nonno of the family, Anton. Try to persuade them both.'

'I will do my best, Holiness. I can promise no more.'

With the old imperious gesture, the Pontiff dismissed them.

'Thank you all. You have our leave to go. Sister Pauline, I am ready for you now.'

As he walked slowly back into the house, the familiar

melancholy descended on him like a black cloud. Oblivious even of Sister Pauline, he muttered to himself.

'I don't believe it. I simply don't believe it. The world wasn't always like this – or was it?'

'I'm sure it wasn't,' said Sister Pauline cheerfully. 'Our old parish priest used to say the madmen have taken over the asylum; but they'll get tired of it very soon and hand it back.'

In the chapel of Cardinal Drexel's villa, designed, so the records said, by Giacomo della Porta, the members of the colonia were assembled: the young ones in front, parents and teachers behind them and, left standing against the rear wall, the few members of the Curia to whom Drexel, the old fox, had offered a personal compliment and a test of their sympathies. Agostini was there, and Clemens from the Doctrine of the Faith, and MacAndrew from the Propagation of the same Faith, and – a long reach from the power-base – Ladislas from the Congregation for the Oriental Churches. Few as they were, they made a crush in the chapel. They also made a sharp reversal of protocol: the people before the princes.

The Pontiff entered, with Drexel as his deacon, Sister Pauline as lector, with a spastic boy and girl as acolytes.

Some, but not all, of the ritual subtlety was lost on Sergio Salviati and Tove Lundberg, who sat, with Britte between them, in the front row of the congregation. Salviati was wearing his yarmulke. Tove was wearing a veil and carrying her father's old order of service. One of the mothers handed them a Mass-book. Salviati riffled through it and then whispered to Tove: 'My God! They've stolen most of it from us!' Tove, stifling a laugh, cautioned him: 'Keep an eye on your patient. This is his first appearance in public.'

It was more than that – much more. It was the first time in thirty years that he had said Mass as a simple priest. It was the first time he had talked to an audience within hand's touch and heart's reach.

Knowing how quickly he tired, he began the ritual at a steady pace; but by the time he came to the readings he was glad to sit down. Sister Pauline read the lesson in her emphatic and inaccurate Italian and ended with the exhortation of Paul to the Corinthians:

'While we are still alive, we die every day for the sake of Jesus, so that, in our mortal flesh, the life of Jesus, too, may be openly shown.'

Then they held the book for the Pontiff. He kissed it and in a firm, clear voice read the Gospel.

'One Sabbath day, Jesus happened to be walking through the cornfields and, as they went along, His disciples picked the ears of corn and ate them. And the Pharisees said to Him: "Look, why are they doing that which is forbidden on the Sabbath?" And he said to them: "The Sabbath is made for man, not man for the Sabbath . . ."'

Pale but composed, he stepped forward to face the small assembly. Salviati watched him with a clinical eye, noting the bloodless lips, the knuckles white with tension as he grasped the edges of the lectern. Then, in the midst of an eerie calm, he began to speak.

'I looked forward to this visit with you as I have looked forward to few pleasures in my life. From the moment I arrived I felt surrounded by love. I felt love welling up in my own heart, like a miraculous spring in a desert. Now, abruptly, I am called away. My brief happy time with you is ended. I lay awake last night, asking myself what gift I could leave you to say my thanks – to you, Anton, my old adversary, who has become my dear friend; to you, Sergio Salviati, my stern but careful physician; to you, Tove Lundberg, who gave wise counsel to a man much in need of it; to you, my children; to you all who care for them with so much devotion and who have made me for these few days a privileged member of this family. Then I realised that the only gift I have is the gift of which Paul speaks, the good news that in and with and through Christ we are all of us – believers and unbelievers alike – made members of the family of God our Father.

'There are no conditions to this gift. It was given to me. I pass it to you – but you have it already and already you have shared it among yourselves and have passed it back to me. This is the mystery of our communion with the Creator. It has nothing to do with laws, prescriptions, prohibitions. And this is what our Lord Himself emphasises when he says: "The Sabbath is made for man, not man for the Sabbath."

'One of the great mistakes we have made in the Church, a mistake we have repeated down the centuries – because we are human and often very stupid – is to make laws about everything. We have covered the pasture-land with fences, so there is no place for the sheep to run free. We do it, we say, to keep them safe. I know, because I have done it all too often. But the sheep are not safe: they languish in a confinement that was never their natural habitat . . .

'For most of my life I have been a celibate priest. Before that I was a lonely boy, brought up by my mother. What do I know of the complex and intimate relationships of married life? I confess it: nothing. You are the ones who know. You are the ones who confer the sacrament on each other, who experience the joy, the pain, the confusions. What can I, what can any one of my wise counsellors, my brother bishops, tell you that you do not know already? I am sure my friend Anton will agree with me. He did not legislate this family into being – he created it, with you, out of love.

'So what am I saying to you? You do not need me, any more than you need the vast edifice of St Peter's, the complex organisation that takes two thousand pages of the Annuario Pontificio to describe. The Lord is present with you in this place. You are a light to the world because you live in the light of His countenance. You need no law because you live by love – and if you stumble as we all do, fall as we all do, there are loving hands to lift you up.

'If you ask me why the innocent among you, the children, are stricken, why they must carry a lifetime handicap, I cannot answer you. I do not know. The mystery of pain, of cruelty, of the jungle laws of survival, have never been explained to us. God's secrets are still God's secrets. Even his Beloved Son died in darkness, crying to know why God had abandoned him. It would be a shame to me to claim that I am wiser or better informed than my Master.

'In this, perhaps, I am most your brother. I do not know. I walk often in darkness. I ask not whose hand is stretched out to guide me. I touch it and from the bottom of my heart I am grateful . . . God keep you all!'

'Thank you,' said Tove Lundberg. 'Thank you for offering us a refuge; but Britte and I are agreed, we live as we are. She stays here in the colonia, Sergio and I continue working as we have always done.'

Anton Drexel smiled and shrugged resignedly.

'I can't say I'm sorry. I would have hated to lose my granddaughter.'

Sergio Salviati obviously felt some explanation was needed.

'At first I thought it would be a good idea to have both of them out of the way. Our people advise it anyway. Then, when we thought about it, we came back always to the same question: why should we retreat? Why should we surrender to these obscenities? So we stay.'

'Then we shall see each other again. You, my prickly friend, have to keep me alive; Britte must deliver my portrait; and to you, my dear counsellor, my house is open always.'

He embraced them all; then Drexel led him away for a brief private talk. He told him:

'While you were speaking, I was watching our colleagues. Clemens disapproved, Ladislas too. MacAndrew was surprised, but pleasantly so I think. Your secretary was very surprised. He was trying to read everyone's reaction.'

'Agostini?'

'He was neither shocked nor surprised; but that's his style. Tell him the sun failed to rise, he'll deal with it. However, there is one thing you have to remember. From this moment on, every member of the Curia, except the few geriatrics like myself, will see himself as a potential candidate at the next Papal election. You look very tired this morning, so it's natural that people will ask whether you'll really make old bones . . . So, being human, they'll begin building alliances for the next conclave. It's a point to keep in mind when you start gathering forces for a spring-cleaning.'

'I'll remember it. You still haven't told me what you thought of my sermon.'

'I thanked God for the good word. I'm proud it was spoken in my house. Now I have a favour to ask of Your Holiness.'

'Ask it, Anton.'

'Let me go now, Holiness. Relieve me of all my duties in Rome. I am long past retirement age. I desire desperately to spend the rest of my life with my little family here.' He gave a small, embarrassed laugh. 'As you see, there's a lot of work to do around the place.'

'I shall miss you very much; but yes, you are free. I shall be very much alone now, Anton.'

'You will find others, younger and stronger. From this moment I should only be an obstacle in your path.'

'And how in God's name do I reach the young ones?'

'As you did this morning. Let your own voice be heard, let your own authentic utterance be read. You can do it. You must.'

'Pray for me, Anton. Have the children pray for me.'

They clasped hands, two old adversaries united after a long campaign. Then the Pontiff gathered his strength, straightened up and, with Drexel beside him, walked briskly outside to the waiting prelates.

Book 3

Lazarus Militans

'A man's enemies shall be the folk of his own household.'

Matt. x: 36

Ten

For the next three weeks, the only reports on the Pontiff were the medical bulletins, the gossip of the Papal household at Castel Gandolfo and the occasional garrulities of Monsignor Malachy O'Rahilly.

The bulletins were studiously uninformative: the Holy Father was making steady progress but, on the advice of his physician, he had cancelled all public appearances until the end of August. The Mass of the Assumption in St Peter's on 15 August would be celebrated by His Eminence Cardinal Clemens.

The household gossip was meagre enough. His Holiness rose late and bedded early. He said his Mass in the evening instead of the morning. He was on a strict diet and was losing weight rapidly. Every day a therapist came to supervise him in an hour of exercise. For the rest – he received visitors from ten till eleven in the morning, walked, read, rested and was in bed by nine every night. One change, however, was noted by everyone. He was less tetchy, less demanding and much more gentle in manner. How long it would last, of course, was anyone's guess. After all, an intervention like that reduces a man's vitality.

The garrulities of Monsignor Malachy O'Rahilly were much more revealing. Life at Castel Gandolfo was a bore at the best of times. There was a castle, the village and the black lake below; damn small diversion for a gregarious Celt who loved convivial company. '. . . but with the old man in this mood it's Tombstone Terrace, believe me! He won't read letters. I have to send holding notes. He's become quite obsessive about what he eats and how much exercise he does, and I wish I could drop the weight off the way he's doing. But he's very quiet. When his visitors come, he doesn't talk more than courtesies: 'Thank you and how's your father', that sort of thing. He's not fey, just distant and abstracted. He reminds me sometimes of Humpty Dumpty, trying to put the pieces of himself together again. Except he isn't fat any more – and the Pontifical tailors are working overtime to refit him before he goes back to the Vatican . . . I notice he reads a lot more than he used to, prays a lot more too – which doesn't exactly leap to the eye, but you become aware of it, because he's in another world, if you take my meaning. It's as if he'd put himself in retreat, a self-imposed solitude . . .

'What is he reading? Well now, that's interesting. He's reading the very fellows that have been in trouble with Doctrine of the Faith – the Dutch, the Swiss, the Americans. In a moment of boldness – or excessive boredom – I remarked on it. He gave me the oddest look. He said: "Malachy, when I was young, I used to watch the test pilots streaking along the Po valley and out to sea. I used to think how wonderful it would be to risk oneself like that to discover something new about a machine or about myself. As my life settled into its pattern, I forgot the wonder. Now that my life has become less important, I am reliving it again . . . Time was when we burnt men like Giordano Bruno who speculated about plural worlds and the possibility of men travelling between them. Of course, we don't burn our speculative thinkers any more. Instead, if they're clerics we silence them, remove them from their teaching posts, prohibit them from public utterance on contentious matters. All this we do in the name of holy obedience. How do you feel about that, Malachy?"

'That stumped me for a minute. I didn't want to put my foot in a cowpat, so I said something like: "Well, Holiness, I suppose there's some kind of principle of progressive enlightenment." To which he said: "Malachy, you're not half the fool you try to be. Don't play games with me. I haven't the time!" Needless to say, I ducked for cover; but he didn't make a big issue of it. It's hard to know what he's really thinking. I'd love to get a look at his diary. He writes in it every evening before he goes to bed. The rest of the time it's locked in his private safe . . .'

'As a young bishop, I was asked to bless a new ship, about to be launched from the slips at La Spezia. Everyone was there: the builders, the owners, the shipwrights and their families. The tension was quite extraordinary. I asked one of the executives of the *cantiere* to explain it to me. He said: 'Once they knock the chocks away and she slides down the slipway, all our lives are riding with her. If our calculations are wrong and she broaches, we're as good as dead . . . so give us your best blessing, please Excellenza . . ." I am like that now. All my temporary supports have been taken away – Drexel, Salviati, Tove Lundberg, the staff at the clinic. I am launched. I am afloat. But I am a hulk without fittings, without crew, dead in the water . . .

'The sense of isolation weighs on me like a leaden cope. Castel Gandolfo, Vatican City – these are my empire and my prison house. Outside, I move only by the permission of others. But my confinement is not by frontiers, it is by the identity to which I was elected Bishop of Rome, Successor to the Prince of the Apostles, Vicar of Christ . . . thus and thus and thus, every title a new barricade between me and the commonality of humankind. There is another confinement too – the Lazarus syndrome. I am not, nor can I ever be again, the same as other men. I have never understood until now – how could I? – the trauma of a young woman who can no longer breed because of a surgical intervention . . . the anger and despair of the soldier maimed in a minefield. They have become as I have: irretrievably *other* . . .

'I can share these thoughts only with those who have shared the experiences; but they are not accessible to me . . . I do not see myself making the rounds of hospital wards and prison cells, patting hands and mumbling platitudes. Neither can I see myself closeted with Clemens as I have been in the past, sniffing out heresies, putting this academic and that under silence and obedience to test their faith. That is a torture more acute than the rack and the thumbscrew. I will have no more of it . . .

'Now comes the rub. Clemens is where he is because I put him there. I put him there because of what he is, because of what I was. What do I say to him now? Everything is changed because I have seen a great light? He will face me down – because he does not lack courage. He will say: "This is the oldest heresy of all. You have no right to impose your private gnosis upon the People of God." I will be vulnerable to that, because even now I cannot explain the change in me . . .

'And that, dear Lord, is the strangest irony of all. I procured the deposition of Jean Marie Barette because he claimed a private revelation of the last things. I cannot move forward or backward until I am convinced that I am not myself entrapped in the ancient pride of private knowing. Against this kind of evil there is no remedy but prayer and fasting. I am fasting! God knows, I am fasting! Why does the prayer refuse to frame itself on my lips? Please God, put me not to the trial of darkness. I do not think I shall be able to bear it!

'I woke this morning with this same fear hanging over me. There is no one here to whom I can communicate it, as I did to Tove Lundberg, so I must grapple with it alone. I went back to that marvellous first letter of Paul to the Corinthians, where he speaks first of offices and functions in the community: "God has given us different positions in the Church; apostles first, then prophets, thirdly teachers; then come miraculous powers, gifts of healing, works of mercy, the management of affairs . . ." Then he speaks of the better way which transcends all others: "Though I speak with the tongues of men and angels, and have not charity, I am like sounding brass and tinkling cymbal . . ."

'This is what I must remember every day when, after the summer vacation, I begin my personal dialogues with the Church. I must not be the man who tears it apart with contention. I must heal the grievous wounds within it.'

For Nicol Peters, the tag-end of summer had settled into its somnolent routine. The Miriam Latif story was dead. The Sword of Islam was no longer a headline item. The Pope was safely home. Mr Omar Asnan was living the agreeable life of a prosperous merchant. The Israeli Ambassador was on vacation, the Mossad man, Aharon ben Shaul, had faded back into his grey netherworld and was no longer available. This was the way life rolled in the news game. You learned to roll with the rhythm of events and non-events. You kept your story-files up to date and hoped to be ready when the next rocket went up.

Katrina was busy at the boutique. The summer visitors were out in force and the cash register was playing merry little tunes every day. The Romans had a proverb: only *cani* and *Americani* – dogs and Americans – could tolerate summer in the city. There was, however, an art to it. You worked in the morning. At midday you swam and lunched at the swimming club, where you also entertained your contacts. You worked again from five until eight, then rounded off the evening with friends at a taverna where you were well enough known to get a reasonably honest bill.

Their friendship with Sergio Salviati and Tove Lundberg was maturing slowly. Distance was a problem. It was nearly an hour's drive from Castelli to the city, longer in the peak hour traffic. The shadow of the terrorist threat still hung over them. They travelled to and from the clinic at staggered hours in a Mercedes driven by a former member of the highway police trained in evasive driving.

On Saturdays, Tove worked with the other parents at the colonia. Sundays she kept for Salviati, who was busier than ever at the clinic and more and more dependent on the brief tranquil time they spent together. It was Katrina who made the astute comment: 'I wonder how long they can keep it up, both so dedicated and controlled. It's like watching a trapeze act at the circus . . . You know if one mistimes, they both go. Somehow I think she's in better shape than he is, even though she's the one under threat.'

Matt Neylan had become something of a fixture in their lives. His affair with the lady of the mysteries had run its cheerful little course and ended with a touching farewell at the airport, after which Neylan drove back to Rome to lunch with his New York editor and drive her up to Porto Ercole for a weekend editorial conference.

It was all good clean fun and the book – a popular study of Vatican diplomacy and the personalities involved in it – was beginning to take hold of him. However, he was becoming more and more aware that not all the attention he was paid was due to his wit or good looks.

There was a steady trickle of invitations through his mailbox; to embassy affairs, to seminars, to art shows sponsored by this or that cultural committee, screening of obscure films, appeals for victims of sundry wars and permanent famines. It was a useful antidote to boredom, provided you were not infected – as Matt Neylan knew himself to be – with the massive cynicism of the ex-believer. Once you had renounced the Almighty and all his prophets, it was hard to pin your faith to the petty propagandists of the cocktail circuit, or the recruiters of the flyblown intelligence networks who infested the city.

So, while he took full advantage of the free food and liquor and company, Matt Neylan devoted half his days to the demanding business of authorship and the other half to the passionate pursuit of women. Since he was proficient in five languages and haltingly adequate in three others, he was offered a wide range of choices. The odd thing was that he felt obliged, sooner or later, to run them past Katrina Peters for her nod of approval. Katrina found it beguiling. Nicol was not amused.

'Don't kid yourself, sweetheart. Matt's naive but he's not stupid. You're his mother hen. He's relying on you for his sentimental education.'

'I find that rather flattering, Nico darling.'

'It's a warning, lover. Matt's an agreeable friend but, like a lot of men with his history, he's a user. All these years he's lived a protected and very privileged bachelor life. He's never had to worry where his next meal was coming from; his career was laid out by the Church, he didn't have to battle for it, people paid him the respect they always give to the clergy and he didn't have to dirty his hands to get it. Now that he's out – and moderately well off by all accounts – he's doing exactly the same thing: freeloading, and freeloading emotionally, too . . . I get a little bored watching the game and I get irritated when I see you involved in it. There now! I've said my piece!'

'And I've listened very politely; so now let me say mine. Everything you've said is true – not only about Matt, but half the clerics we meet here. They're like Oxford dons, living in their own very comfortable bunkers while the world goes to hell in a basket. But there's something about Matt that you're missing. He's a man with a great black hole in the middle of himself. He doesn't have faith any more and nobody's ever taught him about love. He's grabbing for sex as if it were being taken off the market; then when the girl goes home or he sends her – whichever is the scenario of the day – he's back in the black hole. So don't be too rough on him. Times are, my love, when I could strangle you with my bare hands; but I'd hate to wake up and find you weren't there!'

For Matt Neylan, there were other and more subtle problems than those diagnosed by his friends. The work he had taken on, for which his publishers had paid him a very substantial advance, was easy to outline; but to finish it required a great deal of documented research for which the most necessary source was the Vatican Archive itself where, classified in various degrees of secrecy, a thousand years of records were preserved. As an official insider he had access by right; as an outsider, a recent renegade from the ranks, he could hardly claim even the privileges granted to visiting scholars and researchers.

So, well trained in the shifts and stratagems of diplomacy, he set about building a new set of alliances and communications, with junior clerics in the Secretariat of State, with lay members of the Archive staff, with foreign academics already accredited as researchers in the Archive and in the Vatican Library itself.

In this enterprise he found help from an unexpected quarter. After several feints, the Russian Ambassador made what seemed like a straightforward proposition.

'You are a citizen of a neutral country. You have long experience in a specialised field of religious and political diplomacy. You have no present affiliations. You are continuing your studies in the same field. We should like to retain you, quite openly, on a written contract, as adviser to our Embassy here. The pay would be generous . . . What do you say, Mr Neylan?'

'I'm flattered, of course. However, I need to think about it very carefully.'

'Take all the time you need. Talk to whomever you choose. As I said, this is a matter of considerable importance in the future development of our European policy.'

In the end, Matt Neylan decided to take the Ambassador at his word. He sought and obtained a meeting with the Secretary of State, who received him in the bleak conference room reserved for casual visitors. Neylan came straight to the point.

'I am offering you a courtesy, Eminence. I need a favour in return.'

'So far,' – Agostini made a little spire of his fingertips and smiled at him over the top of it – 'so far you are admirably clear. What are you offering me?'

'A piece of information. The Russians have invited me to advise them on what they call religious and political diplomacy. They offer good money and an open contract – presumably to save me the taint of espionage.'

'Will you accept the offer?'

'I'll admit it has a certain fascination – but no. I'm turning it down. However, I think it determines for your department where certain emphases are being laid in Soviet policy.'

'You could be right. It could also be that you are doing exactly what they expected. You are the bearer of a signal from them to us. Either way, I am in your debt. How can I repay you?'

'You know the work on which I've embarked?'

'Yes.'

'I need access to the Archive – the same access which would normally be granted to any scholar or researcher.'

Agostini was puzzled.

'Has it ever been denied you?'

'No; but I thought it more tactful not to apply so soon after my exit.'

'I'll send a note to the prefect tomorrow morning. You can begin work whenever you choose.'

'Thank you, Eminence.'

'Thank you. How are things with you? I hear on various authorities that you are much in demand socially.'

'I'm enjoying myself,' said Matt Neylan. 'And Your Eminence? It must be a relief to have His Holiness safe behind the ramparts.'

'It is; though I do not believe the threat to him is past. That is something you could do for me. If you hear any news, any rumour of terrorist activity that makes sense to you, I should be grateful if you would contact me. Also His Holiness has personal concerns about Tove Lundberg and her child . . . This is a small town. News and rumour alike travel fast. Thank you for coming, Matt.'

'Next time, Eminence,' said Neylan with a grin, 'could you invite me into your office? I'm not a travelling salesman.'

'My apologies.' Agostini was urbane as ever. 'But you must admit it's a little hard to define what you are.'

In his search for a sexual identity, Matt Neylan was making discoveries that to men half his age were already clichés. The first was that most of the women he met at official functions were married, divorced, dedicated to dreams of permanent union, or otherwise disqualified from listing in a bachelor's telephone directory. He had also discovered that it was sometimes less expensive and less exhausting to buy the obligatory two drinks at the Alhambra Club and watch the floor show than to waste an evening and a dinner at Piccolo Roma with a bore, a bluestocking or a featherhead.

The Alhambra Club had another advantage, too: Marta the cigarette girl, who was always ready for a laugh and a few moments of gossip when business was slow. She was small, dark, and lively and, she said, a Hungarian. When he asked her for a date, she demurred. She worked the club every night. She couldn't leave until three in the morning. However, if he felt like taking her out to lunch one day . . .

Which he did, and was happy with the experience, and they both decided to repeat it, same day, same time, same place, next week.

And that was how Matt Neylan, one time Secretary of Nunziatures in the Vatican service, author to be, heir to a prosperous little holding in the Ould Sod, came to bed once a week with Marta Kuhn, Mossad agent assigned to surveillance duty in the Alhambra Club, the contact point for members of the Sword of Islam.

At ten o'clock on a warm summer morning, Leo the Pontiff was taking coffee on the terrace and wrestling with the problem of Cardinal Clemens, a man whom he himself had appointed, who had fulfilled punctually the brief he had been given, but who now was an obstacle to his master's plans.

A flight of birds passed overhead and he looked up to see a man scrambling precariously around the dome which houses the telescope of the Vatican observatory. He recognised him as Father John Gates, the director of the observatory and superior of the small community of Jesuits who ran it. He signalled to Gates to come down and join him for coffee.

Even though the observatory was perched high in the hills, on top of the castle itself, it was almost at the end of its usefulness, because the air above Rome and its environs was so polluted that the old-fashioned equipment could hardly function. Gates and his colleagues spent most of the year at the Astrophysical Institute in Huston, Texas. If the Pontiff was in residence at Castel Gandolfo Gates presented himself to pay his respects. After that he became a figure in the landscape, like the household staff and the farmhands.

He was a sturdy man in his late forties, with a ready smile and a quiet wit. His Italian was fluent and accurate. He had the easy confidence of a man secure in himself and in his scholarship. The Pontiff, hungry for company and eager for distraction from his own dark thoughts, plied him with questions, polite and casual at first, then more and more probing.

'I've always wondered how the astronomer thinks of time, of eternity. How he conceives of the Godhead?'

Gates considered the question for a moment and then, like a good Jesuit, tried to define the terms.

'If Your Holiness is asking whether I think differently from other believers, the answer has to be yes. In science we are faced always with new revelations about the universe. We are forced therefore to entertain new hypotheses and invent new terms to express them. We are always bumping our heads on the limitations of language and of mathematics. That was the last cry of Einstein: "I have run out of mathematics." Goethe made the same plea in different words: "More light!" You ask me how I conceive of the Godhead. I can't. I don't try. I simply contemplate the immensity of the mystery. At the same time, I am aware that I myself am part of the mystery. My act of faith is an act of acceptance of my own unknowing.'

'Are you saying that the traditional formulae of faith have no meaning for you?'

'On the contrary. They mean much more than they can say. They are man-made definitions of the indefinable.'

'Let's take one formula then.' The Pontiff pressed him. 'That which is at the root of our Christian faith. "*Et verbum caro factum est*. And the Word was made flesh and dwelt amongst us". God became man. What does that mean to you?'

'What it says – but also much more than it says; otherwise we should be making human words a measure of God's infinite mystery.'

'I'm not sure I understand you, Father.'

'I look at the heavens at night. I know that what I am

238

witnessing is the birth and death of galaxies, light years away from ours. I look at this earth, these hills, that dark water down there. I see another aspect of the same mystery, God literally clothing himself with his own creation, working within it like yeast in a dough, renewing it every day and yet still transcending it. The Godhead clothing itself with human flesh is only part of that mystery. I find myself moving further and further away from the old dualist terms – body and soul, matter and spirit – in which much of our theology is expressed. The more the limits of knowledge recede from me, the more I experience myself as a oneness.'

The Pontiff gave him a long shrewd look and then lapsed for a while into silence. When finally he spoke, his words were mild, but there was a winter chill in his voice.

'Why is it that when I hear these very personal formulations, I am uneasy? I ask myself whether our faithful recognise in them the simple gospel which we are called to preach.' He tried to soften the blow. 'That is not intended as a reproof, believe me. You are my guest. You honour me with your openness. I seek simply to understand.'

The Jesuit smiled, took out his pen and notebook and scribbled an equation. He passed it across to the Pontiff.

'Can you tell me what that means, Holiness?'

'No, I cannot. What is it?'

'It's a mathematical expression of the Doppler effect, the change of wavelength caused by any motion of a light source along a line of sight.'

The Pontiff smiled and spread his hands in despair.

'Even that description means little to me!'

'I could explain it to you; but since you have no mathematics, I would have to use metaphor. Which is exactly what Jesus did. He didn't explain God. He described what God does, what God is, in the images of a rural people in an earlier age. You and I are people of another age. We have to speak and reason in the language of our own time, otherwise we make no sense. Look! It is part of my job in America to help train men to be astronauts, space travellers. Their imagery is quite different from yours or mine or that of Jesus himself. But why, for that reason, be suspicious of it? Why in this day and age try to put the human spirit in a straightjacket?'

'Do you truly believe that is what we are trying to do?'

Father Gates shrugged and smiled.

'I'm a guest at your table, Holiness.'

'So you have the privilege of a guest. Speak freely. And remember that I am supposed to be the servant of the servants of God. If I am delinquent, I deserve reproof.'

'Which I am not charged to administer,' said the Jesuit with surprising firmness. 'Let me try to approach the question differently. I've travelled a great deal. I've lived in Asia, in South America, in Africa, here in Europe. In the end, I find that all human experience is unitive. The tragic cycle – propagation, birth, death – is always completed by a metamorphosis. The graves are covered with flowers, wheat fields flourish over ancient battlefields. The techniques of modern storage and retrieval confer a continuity which is analogous to our notions of immortality, even of resurrection. Dead beauties come to life again on the television screen. I sometimes ask myself – I know this is a thorny subject right now – what might the television cameras have seen had they been trained all night on Jesus's burial place?'

The Pontiff gave a small, relaxed chuckle.

'A pity we'll never know the answer.'

'I take the opposite view. A lifetime of scientific exploration has made the act of faith much easier for me. I demand always to know more, but I am prepared to risk much more on creative ignorance.'

'Creative ignorance!' The Pontiff seemed to savour the phrase. 'I like that. Because we are ignorant we seek to know. Because we are in darkness, we cry for light. Because we are lonely, we yearn for love . . . I confess to you, my friend, that, like Goethe, I have great need of light. I envy your starwalkers. It must be easy to pray up there.'

The Jesuit grinned happily.

'When I was a boy, I couldn't make any real sense of the Doxologies – Glory to God in the Highest, and so on. It sounded like people cheering at a football match, flattering the Creator by telling Him what a great fellow he was. But now, when I look through the telescopes and listen to the myriad signals that come to us from outer space, the prayer of praise is the only one I can utter. Even the wastage and the horror of the universe seem to make a kind of sense, though the haunting presence of evil rises always like a miasma from a swamp . . . I am talking too much. I should leave Your Holiness in peace. Thank you for the coffee.'

'Thank you for coming, Father. Thank you for sharing yourself with me.'

When he had gone, Leo the Pontiff asked himself an almost childish question: why he had denied himself so long the pleasure of such men at his table. Why had he not given himself – stolen if need be – the leisure to learn from them? In the mood of depression that descended upon him, he found only a sad answer: he was a peasant who had never learned to be a prince.

Katrina Peters's reading of the situation between Tove Lundberg and Sergio Salviati was very close to the truth. Each for a different reason was living under stress and the stress was evident even in that part of their lives which they shared most fully and intimately.

Salviati was deeply angered by the fact that, once again, in the country of his birth, he and those close to him were under threat simply because he was a Jew. Every time he stepped into the Mercedes, said good morning to the driver, checked the alarms on his house, monitored Tove's comings and goings, he felt a fierce resentment. This was no way for a man to live, haunted by another man he had never seen, who by all accounts lived like a pasha, doing big business under the protection of the Italian government.

His resentment was all the greater, because he knew it was beginning to affect his work. In the operating theatre he was still the cool technician, totally concentrated on the patient. Outside, on ward rounds and the 'white glove' inspections, he was edgy and impatient.

Tove Lundberg was worried enough to confront him over dinner.

'You can't go on like this, Sergio. You're doing exactly what you tell your patients not to do – driving yourself, living on adrenalin. You're alienating the staff, who would do anything for you. You've got to take a break.'

'And tell me, pray, how do I do that?'

'Invite James Morrison down from London. He'd come like a shot. Move young Gallico up beside him. He could use the experience with another man. The administration works pretty well anyway – and I can always keep an eye on things for you. I know how the place runs.'

'You wouldn't come on vacation with me?'

'No.' She was very definite. 'I think you need to go alone, feel absolutely free. At this moment I'm part of your burden, precisely because I'm threatened and you feel you have to protect me. Well, I am protected, as much as I ever can be. If it would make things easier, I could take off and work full time at the colonia while you're away . . . I've got some problems of my own to work out.'

'Look, my love!' Salviati was instantly penitent. 'I know I'm hard to live with these days –'

'It isn't you. It's Britte. She's a young woman now. I have to work out what kind of a life I can make for her and with her. The colonia isn't the final answer, you know that. It's given her a wonderful start; but it's a small, elitist group.

Once Anton Drexel dies who's going to develop it and hold it together? The property is mortgaged to the Church. I'm sure one could make some arrangement with them; but much more is needed: a plan, development funds, training of new teachers.'

'Is that what you see yourself doing?'

'It isn't. That's the point. I'm thinking of something much simpler – a home for Britte and myself, a career for her. It would be a limited one, but she is a good painter.'

'And what about you?'

'I don't know yet. Just now I'm living from day to day.'

'But you're putting me on notice there's a change coming?'

'There has to be. You know that. Neither of us is a totally free agent.'

'Then why don't we do what I've suggested before – get married, join forces, make a family for Britte?'

'Because I'd still be denying you the chance to make a family for yourself.'

'Suppose I accept that.'

'Then one day, sure as sunrise, you'll hate me for it. Look, my love, we're still friends, we still support each other. Let's go on doing that. But let's be honest. Things are out of our control. You got the most prominent man in the world as a patient in your clinic. It was a triumph. Everybody recognised it. Now we drive back and forth with an armed guard and pistols taped under the seats . . . Britte's an adolescent. She can't be managed like a child any longer. And you, my love, have spent so much of yourself that you're wondering just what's left . . . We have to make a change!'

Still he would not admit the need. It was as if, by admitting the process of evolution, he might suddenly call on the earthquake. There was no easy solace for either of them any more. The good taste of loving was gone, all that seemed to be left was the bitter aftertaste of lost illusions.

She tried to talk about it to Drexel, who for all his ripe

243

wisdom had his own quirks and quiddities. He did not want to lose his little family. He did not want to consider any alienation of the villa property during his lifetime. He would happily work with Tove to extend and organise the colonia; but she would have to make a total commitment to it . . . All of which meant another set of barriers to what had once been open and affectionate communication.

Then she realised that, although he was scarcely aware of it, Drexel himself was dealing with another set of problems. Now that he was truly pensioned off, he was lonely. The rustic life for which he had longed so ardently was not nearly enough to satisfy his active mind and his secret yearning for the excitements of the power game in which he had played all his life. This was the meaning of the transparent little strategy which he proposed to Tove Lundberg.

'Britte has finished her portrait of His Holiness. Why don't I arrange for her to present it to him? I'm sure he would be happy to receive us together at Castel Gandolfo.'

As it turned out the strategy was unnecessary. Next morning he received by telephone a summons to wait upon the Pontiff before midday.

'Read this!' The Pontiff slammed the flat of his hand on the pages of *Osservatore Romano* laid open on his desk. 'Read it very carefully!'

The article was headed 'An Open Letter to the Signatories of the Tübingen Declaration' and it was a blistering attack, in the most formal terms, on the content of the document and what it called the 'arrogant and presumptuous attitudes of clerics who are entrusted with the highest duties of Christian education'. It ended with the flat pronouncement: 'The luxury of academic argument cannot be allowed to undermine the loyalties which all Catholics owe to Peter's successor or to obscure the clear outlines of Christ's message of salvation.' It was signed Roderigo Barbo.

244

Drexel's first question was the obvious one: 'Who is Roderigo Barbo?'

'I have asked. I am informed that he is, and I quote: "A layman. One of our regular and most respected contributors."'

'One has to say,' observed Drexel mildly, 'he has a very good grasp of the official line.'

'Is that all?'

'No. If Your Holiness wants me to speculate . . .'

'I do.'

'Then I detect – or think I detect – the fine Gothic hand of Karl Clemens in this matter.'

'I too. You know I met with him in the clinic. I told him there should be a cooling off period before any contact is made with the signatories of the Tübingen Declaration or any action taken against them. He disagreed. I overruled him. I believe he chose this method to sidestep my direct order.'

'Can you prove that, Holiness?'

'I am not required to prove it. I shall ask him the question direct. In your presence. He is already waiting to see me.'

'And what does Your Holiness expect me to do?'

'What good sense and equity tell you to do. Defend him if you think he merits it. I do not wish my judgement in this matter to be clouded by anger – and I have been very angry this morning.'

He pressed a buzzer on the desk. A few moments later, Monsignor O'Rahilly announced His Eminence, Karl Emil Cardinal Clemens. The ritual greetings were exchanged. The Pontiff made a curt explanation.

'Anton is present at my behest.'

'As Your Holiness pleases.' Clemens was steady as a rock.

'I presume you have seen this piece in *Osservatore Romano*, signed by Roderigo Barbo.'

'I have seen it, yes.'

'Do you have any comment on it?'

'Yes. It is in line with other editorials published in Catholic papers around the world: in London, in New York, Sydney Australia and so on.'

'Do you agree with it?'

'Your Holiness knows that I do.'

'Did you have any hand in its composition?'

'Clearly, Holiness, I did not. It is signed by Roderigo Barbo, and would have been commissioned directly by the editor.'

'Did you have any influence, directly or indirectly, by suggestion or comment, upon its commissioning or publication?'

'Yes, I did. Given that Your Holiness was not in favour of official action at this moment, it seemed to me not inopportune to open the matter to public discussion by the faithful – which the authors of the original document had done in any case. In short, I believed that the other side of the case should at least be heard. I believed also that the climate should be prepared for any action that might later be taken by the Congregation.'

'And you did this in spite of our discussion at the clinic, and my clear directive on the matter.'

'Yes.'

'How do you explain that?'

'The discussions were too short to cover the whole range of issues. The directive was a limited one. I followed it to the letter – no official action or response.'

'And *Osservatore Romano* is not official?'

'No, Holiness. It is sometimes a vehicle for the publication of official announcements. Its opinions are not binding.'

The Pontiff was silent for a long moment. His strange predator's face, lean now from illness and dieting, was tight and grim. He turned to Anton Drexel.

'Does Your Eminence have any comment?'

'Only this, Holiness. My colleague Karl has been very frank. He has taken a position which, though it may not be palatable to Your Holiness, is still understandable, given the temper of his mind and his concern for the maintenance of traditional authority. I believe also Your Holiness must credit him with the best of intentions in trying to spare you stress and anxiety.'

It was a lifeline and Clemens grasped it as eagerly as a drowning man.

'Thank you, Anton. I should have been hard put to defend myself so eloquently. There is only one more point I should like to make, Holiness. You put me in this office. You gave me a clear commission to examine rigorously – and the word is yours – any persons or situations dangerous to the purity of the faith. You quoted to me the words of your distinguished predecessor Paul VI: "The best way to protect the faith is to promote the doctrine." If you find my performance unsatisfactory, I shall be happy to offer you my resignation.'

'We take note of the offer, Eminence. Meantime, you will refrain from further prompting of the Press – sacred or profane – and interpret our instructions broadly, according to their spirit and not narrowly, according to the letter. Do we understand each other?'

'We do, Holiness.'

'You have our leave to go.' He pressed the buzzer to summon Malachy O'Rahilly. 'Anton, you will wait. We have other matters to discuss.'

The moment Clemens had left the room, the demeanour of the Pontiff changed. The tense muscles in his face relaxed. He folded the newspaper slowly and laid it aside. Then he turned to Drexel and asked a blunt question.

'Do you think I was too hard on him?'

Drexel shrugged. 'He knew the risk. He took it . . .'

'I can forgive him. I can't trust him again.'

'That is for Your Holiness to decide.'

A slow smile dawned in the eyes of the Pontiff. He asked: 'How does it feel to be just a farmer, Anton?'

'Less interesting than I had hoped.'

'And the children?'

'There, too, I have problems which I had not foreseen.' He told of his conversations with Tove Lundberg, and the question which loomed for her and for all the other parents: what future could be offered to these brilliant but terribly handicapped children? 'I confess I have no answer to it – nor, I fear, are we equipped in this country to deliver one. We may have to look outside for models and answers . . .'

'Then why not do it, Anton? Why not propose that to Tove Lundberg? I would be willing to find some funds from my private purse . . . But now to other matters. You are retired. You will remain retired. You will, however, remain as a member – *in petto* as it were, private and unobserved – of the pontifical family . . . Today is the beginning of change. Clemens did a foolish thing and I am very angry with him. Yet, the more I think about it, the more clearly I see that he has done us all a great favour. He has put into my hands exactly what I need: the instruments of change, the lever and the fulcrum to get the Church moving again. I lay awake for hours last night thinking about it. I got up early this morning to say the Mass of the Holy Spirit to beg for guidance on it. I'm sure I've made the right decision.'

'I hope Your Holiness will permit me to reserve judgement until I've heard it.'

'Let me reason it through with you.' He pushed himself out of his chair and began to pace the room as he talked. Drexel was amazed to see how much weight he had lost and how vigorously he moved so early in his convalescence. His voice was strong and clear and, best of all, his exposition did not falter. 'Clemens goes. He has to go. His argument was casuistry and unacceptable. He defied authority more blatantly than the Tübingen signatories who complained publicly about the alleged misuse of it . . . So now we need a new prefect for the Congregation for the Doctrine of the Faith . . .'

'Do you have anyone in mind?'

'Not yet. But you and I know that that Congregation is the most important and the most powerful instrument in the Church. All of us bend to its demands, because its purpose is to defend that upon which the existence of the Church depends – the purity of the teaching given to us by Christ and handed down from apostolic times . . . Clemens thought I would bend too, because I am still not wholly recovered and I dare not alienate the heritage of the ancient faith. But he was wrong – as the Congregation has been wrong, grievously wrong so many times down the centuries. I am going to reform it, root and branch. I am going to abrogate the dark deeds of its history, the tyrannies of the Inquisition, the secrecy and the inequities of its procedures. It is and always has been an instrument of repression. I am going to turn it into an instrument of witness, against which not only our doctrine, but our charity as a Christian Assembly, may be judged by all.'

He broke off, flushed and excited, then sat down, mopping his hands and his brow. Drexel passed him a glass of water and then asked quietly: 'How do you propose to do all this, Holiness?'

'By *motu proprio*. I need your help in drafting it.'

'You need more than that, Holiness.' Drexel gave a little rueful laugh. 'There are fourteen cardinals and eight bishops running the Congregation. You can't dismiss them all. And what will you do with Clemens? He is known as your man. You can hardly stick his head on a pike outside the Porta Angelica!'

'On the contrary. I shall draw him very close to me. I shall give him your place as Cardinal Camerlengo and make him, in addition, prefect of my household. How does that sound?'

'Very much in character,' said Drexel with wry humour. 'Your Holiness is obviously much recovered.'

'Be glad I am.' The Pontiff was suddenly grim again. 'I am

changed, Anton, changed to the core of my being. I am setting out to repair the damage I have done to the Church. But in one thing I have not changed. I am still a country bumpkin, a hard-head. I don't want a fight; but if I'm forced into it, I have to win or drop.'

At which point Anton Drexel deemed it prudent to change the subject. He asked: 'Before you return to the Vatican, may I bring Britte and her mother to see you? Your portrait is finished. It's very good . . .'

'Why don't we do it tomorrow at eleven?'

'We'll be here. And, Holiness, Tove Lundberg herself is going through a difficult time. It would help if you could encourage her to talk about it.'

'By all means. You can take Britte into the garden. Leave Tove to me.'

As he was driven back from Castel Gandolfo to his own villa, Drexel replayed the events of the morning. First and most dramatic was the emergence of the old Leo, the man who knew how the vast machine worked and where to put his finger on the nerve-centres that controlled it. He had shed uncertainty. The fire was alight in his belly. He would thrust forward relentlessly towards the goal he had set himself. How wisely he had decided was another matter; but there was no gainsaying the sense of history that determined his choice.

Before the sixteenth century, the affairs of the Universal Church, including doctrinal matters, were handled by the Apostolic Chancery. In 1542 Paul III, Alessandro Farnese, founded the Sacred Congregation of the Inquisition. It was in the beginning a temporary institution, replaced by secular commissions under Pius IV, Gregory XIII, Paul V. But the first stable one, with an organic plan, was set up by Sixtus V, who had himself served as an inquisitor in Venice and who, as Pope, ruled with Draconian severity; imposing the death penalty for thievery, incest, procuration, adultery and sodomy. It was he who planned with Philip II of Spain to send the Armada against England, and when the Armada was sunk, defaulted on the payments to his ally. Pius X changed the name to the Holy Office, Paul VI changed it again to Doctrine of the Faith.

But the essential character of the institution had not changed. It was still essentially authoritarian, repressive, penal, incurably secretive and, in its procedures, inequitable.

In an institution like the Roman Catholic Church, built solidly on the old imperial model, relentlessly centralised, this inquisitorial institution was not only enormously powerful, it was a symbol of all the scandals of the centuries: the witch-hunts, the persecution of Jews, the burning of books and of heretics, the unholy alliances between the Church and the colonisers.

In the post conciliar world it was identified with reaction, with the concerted attempt to hold back reform and developments which the Council had set in motion. Leo XIV had used it himself precisely for those purposes. He knew its importance. His attempt to reform it was a true measure of the change in him.

The means he had in mind were interesting, too. A *motu proprio* was a document issued by a Pope on his own initiative over his own signature. It was, therefore, in a special sense a personal directive. It laid him open to challenge from the Sacred Congregations and the senior hierarchy; but it also put his pontifical authority on the line in a matter on which he held strong personal convictions.

By the time the car turned into his own driveway, Drexel was convinced that there was stormy weather ahead but that Ludovico Gadda had a reasonable chance to survive it.

Eleven

Matt Neylan was coasting towards the end of a very satisfactory day: a morning's work on the book, lunch, tennis and a swim, and a reconciliation dinner at Romolo's with Malachy O'Rahilly. The Papal Secretary was eloquent as always, but obviously bruised from a series of recent encounters in the service of the Lord and his Vicar on earth.

'I'm still haunted by that security meeting and what happened to poor Lorenzo de Rosa and his family. I must have been pissed out of my mind, holding forth like that with all the Eminences around. I haven't been allowed to forget it, either. This very evening, when I was coming into town, I got a little lecture from the Man himself . . . "Malachy," he says, "I have no personal complaints; but little birds whisper to me what I know is half scandal and you know is half truth. The downfall of the Latins is women and the Celts tend to drown their lusts and their sorrows in alcohol. So you will be careful, won't you? And you'll promise me never to drive these mountain roads with more than a glass taken." They're on to me, Matt. That was just a warning of things to come, a shot across the bows so to speak. So maybe it's time I made a change – or a connection with Alcoholics Anonymous. What's your advice?'

'I'm out of the club,' said Matt Neylan firmly. 'You and I are reasoning in different categories now. But the old rule still holds: if you can't stand the heat, get out of the boiler-room. And if you can't tolerate liquor, don't drink.'

'Are you happy where you are, Matt?'

'Sure. I'm very content.'

'When are you going home?'

'That I'm not sure of – probably early autumn. The manager's doing a good job with the farm. I'm happy working here – for the moment, at least.'

'Are you still – you know – living alone?'

'I don't have a live-in lady, if that's what you mean. For the moment I'm doing fine with temporary help . . . And what's happening on Vatican Hill?'

'At this moment, nothing; but all my instinct tells me there's going to be fun and games when the Old Man comes back into residence. He's getting stronger every day. He had Clemens on the carpet yesterday. You know what a tough customer he can be. Well, he was only in for five minutes, but he came out like a man on his way to the gallows. Drexel's retired . . . It's like waiting for a thunderstorm. You wish the damn thing would start. Which reminds me. Drexel and the Old Man are very worried about Tove Lundberg and her child. She's the one who . . .'

'I know who she is. I've met her.'

'The security people say she's on a kidnap list. She goes everywhere under protection. The Old Man offered them refuge in Vatican City. They refused. I don't blame them. They'd wonder what hit 'em in our celibate metropolis. But I had a way-out thought which I've mentioned to no one . . . You wouldn't think perhaps of inviting them as paying guests to your house in Ireland? Just until the whole thing blows over, of course!'

Matt Neylan threw back his head and laughed until the tears came.

'Malachy, my boy, you're transparent as water! I can just hear the dialogue now . . . "A wonderful idea, Holiness! It came to me in sleep, like the visions of Joseph. I spoke to my old friend Matt Neylan – he's a good soul, though he doesn't believe he's got a soul any more –

253

and he's offered bed, board and refuge to mother and child!'"

'So will you do it? Will you now?'

'The refuge is for you, isn't it, Malachy? You're scared they're going to ship you home to your bishop and make you do a little pastoral work for a change. Admit it now!'

'I admit it. You don't have to rub my nose in it.'

'All right, I'll do it. Tell Drexel. Tell His Holiness. If I chance to meet the lady again, I'll make the offer myself.'

'You're a prince, Matt!'

'I'm a footloose infidel with time and money he's never had before. I'll wake up to myself one day . . . You're paying the check, remember?'

'How could I forget a simple thing like that?'

When Malachy O'Rahilly had left him, he crossed the river, strolled for a while in the Piazza del Popolo and then took a taxi to the Alhambra Club. This was the hour that bothered him most in his new existence, the hour of the full belly and the empty bed and the craving for a woman, any woman, to share it with him. In the Alhambra he could join all the other males in a public confession of his need and sort through the offerings with offhand bravado. There were a thousand other solutions, of course. The evening papers carried columns of advertisements for masseuses, manicurists, secretary-companions; there were a dozen other clubs like the Alhambra, the tables along the Veneto, outside Doneys and the Café de Paris. He had tried them all; but the confession they demanded was too public, the encounters too prone to accident or boredom. At the Alhambra he was known. The girls acknowledged him with a smile, vied for his attention – and Marta had assured him with a certain seriousness that they had to be clean because the management insisted on a weekly medical certification and any girl who passed on something nasty to a regular client would have something very nasty happen to her. It was cobweb insurance at best;

but it gave him the sense of security and belonging which his late-flowering emotions demanded.

It was a slack night. There was time for a chat with Marta at her little booth near the entrance. The girls were waiting in little groups, ready to pounce as soon as he sat at a table, so he perched himself on a stool at the bar and started a dialogue with the barman, a cheerful fellow from Tunis, who knew how to protect a quiet drinker and a generous tipper.

Neylan was halfway through his second drink when a man took the stool beside him and asked: 'May I join you? I can't cope with all these women at once.'

'I know how you feel. Be my guest. What will you take?'

'Coffee please, and mineral water.' He introduced himself formally. 'I have seen you often. We have never spoken. I am Omar Asnan.'

'Matt Neylan.'

'English?'

'No. Irish.'

'I myself am from Iran. You live here in Rome?'

'I have for many years. I'm a writer.'

'I am something much more prosaic. I'm a merchant, import and export. And what sort of books do you write, Mr Neylan?'

'At this moment I'm working on a study of religious and political diplomacy, with special reference to the Vatican.'

'You are familiar with the Vatican, Mr Neylan?'

'Reasonably, yes. I do a certain amount of my work in the Archive.'

'How interesting. I am, of course, Muslim; but I should be fascinated to visit some time.'

'There are daily tours: St Peter's, the Museum, the usual things. You can also get permission to visit the Library and other places . . .'

'I must certainly think about it. You have contacts there. You must have of course.'

'Some, yes . . .'

'I am fascinated by this idea of the totally religious society. It has, of course, taken hold again in Islamic countries, most notably in my own.'

'I find I need to get away from it for a while.' Matt Neylan wanted to get off the subject as quickly as possible. 'That's why I come here. But it looks like a dull evening that could get expensive. I think I'll be pushing along.'

'No, wait!' Asnan laid a detaining hand on his sleeve. 'You are bored, so am I. We can easily remedy that. Do you know a place called Il Mandolino?'

'No.'

'It's in an old house in a tiny square just behind the Piazzo Navona. Lots of people go there. Two young men and a girl make music there every night, folk songs from all over the country. You buy drinks, sit in armchairs or on a cushion, and listen. It's very simple, very restful . . . If you're looking for a woman, of course, that's not the place to be; but to relax at the tail-end of an evening . . . Would you like to try it?'

After a good dinner and a brace of brandies, Neylan was relaxed enough to welcome the idea. It was made more attractive when Omar Asnan told him that his chauffeur was waiting and would drive him home afterwards. On the way out he stopped by Marta Kuhn's booth to buy cigarettes. Neylan bade her a discreet goodnight and managed a hurried whisper to confirm their lunch date.

When they had gone she went to the public phone in the foyer and made a call to the contact number of Aharon ben Shaul.

One of the less pleasant phenomena of the Pontiff's convalescence was broken sleep. He would go to bed utterly fatigued. Three hours later he would be wide awake and lie reading for another hour until sleep claimed him for another two hours. Salviati had warned him that the syndrome was common after cardiac interventions, but had warned him also against becoming dependent on opiates. It would be much better if he could do without them until a normal and natural rest pattern re-established itself. Now he kept a book and a diary by his bedside. If his mind began to spin, as it often did, with preoccupations about his future role, he would force himself to write through them, as if the act of definition would exorcise their latent terror:

'I was not proud of myself today. I knew, and Drexel knew, that I had slipped back into the old tactics of the power game. There was an element of fear in my handling of Clemens. He had done wrong. I felt threatened and vulnerable. I struck out hard and brutally, knowing that I might not have strength for a long combat. I regret the hurt I inflicted on him less than my own failure to behave with Christian restraint and charity. I am far from recovered, it seems. I am far from ready to pick up the full burden of office.

'On the other hand, I am still firm in my conviction that I have found the starting point for reform. I am dealing with an organism within the Church whose methods and functions have been a matter of dispute and discontent for a very long time. I am setting out to remodel it. If I succeed in doing so, I shall have done what Salviati has done for me: bypassed a block in the vital blood-flow of the body of the Church.

'I shall not be attacking any person. I shall not be clouding an essential doctrine of the faith. I shall not be creating confusion by seeming to reverse the decrees of earlier pontiffs – or even my own rigorous policies. I believe that I can begin the process of decentralisation in a fashion which Drexel has not foreseen.

'High hopes? Very high and I must beware of them. Nevertheless, the logic makes sense. Once the rules are changed, once it is impossible to make secret denunciations of a man or a work, once an accused has the right to know in detail the charges against him, the name of the accuser, once he has the right to a competent defender and an open debate upon the issue and the free exercise of his functions until the issue is decided, then the whole picture changes and it will begin to change in other sectors.

'The mediaeval traps will be taken out of juridical procedures. In marriage cases, the old principle of favouring the bond over the person is fundamentally inequitable; though I have to confess, time was when I judged otherwise. In issues which must sooner or later become urgent within the Church – a married clergy, women priests, the development of doctrine – it will be possible to have at least open discussion between competent scholars and competent authority, and an open forum even in the dicasteries of the Church.

'This is where I believe I am being led: back to the path opened by Vatican II and by the man who convened it, John XXIII. Like him, I must expect contention – and even conspiracy – against the grand design. I must expect, too, that I myself may prove my own worst enemy. Even so, I must move forward. But not tonight, not even tomorrow . . .'

Matt Neylan's evening at Il Mandolino turned out to be a pleasant experience. The setting was an old sixteenth-century house, with vaulted underpinnings from Roman times. The walls were decorated with antique musical instruments. The *salone* where the music was dispensed held no more than thirty people, who were comfortably settled in armchairs, cushioned alcoves and banquettes. The trio were talented and their music was a pleasant hour of tune-travel round the byways of the Italian peninsula.

Omar Asnan himself was an agreeable companion, good-humoured and unobtrusive. He talked vividly of the perils, pitfalls and occasional comedies of Middle Eastern trade. He explained to Matt Neylan the phenomenon of Islamic resurgence and the conflicts between Sunni and Shiite. He was interested to hear of Matt Neylan's rejection of his natal faith and suggested, with appropriate deference, that one day he might be interested to begin a study of Islam.

Neylan for his part offered to arrange a tour of the Vatican through one of his own friends: Peter Tabni, a consultor to the Commission for Religious Relations with Islam. Omar Asnan seemed astonished that such an organisation even existed. He would be delighted to accept such an invitation whenever it was offered.

As he rode home in Asnan's limousine, he felt a sense of well-being, of having assisted at one of the minor rites of civilisation in a city that was becoming more and more barbaric. He made a note on his desk pad to call Peter Tabni, laid Omar Asnan's card beside it, and then made ready for bed. At least tonight he would not have to worry whether he had caught more than a cold. To which he added, as a last waking thought, that he really had been wasting a lot of time and money in some very sleazy hangouts.

The principal item which Monsignor Malachy O'Rahilly noted in the Pontiff's diary was his appointment with Tove Lundberg, Britte and Cardinal Drexel. This was his cue to mention his dinner with Matt Neylan. The response was cordial and interested.

'I'm glad you're keeping in touch with him, Malachy. Cardinal Agostini spoke very highly of him, in spite of his defection.'

'He's bright, Holiness – and he's generous. I asked him a big favour last night.'

'Indeed?'

'We were talking about Tove Lundberg and the threat she's under. As it happens, he knows her. They met at the house of a journalist friend. Anyway, it seems he has a small farm property in Ireland. I asked him whether he'd have the Lundbergs there, if they wanted to go. It seemed to me at least a viable alternative to the offer Your Holiness made. He said he'd be happy to receive them.'

'That was very thoughtful of you, Malachy – and most generous of Neylan. I'll inform Tove Lundberg. If she's interested, then she can discuss it directly with Neylan. Now, Malachy, you and I must talk.'

'Holiness?'

'Please, sit down. How long have you been with me, Malachy?'

'Six years, Holiness; three years as junior, the last three as principal private secretary.'

'You've served me well.'

'I've tried, Holiness.'

'And I have never been the easiest of masters . . . I know you've told me before, you were always happiest if you had to fight a little . . . However, I think the time has come for us both to make a change.'

'You are dissatisfied with my work, Holiness?'

'Your work is excellent, Malachy. It's a pleasure to have you near me. You have an excellent sense of humour. However, you have two shortcomings, which unfortunately have become apparent to senior members of the Curia. You have a loose tongue and a low tolerance for liquor. Either of these is an impediment. Both together constitute a grave danger – to me and to you.'

Malachy O'Rahilly felt a small, cold finger probing at his heartstrings. He sat in silence, staring down at the backs of his big hands. Finally, with more calm than he had ever thought to command, he said: 'I understand, Holiness. I regret that you have been put to the embarrassment of saying it. When do you want me to quit?'

'Not until we have moved back to the Vatican, and you have had time to move your successor into place.'

'And who will that be?'

'Monsignor Gerard Hopgood.'

'He's a good man, an excellent linguist. He's quite up to the job. I could hand over a week after we get back.'

'I should like to find you a congenial posting.'

'With great respect, Holiness, I'd rather you didn't.'

'You have something in mind?'

'Yes, Holiness. I want to be suspended from all duties for three months. I'm going to put myself into a place I know in England to be detoxified. Then I want to see whether I'm fit for the priesthood and whether it's a life I can endure from here to eternity. It's a rough choice to make after all these years, and all its cost in time, money and work to turn me into a Papal Secretary. One thing I'm sure of, however; I don't want to end up a whisky-priest with soup-stains down his cassock and no one to take him in but a convent of ageing nuns!'

'I had no idea you felt like this, Malachy. Why didn't you speak to me before? I am, after all, your pastor.'

'No you're not, Holiness! And with great respect, don't believe that you are. You're the successor to the Prince of the Apostles. I'm the prince's minion. You're the Supreme Shepherd, but you don't see the sheep – only a vast carpet of woolly backs stretching to the horizon! It's not your fault. It's the way this institution has grown over the centuries. Talk about the Russians or the Chinese – we're the biggest collective in the world! And until you got sick and were stripped down to the skin, that's the way you thought about it and ran it. That's why it's in the parlous state it is . . . I'm sorry! I have no right to sound off like this; but it's my life, my soul's salvation that's on the line!'

'I don't blame you, Malachy. God knows, I have enough

guilts of my own. But please trust me if you can. Is there anything I can do to help?'

'Yes, there is one thing.'

'Name it.'

'If, at the end of my purgation – which I'm not looking forward to – I find I can't take the life any more, I want you to let me go – you personally, because you've got the power. I don't want to be besieged by compulsory counsellors, put through the meat-grinder of the tribunals. If I come in good conscience, I want a clean exit. Will Your Holiness give it to me?'

'Why do you ask now?'

'Your Holiness knows why.'

'I want to hear you say it, Malachy.'

'Because this time, I want to make the choice of a free man.'

For the first time the Pontiff was taken aback. He had not expected so curt an answer. He asked again: 'Are you saying you were not free when you entered the priesthood?'

'That's the root question, isn't it? That's what I'm going into the desert to answer. But given my background in Holy Ireland, given all the pressures and conditionings of my education since the nuns first got hold of me at four years old, I'm not sure at all. I know it's not the sort of statement that will cut much ice with the tribunal, but it's the truth; just the same as it's the truth with a lot of marriages that turn into hell on earth because they were defective from day one. But what do we do? We turn the lawyers loose on 'em and not the compassion of Christ we're supposed to dispense! I'm not sure any of this is making any sense to you. I hope it is; because I'm bleeding. You've just done what this blasted bureaucracy always does. You've fired me on an anonymous denunciation. I think I deserved better than that.'

Leo the Pontiff was at first stunned by the vigour of the attack, then overwhelmed by shame and guilt. He had done exactly that: damned a faithful servant on hearsay. And, remembering his own childhood, remembering how early and how rigidly his own mindset had been formed, he knew that O'Rahilly was right. He groped for the words to express his confused emotions.

'I understand what you're telling me, Malachy. I've handled this badly. I hope you will be able to forgive me. I shall pray every day that you may be able to live in peace in your vocation. If not, then I shall release you by my own rescript. One thing I have learned the hard way: there should be no slaves in the City of God.'

'Thank you, Holiness. Is there anything else?'

'No, Malachy. You may go.'

It was a melancholy moment and it called up memories of Lorenzo de Rosa, the defection of Matt Neylan and, beyond these local images, the large and distant ones of empty seminaries, convents without postulants, churches with aged priests and ageing congregations, men and women of ardour and goodwill frustrated by clericalism, creating small, self-protective cells within an assembly they did not trust any more because it was ruled by fiat and not by faith.

His mood was not lightened, either, by the visit of Tove Lundberg and Britte. The portrait pleased him very much. The girl was pleased that he was pleased, but communication was difficult and he was glad when Drexel took her out to show her the pleasances of the castle. Tove herself was trying hard to turn her problems into a piece of black humour:

'Except for the fact that I'm being hunted by some mad mullahs, I'm the luckiest girl in the world. One man wants to marry me. Another wants to set me up on a farm in Ireland. Nonno Drexel wants to send me to study in America. Your Holiness wants to give me money. My daughter thinks she's ready to live away from home. I wonder why I'm not happy?'

'You're really very angry, aren't you?'

'Yes, I am.'

'Why?'

'Because everyone has a private purpose for me. No one seems to have given a thought to mine.'

'Do you think that's quite fair? All of us are deeply concerned for you and Britte!'

'I know that, Holiness. I am grateful for it. But my life is my own. Britte is my daughter. I have to decide what is best for us both. At this moment I'm being tugged this way and that like a rag doll. I can't take that any more. I just can't.'

Suddenly she was weeping and Leo the Pontiff stood beside her, stroking her hair, comforting her as she had comforted him, with small soothing talk.

'There now! It's not nearly as bad as you think! But you mustn't shut out the people who love you. You told me that, right at the beginning. I trusted you. Can you not trust me, even a little? Why not think about this house in Ireland – even as a holiday?'

Through the tears a small uncertain smile dawned and, as she dried her eyes, she told him: 'I'm not sure I should risk it.'

'What's the risk?'

'Didn't you know, Holiness? The Vikings burned Dublin, centuries ago. The Irish have never forgotten it!'

There was one more visitor listed in his appointment book: the Abbot of the Byzantine monastery of St Neilus, which lay only a few kilometres away at Grottaferrata. The Abbot Alexis, who functioned as bishop of the surrounding countryside, was an old man, still vigorous, still witty, but radiating an air of extraordinary calm and spiritual ease. His visit to Castel Gandolfo was an annual affair, made always in a private and neighbourly fashion.

The monastery had existed for a thousand years and traced its origins back to the early Hellenic communities of Calabria and Apulia. The original Greek stock was mixed with Albanian and other races from ancient Illyria who, in spite of constant difficulties and frictions, managed to preserve their rites, customs and privileges, and their union with Rome, even after the Great Schism.

The present monks were mostly Italo-Albanians; but their rite was Greek. They had a library of valuable manuscripts. They conducted a seminary for priests of the Byzantine rite. They ran a school of palaeography, illumination and restoration. For Leo the Pontiff, the place had always had a special significance, as a possible stepping stone on the long river of time back to reunion with the Orthodox churches of the East. But somehow he had never found the inspiration to make use of its resources. Too late perhaps, he was now prepared to admit that, at his first encounter, he had found the Abbot's humour a trifle too barbed.

This was the man who, asked to compare the Greek practice of married clergy with the Roman one of clerical celibacy, had remarked: 'We think ours works better. After all, if you want labourers in the vineyard, why stop them bringing their lunch?' Speaking of the Roman passion for legislation, he coined the aphorism: 'It is not the Church which leads people to God. It is God who draws them to Himself, sometimes through the visible witness of his Church – and sometimes in spite of it!'

In his later years, however, the old man had become a contemplative, and there were tales abroad about his power of divining human hearts and endowing them with the gift of peace. After the stress of his recent encounter, the Pontiff found him a very easy guest. He had brought a gift – a facsimile edition of the monastery's greatest treasure, a *typikon*, or liturgical compendium of the eleventh century. With the gift was a graceful dedicatory note quoting from the Epistle of John: 'Beloved, I wish above all things that thou mayest prosper and be in health.'

They walked together in the garden and, as Tove Lundberg had taught him to do, the Pontiff talked without embarrassment of the problems that loomed up before him.

'There's a great irony in my situation. I see all the mistakes I have made. I see even more clearly how little time I have to make them good.'

The old man laughed, a light silvery sound like the laughter of a child.

'God's people are God's business. Why don't you trust Him?'

'Would it be so simple!'

'It is. That's the point. What else do the parables tell us? "Consider the lilies of the field. They labour not, neither do they spin . . ." It is the passion for action that destroys us all. We are so busy organising and engineering and legislating that we lose sight of God's own purposes for us and for this planet of ours. You are still frail – frailer than I, who have fifteen years on you. Give yourself more time before you start work again. Don't let them bury you under a mountain of detail, as they try to do. A word from you at the right moment will do more good than a week of flurry in the Congregations.'

'The problem is that I'm having difficulty with the words. The simpler they need to be, the harder it is for me to say them.'

'Perhaps,' said the Abbot mildly, 'perhaps because you are trying to speak two languages at once: that of the heart and that of authority.'

'And which one would you have me use, my Lord Abbot?'

'May I presume a little, Holiness?'

'Please!'

'In a way which you do not and, indeed, cannot experience, I face this question every day that I am in office. I am an old man now. My strength is limited. Consider a moment. We are, like our sister monasteries in Lungro, San Demetrio,

Terra d'Otranto and other places, a small group of ethnic survivors – from Greek colonies and from scattered Balkan tribes. As priests and monks, we are custodians of the cultural identity of our peoples, what is left of their language, their traditions, their iconography. In the eyes of Rome – in the old days at least – this was granted as a privilege. We held it then, and hold it now, as a right. To maintain that right we have to demonstrate that we deserve it. So I as Abbot have to keep in our community a discipline that puts us beyond criticism or challenge from the Vatican. It is not always easy for my people or for me. But I have found over the years that it is better to persuade than to impose. The difference between you and me is that I can have, all the time, a face to face dialogue. Except in your own household, that is impossible for you. You are interpreted by rhetors and officials and translated by journalists. Your authentic voice is never heard. Look at the pair of us! Except for this one day of the year, this one brief hour, you and I might be on separate planets . . .'

'One advice which has been given me,' said the Pontiff slowly, 'is that I should begin to decentralise, give back to local bishops their authentic apostolic authority. What do you think of that?'

'In theory it's possible and desirable. We Byzantines are a case in point. We acknowledge the authority of the Pontiff, yes. We preserve our identity and our authority as an apostolic church. It works because the barriers of language and custom save us from too much interference. But if you try to do the same thing with the Germans, the British, the French, you will find opposition from the most unexpected quarters. Look what happened in Holland all those years ago! The Dutch claimed the freedoms affirmed in the decrees of Vatican II. Immediately the prophets of doom were crying from the roof-tops. Reaction set in, Rome applied the thumbscrews. The Dutch Church was split and nearly ended in schism . . . But slowly, slowly, yes, it will work, it must work. I say to my monks: "Before you stage a revolution, think what you have to put in its place – otherwise you are left with a vacuum and seven devils rush in to take possession!"'

Their walk had brought them to a small arbour with a stone bench and table. A gardener was working a few paces away. The Pontiff called him and asked him to order coffee and mineral water from the kitchen. When they were seated, he asked simply: 'My Lord Abbot, would you hear my confession?'

The old man showed no surprise.

'If Your Holiness wishes, of course.'

They sat side by side, leaning on the table while Leo the Pontiff poured out, sometimes haltingly, sometimes in a rush of words, the guilts and confusions that had piled up like windblown leaves in the crannies of his conscience.

He spoke without reserve, because this time he was not asking for counsel or judging the advice given, or weighing its possible consequences. This was another act altogether; this was the completion of the *metanoia*, the purging of guilt, the acceptance of penance, the resolution to begin anew. It was an act anonymous, secret and fraternal, brother mediating for brother with the Father of all. When the act was done, Leo the penitent bowed his head and heard the old man's voice pronounce in Greek the words of absolution.

Late the same morning, Matt Neylan called Monsignor Peter Tabni, consultor to the Commission for Religious Relations with Islam. His request was couched in very cautious terms.

'Peter, there's a casual acquaintance of mine, an Iranian Muslim called Omar Asnan. He's expressed interest in a visit to the Vatican. He's a permanent resident in Rome, a merchant, obviously rich and well educated. I'm wondering if you could perhaps give him an hour or two of your time.'

'Sure! I'll be happy to give him a morning. How do you want to arrange it?'

'I'll call him and tell him you'll be in touch with him. You make your own arrangements.'

'You won't come?'

'Best I don't, Peter. I've been granted Archive access. I don't want to push my luck.'

'I understand. You're well and happy?'

'For today, I'm both. Let me know how it goes with Asnan. I'll buy you a lunch. *Ciao, caro!*'

Next he telephoned Omar Asnan, who was effusive in his gratitude.

'You are a most punctual man, Mr Neylan. I shall not forget your kindness. You will be joining us, of course.'

'Regrettably, no, but Monsignor Tabni will take very good care of you. We'll see each other very soon at the Alhambra.'

Then Malachy O'Rahilly called him from Castel Gandolfo. He was obviously distressed.

'You must have the second sight, Matt.'

'How come?'

'I've been fired; just as you guessed I might be. Oh, it was all very kind and compassionate. I've got three months' leave to dry out and make a conscience decision. If I can't cut it after that, I get a quiet pass-out by private rescript.'

'Malachy, I'm sorry.'

'Don't be. I'm not. I'm taking the Man back to the Vatican, settling my successor in the hot seat. Then I take leave.'

'If you want to hang your hat for a few days, come to my place.'

'I'll think about that. Thanks anyway. And there's one other thing: Tove Lundberg. Your offer was passed on to her this morning. She's very grateful. She wants to think about it. She'll call you direct to discuss it.'

'So what else is new?'

'Not much. Britte Lundberg's portrait of the Man is quite wonderful. We had the annual visit of the Abbot of St Neilus

– nice old boy, transparent as old porcelain. On his way out, he stopped by my desk and gave me a funny, sidelong smile and said: "Don't be too angry, Monsignore! His Holiness is doing you a favour." Then, would you believe, he quoted Francis Bacon: "Princes are like to heavenly bodies which cause good or evil times and which have much veneration but no rest."'

'I've never met the man. It sounds as though one should invite him to dinner.'

'Invite me instead, Matt. It's your turn anyway and I'm needing a shoulder to cry on.'

By then it was midday. He was just getting ready to go out when the doorbell rang. Nicol Peters was standing on the mat. Behind him were Marta Kuhn and a lean, vulpine fellow he had never seen before. Peters had obviously been named master of ceremonies.

'Do you mind if we come in, Matt? There are things to explain.'

'It would seem so.' He waited for a word from Marta. She said nothing.

He stood aside to let them pass into the apartment. When they were seated, he remained standing, looking from one to the other. It was Nicol Peters who made the introductions.

'Marta Kuhn you know.'

'Not, it seems, as well as I thought.'

'And this is Aharon ben Shaul, attached to the Israeli Embassy in Rome.'

'That's the identification, Nico. I'm still waiting for the explanation.'

'I'm the explanation, Mr Neylan.' Aharon ben Shaul was in command now. 'I work for Israeli intelligence. Miss Kuhn works for me. Part of our job is anti-terrorist activity. You frequent the Alhambra Club. Last night you left the club with a certain Omar Asnan. Miss Kuhn reported the matter to me. This morning I had a call from the International Clinic indicating that you had offered refuge in your house in Ireland to Tove Lundberg and her child. The connection was puzzling until I discovered you had met her at the house of Mr Nicol Peters, who filled me in on your background. That encouraged me; but still left some areas of doubt.'

'About what?'

'Your political sympathies.'

'Which are my own bloody business!'

'And your Roman activities, which are very much the business of the Italians, ourselves and the Vatican. Where did you go last night with Mr Asnan?'

'We went to a little music club near Monteverde Vecchio called Il Mandolino. We stayed for an hour. We left. He dropped me off at my house.'

'Why did you go with Mr Asnan?'

'It was a casual encounter on a dull night. No more.'

'But you both frequent the Alhambra.'

'We had seen each other. We had never talked. I believe Miss Kuhn can confirm that.'

'She already has. What did you talk about?'

'Trivia mostly. I told him I was writing a book. He told me he was a merchant. When he heard I was working in the Vatican Archive, he expressed a wish to visit the City. This morning I arranged for him to be in touch with a friend of mine, Monsignor Tabni, who runs the Commission for Religious Relations with Islam. Tabni was going to give him the ten-dollar tour. End of story.'

'Not the end, Mr Neylan, just the beginning. Mr Omar Asnan is the leader of an extremist Muslim group called the Sword of Islam, about which our friend Nicol Peters has been writing at some length. I hate to tell you, Mr Neylan, but you have just given an assassin the keys of Vatican City.'

Matt Neylan groped for the nearest chair and slumped into it.

'God in heaven! I'm the fine Vatican diplomat! And I can't see past the end of my own nose!'

'Don't be too rough on yourself, Mr Neylan.' Ben Shaul gave him a thin smile. 'You were looking for the pleasant things – not the shit we deal in. Just a month ago, Asnan murdered one of our men. We couldn't move then without blowing a much bigger operation of which the Alhambra is the centre. Marta's been the agent in residence for months. Then you showed up . . .'

'And she did a very good job of checking me out – full profile, physical and mental! Congratulations, sweetheart!'

'Hold it, Matt!' Nicol Peters thrust himself into the argument. 'You were playing; the girl was risking her life.'

'Let's get the priorities straight.' Suddenly the Israeli took over. 'Two things are about to happen: a woman's going to be kidnapped; there will be an attempt on the life of the Pope. You can help prevent both crimes. Are you willing or not?'

'Do I have a choice?'

'Yes. If you want out, we can get the Italians to deport you back to Ireland as an undesirable alien.'

'On what charge?'

'You're associated with a known terrorist. You've left the Vatican Secretariat of State under a cloud. Nobody will say what it is, but we can make it look pretty black. We also have reason to suspect you might have sympathetic connections with the IRA, who often come here to shop for arms with Libyan money. How does that sound?'

'It's a load of rubbish.'

'Of course it is; but it will make a hell of a *denuncia!* And you know how messy things can get after you're on the books of the security boys. On the other hand, you can join our nice exclusive club here and help us clean up this mess.

So what's it to be, Mr Neylan? Hurt pride or help for the righteous?'

In spite of himself, Matt Neylan laughed.

'That's the worst piece of salesmanship I've heard in years! . . . All right, I'm in. What do you want me to do?'

Twelve

'You're booked out tomorrow.' In his usual peremptory fashion, the Mossad man recited the details to Salviati and Tove Lundberg. 'Aer Lingus direct to Dublin, departure 1405 hours, arrival 1620 local time. Italian security will handle your transport from here to the colonia to pick up your daughter, thence to the airport. You will be taken directly to the VIP lounge, where you'll be in care of the Carabinieri until departure time. Mr Matt Neylan will meet you there and travel with you. Your tickets will be handed to you at the airport. I wish you a safe journey and a happy return when this mess is cleared up.'

Then he was gone, and Tove Lundberg and Sergio Salviati were left alone. It was a curiously dry and vacant moment, all argument over, all passion spent, each anchored in a bleak private haven of solitude. Finally, Tove asked: 'Have they told you what's going to happen when I'm gone?'

'Nothing. All they've said is that things are coming to flash-point, and they want you out.'

'And you?'

'I'm the one everyone wants to keep alive — it seems even terrorists can't do without a plumber!'

'I'm more scared to be going than I ever was of staying.'

She shivered involuntarily and seemed to be trying to draw an invisible cloak about herself. Salviati knelt in front of her, cupping her face in his hands.

'We've had good times, rich times. We'll have them again.'

'I'm sure we will.'

'And I'm writing around to colleagues in Europe and America to get the best advice we can for Britte's future.'

'That's the part I'm dreading; being totally alone with her, in a strange place. There's something terrible in the sight of all that passion welling up in her with no hope of satisfaction. I see it even in the way she paints – she almost attacks the canvas!'

'Drexel's going to miss her.'

'He's going to miss a lot of things. But he will never complain. He's much more passionate and proud than you would ever imagine – and in his time he's been a very powerful man.'

'I'm much more fascinated by his master. I keep asking myself what kind of terrible mutation I've loosed upon the world.'

'You keep using that word. I've never found him terrible.'

'What are you telling me, sweetheart? That you coaxed an angel out of him?'

'No; but there were moments when it almost seemed I was dealing with my father – all that repressed affection, the compassion he could never find words to express. Anyway, I must go. The car's waiting. I've got a lot to do tonight. We have to pack for autumn and winter now.' She reached out and drew his face towards her own and kissed him. 'No more talk, my love. Let's cut clean. It heals quicker. You taught me that.'

The next moment she was gone, and Sergio Salviati wondered why his eyes were wet and his hands were unsteady, and how the hell he would face a triple bypass at seven in the morning. He was still trying to get a grip on himself when the Mossad man came back.

'Stage one is completed. We've got them covered from now until embarkation time. We're putting the word about Rome that you and Tove have broken up and she has left for a long holiday with her family in Denmark. Her car is gone, stored in the Embassy garage. Our people in Israel are releasing Miriam Latif. She'll be delivered safe into the care of her parents in Byblos. She's given us all the useful information she's got, and she'll take some time to recover from the mind-washing, so she's out of play as well as Tove Lundberg. That forces Asnan to concentrate on his operation against the Pope and leaves us free to concentrate on him and the Sword of Islam group . . .'

'And where does that put me?'

'It allows you, my dear Professor, to continue the fiction – that Tove Lundberg is out of your life and you are beginning to be interested in other women. That, of course, confirms the fairytales we'll be spreading. So while Omar Asnan is setting up his strategy for assassination, we'll be drawing the net tighter and tighter round him and his group.'

'That sounds to me like a very risky race. Who pulls the pin out of the grenade first?'

'I can think of a pleasanter metaphor,' said the Mossad man. 'It's a very elaborate chess game. The players both know what is going on. The art is to choose the right move and judge all its consequences.'

Leo the Pontiff was already laying out in his head a different chess game.

Tomorrow, in the mid-afternoon, he would go home to the Vatican. The journey would be made by helicopter, courtesy of the Italian airforce. It would save time, risk and the expense of a public procession from the mountains to the city. The Secretary of State was giving him the situation report.

'The Sword of Islam are already moving towards an attempt on Your Holiness's life. We are mounting a combined protective operation with the Italian Government and the Israelis. You will find on your return to the Vatican that internal security measures are somewhat more stringent. Apart from that, there will be no perceptible change in your administrative routine. We have noted your appointment of a new Senior Secretary and the retirement of Monsignor Malachy O'Rahilly, which, if I may say it, was generally regarded as a prudent step.'

'I am glad.' The Pontiff's tone was dry and formal. 'For me, it was a painful decision . . . You should know that there will be other changes when I get back.'

'Perhaps we should begin to set the machinery in motion immediately.'

The Secretary of State could not have been more tentative, nor the Pontiff more abrupt.

'What machinery, Eminence?'

'If Your Holiness is thinking of a Curial Consistory – a meeting of all the cardinals residing in Rome – then notices should be sent out, an agenda prepared and circulated. If it's a question of a full Synod, that's at least twelve months of preparation.'

'Matteo, I have never thought of you as an obtuse man.'

'I trust not, Holiness.'

'Then let's be clear. I have no intention of using those procedures, which so easily can be an excuse for deferring action. I am living on borrowed time. I am driven to use every moment. Look! We have command of every modern communication. We have, unless our balance sheets lie, even a substantial stake in satellite communications. I can talk by telephone or send a facsimile letter to all our senior bishops around the world. The contact is immediate. I propose to work with these tools. My Curia has a simple choice – work with me or wait around until they can elect a more complaisant candidate. I am prepared to be open with them. They have to be open with me.'

'And if they oppose you?'

'I shall respect them as the loyal opposition, take their opinions under advisement and act according to my conscience.'

'Then we are back to papal absolutism and collegiality goes out the window for good and all!'

'The Curia already rejects it *de facto!*' Once again he was the raptor, poised on the topmost branch ready to dive on the prey. 'Most of our brethren in the Curia want it both ways. They pay lip-service to collegiality, the consensus of the bishops as apostolic successors in union with the Bishop of Rome. But that's not what they really mean, Matteo. They want what they have, a self-perpetuating oligarchy with all real power vested in them – because the Pope can't move a metre past the barriers they put up around him! I know that. You know it. It's a set-piece game. So I will play it exactly as it is laid out. I am the Successor of Peter, Supreme Pontiff and Pastor. So I am called; so I shall act: with love, because I have learned love, Matteo, but without fear, because I have looked into the face of Brother Death and seen a smile on it. I wish, I wish so much, that you may understand me!'

'I do, Holiness, believe me. You have the same loyalty as you had the day I kissed hands as your Secretary of State.'

'I have demands to make on you, too, Matteo.'

'I shall do my best to meet them; but I, too, am what I am. The only art I know is the art of the possible. Come the day when you want me to swear that the impossible is the possible, I will not do it.'

'I ask no more. I expected no less. But I tell you truly, I am dreading my return to duty. I feel like a prisoner being walked back to his cell after a brief hour in the sunlight.'

Agostini gave him a swift, appraising look and uttered the now familiar caution: 'Salviati warned you, Holiness. This is only the first stage of your recovery. You must not try to do too much.'

'It is not the doing, Matteo. The real burden is the knowing. I understand the workings of the Church better than any man alive, certainly better than my two immediate predecessors. But that's the problem: I understand it too well. On the one hand, Vatican City is the Sedes Apostolica, the See of Peter; on the other, it is an apparatus of power which we try always to endow with a sacred character, to justify our own mistakes and excesses. This is propaganda, not religion. It is a political conjuring trick, which impresses the faithful less and less each year. Look at me! Look at yourself! I am dressed in the white of innocence, you in the scarlet piping of a prince. Our Master walked the dusty roads of Palestine, slept under the stars, preached from a fishing boat. I am shamed by what we have become and by my personal contribution to it. Oh, I know what you will tell me. I cannot demean my office. I cannot cancel two thousand years of history. I cannot vacate the City and turn it over to the Vandals. But the plain fact is, Matteo, we cannot afford to go on as we are, a bloated bureaucracy riddled with jealousies and intrigues. I am sure even this long-awaited study of our finances will tell us the same thing in banker's language. And that brings me back to my first proposition. I propose to act, not sit as chairman of a Curial debating society.'

'In that case, Holiness, permit me to offer you the advice my father gave me. He was a colonel in the Carabinieri. He used to say: never point a gun at a man, unless you're prepared to fire it. If you fire, don't miss, because one shot is all you get.'

It was the warning which Abbot Alexis had given him, expressed in other terms: 'It is the passion for action that destroys us all!' Yet he could see no other way of breaking out of the blockade which he himself had imposed. Expedient and not expedient, opportune, inopportune – these were the most potent words in the lexicon of Church government. They opened the floodgates of eternal debate; they could retard any decision until judgement day, on the pretext that its ultimate consequence had not yet been explored.

And yet he understood very well what Agostini was telling him: the more questions you could leave open, the less danger there was of having your mistakes cast in bronze to endure for centuries. Which reminded him of another proposition of Abbot Alexis: 'You are interpreted by rhetors and officials and translated by journalists. Your authentic voice is never heard!' He put the same proposition to the Secretary of State, who gave it only a qualified answer . . .

'It's true; but how can it be otherwise? How can you guarantee the accuracy of a translation from your Italian into all the languages under heaven? Impossible. And with every new Pontiff we get the same old comedy in the press: "The Holy Father is a great linguist. He can say 'God bless you' in twenty languages." And then he gets ambitious and starts stumbling through his public discourses like Linguaphone lessons! Your Holiness has been wise enough to know his own limitations!'

Leo the Pontiff laughed. It was an old Vatican horror story. Eight, ten different language versions of the same six-minute *discorso* used to be given to polyglot pilgrim groups in St Peter's Square, just to prove that the Holy Father had the gift of tongues! Then there was the other cautionary tale about himself. Suggestions had been made, very sane and sensible suggestions, that he might make a series of sub-titled cassette programmes for worldwide television. However, the final impediment was his own incurable ugliness and the habitual severity of his expression. He could still chuckle over everyone's embarrassment as they tried to tell him. Agostini profited by his good humour to add an extra caution: 'Your Holiness is aware of another lesson we have learned: the debasement of currency, the over-exposure of the Pontiff just to demonstrate his concern and involvement. Even in your dealings with the Curia, nice judgements have to be made; and your first policy statement will be crucial. That's the one shot which will win or lose the war.'

'So tell me, Matteo; do you really believe I can win my war?'

'If it is your war, no. You will lose it. If it is God's, you will win it – though not, perhaps, in the way you hope.'

The which, as the Pontiff mused on it, cast new light on the character of Matteo Agostini, Cardinal Secretary of State, a man dedicated to the art of the possible.

In the VIP lounge at Fiumicino, Matt Neylan took custody of his temporary family. He tried to be casual and good-humoured about it, but the spectacle of Britte, with her shambling body and her angelic face and the piercing intelligence that could not assemble the words to express itself, moved him strangely. She was both scared and excited in the unfamiliar surroundings and was making frantic efforts to communicate verbally with her mother, who had her own preoccupations and was unable to concentrate enough attention on the girl. Matt Neylan himself was walking on eggs. He dared not risk an untimely gesture towards mother or daughter and he was wondering how they would rub along together in a farmhouse in County Cork, with an old-fashioned Catholic housekeeper as chaperone – and she already in grief for a spoiled priest! Then Britte's small, clawlike hand stroked his cheek and her spindly body snuggled close to him. The words sprang unbidden to his lips: 'You're not scared now, are you? This place we're going to is very friendly: green meadows and old stone walls and a path that runs down to a white beach. There are cattle and horses and an apple orchard, and the house is painted white and it has a big attic where you can paint to your heart's content . . . The place is large enough so you can be private and small enough to be cosy when the winter comes. Your bedroom, and your mother's, look towards the sea. My bedroom and study are on the opposite side, There's a living-room and a dining-room and a big, old-fashioned farmhouse kitchen. Mrs Murtagh and her husband live next-door in the cottage. He manages the farm, she's my housekeeper, and I gather they're both much scandalised because I've left the Church. Still, they'll get used to it . . . I've ordered a new car to be delivered to me at the airport and there's a Range Rover at the house, so you won't be anchored or isolated . . . I hope I'm getting through to you, young lady, because I'm talking my silly head off . . .'

'You're getting through, Mr Neylan. And you don't have to try so hard. We're both grateful; we both trust you.'

'In which case, would you mind if we used Christian names?'

'We'd both like that.'

Britte made her own sound of approval and turned to kiss him. Neylan caught the swift shadow of concern on Tove's face. He stood up, drew her with him out of earshot of the girl and told her curtly: 'The girl's scared. She needs assurance. What do you think I am – an abuser of children?'

'Of course not! I didn't mean . . .'

'Listen! Until I get you two settled, we're going to be living like a family in the same house. I don't have much practice at that, but I do have a lot of practice at self-control. I drink only in moderation and the men of my family have the reputation of being good to their women. So why the hell don't you relax, madam, and pay me the compliment of simple trust . . . If your daughter wants to spend a little of the warmth she's got piling up inside her, I'm probably the safest man around to spend it on. Which, by the way, is not an assurance I'm giving to you or any other woman . . . If we can be clear on that, we should all have a pleasant holiday!'

Tove Lundberg gave him a small uncertain smile and then held out her hand.

'Message received and understood. I'm relieved. For a moment I thought you were going to blame me for the burning of Dublin!'

'That's for the winter. Every night I'll recite you a litany of the wrongs of Ireland.'

'I'd rather you sang to me.'

'Why not? There's a piano in the house – though it probably needs tuning. We'll have a come-all-ye.'

'And what's that?'

'An Irish party. An open house: all your friends, and all your neighbours, and any wandering folk who happen by. It'd be interesting to see who turns up and what they think of the infidel priest and his two women!'

Nicol Peters was sitting on his terrace watching the swifts circling the cupolas of the old city and making the last adjustments to the latest edition of 'A View From My Terrace'. This time it was a somewhat eccentric piece, since he had agreed, in deference to a joint request from the Italians and from Mossad, to feed into it certain factual but provocative material:

'Miriam Latif, the young laboratory technician who disappeared under mysterious circumstances from the International Clinic, has now appeared, in equally mysterious circumstances, in Lebanon. According to reports, she simply walked into her parents' house in Byblos and announced that a man and a woman had brought her there. She could give no coherent account of her previous movements. She appears to have suffered no physical ill-treatment or sexual invasion and her parents have placed her in psychiatric care for observation and treatment. They have refused to disclose her whereabouts to the press.

'Meantime, reliable intelligence sources and the Vatican Secretariat of State confirm that terrorist threats against the Pope are being taken very seriously. Special security measures are in force. His Holiness has returned by Army helicopter from Castel Gandolfo. The Pontiff is said to be untroubled by the threat, but irked by the restrictions imposed on his public appearances and even his movements within Vatican City itself.

'However, his health continues to improve. He has lost a great deal of weight and he exercises for an hour every day under the supervision of a therapist. Although His Holiness is still on a restricted schedule of work, there are strong rumours that winds of change may soon be blowing through Vatican City. Usually reliable sources suggest that the Pontiff has been deeply affected by his recent experiences and, indeed, has taken a revisionist view of certain important current issues. A well-known Vatican prelate made a pun about it: "They told us he was having a bypass. Now it seems he has had a complete change of heart."

'Hard evidence is, as usual, difficult to get, but already there have been two important changes. Anton Cardinal Drexel, the Camerlengo or Papal Chamberlain, has retired to his country estate. A new appointment must be made. Monsignor Malachy O'Rahilly, Senior Private Secretary to the Pontiff, is leaving Rome. His place will be taken by an Englishman, Monsignor Gerard Hopgood.

'To ordinary folk like you and me these are clerical matters, relevant only to the strange celibate world of those "who have made themselves eunuchs for the sake of the Kingdom of Heaven". In fact, they may well be portents of greater happenings in the worldwide organisation.

'The most important bodies in the bureaucracy of the Roman Church are the Congregations, which function like the Departments in a normal Civil Service. However, unlike the Civil Services, the Roman Congregations are organised on what is best described as an interlocking grid system. Thus the same names pop up in a variety of appointments. The Cardinal Secretary of State heads up the Council for the Public Affairs of the Church. A senior member of this Council is also a member of the Congregation for the Doctrine of the Faith. The same man sits on the Congregation for the Bishops. So to change any key personage is like pulling a thread in a piece of knitting – the whole pattern may unravel before your astonished eyes.

'So the Roman observer has to read, not only what seems

to be happening, but what is happening in reality. I find it hard to believe that a man so fixed in his ideas as Leo XIV will commit himself to any relaxation of present disciplines. Yet he cannot fail to see that the Church is bleeding at every pore – people, clerics and even financial revenues.

'Vatican finances are in a parlous state. The place is running on a deficit of at least fifty million dollars a year. It is being constantly hit with rises in the cost of living and currency depreciations in every country of the world. It has never recovered from the sorry scandals of a recent era. Donations from the faithful are notably reduced. A full report by an international firm of auditors, commissioned by the present Pontiff, is to be delivered shortly. It is not expected to offer much hope of immediate improvement.

'Now to lighter, if not happier, matters. Professor Sergio Salviati, surgeon to His Holiness, seems likely to lose the services of his most respected colleague, Ms Tove Lundberg, who acts as counsellor to cardiac patients. Ms Lundberg left Rome with her daughter Britte for an extended holiday in Denmark.

'Matt Neylan, recently Monsignor Matt Neylan of the Vatican Secretariat of State, now very much a man about this town, has just signed a six-figure two-book contract with an American publisher. Subject: personalities and policies at the Vatican Secretariat of State . . . Since Matt Neylan has severed all ties, not merely with the priesthood but with the Catholic Church, the book could prove an interesting investment for publishers and readers alike.

'One final item – and a caution for autumn tourists in Rome. The Guardia di Finanza have begun a new crackdown on drugs in this city. This week they seem to be concentrating their attention on the more expensive nightclubs. Latest to be gone over with a fine toothcomb was the Alhambra, a plush and pricy resort just near the Veneto. It is much frequented by Arab and Japanese businessmen and its floor shows are as expensive and raunchy as the traffic will allow. Patrons were patted down but not bothered too much; but staff got a real going over and the hat-check-and-cigarette girl was taken into custody. Latest reports say she is still being questioned . . .'

'They are playing games with us!' Omar Asnan was furious; but his anger was masked by a glacial calm. 'The Lundberg woman left Rome on an Aer Lingus flight bound for Dublin. Our airport contacts identified her and her daughter, who was taken aboard in a wheelchair. Miriam Latif has been dumped back in her parents' lap, brainwashed and full of psychotropic drugs. The raid on the Alhambra was a blind – harassment and intimidation. That cigarette girl never handled anything stronger than tobacco! My servant reports two visits from the electricity company, checking the meter and the fuse-box . . . Then I have a call from the Vatican. My guided tour was cancelled because Monsignor Tabni was down with influenza. To cap it all, my friend Mr Matt Neylan is suddenly called out of town, but he finds it necessary to telephone me, a man with whom he has passed one evening in a lifetime . . . That little thing bothered me like a flea-bite until I decided to call the airport again. Then I discovered that Mr Matt Neylan left on the same flight as the Lundberg woman and her daughter.' He broke off and surveyed the three men seated with him in the back of the limousine, which was parked on a dirt road in the pine woods near Ostia. 'The conclusion is obvious, my friends. They are trying to drive us into a trap, like one of those tuna traps the fishermen use along the coast. It is constructed like a maze. The fish get in; they can't get out. They thresh about waiting for the *mattanza*, the bloody slaughter.'

'So what are we going to do about it?'

'Abdicate,' said Omar Asnan calmly.

'Abandon the project?'

'No. Sub-contract it.'

'To whom?'

'I'm investigating possibilities.'

'We have a right to know.'

'You shall, at an appropriate time. But since I am under-writing the operation, I claim the privilege of arranging it to my own specifications. Besides, if any one of you is picked up as Miriam Latif was, all four of us – and the plan itself – are compromised.'

'Are you saying you would hold out longer than the rest of us?'

'Not at all. Only that I am the last one they will pick up. They know about us all from Miriam; but they know most about me – where I live, where I do business, my bank accounts, and the important fact that I make a lot of money here and I'm not going to walk away from it. So trust me, gentlemen – and have a good flight to Tunis. We'll drop you in Ostia. You can take a taxi from there to the airport.'

An hour and a half later, he was back in Rome lunching at Alfredo's with a Korean businessman who bought and sold container space, financed the cargoes to fill it and guaranteed to provide any service his clients needed, anywhere in the world.

The homecoming of the Pontiff was an event limited by a protocol which he himself had prescribed a long time ago and which he now regretted, with an almost childish anguish.

'At Drexel's house there were flowers in my bedroom and in the *salone*. From the first day of my accession, I forbade them here. I wanted to impress on all my household the notions of austerity and discipline. Now I miss them. I understand, as I never did before, that I have denied the Sisters who look after me the simple pleasure of a welcoming gesture. The youngest of them, a simple country girl, blurted it out: "We wanted to put in flowers, but Mother Superior said you didn't like them." Which at least gave me the opportunity to make the first small retreats from my old self. I told her that was an example of how wrong even a Pope could be. I would love to have flowers in my study and on the dining table. Only afterwards did it occur to me to ask myself what pleasure I could offer to them. Their lives are so much more confined, so much more under scrutiny than those of their sisters outside the Vatican. They still wear the old-fashioned habits – my orders again! – and their housekeeping tasks are boring in the extreme. Before I think about the big changes, here is a small but necessary one, right under my pontifical nose! If I feel confined – and tonight, dear God, I feel as though I am locked in a box – how much more must they feel it, in this kingdom of professional bachelors.

'Malachy O'Rahilly has already instructed them on the routines of my convalescence. He has set my desk in order, laid down a list of priorities. He has also presented his successor, a blond, square-jawed Englishman, very reserved, very cool, totally in command of himself. His Italian is more polished than mine. He writes Ciceronian Latin and Plato's Greek. He has French and Spanish, German and Russian, and a doctorate in Ecclesiastical History.

'To make conversation, I ask him what he presented as a doctoral thesis. He tells me it was a study of Pope Julius II, Giuliano della Rovere. That takes some of the stiffness out of our first talk, because there is a curious connection between this formidable warrior-pope and my home place of Mirandola. In the Palazzo Chigi in Rome there is a strange portrait of Julius in winter armour, painted during his siege of Mirandola in 1511.

'It is a tiny footnote to history, but it helps to soften the bleakness of my homecoming. It also encourages me to believe that in place of my very companionable

Malachy O'Rahilly I may have found a tough young disciple with a sense of history.

'No sooner had I sent him off with Malachy O'Rahilly than I began to feel restless, claustrophobic. I wanted desperately to be at work, even though I knew I was not capable of it. Instead, I went into my private chapel and forced myself to sit in meditation for nearly an hour.

'I focused my mind on the Psalmist's words: "Unless the Lord build the house, they labour in vain who build it." I was immediately reminded of Agostini's warning, so unexpected from that very pragmatical man: "If it is God's war, you will win it, though not, perhaps, in the way you expect." Came the sudden awareness that all my thinking recently has been in terms of conflict and confrontation. Then, soft and insinuating, like the sound of distant bells, I heard the words of Jesus: "A new commandment I give you: that you should love one another, as I have loved you."

'How can I, an ugly man, possessed so long by an ugly spirit, gloss or change that luminous simplicity? So be it then! This will be my first text, on which I shall build my first colloquy . . .'

Yet, for all the brave confidence of the writing, his sleep was haunted by nightmares, and he woke next morning in the grip of a black and almost suicidal depression. His Mass seemed a sterile mummery. The nun who served his breakfast was like a character out of some oafish miracle play. He flinched at the pile of papers on his desk. Then, because he dared not any longer be seen as a maimed and halting spirit, he summoned his two secretaries to his desk and issued his directives for the day.

'Monsignor Hopgood. You will reply to all my well-wishers in the Hierarchy. A short letter in your best Latin, offering my thanks, telling them they will hear from me again, very soon. You will also go through these documents from the dicasteries. Give me a thumbnail summary of each, in Italian, and a draft reply, also in Italian. If you have problems, discuss them with Malachy. If you can't solve them between you, bring me what is left. Any questions?'

'Not yet, Holiness; but it is very early in the day.'

He gathered up the trays of documents and left the room. The Pontiff turned to O'Rahilly. His voice was very gentle.

'Are you still bleeding, Malachy?'

'Yes I am, Holiness. The sooner I can be gone, the better I'll be pleased. Hopgood's in place now. As you've seen, he's a fast learner and he's ten times better qualified than I am. So, will Your Holiness not make it easy for me?'

'No, Malachy, I will not!'

'In God's name, why?'

'Because, Malachy, I know that if you walk out of here in anger, you'll never come back. You'll shut your mind and lock up your heart and you'll be unhappy until the day you die. You were meant to be a priest, Malachy – not a Papal Secretary, but a pastor, an understanding heart, a shoulder for folk to cry on when the world gets too much for them. It may get too much for you – and I know that's what you're afraid of – but what if it does? You and I are imperfect men in an imperfect world. You may not believe this; but I swear it is true. When I finished Mass this morning I was in so deep a despair that I wished I had died under Salviati's knife. But here I am and here you are and this sorry old world has work for both of us. Now, please, will you help me write a letter? It may be the most important one I've written in a lifetime.'

There was a long moment of silence before Malachy O'Rahilly raised his eyes to confront his master. Then he nodded a reluctant assent.

'I am still in service, Holiness; but will you permit me to

tell you something? If I don't get it out now it will never be said and I'll be ashamed of that always.'

'Say whatever you want, Malachy.'

'Here it is then, for better or worse, richer or poorer! You're just home from a long journey, a trip to the end of time, where you nearly dropped off the edge. The wonder of that and the fear of that are still with you. You're like Marco Polo, back from far Cathay, itching to share the strangeness and the risks of the Silk Road . . . You're convinced, as he was, that you've got knowledge and experience that will change the world. It will, it can, but not by the simple telling; because, as Marco Polo found and you'll find, very few even of your own brother bishops are going to believe you!'

'And why not, Malachy?'

Malachy O'Rahilly hesitated for a moment, then gave a rueful grin and threw out his hands in despair.

'Do you know what you're asking, Holiness? My head's in the lion's mouth already!'

'Answer the question, please. Why will they not believe me?'

'You're going to write them a letter first, an eloquent personal letter explaining this experience.'

'That is my intention, yes.'

'Holiness, believe me, you are the world's worst letter writer. You're too commonsensical. Too . . . too concrete and orderly. It takes a lot of work to polish your style, and even then it's never emotional or eloquent enough to be more than a document. It certainly doesn't speak with the tongues of men and angels. But that's only the beginning of the problem . . . The crux of it is, you're suspect, you will be for months yet. This cardiac intervention is a commonplace now. The sequelae are well documented. All your brother bishops have been warned that, for the time being at least, there will be a lame duck administration. You won't find it anywhere in writing; no one will admit to being the source of the information; but it's out there and for the present it taints everything you do or say. Right or wrong, Holiness, that's my testimony . . .'

'And your head is still on your shoulders, is it not?'

'It feels like it, Holiness.'

'So answer me one more question, Malachy. I'm a suspect leader. What should I do about it?'

'Are you seeking an opinion, Holiness – or do you just feel the need to pin my ears to the wall?'

'An opinion, Malachy.'

'Well, look at it from the outsider's point of view. You've been an iron-fisted Pontiff. You've installed some iron-fisted fellows in the Curia and in the national churches. Now suddenly your Grand Inquisitor, Cardinal Clemens, is out of favour. He's put that word about, all by himself. So now there's doubt. Everybody's wondering which way the cat will jump. Fine! Let 'em wonder! Do nothing. Gerard Hopgood will keep your desk clean and demonstrate that you're working as efficiently as ever. Meantime, develop the one big *motu proprio* that says and does everything you want and when it's ready, summon a short-notice full Consistory and publish it – tic-tac! – in your old style. That way, you're not putting yourself forward as Lazarus, straight out of the tomb and shaky on his pins! In this most Christian Assembly, we hate innovators – even when they sit in Peter's Chair. You can lock a saint up in a monastery; you can sack a mere monsignor; but a modernising pope is a long-term embarrassment! Now, Holiness, I beg you, please let me go!'

Forty-eight hours later, Monsignor Malachy O'Rahilly left Rome, with ten thousand dollars in his pocket – a gift from the Pontiff's privy purse. At the same time, the Pontiff announced a private Consistory of the College of Cardinals, to be held November 1st, the Feast of All Saints. At this Consistory the

Pontiff would promulgate new appointments and deliver an allocution entitled *'Christus Salvator Homo Viator'* – Christ the Saviour, Man the Pilgrim.

Thirteen

Summer wore swiftly into autumn. The *maestrale* stopped blowing. The seas lay slack and listless. The mists gathered in the river valleys. The late vintages were in and the stubble was ploughed under. In Rome, the final waves of tourists arrived – the wise ones who had missed the summer heats to travel in the mild, sunny weather. The pilgrims gathered on Sundays in St Peter's Square and the Pontiff stood at his window to bless them and recite the Angelus, because his guardians would not let him descend into the square as he had done in former times. The terrorist threat was still marked 'probable' in the intelligence records.

Inside the Vatican, there was an Indian summer. His Holiness was proving a docile patient. He was still following the strict regimen of diet, rest and exercise. His physician was pleased with his progress. His surgeon did not need to see him for another six months. The work that passed across the papal desk was handled promptly and efficiently.

The new secretary was discreet, serviceable and, so rumour had it, a linguist to rival the fabulous Cardinal Mezzofanti. Most important of all, the Pontiff himself gave an impression of calm, of optimism, of lively but benevolent curiosity. He had even suggested to the Mother Superior that the nuns of the Papal Household might be more comfortable in modern dress, and that they should be given more leave time outside the precinct of the City.

For the rest, the routines of the Apostolic Palace and the Papal Household had settled back to normal. His Holiness gave audience to foreign dignatories, to bishops making their *ad limina* visits to pay homage and make the offerings of their people to the Successor of Peter. They found him thinned down, less brusque than they remembered him, more generous with his time, more searching in his enquiries. He asked, for example, how matters stood between them and the Apostolic Delegates or Nuncios in their countries. Was there harmony, open communication? Did they feel spied upon? Were they given copies of reports made to Rome about the local church and clergy? Did they feel totally free to announce the Good News, interpret it to their people boldly, or did they feel constrained by fear of delation or denunciation to Rome? How well or ill did Rome understand their problems, the special conditions of their flock? And the last question of each audience was always the same: What do you need from us? What can we do for you?

Sometimes the answers were bland; sometimes they were almost brutally frank; but every night Leo the Pontiff set them down in his diary. Each day he tried to incorporate them into the allocution, which was growing slowly, page by page. It was like putting together a jigsaw puzzle as big as the world. How did the problems of bio-ethics in prosperous societies fit with the appalling toll of famine in the desert fringes? What moral definitions should be applied to the destruction of rain-forests and the genocidal land-grabbers of Brazil? How boldly was he prepared to speak about a married clergy, the rights and status of women within the Christian assembly, the vexed question of a female priesthood? Then, one day, Monsignor Gerard Hopgood brought back a pile of typescript, the compilation of the Pontiff's handwritten notes. By accident or design, he found, stuck in among the pages, a scrap of paper on which was written in Hopgood's clear cursive script: 'Round and round the mulberry bush! Why don't we say it plainly, once and for all? We have the message of salvation, total and complete. We do not and never will have the answer to every ethical problem that may arise . . .'

The next time Hopgood came in with letters to be signed, the Pontiff handed him the paper with an offhand remark: 'I think you dropped this.'

Hopgood, cool as ever, simply glanced at the torn piece of foolscap and nodded.

'Yes, I did. Thank you, Holiness.'

His Holiness went on signing the letters. He spoke without raising his eyes from the paper.

'What do you think of my allocution, so far?'

'So far,' said Hopgood carefully, 'it seems as though you are writing your way towards a document. You are a long way from the document itself.'

'As bad as that, eh?' The Pontiff went on writing assiduously.

'Neither bad nor good. It should not be judged in its present tentative form.'

'Monsignor O'Rahilly told me I was the world's worst writer. Any comments?'

'None. But if Your Holiness would entertain a suggestion . . . ?'

'Make it.'

'Writing as you are doing it is brutal labour. Why inflict it on yourself? If you will give me an hour a day, and talk out to me what you want to say, I'll write it for you in half the time. Then you can cut it about to suit yourself. I'm good at that sort of thing. I've written and directed theatre at Oxford; so the rhetoric of the thing is easy for me . . . Besides, I very much want this Consistory to be a success.'

The Pontiff put down his pen, leaned back in his chair and studied Hopgood with dark, unblinking eyes.

'And how would you define a success?'

Hopgood considered the question for a few moments then, in his precise, donnish fashion, he answered it.

'Your audience will be men powerful in the Church. They can, if they choose, remain totally indifferent to anything you say. If they dislike it, they can obstruct you in a thousand ways. But if they go out into St Peter's Square and look at the people and feel a new kinship with them and a new care for them . . . then your allocution will have meant something. If not, it will be windblown words, lost the moment they are spoken.'

'You seem to me to be a very dedicated but rather reclusive young man. What is your own contact with the people?'

It was the first time the Pontiff had seen Monsignor Gerard Hopgood embarrassed. He blushed, shifted uneasily on his feet and made the surprising confession.

'I'm a runner, Holiness. I train on my days off with a club over on the Flaminia. A friend of mine is the priest there. He set up the club to keep the kids off the drug circuit and out of the thieves' kitchens. So the answer is that I do see quite a lot of the people.'

'Are you a good runner, Monsignore?'

'Not bad . . . which reminds me: you've been missing your morning exercises, Holiness. You can't afford to do that, it's dangerous! If it helps, I'll do them with you.'

'I am rebuked in my own house,' said Leo the Pontiff. 'And by my own secretary! A runner indeed!'

'"Let us run with endurance",' said Monsignor Hopgood innocently. 'St Paul to the Hebrews. I wait on Your Holiness's decision about the allocution – and the exercises. Personally, I'll settle for the exercises, because they at least will keep you alive. In the end, it's the Holy Spirit who takes care of the Church.'

The Pontiff signed the last of the letters. Hopgood gathered them into the file and waited for his formal dismissal. Instead, the Pontiff waved him to a chair.

'Sit down. Let us go through the text we have so far . . .'

On Matt Neylan's farm, it was another kind of autumn, warm

and misty from the wash of the Gulf Stream, cloudy most days, with the air smelling of sea wrack and peat smoke and the trodden grass of the cow pastures. It was a lonely place, halfway between Clonakilty and Courtmacsherry, thirty-five acres of grazing land, with an orchard and a kitchen garden and a view across the bay to Galley Head.

The house was larger than he had remembered, with a tree-break planted against the westerlies, and central heating, and a walled garden where roses grew and pears and apples were espaliered along the walls. Inside, it was spotless. His mother's ornaments were all in place, his father's books dusted, the pictures square on the walls. There was a Barry over the mantel and a David Maclise in his study, which was a pleasant windfall to be going on with.

The welcome the Murtaghs gave them was like the climate, grey and tepid; but once Neylan had told them the story: how this brave woman had nursed and counselled His Holiness and was now threatened with kidnap and worse, and how this dear child was the ward and the adoptive granddaughter of the great Cardinal Drexel himself – then they warmed up and Mrs Murtagh fussed around the pair like a mother hen, while Neylan and Mr Murtagh drank Irish whiskey in the kitchen.

Which left only the problem of his own defection from the faith which, as Mr Murtagh put it, didn't worry him too much but bothered his old woman somewhat, she having a sister in the Presentation convent at Courtmacsherry. But then – he conceded after two whiskies – a man's belief was his own business, and wasn't he giving shelter and protection to these two threatened creatures? Which prompted the next question: did Neylan think they'd be pursued to this neck of the woods? Neylan admitted that it was possible, but hardly likely. However, just in case, it might pay to pass the word around the villages that an early warning of strangers would be appreciated. And – this was Murtagh's contribution – there was a twelve-bore shotgun and a rook rifle that used to belong to his father. It would be wise to keep them oiled and clean. And, by the way, how did he want to be addressed, now that he wasn't a priest any more? And what about the ladies, Missus or Miss? Christian names, Matt Neylan told him – and wondered what it was that made a name Christian when its owner wasn't.

After that, life was easier. They were fed like kings. Britte was coddled. They explored the coast from Skibbereen to Limerick and down across the counties to Waterford. They ate well and drank well and slept warm, though separate. It was only when the first gales hit that they looked at each other and asked what the devil they were doing in this place and how did they expect to get through the winter?

Two telephone calls gave them the answer. Salviati said without hesitation: 'Stay put. It hasn't begun yet.' The Israeli Embassy gave them even plainer warning: 'Don't move. Keep your heads down. We'll tell you when it's safe to return!' Then for good measure they gave them a telephone number in Dublin where Mossad maintained a station to watch the arms runners from Libya and elsewhere.

So, Britte began to paint. Matt Neylan picked up his writing and Tove Lundberg fretted in silence until she read that a German manufacturer of pharmaceuticals, enjoying a tax holiday in Ireland, had decided to endow a cardiac unit at the Sisters of Mercy hospital in Cork. They would need skilled staff. She had the best possible references. Any objections? From Britte, none. Matt was working at home. The Murtaghs kept the house and the farm going. From Matt Neylan?

'What can I say? If it's a choice between going crazy here or sticking your head up a little – and who, for Christ's sake, reads about Cork in Rome? – then go to it, by all means. It's a forty-mile drive from here to Cork. They'll probably give you a room at the hospital. Why not apply?'

'You don't mind looking after Britte?'

'What's to look after? Mrs Murtagh mothers her and

does the girl things she needs. I entertain her and cart her about with me when she isn't painting. It seems to work for her. You're the one who has to be happy with the arrangements.'

'What about you?'

'I'm fine. I'm in my own home. For the moment, I'm happy. I'm working well.'

'And that's all?'

'No, it isn't. One day I'm going to get a twitch and an itch and I'll drive to Dublin and take a flight to somewhere and come back when I've played myself out. The Murtaghs will see to Britte. You'll be around. That's my end of the bargain. Do you have any problem with it?'

'No, Matt. But I think you have.'

'Sure, I've got problems!' Suddenly the urge was on him to talk. 'But they're mine. They have nothing to do with you and Britte. I looked forward to coming back – and in one way I wasn't disappointed. It's a comfortable living. It's a nice cushion to have at my back if the bad times come. But that's it! There's no future for me here, no continuity. The taproot's been cut. I don't belong to the old Catholic Ireland; I've no taste for the new rich and the tax-haveners from Europe. When the day comes that I fall in love and want to settle down with a woman, I know it isn't going to be here . . .'

'I understand how you feel.'

'I believe you do.'

'Don't you see? Our lives run parallel to each other. We both left an old, harsh religion, a small country, a small language, a narrow history. We both became mercenaries in a foreign service. I couldn't live in Denmark now, any more than you could live here.'

'That's the country. What about marriage?'

'Out of the question for me.'

'Where does that leave Salviati?'

'Where he needs to be: free to make a new start with a new woman.'

'That's noble of you!'

'For God's sake! It's a selfish choice right down the line. I couldn't ask any man to share the responsibility of Britte. I don't want to risk another child at my age. And even if I had one, it would put Britte into a kind of permanent exile. I've seen it happen in many families. The normal children resent the maimed one.'

'It seems to me,' said Matt Neylan quietly, 'you're predicating everything on a perfect world, which we both know doesn't exist. For most of us, life's a make-and-mend affair. I'm sure many of my former colleagues see me as a happy-go-lucky infidel with alley-cat morals and all the women in the world to play with. Given the headlong way I've been living lately, I don't blame them. But the real truth is something different. I'm like the camel-driver who fell asleep under a palm tree and woke to find the caravan gone and himself alone in the middle of a desert. I'm not crying about it, just trying to make a point.'

'Which is?'

'Britte and I. We get along very well. We manage to communicate. We're companionable. I'm at least a useful father figure to take the place of Nonno Drexel. Inside that beautiful head and behind all that gobbledegook muttering is a mind like a razor and I know she's slicing me up every day and putting me under a microscope. Right now, we're talking about an exhibition in a good gallery in Cork or Dublin.'

'I presume you were going to consult me at some stage?'

'At some stage, sure; but it's too early yet. As far as you and I are concerned . . . Oh hell! How did we get into all this?'

'I don't know; but you've got the floor, Matt. First, your speech!'

He plunged ahead recklessly.

'Then I'll say it fast and if you don't like it you can spit in my eye. You're a thousand times welcome under my roof. Whether I'm here or not, this house is your house and there's neither rent nor board to be thought of. But I sleep just across the hall and I lie awake at night wanting you and knowing I'd take you on any terms, for as long or as little time as you wanted me, because you're a very special woman, Tove Lundberg, and if I thought they'd make you happy I'd pull the stars out of the sky and toss them in your lap! There now, it's out! You'll hear no more of it. Would you join me in a drink, madam? I think I need one!'

'I'll get it,' said Tove Lundberg. 'You Irish make such a big mouthful of simple things. Why didn't you just ask me, instead of wasting all this time?'

Late in September, His Excellency Yukishege Hayashi, Ambassador Extraordinary and Plenipotentiary to the Holy See, received a letter from Tokyo. The letter informed His Excellency that a team of independent film-makers would be visiting Rome during October and November. Part of their assignment would be to make a two-hour documentary for Japanese television on the Vatican and its treasures. His Excellency was asked to facilitate this work and secure the good offices of the Pontifical Commission on Social Communications, through whom all the required permissions must be secured.

The letter was accompanied by a copy of a recommendation from the Pro-Nuncio Apostolic Archbishop, Paul Ryuji Arai, to the President of the Commission, requesting his personal interest in the project.

It was one of hundreds of such requests the Commissioners received during a year. Its provenance was impeccable. There were very sound reasons for extending special courtesies to the Japanese. His Excellency was assured that permissions would be issued as soon as the team arrived in Rome and had filed the usual information: number of persons in the team, subjects to be photographed, equipment and transport, thus and thus and thus.

At the same time, the President wrote personally to the Ambassador, pointing out that, on the Feast of All Saints, the whole College of Cardinals would assist at a Pontifical High Mass in St Peter's and that the Diplomatic Corps would be invited to attend. This would seem to be a ceremony, unique in character, which would recommend itself to the film-makers, especially since His Excellency himself would be present, representing the Emperor.

The information was mentioned casually in a conversation with Nicol Peters, who had called on the Commission to discuss the announcement of the Consistory and how it fitted into the hidden subtext of Vatican affairs. On that question, the President was bland but vague. To inform himself more fully, Peters telephoned Cardinal Drexel and was promptly invited to lunch. The old man was trenchant and vigorous as ever, but admitted frankly that there was a gap in his life.

'I miss my Britte. I miss her mother too. Still, I am glad they are safe and they appear to be happy. Britte sends me sketches and watercolours and they are cheerful pieces. Tove writes regularly. She speaks very warmly of your friend Neylan and his care of them both. I never knew the man, of course. There was never any scandal about him as priest . . . However, you didn't come here to talk about my family affairs. What do you want to know?'

'This Consistory. It seems an old-fashioned, almost retrograde, step. After Vatican II the notion was always to continue and to emphasise collegiality, the role of the bishops. So far the Synods have produced more window-dressing than results; but at least the principle has been affirmed. Now this private Consistory, as I understand it, is to be limited to members of the College of Cardinals. Why?'

Drexel did not answer immediately. He sat slicing a piece of country cheese and selecting a pear to go with it. Finally, he set down his knife and explained carefully.

'You will not quote me on this. That would create jealousy and do harm, since I am retired and I must not seem to be trying to intrude into Curial affairs. On the other hand, I would like you to record very accurately what I am about to tell you. It is important. You know that this Pontiff is by nature an old-fashioned man. He is changed, profoundly changed; but instead of trying to create a new image for himself, he has chosen to live with the old one of which – you may not know this – he is often ashamed. He thinks of himself as an ugly man with an ugly nature. For a long time he was just that. Now, however, he has made a decision, a wise one I believe, not to concern himself with image, but with fact and practice in the Church today. He is also holding strictly to protocol. A Consistory, by tradition, is not a consultative assembly. It is a meeting at which the Pontiff promulgates appointments, makes known his personal sentiments on matters of concern, forewarns of his personal decisions. A Synod is another matter. It is a discussive, deliberative, deciding body of bishops in union with the Bishop of Rome. Its acts are collegial acts.'

'So, on the face of it,' said Nicol Peters deliberately, 'Leo XIV is abrogating the collegial procedure and going straight to promulgation.'

'That's what they think he will do. It's absolutely in character. He will begin by announcing changes and appointments within the Curia.'

'Do you have any information on those, Eminence?'

'Some, but I cannot discuss them. After that announcement, His Holiness will deliver an allocution, an address outlining his views on matters of importance. That address will foreshadow a more formal document, the *motu proprio*, which will be issued shortly afterwards.'

'Will there be debate or discussion after the speech?'

'That will depend entirely on the Pontiff.'

'Will the speech be available to the press?'

'No.'

'Why not?'

'Protocol again. This is a private and not a public Consistory. However, His Holiness may well direct that a summary be published by *Osservatore Romano* or distributed through the Sala Stampa . . . Try some of this cheese, it's very good. Coffee?'

'Please.'

'Any more questions?'

'May we talk now, off the record?'

'If you wish.'

'The policies of Leo XIV have been both rigorous and divisive.'

'No comment.'

'Will he reverse those policies?'

'He will try, yes.'

'Will he be able to heal the rifts in the Church?'

'Some, yes. Others, no. In any case, none of it will happen overnight. You see, my friend, we call ourselves the One, Holy, Universal and Apostolic Church. We are all of those things and none of them. That's the paradox and the mystery. In and through Christ we are one, we are holy, we are brothers and sisters in a worldwide family and the word we preach is that preached by the first Apostles who heard it from the lips of the Lord. But away from Him, without Him, of ourselves only, what are we? A lost race in a tiny planetary system, vagrant in the deeps of space.'

'And how does Your Eminence regard those millions who do not, and cannot, share this Faith? How does His Holiness regard them?'

'I can answer only for myself,' said Anton Cardinal Drexel. 'This time we have is a bridge between two eternities. This light we have has been travelling to us for uncounted years.

The tongues we speak, the symbols we use, are human inventions, inadequate for anything but the uses of the moment, yet always seeking to express that ineffable mystery of a Godhead which contains and maintains and sustains us all. When you get old, my dear Nico, you are much less conscious of difference than of identity. Plant us in the ground and we all turn into daffodils!'

'Which brings me to my last question, Eminence. The threat to assassinate the Pontiff was made by an Islamic group. Is it possible that he is hated enough to be killed by one of his own?'

Anton Cardinal Drexel knew this man too well to dismiss the question. He frowned and said: 'We've known each other too long to play games, Nico. What exactly is on your mind?'

'The terrorist threat has been widely publicised. I'm asking whether another group, or another person even, might take advantage of that to stage a private execution.'

'It's possible. Anything is possible in this crazy world. Do you have any ideas?'

'Do you remember Lorenzo de Rosa?'

'Only too well.'

'I was going through my files the other day and it occured to me that I'd never bothered to follow up that story. De Rosa, his wife, their children, were dead. The police had taken over. *Basta!* End of story.'

'Not quite. His Holiness is moving towards reforms prompted by that sad business.'

'Good! But that's not what I was thinking about. There were families involved, parents, aunt and uncles, cousins. Lorenzo was Tuscan, his wife was Sicilian, old family from Palermo, lots of relatives.'

'Are you telling me they have made threats?'

'No. But all of us in the Press Club got one of these and there was one pinned to the message board.' He fished in his wallet and brought out one of those small obituary cards, with a black cross and a black border which friends and relatives of the deceased kept in their prayer books. There was a photograph of Lorenzo de Rosa with his wife and children, the date of their deaths and the place of their burial. The inscription read: 'God has a long memory. He demands to be paid. May these we loved rest in peace.'

Drexel handed back the card and said, almost pleadingly, 'Once before we called up the ghosts and look what happened. Forget it, my friend! Tear it up and forget it! We know where the real threat comes from. This is just the excuse people would use to avoid trouble with the Islamic world. We cannot bow to terror, whoever practises it.'

In the most secure room at the Israeli Embassy, Menachem Avriel was in conference with the man who called himself Aharon ben Shaul. They had a decision to make. It was Aharon who laid down the terms of it.

'Do we deal with the Sword of Islam ourselves or do we leave it to the Italians?'

'Can we be sure they'll take the action we want?'

'No.'

'Even with an extra push from the Vatican?'

'No again.'

'Once more, please, walk me through what we've got.'

'Item one. Omar Asnan is the head of the organisation in this country. Item two. His three lieutenants are no longer in Italy. Two are in Tunis, one in Malta. The other members of the group, those we've identified at the Alhambra Club and other places, are still here, though inactive. Which brings us to item three. There is strong evidence to suggest that Omar Asnan has not abandoned his operations, but sub-contracted them. It's not an uncommon practice, as you know. Terror is big business, international business. The currencies are arms, cash, drugs and the barter of facilities.'

'With whom is Asnan dealing?'

'This man.' He shoved a photograph across the table. 'Hyun Myung Kim, a Korean who peddles shipping space and sells spot cargoes around the world. He's a travelling man, who's known for driving hard bargains but delivering what he sells. Omar Asnan met him over lunch at Alfredo's the same day his henchmen left for Tunis . . . We weren't able to bug him, but we had a camera on him. Money was passed, as you see.'

'The Italians have this information?'

'Sure. We're playing strictly according to the book. Their question was: what had we really got to take to court? Then I played them the tapes from the bugs in Asnan's house. They agreed they meant what they seemed to say, but again the question: how would they sound in court? We'd have to admit they were composites and, knowing the risks involved of reprisals against aircraft, shipping, Italian citizens travelling in Islamic countries, the Italians wouldn't buy anything but a watertight case – the smoking gun, the assassin standing over the body. They're willing to deport Asnan quietly; but that gets us nowhere. We need to sweat him for information.'

'So Asnan goes scot-free.'

'Unless we lift him ourselves.'

'How the hell do you do that? The man's a permanent resident. He goes to Embassy functions. He maintains an expensive life style . . .'

'He also killed our man and made him disappear very effectively.'

'Which isn't the hardest thing in the world in that archaeological zone. There are three major catacombs and a whole series of others never opened to the public. There's even one called the Catacomb of the Jews, in case you're interested!'

'I'm very interested,' said Aharon ben Shaul. 'So interested that I staged a power failure at Mr Asnan's villa and put a couple of electricians in to check the wiring. They discovered a reverse cycle air conditioner that's much too big for a villa that size, with wiring and ducting that doesn't fit the registered plan . . .'

'So?'

'So before I go back to the Italians or you decide we'll go without them, I'd like to do a real job on Mr Asnan's villa.'

'What sort of job?'

'Old-fashioned break and enter. Put the dogs and the servants to sleep, strip out the valuables. The Appia Antica is a very vulnerable area. Insurance premiums are high. And they haven't had a decent robbery for nearly three months!'

'And where will Omar Asnan be while all this is happening?'

'Good question, Mr Ambassador. When I have the answer, I'll let you know.'

'Please don't,' said Avriel. 'Please, don't even tell me the time of day!'

'I'm not looking forward to this session.' The Pontiff sat at his desk, tapping an impatient rhythm on the documents Hopgood had laid in front of him. 'Clemens will be here exactly at ten. Make sure he is not kept waiting.'

'How much time shall I allow for the meeting, Holiness?'

'As long as it takes. Offer coffee when he arrives; then don't come in unless I ring.'

'A suggestion, Holiness.'

'Yes?'

'The leatherbound volume under your hand is the report on the financial condition of the Church; three hundred and fifty pages of it, with figures, graphics and comments on every item.'

'I can't even begin to think about this today.'

'With respect, Holiness, I think you should read the last ten pages before Cardinal Clemens arrives. They deal with conclusions and recommendations and they confirm the main lines of the arguments you will be presenting to His Eminence.'

'Who else has seen this document?'

'Copies were delivered simultaneously yesterday evening to Your Holiness, to the Prefecture for the Economic Affairs of the Holy See, the Institute for Works of Religion and the Administration of the Patrimony of the Apostolic See. No one will have had time to read or digest it; Your Holiness should, I believe, have the advantage of a first glance. There's an old English proverb which translates quite well into Italian: "Twice armed is he whose cause is just; thrice armed the one who gets his blow in first."'

'And that, I would remind you, my dear Hopgood, is still the language of confrontation, which is exactly what we are trying to avoid.'

'With great respect, Holiness, I doubt you'll be able to avoid it this morning.'

'How long before Clemens arrives?'

'Forty minutes.'

'Let me take a look at this report. I'll ring when I'm ready.'

The authors of the document wrote in the dry, passionless style of money-men everywhere, but their final summation took on, perforce, a bleak eloquence.

'It is difficult to avoid the conclusion that those Catholic congregations which are expanding most rapidly in Third World countries are also the most needy, while those with a no-growth or low-growth rate are the most prosperous and the least generous in the traditional gift-giving.

'In so-called Catholic countries like the South Americas, Spain, Italy, the Philippines, where there is a traditionally wealthy and privileged class, still loyal to the Church, there is an often quite appalling disparity in social conditions, and a hostility born of fear between the privileged and the deprived, the exploiters and the exploited. The privileged use their surplus to improve or protect their position. There is no noticeable increase in the revenues available for education, works of charity or social betterment.

'It has to be said also that in those dioceses and parishes where accounts are published and expenditures thoroughly documented, the level of donations is appreciably higher than elsewhere. So far as the central administration is concerned, it suffers and will continue to suffer from pandemic secrecy and the long consequences of well known scandals and affiliation with known criminals.

'Finally, with the increasing conglomeration of large corporations with diverse interests, it is becoming more and more difficult for those who handle Church funds to find untainted investments – e.g. a chemical company that does not manufacture toxic substances; a manufacturer not connected with arms or military equipment; a pharmaceutical company which does not manufacture birth control products, which Catholics are specifically forbidden to use . . . With the best will in the world, scandal can hardly be avoided; but in the end, secrecy breeds suspicion and suspicion causes the fountain of charity to dry up very quickly . . .'

There was more, much more in the same vein, carefully cross-referenced and footnoted, but the import was the same. Needs were growing, revenue was declining. The traditional sources were drying up. The traditional methods of funding from the worldwide congregations were no longer effective, because the congregations in the affluent countries were getting smaller.

But the nub of the matter was the 'why'. The money-men touched only the outer skin, they could not reach down for heart's reasons. In the old days, when the faithful were lapsing into indifference or their offerings were falling off, the bishop would call in missionary preachers, fiery, eloquent men who set up a cross in the market square and preached hellfire and damnation and the love of God that snatched folk like burning brands from the pit. Some were converted, some were changed for a while, no one was quite unmoved and nine months later the birthrate showed a marked increase. But those were other times and other manners, and it was very hard for the most eloquent of men to get past the glazed eyes and numbed imaginations and atrophied reason of a generation of television addicts and victims of media saturation.

He himself was faced with the same problem. He was a man framed in splendour, endowed with the mighty numen of an ancient faith and yet he rated less attention than some shouting clown with a guitar or a drunken riot at a soccer match.

Hopgood ushered in His Eminence Karl Emil Cardinal Clemens. Their greeting was cordial enough. Time had passed. Tempers had cooled. Clemens opened the talk with a compliment.

'Your Holiness looks well and very trim. At least fifteen years younger.'

'I train like a footballer, Karl – and eat like a bird! No fat, no red meat . . . Never talk to me about the penitential life. I'm compelled to it. And you?'

'I'm well. A touch of gout sometimes. My blood pressure's a trifle high; but my doctor tells me I'm a hypertensive character.'

'And does he tell you where that can lead?'

'Well, he gives me the usual warnings.'

'If you don't heed them, Karl, you'll end up exactly where I did. At your age you can't afford to play dice games with your health. Which brings me to the reason for this morning's talk. I am moving you from the Congregation for the Doctrine of the Faith. I am appointing you head of my household: Cardinal Camerlengo. You will retain your appointments with the Congregation for the Oriental Churches and for the Propagation of the Faith. These changes will be announced at the Consistory on November first. I trust that is agreeable to you?'

'It is not agreeable, Holiness, but I bow to Your Holiness's wishes.'

'You have a right to know the reason.'

'I have not asked for it, Holiness.'

'Nonetheless, I shall give it to you. I propose to make certain drastic changes in the constitution and the functions of the Congregation. You will not agree with them. It would be quite unfair to ask you to implement them. Further – and I want you to know this – I appointed you because I saw in you the mirror image of the man I believed myself to be: the stalwart guardian of the Faith committed to us all. You have been that. You have discharged exactly the commission I gave you. Your lapse with *Osservatore Romano* angered me; but that alone would not have brought me to this decision. The fact is, Karl, I believe I misread my own duty and gave you the wrong brief!'

Clemens gaped at him in utter disbelief.

'If Your Holiness is saying that it is no longer his duty to guard the Deposit of Faith . . .'

'No, Karl. I am not saying that. I am saying that the Congregation in its present form and function is not an appropriate instrument. As a matter of historic fact, it never has been. In my view it never can be.'

'I don't see that at all.'

'I know you don't, Karl. That's why I'm moving you; but you are going to hear my explanation, because it has references far beyond this present matter. Suppose you walk me through the procedures.' He laid open on his desk the large volume of the Acta Apostolicae Sedis for the year 1971. 'A denunciation is made of a book or publication which is deemed contrary to the Faith. What happens?'

'First, the denunciation has to be serious and it has to be signed. If the error is obvious and – I am quoting now – "if it contains certainly and clearly an error in Faith and if the publication of that opinion would do harm to the faithful", then the Congregation may ask the bishop or bishops to inform the author and invite him to amend the error.'

'Let's pause there a moment. I need to be very clear. At this stage, the author knows nothing. Someone has denounced his writing. The Congregation has judged it erroneous and asked for a correction.'

'That's right.'

'He hasn't been heard, offered a right to reply. He is already presumed guilty.'

'Effectively, yes. But that is only so in the case of blatant error, one immediately visible.'

'So, let us pass to a more complex issue. A controversial opinion is published. The Congregation is required to decide whether it is or is not – and here I quote – "in harmony with divine revelation and the *magisterium* of the Church". Immediately, it seems to me, not only the author but we are in real trouble . . . Divine revelation is one thing. The *magisterium*, the general authority of the Church, is quite another. Under that authority, things can be and have been done quite contrary to divine revelation: witch-hunts, the burning of heretics. You see the problem?'

'I point out,' said Clemens stiffly, 'that these anomalies have existed for a long time and Your Holiness has never found it necessary to object to them.'

'Exactly what I have told you, Karl. I see them now in a different light. I propose to exercise my authority to change them. But let us go on. The author is aware of the doubts cast on his work?'

'Not yet. But we appoint a spokesman for the author; you'll find him described in the Acts as *relator pro auctore!* His function is also described: "To indicate in a spirit of truth the merits and positive aspects of the work; to help reach the true meaning of the author's opinions . . ." and so on and so on . . .'

'But this spokesman,' the Pontiff's tone was mild, 'is quite unknown to the author. He is, in fact, forbidden to communicate with him. How can he possibly give an accurate rendering of his opinions, his merits, all the rest?'

'He can do so, Holiness, because he is in exactly the same position as any member of the public reading the book. He rests on the text.'

The Pontiff did not answer directly. He held up two volumes which had been lying on his desk. One was entitled *The Nature of Faith*, the other *The Word Made Flesh*.

'You yourself wrote these, Karl.'

'I did.'

'And you kindly inscribed them to me. I read them with interest. I did not object to them, but I marked certain passages which seemed to me to be obscure, or which could be interpreted as not quite orthodox . . . Now, let me ask you: would you like to have these works judged by the same criteria and by the same secretive, inquisitorial methods as are presently employed?'

'If Your Holiness required it, yes.'

'Would you feel justice had been done or could be assumed or seen to be done?'

'There are, I admit, certain shortcomings . . .'

'Which my predecessors and I have condoned but which I can permit no longer. We can go further if you want. I have a long list of objections. Shall I recite them all?'

'It will not be necessary, Holiness.'

'But it will be necessary for you to understand better, Karl. We, you and I, the rest of our brother bishops, we are the City set on a mountain-top. We cannot hide our deeds, our commission is to be a witness to the world – and if we do not give witness to truth, to justice, to our free search for God's meaning in God's world, then people will call us liars and hypocrites and turn away. We are going to be living very close together, you and I. Can we not be friends?'

'Your Holiness asks me to deny something I have believed all my life.'

'And what is that, Karl?'

'That the doctrine we hold is a treasure beyond price. Our

martyrs died for it. Nothing and no one should be permitted to corrupt it.'

'I have come, by a long road, to another point of view, Karl. The truth is great and it will prevail. We make confession of it every day. But if there are no eyes to see the truth, no ears to hear it, no hearts open to receive it . . . what then? My dear Karl, when Our Lord called his first Apostles, He said: "Come with me and I will make you fishers of men!" Not theologians, Karl! Not inquisitors, not popes or cardinals! Fishers of men! The greatest sadness of my life is that I have understood it so late.'

There was a long and deathly silence in the room. Then Karl Emil Cardinal Clemens stood up and made his own confession of Faith.

'In all that conscience allows, I am at the service of Your Holiness and of the Church. For the rest, God give me light! I beg Your Holiness's leave to go.'

'You have our leave,' said Leo the Pontiff. Even as he said it, he wondered how many others would walk away and how he himself would endure the solitude.

Fourteen

The Old Appian Way was once an imperial highway, that ran south to Naples and across the Appenines to Brindisi. The Romans, courting immortality, lined it with funerary monuments, which were gradually defaced and in part demolished by time and sundry invaders. The Belle Arti put covenants upon the surrounding land, naming it an archaeological zone, where villas might be built only on the sites of existing – structures. Between the battered monuments, the pines grew tall and the grass was lush, so the lovers of Rome turned it into a tail-light alley, which every morning was littered with condoms, Kleenex, assorted underwear and other debris. It was no place to make a promenade or a picnic with the children, but for a population crammed into apartments, with a minimum of privacy, it was a splendid place to make love. Even the highway police were discreet and voyeurs tended to get short and violent shrift.

It was here, just across the road from Omar Asnan's villa, that Marta Kuhn and a male Mossad agent spent ten nights of vigil, plotting the movements of the servants, the dogs and the master of the house. Asnan came home every evening at seven-thirty, driven by his chauffeur. The garage gates opened and closed electrically. A little later, the watchman came out with two big Dobermans on leash. He did not walk them, but trotted them down the grassy verge, across Erode Attico and down the Appia, almost to the ring road. Then he turned back. The whole run took between fifteen and twenty minutes. The watchman let himself back into the villa through the front gate, using a key. Omar Asnan generally went out again at ten-thirty or eleven, returning at one or two in the morning. Agents who picked up his surveillance from the Porta Latina reported that he went to one of two places: the Alhambra Club or an expensive house of appointment on Parioli patronised by Middle Eastern tourists. The only staff at the villa were the housekeeper, the chauffeur and the watchman, who appeared to be the husband of the housekeeper. All were listed in the files of the local carabinieri as Italian residents of Iranian nationality, working under special permissions and paying full local taxes.

Armed with this and other information, Aharon ben Shaul made a personal visit to the International Clinic to talk to Sergio Salviati. He had a special and unusual request.

'I'd like to borrow your medical skills for one night.'

'To do what?'

'Supervise an interrogation. There will be no violence involved; but we'll be using a new Pentothal derivative developed in Israel. It can, however, have certain side effects. In some patients it produces marked arrhythmia. We need an expert to monitor the procedure.'

'Who's the subject?'

'Omar Asnan, mastermind of the Sword of Islam. We're going to lift him, question him and free him.'

'Which tells me nothing.'

'Our sources tell us that he's still planning the assassination of the Roman Pontiff, but that he's sub-contracting the hit to another group, probably Oriental. We've got to get detailed information on who they are and how they operate. Will you help us?'

'No!'

'Why not?'

'Because everything about the suggestion stinks to me. It reminds me of all the bloody perversions our profession has been through in this century: the torture rooms in Argentina, with the doctor standing by to keep the poor bastards alive, the medical experiments in Auschwitz, the confinement of dissidents in Soviet mental institutions, what you're doing now to the Palestinians. I want no part of it!'

'Not even to prevent the assassination of your patient?'

'Not even! I gave the man a new lease of life. After that, he's on his own like the rest of us.'

'If Omar Asnan has sub-contracted, he will have covered the whole operation – including Tove Lundberg, possibly her daughter as well.'

'They're out of the country. Tucked away in the Irish countryside.'

'Which is an easy place to get to and where killings are planned everyday of the week! Come on, Professor! What's this sudden hot flush of morality? I'm not asking you to kill anyone, just to keep a man alive so he can spill his guts about an upcoming assassination. Dammit man! We kept your distinguished patient safe. We lifted the woman who was named to kill him. You owe us – and we're taking a big discount on the payment.'

Salviati hesitated and was almost lost. Then he saw the mantrap.

'Why me? Any half-baked student can monitor a heartbeat.'

'Because we're doing this without the Italians. We need one of our own to help.'

'You forget!' Salviati's anger boiled over. 'I am Italian! Our people have been here for four centuries. I'm a Jew, but I'm not an Israeli. I'm a son of the Law but I'm not a son of your house. In Italy, we've taken all the shit that's been handed to us here down the centuries right up to the final Black Sabbath when the Nazis trucked us out of the Roman ghetto to the death camps in Germany. But we stayed, because we belong, from antique Roman times until now. I've walked a very thin line to help you and to help Israel. Now you're insulting me, blackmailing me with Tove Lundberg. You do your own business your own way. Leave me to mine. Now get the hell out here.'

Aharon ben Shaul simply smiled and shrugged.

'You can't blame me for trying! Funny though! None of this would have happened if you hadn't got caught up in all this *goyische papisterei*!'

When he had gone, Salviati had an angry conversation with Menachem Avriel, who apologised profusely and disclaimed all knowledge of the affair. Then he made a call to Ireland and spoke briefly to Tove Lundberg and, for a much longer time, to Matt Neylan.

Now another word was being bandied about the corridors of the Vatican, and in the private correspondence of the hinge-men of the Church. The word was 'normative', and it had a very precise meaning: 'creating or establishing a standard'. Every prelate knew it. Everyone understood exactly the question which Clemens and his friends were asking: 'What is now to be normative in the government of the Church: the codex of Canon Law, the Acts of the Apostolic See, the Decrees of Synods or the subjective judgements of an ailing pontiff – delivered informally and without consultation?' It was a two-edged blade that cut to the heart of two issues: the value of papal authority and the power of the institution itself to enforce its own decrees. It was precisely this power which the Congregation for the Doctrine of the Faith, formerly the Holy Inquisition, had been established to preserve and reinforce.

From its earliest days the Church had been infiltrated by alien ideas, Gnostic, Manichaean, Arian. Their vestiges lingered still, colouring the attitudes of this group or that – the charismatics, the traditionalists, the literalists, the ascetics. In the first centuries the instruments of purification had been public debate, the writings of the great Fathers, the decisions of Synods and Councils. Then, when imperial power was claimed as an endowment of God through His Vicar, the Pope, all the instruments of repression were available: the crusading armies, the public executioners, the merciless inquisitors, absolute in their conviction that error had no right to exist. What was left at the end of the second millennium was a pale shadow of those powers and it seemed to many a folly to surrender them in favour of a purely humanist conception of human rights.

Leo the Pontiff was made aware of the dissension in his talks with Curial Cardinals about new appointments, but only Agostini was prepared to be totally frank.

'In purely political terms, Holiness, it is a folly for any ruler to surrender any instrument of power, even though he may never see the need to use it. I don't like what you are asking me to do – reduce the powers of Apostolic Nuncios, oblige them to make the local bishops aware of any complaints they make to Rome. I know why you are doing it. I know there are as many causes of friction as there are advantages in the present system; but as a pure matter of political practice, I don't like to let go what I have. I'm like the museum curator who would rather hang on to five pages of a valuable manuscript than see them restored to the whole book in another place!'

'At least you are open about it, Matteo.' The Pontiff gave him a smile of weary approval. 'For a long time I held exactly the same view. This is what Clemens will not accept; I am not, overnight, his enemy or a danger to the Church.'

'He thinks you are.'

'And you?'

'I think you could be,' said the Secretary of State.

'Explain why and how.'

'We begin with a truth. Our Act of Faith, our submission to God, our confession of Jesus as the Lord, is a free act. It is the act which gives us fellowship in the Assembly of

321

believers. The capacity to make the act is a gift. The act is free.'

'And it must remain so. We choose every day.'

'But this, I believe, is where Your Holiness is mistaken. You think that men and women want to be free, that they want to exercise their right of choice. The plain fact of life is that they don't. They want to be directed, they want to be told, they want the policeman on the corner, the bishop in his mitre proclaiming the Good News with authority and certainty. That's why they get dictators. That's why your predecessors ruled like Jove's thunderbolts! They split the world and the Church, but they bespoke power. The risk you run is quite different. You hand the people the first fruits of salvation, the liberty of the Sons of God. To many, as to Clemens, it will taste like Dead Sea fruit.'

'So!' There was winter chill in the Pontiff's voice. 'We are back to the old catchcries: It is not expedient. It is not timely!'

'I am not saying that.' Agostini was unusually vehement. 'I am delivering, as I am obliged to do, a counsel and a warning. But as it happens, I agree with Your Holiness – in principle at least! I read last night, for the first time in many years, the decree of Vatican II on the Dignity of the Human Person. I made myself recite it to fix it in my memory. "Authentic freedom is an exceptional sign of the divine image within man . . . Hence man's dignity demands that he act according to a knowing and free choice." It may be wise to remind our brethren that this is a conciliar document and not a private papal opinion.'

'One wonders why it is necessary to remind grown men of such simplicities!'

'Because, for most of their lives, they never have to address them. They are protected species, living in hot-house conditions. In this allocution, do you propose to say anything about the position of women in the Church?'

'I am working on that section now. Why do you ask?'

'Because it seems to me, Holiness, we're talking to and about only half the world. We're a patriarchal society whose dialogue with its womenfolk is becoming more and more attenuated, less and less relevant. The heads of major states are women. They are legislators and judges and heads of major business enterprises. Our only recognition of their existence is through the Pontifical Commission on the Family, on which married couples serve but which meets only once a year. Women in religious communities are still "protected" by a Curial Cardinal, who is hardly an adequate voice for their interests or concerns. Matrimonial questions, bio-ethical ones, have to be dealt with by women themselves. The question of women priests is still a taboo subject, but it will come more and more into debate and even on biblical and traditional grounds it is hard to see that it is finally closed . . .'

'So far,' said the Pontiff carefully, 'I have reached a point where I admit our inadequacies and our willingness to reach out for remedies. The remedies themselves are not so easy to come by. Look at this place! We are so busy protecting our unchallenged chastity and our reputation as virtuous priests that it is impossible to have a normal conversation, let alone a stroll in the sunlight with a member of the opposite sex! Inevitably we are going to be forced to admit a married clergy in the Roman rite, as we have already admitted it among the Uniats; but even I am not bold enough to broach the question at this moment. But to answer you: yes, I shall be opening the question of women in the Church, and I shall try not to embellish it with too much Marian imagery. The Mother of Jesus was a woman of her time and of her station. That is the essence of her mystery and it needs no fairytales to decorate it.'

Agostini shook his head in wonderment and disbelief.

'There is work for two lifetimes in all this. Why not settle for less and spare yourself some heartache?'

The Pontiff laughed, a free, open sound that Agostini had never heard from him before.

'Why? Because I'm a farmer's son, Matteo. You plough the ground. You harrow it. You cast the seed and what the birds don't eat and the rains don't rot and the mildew doesn't get, is what you have left to harvest. Besides, for the first time in my life, I think, I'm a truly happy man. I'm gambling everything I am and have on the Gospel truth.'

Even Agostini, the pure pragmatist, had not the heart to remind him that, win or lose, the reward would be the same: they would nail him to a tree and watch him die, very slowly.

By a series of Irish progressions – Murtagh, to Murtagh's cousin on his mother's side, from his cousin's wife to her brother, who was known to have connections in the Irish Republican Army and maybe, just maybe, with the Provisionals – Matt Neylan found himself one Thursday morning sitting in the office of Constable Macmanus in the Garda station at Clonakilty.

He came as a recommended man, which meant that his story would be taken for truth – even though he'd be a fool if he took for gospel everything that was told to him. His request was quickly stated.

'I'm an unfrocked priest, as you know; but I'm looking after two ladies who are very precious to certain high persons at the Vatican. One of them's a cardinal, no less, and the other's a grade higher, you might say. I had a call from Rome to tell me we might be getting some unwelcome visitors. So first I'm looking for some advice. What sort of warning can I get if strangers come asking for me? And what can you do to stop 'em getting to me?'

Constable Macmanus was a slowish thinker, but it took him no time at all to give the answer.

'Not a lot, either way. Unless someone asks for you by

name, who's to know whether they're here for the fishing or the tourism or a bit of business investment? We get all sorts in Ireland nowadays: Germans, Dutch, Japanese, the whole bloody colour chart. What can we do to stop 'em getting to you? Nothing, unless they're carrying a banner with "Kill Neylan" printed on it, or a bazooka for which they don't have a licence. You take my point, I'm sure.'

'It couldn't be plainer,' said Matt Neylan agreeably. 'So I'll pass to my next question. Where do I get some guns and the licence to carry and use them?'

'I notice you're using the plural. Why would that be?'

'Because there are two of us who can use 'em, Murtagh and myself. Because I think we should each have a pistol; and, if possible, I'd like a couple of semi-automatics in case there's a sudden surprise attack on the farmhouse itself.'

'Which I hope there won't be. I'd hate to deal with the paperwork for a thing like that . . . Let me think now. Before we go further, you'd be prepared to pay for these items?'

'Unless the Garda wanted to donate them to the cause of law and order.'

'You must be joking!'

'Then, of course, we pay.'

'For the weapons and the licences – and the procurement service of course.'

'One always pays for that,' said Matt Neylan – and was glad the constable seemed to miss the point. 'How long before delivery?'

'Do you have the cash about you, by any chance?'

'No; but I can get it at the bank.'

'Then fine. We'll take a small drive into the country. You can collect the goods and take 'em home with you. And while we're about it, we should get you a dog – a big one, like a wolfhound. A friend of mine breeds 'em. He'd make you a good price.'

'And the licences?'

'I'll make 'em out before we leave and fill in the particulars later. Which reminds me, can you use a typewriter?'

'Sure.'

'Then sit yourself down and type me out a complaint, about person or persons unknown, for threats made against yourself and the ladies. Mention their high connections and the warnings you've just had. Lay it on as thick as you like, and sign it in your best hand.'

'And what's that for?'

'It's called covering your backside, Mr Neylan. Yours and mine. The guns are no problem. There's more than one shipment for the IRA been landed in Clonakilty Bay and there's like to be more yet, so long as the war goes on. But in this little corner of Holy Ireland bodies with bullet holes are very hard to explain. So it's as well to have all the paperwork done in advance.'

'I see that,' said Matt Neylan fervently. 'I see it very clearly.'

Tove Lundberg, on the other hand, did not see it at all. She was aghast at the thought of gun battles in the misty mornings, of blood on the pastures where the placid cattle grazed. She demanded to know: 'What is this, Matt? Some cheap melodrama that is being invented for us? Let's pack tonight and go to Dublin. We can fly from there anywhere we want, change planes, cover our tracks. Who knows or cares where we are?'

'It doesn't work like that,' Matt Neylan explained patiently while Britte listened, nodding and muttering with desperate eagerness to be heard. 'In this game we're demonstration models. Wherever we are, we have to be eliminated to show the power of the Sword of Islam. Do you want to live all your lives in hiding?'

Britte clung to him, signalling desperately: No, no, no! Tove sat immobile, watching them both. Then she thrust herself out of the chair and grasped them both with urgent hands.

'So we fight! Good! In the morning you take me out and teach me to shoot! I refuse to be a spectator any longer!'

The raid on Omar Asnan's villa took place on the sixteenth day of October. This was the manner of it. Omar Asnan arrived home at seven-thirty. Immediately afterwards the watchman came out to run the Dobermanns. Just past Erode Attico, he was overtaken by a closed van which forced him and the leashed dogs against a stone wall. The dogs were dropped cold by anaesthetic darts. The watchman was overpowered by masked men. His eyes, mouth, wrists and ankles were taped. His keys were taken. He was driven, with the animals, to a deserted spot in the pine woods near the sea and dumped there. He was discovered late next morning by a pair of joggers. The dogs were beside him, whining and licking his face.

Meantime, Aharon ben Shaul and three assistants, dressed in black tracksuits and ski masks, entered the villa, overpowered the chauffeur and the woman, drugged them both, then proceeded to deal with Omar Asnan, who was taking a bath before dinner. Naked, shivering and blindfolded, he was taken down to the cellar, laid on the carpet which covered the stone floor and injected with the Pentothal derivative. Forty-five minutes later he had revealed the murder of the Mossad agent and the existence of the underground granary where his body was entombed. He also exposed the nature of the deal with the Korean who had engaged to import one hit team to kill the Pontiff and another to kidnap or kill Tove Lundberg in Ireland. As to how or when the events would take place, Asnan knew nothing. That was the nature of the deal: half the money down, plus expenses, the rest on completion; everything left to the discretion of the hit teams, who could work without fear of betrayal.

It wasn't totally satisfactory, but it was the best they could hope for – and Omar Asnan was already in acute discomfort from the heavy dose of the drug. So they rolled back the carpet, lifted the stone that covered the entrance to the crypt and carried him into the chamber where the antique grain jars were stored. Then, single-handedly, Aharon ben Shaul lifted the small brown body, put it in one of the grain jars and closed it with the lid.

'He'll die,' said one of the assistants.

'For sure,' said Aharon ben Shaul. 'Our friend Khalid died too. That's the law, isn't it? Life for life, limb for limb. Now let's get out of here. There's still work to do upstairs.'

They closed the chamber, sealed and covered the entrance, then systematically burgled the house, carried their booty to the garage in pillowcases and stowed it in the trunk of Asnan's Mercedes. The chauffeur and the housekeeper were still sleeping. Aharon ben Shaul administered an extra shot of opiate, untaped their mouths, loosened their bonds and left them. The intruders drove away in the Mercedes, which was discovered a week later in a disused marble quarry on the road to Hadrian's Villa. Most of Asnan's possessions found their way, by devious routes, to Thieves' Market and were put up for sale to Sunday morning visitors.

The disappearance of Omar Asnan caused a brief ripple of interest among local investigators and certain confusion among his business associates. His servants were rigorously questioned. Their sojourn permits were withdrawn and they were quietly repatriated. The house and the funds in Asnan's bank and the contents of his safe were committed to the care of a procurator appointed by the Republic.

Aharon ben Shaul congratulated himself on a good night's work. He had broken a terrorist ring and eliminated its leader. The Pope could look after himself and Tove Lundberg was outside his bailiwick.

Meantime, since no mention of the proceedings was made in the Press and Hyun Myung Kim was out of the country, two highly efficient teams of hunters prepared to move on their quarry.

The schedule of events for the Consistory – commonly called the *Ordo* – was sufficiently unusual to raise comment among the participants. It would begin at the ungodly hour of eight in the morning, in the new Hall of Consistories in Vatican City. It would open with prayer, the traditional invocation of the Holy Spirit, the Illuminator. His Holiness would announce certain changes in curial appointments. These preludes would finish at eight forty-five, when the allocution would begin. This was timed at one hour. Afterwards there would be half an hour left for questions and comments. At ten-fifteen the cardinals would disperse to vest for the eleven o'clock Mass in St Peter's which His Holiness would concelebrate with six senior cardinals in the presence of the rest of the Sacred College and members of the Diplomatic Corps accredited to the Holy See.

Since nothing was ever done in Rome without a reason, the arrangements were read as a move on the part of the Pontiff to defuse any hasty controversy over his speech, to make a large public gesture of Eucharistic unity and to hold himself available for private audiences over the ensuing days. Their Eminences were informed that His Holiness would be available from five to eight in the evening and from eight till noon on ensuing days, and those desiring audience in private or in groups should register their requests with the Cardinal Camerlengo. Certain sceptics suggested that this was a very good way of counting heads. Certain others called it just another version of *'divide et impera'*: divide and rule.

The simple fact was that for the Pontiff the morning was the only part of the day when he could command a full measure of strength. After a long speech and a very long ceremonial Mass in St Peter's he would be near to exhaustion and would have to rest for at least two or three hours. He knew beyond any doubt that every ensuing conversation with these senior princes of the Church was crucial to his plans. Even a momentary lapse of attention or a flash of irritation could do damage to the grand, but fragile, design. The full extent of his anxiety was expressed only in his diary:

'Of the hundred and forty members of the Sacred College, a hundred and twenty-two will be present at the Consistory; the others have excused themselves on the grounds of illness, age or intolerance of long air travel. All have been in personal contact with me, however briefly, and all are anxious to know the direction my address will take. I have tried to reassure them by describing it as a prologue to a fraternal colloquy on matters of concern to us all. That is what I want it to be, a beginning to open-hearted talks between brothers; but my reputation as an ill-tempered autocrat is too deeply etched in their memories to be erased so easily. So I can only pray – for light and for a golden tongue.

'Gerard Hopgood is proving a tower of strength. Though he lacks Malachy O'Rahilly's wit and bubbling good humour, he is much more solidly grounded in learning and much more confident in his dealings with me. He will not let me shirk an examination of difficult issues in the text. He will not let me take refuge in arguments about expediency and opportunity. He tells me flatly: "It will not do, Holiness. These are all adult men. They cannot have the luxury of papering over the cracks in bad arguments. If you have found the courage to face unpleasant facts, so must they."

'Sometimes, surrounded by pages of heavily scored manuscript, we drink coffee and he talks to me about the tribe of juvenile delinquents whom he is training as athletes. He has a healthy scepticism about his success. The best ones, he tells me, are likely to be hired as purse-snatchers by the criminal gangs who prey on women tourists in Rome; but there are others for whom he and his friend have become surrogate fathers and uncles. However, he adds a shrewd footnote: "I don't have to be a priest to do what I'm doing. I don't have to be celibate either. In fact, it's probably better if I'm not. The point I'm making, Holiness, and I think we should take another look at it in this document, is that we need to define much more clearly the identity of a modern priest, his true vocation in the Church. Believe me, I know what I'm talking about. I know how the casualties start."

'I believe him. I respect him. Let me say it frankly: I have come to love him as the son I never had. I am touched by the small, protective gestures he lavishes on me: Have I taken my pills? I have been sitting too long. I must stand and walk about for a while . . . "Let's take a break and do fifteen minutes' exercise. I know it's a bore, but if you don't do it, you're committing suicide . . ."

'I ask him how he sees his future in the Church. I have the secret thought that one day he will make a splendid bishop. His answer surprises me. 'I'm not sure yet. There are certain dilemmas that present themselves. There's a friend of mine, a priest like me, who works in one of the base communities in a very poor part of Brazil. He couldn't figure out why the womenfolk refused to marry – refused absolutely. They cared for their men, were faithful to them, bore them children, but marriage? No way. Finally, he found out the reason. Once they married they were in bondage. Their men could walk all over them. They could never escape. So long as they didn't marry, they had at least the freedom to walk away from cruelty and take their children with them. I have film of my friend and his bishop – who is also a cardinal, and he'll be here for the Consistory –

administering Communion to these people at a festival Mass. Now I approve that. I'm happy to live and work in a Christian church that lives like that. If it doesn't, then I have to do some very serious thinking."

'This is a revelation which I cannot let pass without comment. I ask him: "How do you justify the administration of the sacraments to people living in formal sin?" His answer comes back instantly: "How do we justify refusing them? And which is closer to the Christian ideal of marriage, a free and caring union in which children are loved and protected, or one that creates a slavery for woman and child?" He laughs then and apologises. "Forgive me, Holiness. You asked. I answered. I don't suggest you make this an issue at the Consistory. You will have enough on your plate already."

'I agree with him; and I note that the Archbishop to whom he refers may well prove a sound ally in the cause I have set myself. As for the quality of the theology involved, I doubt it would recommend itself to Clemens, but at least there must be an open forum within the Church where it can be debated freely and without censure, real or implied.

'So night falls and I am another day closer to the Feast of All Saints. I have a strange dream. I am sitting in the Hall of Consistories looking down at the assembled cardinals. I am speaking to them, although I do not hear the words I am saying. Then suddenly I notice that they have all turned to stone, like courtiers in an enchanted palace.'

Menache, Avriel, Ambassador of Israel to the Republic of Italy, was having a bad day. It was not as bad as some but, in all conscience, bad enough. In the morning, he was invited to a friendly conversation with the Minister for

Foreign Affairs, on matters of mutual interest. It could have been much worse. He could have been summoned. The friendly conversation could have been an urgent conference and the matters of mutual interest could have been questions of singular concern. The Minister was a very urbane man. He liked Avriel. He recognised the usefulness of Israel in Mediterranean affairs. The last thing he needed in the world was a diplomatic incident. So, with infinite tact, he proposed: 'My dear Menachem, we work very well together. Let us continue to do so. This Mossad fellow – what does he call himself, Aharon ben Shaul? – is very heavy-handed. So far, he has been lucky and we have profited from that. Each time he risks a little more. Enough is enough! I would like to suggest – I, personally, not Foreign Affairs – that you ship him out as soon as possible. My friend Agostini at the Vatican agrees with this advice . . . Understand, we are not telling you how to run your business. Send us any replacement you like, provided he has more tact than this one, and we'll accept him without question. What do you say?'

'I'd say it was a very timely suggestion, which I shall take under immediate advisement and refer to my government for instructions. However, my dear Minister, he'll be out of here within forty-eight hours!'

'Please, my dear friend! We do not demand miracles. Seven days would be fine. Even thirty would be acceptable.'

'Forty-eight hours,' said Avriel firmly. 'I always say you should leave the poker table while you're ahead. And so far we're both ahead, are we not?'

'I hope so.' The Minister sounded dubious. 'Will you take coffee with me?'

Back at the Israeli Embassy there was a letter waiting for him. The envelope was embossed with the papal coat of arms and the Embassy sticker noted that it had been delivered by Vatican courier. The letter was handwritten in Italian.

333

Excellency,

I owe you a debt for your personal care for my welfare during my recent illness.

November 1st is the feast day which we call All Saints. It celebrates in a special way the community of all Christian believers with men and women of good will everywhere.

To mark this festival, I shall be celebrating a Mass in St Peter's Basilica at 1100 hours with the College of Cardinals and members of the Diplomatic Corps accredited to the Holy See. Unfortunately, the State of Israel is not yet accredited. However, if circumstances permit, I should like you to come as my personal guest and to take your place among the members of my pontifical household. If this invitation causes you any embarrassment, please feel free to decline it. My hope is that it may prove a first step towards a closer and more formal relationship between the State of Israel and the Holy See. Centuries of unhappy history still divide us. Today's politics ensnare us at every step. But any alliance has to begin with a handclasp.

Mindful always of protocol, my Secretary of State regrets that it is not he who is issuing the invitation, to which, however, he adds his warm personal greetings . . .

Leo

Menachem Avriel could hardly believe his eyes. Decades of drilling and boring and hammering had made no dent in the wall of resistance to Vatican recognition of the State of Israel. Now, for the first time, there was hope that it might be breached. Then, always the diplomat, he asked himself whether there might be any connection between the 'invito' to the Foreign Office and that of the Pontiff. Even the simplest Roman document was a palimpsest, with texts and subtexts and indecipherable fragments laid one upon the other.

When he called Sergio Salviati to share the news, he found that a new refinement had been added to the compliment. Salviati had his own invitation to the ceremony, which he read to Avriel:

> I owe you, my dear Professor, a debt that I can never repay. I write to invite you to join me in a Christian celebration, the Feast of All Saints, which celebrates not only the holy ones in our calendar, but the essential community of men and women of good will everywhere. If the notion embarrasses you, I shall understand perfectly. If you decide to come, you will be seated, along with Ambassador Avriel, among the members of my own household. It would give me great joy to think that, in spite of the horrors of history, you and I could join in common prayer to the God of Abraham and Isaac and Jacob. Always, I wish peace upon your house . . .

Salviati sounded irritable and depressed. He demanded to know: 'Do we go or don't we?'

'I go,' said Menachem Avriel cheerfully. 'Don't you understand what this means?'

'To you, maybe. To Israel, a very big maybe. But why should I roll over because the Pope wants to scratch my belly?'

'I don't know, Sergio!' The Ambassador seemed suddenly bored with the conversation. 'I've got the smell of a big diplomatic coup! All you seem to have is a royal pain in the arse!'

To Anton Drexel, drowsing in the thin autumn sun, a package was delivered: a canvas rolled inside a cardboard tube and, inside the canvas, a letter from Tove Lundberg. The canvas claimed his attention first. It was an interior, executed in a dashing bravura style, of Tove and Matt Neylan drowsing at the fireside, with a wolfhound between them and above, reflected in the mantel mirror, Britte herself, perched on her stool, painting with the brush clenched between her teeth.

The picture told its own story, to which Tove's letter added only commentary and counterpoint.

' . . . Britte wanted very much that you should have this piece. She says: "Nonno Drexel used to say that as an artist grows up, the pictures grow too. This is a happy picture and I want him to be happy with us all!" That's a long speech for her, as you know; but she still needs to share herself with her Nonno.

'Matt has become very important in her life, though in a different fashion. He is – I am searching for the word – very comradely. He challenges her, makes her do always a little more than she is willing to attempt by herself. Before she began this picture, for instance, he sat with her for hours, turning over art books, discussing styles and periods of painting. She has always been frustrated because her disabilities prevent her from working in the finished style of the classic masters. Not that she wants to paint like that, it is a question of being deprived of the capacity. Matt understands this and insists on working through the struggle with her. What surprises me with him is that he distinguishes so clearly the sexual element in her relationship with him, and handles it with enormous care.

'Which brings me, dear Nonno, to Matt and me. I won't ask you to approve, though I know you will understand – and Britte's picture says it – we are lovers and we are good for each other. We are good, too, for Britte. What more can I say? What more, indeed, can I predict? We are still under threat. The Israelis assure us the threat is real. Matt and Murtagh are always armed and there are guns in the house. I have learned to shoot and I can hit a tin can at fifteen paces with a pistol. You see, I talk as if it were a triumph. What a mad world it is . . . Still, this kind of nonsense cannot last for ever. Britte and I look forward to the time when we can visit our Nonno again, and drink the wine of Fontamore.

'Oh, I almost forgot. We had a visit last week from Monsignor Malachy O'Rahilly, the one who used to be the Pope's secretary. Matt and he had quarrelled but they made friends again. He was just out of what he called the "funny farm", where he was taking a cure for alcohol addiction. He looked trim and fit and very confident, though Matt says the priesthood is a dangerous road for a man like him who needs a lot of real family support. We took him touring and fishing. He asked to be remembered gently to you.

'But remembering gently is not enough for Britte or for me. She loves her Nonno very much. I love him too, because he came into our lives at a very important time and opened doors that might have been closed to us forever . . .'

Drexel dabbed at his eyes and wiped the mist off his spectacles. Soon the children would be coming out for their morning break. They would not understand an old man's tears. He folded the letter carefully and put it in his breast pocket. He rolled up the canvas and slid it back into the tube. Then he strode out of the villa grounds and down the road to Frascati, where the Petrocellis – father and son and grandson – still made picture frames for the best galleries in Rome.

Book 4

Lazarus Revocatus

'And Jesus said to them: "The light is among you still. Finish your journey while you still have the light, before the darkness overtakes you." '

John xii: 35

Fifteen

On the twenty-ninth of October, two men and two women in a Volkswagen campervan boarded the ferry from Fishguard in Wales to Rosslare on the south-east tip of Ireland. Their van was hired from a company which specialised in rentals to Oriental tourists.

From Rosslare they drove directly to Cork, where they lodged in a modest, old-fashioned hotel much patronised by coach tours. All that was remarked about them was that they were very polite, spoke passable English and paid in cash. They let it be known that they would use the hotel as their base for a week's tour. One of the men called telephone enquiries and asked for the number of Mr Matt Neylan, a subscriber in the county. Once he had the number it was simple to match it to an address in the directory. A tourist map supplied the rest of the information.

Matt Neylan's address was Tigh na Kopple – Home of the Horses – Galley Head Road, Clonakilty, which put it well off the main road with nothing but open fields between the house and the sea.

So, on the thirtieth of October, in the morning, they did a trial run, identified the house and drove on to Bantry for lunch. In the afternoon they came back the same way. In the garden a girl, grossly handicapped, was painting with a brush held in her mouth. The driver stopped the van. One of the women got out and began to photograph the scene. She was so intent on getting as many shots as possible that at first she did not notice the man standing in the doorway watching.

When she turned and saw him she was totally confused, blushing, stammering, retreating crabwise towards the van. The man gave her a greeting with a big smile and stood waving until the van turned the corner. Then he went inside and made a telephone call to the Dublin number which the Israelis had given him.

A woman answered. She passed him to another woman who assured him she had been fully briefed on the situation, but did not see this incident as cause for panic. A tourist had stopped to take photographs of a girl painting in a garden. What did that signify?

'Possibly nothing. But I can't afford to take any risks.'

'Of course not, Mr Neylan. On the other hand, we can't afford to have essential staff careering around the country chasing moonbeams. You do see my point?'

'I do indeed, madam; but if my people are shot up or kidnapped, what then?'

'We'll send flowers. Officially, that's all we're allowed to do anyway. If anything else untoward happens, please be in touch!'

Which led Matt Neylan to think that someone in Rome had shoved a mighty large spanner in the works. However, Constable Macmanus was rather more helpful. He would 'call around and come back to yez'. Which he duly did and reported that there were two Japanese couples at the Boyle Hotel in Cork. They had driven to Bantry for lunch and had passed the farm going and coming. They were normal as mashed potatoes, no threat to anyone. Four people in a campervan, Orientals at that! How could they stage a crime and get off the island? Relax boyo, relax! Trouble will find you soon enough!

But Matt Neylan was not a believer any more and especially he wasn't a believer in the facile logic of the Celts, who knew

344

with absolute certainty how God ran His world and why it was only idiots and infidels who slipped on banana skins!

The constable was right. Four Orientals in a campervan made a very conspicuous team – so conspicuous, indeed, that everyone who had seen them would swear to it, with absolute conviction. But whether at any one moment there were two or three together, whether one was in the ladies' room or in the bar or had just stepped out to take the air . . . who would know, who would care? In one particular, however, Constable Macmanus was right. If they were planning a kidnap, how the hell would they get off the island with the victim in a campervan? On the other hand, if the kidnap plot had suddenly been upgraded to murder, then the text read quite differently – one or two killers with a back-up of two women to transport them and provide their alibi.

Matt Neylan's imagination was working in high gear. How would they come? When? How would the event be staged? He had never been to war, he had never done police or army training. How far could he trust himself with four lives – because with Britte and Tove there were also the Murtaghs in the cottage. Then he understood that, now or never, this thing must be ended. No one should be forced to live continually under threat. If the only way to end it was by killing, so be it. Let's get the dying over and be done with it. Then, suddenly, he was very angry and he knew beyond all doubt that he was prepared to step on to the killing ground and stay there until the last shot was fired, the last blow struck.

Anger was not enough, however, courage was not enough. He had to choose the killing ground and entice the enemy on to it. The farmhouse, the Murtagh's cottage, the barns and cowsheds were all close to the road, grouped in a rectangle, with the farmhouse as one long side, fronting the road. The cottage and the cow bales formed the two short ends of the rectangle, the barns and storage sheds ran parallel to the main house. The floor of the rectangle was concrete which could be hosed down every day. The buildings were stone, plastered with white stucco and roofed with slate. They were stout enough, but as a defence position they were worse than useless. The barns would burn. A stun grenade or tear gas would turn the house and the cottage into death traps.

Given that he had weapons for close or more distant engagement, they would all be safer in open ground. There were thirty-five acres between the house and the sea, undulating land divided by low stone fences and bordered by a winding path that ran along the cliff edge and down the lower ground to the inlet, where there was a boatshed, invisible from the road. The women could spend the night there while Murtagh and he kept vigil. The assassins would come during the dark, he was sure of that; round midnight or in the small sinister hour before the false dawn. They would park some distance away. The killer or killers would approach on foot.

Just at that moment, Tove and Mrs Murtagh came in with a basket of eggs and a pail of fresh milk. Murtagh was scraping his boots at the door, waiting to be invited in for his evening whiskey. Matt Neylan gathered them round him, poured the drinks and made his announcement: 'I haven't a shred of proof, but I feel in my bones that we're going to have trouble tonight. So here's what I'm proposing . . .'

In Rome, at seven o'clock that same evening, Monsignor Gerard Hopgood laid the final text of the allocution on the Pontiff's desk and announced: 'That's it, Holiness. I've checked every last comma. Now, with great respect, I suggest you get out of here and give yourself a quiet evening. Tomorrow's going to be a heavy day.'

'You mustn't worry, Gerard.'

'I do, Holiness. It's my job to keep you on your feet, with a clear mind, a good text and an air of total confidence. By the way, I've told your valet to shave you at six-thirty in the morning and to trim your hair a little.'

'And you didn't think that was presumptuous?'

'I did, Holiness; but then I thought I'd rather risk your wrath and have you looking spruce at the Consistory. If you'll pardon another presumption, we have a very elegant text and it merits a very elegant spokesman.'

'And that, my dear Monsignor Hopgood, bespeaks a very worldly view.'

'I know; but Your Holiness is going to be addressing some very worldly-wise people. They pay you homage and obedience; but they still remember that they are the princes who elected you and who, had you not survived, would have elected another in your place!'

It was the boldest speech he had ever uttered and there was a reproof on the tip of his master's tongue. It remained unspoken, because Hopgood himself was instantly penitent.

'I'm sorry, Holiness. That was impertinent; but I am concerned for you. I am concerned for the work which you are beginning so late in life. I'm another generation. I see the need for it, I feel the hope in it. I see how easily it can be misrepresented and hindered. Please forgive me.'

'You're forgiven, my son. I know as well as you that our elders are not always our betters; and although in the past I have often exacted it, I no longer believe that obedience should be blind. Your real fault is lack of trust in God. It isn't easy to commit to Him. It's like stepping out of an aeroplane without a parachute. But when you have to do it as I did – not knowing whether I was going to live or die – suddenly it seems the most natural thing in the world. We still have anxieties, the adrenalin still pumps to make us ready, like all animals, for attack or defence. But the essential calm remains, the conviction that, alive or dead, we never fall out of the hand of the Almighty . . . What are you doing for dinner tonight?'

'I'm entertaining my friend, Father Lombardi. He's the one

347

who runs the athletic club. He's been having a bad time lately with his parish priest, who's also having a bad time because he's getting over a stroke and his housekeeper has left . . . So Lombardi needs a little cheering up.'

'Where are you eating?'

'At Mario's. It's just round the corner from the Porta Angelica. I'll leave the number with the switchboard in case Your Holiness needs me.'

'I shan't, Go and enjoy yourself with your friend. I'll see you here at six in the morning.'

When he had gone, the Pontiff lifted the telephone and called Anton Drexel at his villa. They had agreed that Drexel, now wholly retired, should not attend the Consistory. However, a number of the visiting prelates had already telephoned him for a private reading of the situation. The Pontiff was interested to know their frame of mind. Drexel described it.

'They are puzzled. They cannot quite come to terms with the idea of a personal change in you. Clemens, I fear, has let his ill-humour get the better of him. He has presented a picture of you as a quasi-heretic, or at least a risky eccentric, which his colleagues find equally hard to accept. So, on balance, you have the advantage. Everything now depends on your allocution. Are you circulating copies?'

'No. I thought it better not to do so. I am explaining the document as a presentation of my views, an invitation to comment on them and as a prelude to a *motu proprio* on certain of the major subjects. That has to bring responses, for and against.'

'I agree. As soon as I get any comments, I'll relay them to Your Holiness.'

'I appreciate that, Anton. How are you feeling?'

'Lonely. I miss my Britte. She sent me a beautiful canvas, and her mother wrote a very newsy letter. They are still under threat – which bothers me a lot; but there is nothing effective I can do, Neylan is looking after them very well.

348

But the question does arise, Holiness: how effective is your own security?'

'About as good or bad as it ever was, Anton. St Peter's will be filled to overflowing tomorrow morning. People will be milling around the square. Who can control a crowd like that in a building so enormous? In a sense, the token presence of security men is as effective as that of a whole detatchment of armed men who couldn't use their weapons anyway. Believe me, I am very relaxed about the whole affair.'

'Our children are offering their prayers for you.'

'That's the best protection I can get. Thank you, Anton. Thank them, too, for me. Which reminds me. Some time in the near future, I'm going to send my new secretary out to you, Monsignor Gerard Hopgood, the Englishman. It turns out he is a very good athlete who trains a youth club out on the Flaminia. He also has experience with athletic activities for the handicapped. If he is interested and apt for the work at the colonia, he might provide both the impulse and the means of continuity . . . I should hate to lose a good secretary; but I owe you a debt, my friend. I should like to find a suitable way to repay it.'

'You owe me nothing, Holiness.'

'We shall not argue about it, Anton. Pray for me tonight.' He gave a small, wry chuckle. 'I have just read Monsignor Hopgood a homily on trusting God. At this moment I need it more than he does!'

Just before nightfall, Murtagh put out the big milk cans for collection by the co-operative, then moved all the cattle into a paddock midway between the house and the rim of the cliff. Neylan took the women down to the boathouse and settled them with food, blankets, a kerosene heater and the wolfhound and a shotgun for company. Britte was fretful and out of sorts, complaining of the cold and a headache. Tove signalled to Neylan to leave. She would cope better without him. Then he and Murtagh dressed themselves for a cold, long night, made sandwiches and a thermos of coffee, loaded their weapons and drove the Range Rover and the new car into the shadow of the wind-break on the western edge of the property.

Matt Neylan laid out his plan.

'. . . which isn't a plan. It's just what we've got to do any way we can, drop 'em dead in their tracks, but on this property, not outside it. Don't have any illusions now! These are hired killers. They don't fight by Queensberry Rules. They'll know all the martial arts and they'll be fast as cats on their feet. So you can't let 'em get within reach of you . . . And we've got to get 'em all, you understand? Otherwise those that are left will keep coming after Tove and Britte. Do you read me now?'

'I read you; but for a priest you're a bloody-minded bugger, aren't you?'

'A priest I'm not; but bloody-minded, yes. Now let's try to think how they'll come and what we've got to stop 'em.'

'If you're bent on total elimination, then I think I can help you.'

'I'm listening, Murtagh!'

'When I was younger and sillier, and before my wife threatened to leave me, I used to do occasional jobs with the Provos – not for money, mind you, but because I believed in the cause . . . What I was good at was booby traps and ambushes. But after a while it got to me. It wasn't fun any more, just bloody dangerous. Are you understanding me now?'

'I'm understanding you, Murtagh, but I wish to God you'd come to the point.'

'The point is that if you'll go draw off a few gallons of petrol from the drums in the store and then help me fiddle with the electrics, then I think we can give our visitors the surprise of their lives.'

'I don't want 'em surprised,' said Matt Neylan flatly. 'I want 'em dead.'

'They will be,' said Murtagh. 'The booby traps will distract 'em long enough for a killing volley. You'll be up there in the barn. I'll be in the byre.'

'I hope you're not going to burn the bloody house down.'

'No . . . There'll be a little scorching maybe. Nothing a dab of whitewash won't cover. But you'd better pray for a good eye and a steady hand. One burst is all you'll get to bring the buggers down . . . Are you ready?'

'As ready as I'll ever be. All I was taught was priestcraft and statecraft. Neither of them is worth a tinker's curse at this moment.'

'Then think of the child and the women down in the boathouse. That'll steady your nerves. What time do you reckon the bastards will come?'

'Not till after midnight, when the pubs are closed and the roads are quiet.'

'That gives us time enough. Get the petrol now. Use a couple of milk pails. Set one by your own back door, the other by the kitchen of the cottage. I'll need some flex and a pair of pliers and a screwdriver . . .'

Huddled in the boathouse, with a cold wind searching through the cracks and the surf pounding on the shingle, Tove Lundberg and Mrs Murtagh kept vigil over the ailing Britte. She slept fitfully, tossing and mewing. Tove held her hand and wiped the clammy sweat from her face, while Mrs Murtagh fingered her rosary and clucked helplessly.

'She needs a doctor.'

'I know she does.' Tove had learned long since that if you argued with Mrs Murtagh, she would retreat like a rabbit to a burrow and you lost her for hours on end. 'Matt will come for us when it's safe. Just relax now and say a prayer for us all.'

Mrs Murtagh was silent until she could bear it no longer. Then she asked: 'What is it with you and Matt Neylan? Are

351

you going to marry him? If you're not, you're wasting your life, which no woman of your age can afford to do.'

'All the more reason not to make a mistake, wouldn't you say?'

'It seems to me there's been a lot of mistakes already: you with this poor child and no husband to share her with, Matt Neylan with that great career in Rome. They were expecting him to be a bishop one day. Did you know that? And now look at him! Out of the cloth! Out of the Church altogether and every day in danger of damnation!'

'I'm sure God understands him better than we do, Mrs Murtagh.'

'But to throw away all the grace he's been given! Why, only last Sunday Monsignor O'Connell – that's our parish priest at Clonakilty – was preaching on the same thing, rejection of grace. He said it's like refusing a lifebuoy in a raging sea . . .'

'My father was a pastor too, Mrs Murtagh. He used to say: "Men and women close the door on each other, but God's door is always open."'

'Your father, you said?'

The notion of a married priest was too complicated for Mrs Murtagh and in any case vaguely obscene. It was one of 'those Protestant things'.

'Yes indeed. His people loved him.'

'But you left your church too.'

'Like Matt, I found I couldn't believe – not, at any rate, in the way I'd been taught. So I did the only honest thing I could see. I walked away.'

'Into a lot of trouble,' said Mrs Murtagh tartly.

'But that's not the point, is it? If the only reason you hang on to God is to keep yourself out of trouble, what sort of religion is that?'

'I don't know,' said Mrs Murtagh fervently. 'But let me tell you, I'm glad I've got my beads in my hand at this moment.'

Britte gave a sudden sharp cry of pain and woke up in panic. Her mother tried to soothe her, but she clapped her hands to her head and rolled from side to side, moaning. Her eyes turned inward and rolled upward in their sockets. Tove sat beside her and cradled her in her arms, while Mrs Murtagh sponged her face and crooned over her: 'There now, there! The hurt will pass soon.' Outside, the wind made an eerie keening and the pounding of the surf sounded like tramping feet on the shingle.

They came an hour after midnight, all four of them, two from the east and two from the west, masked and dressed from head to toe in black, trotting silently on the thick grass of the verge. When they reached the corners of the property, they stopped to take their bearings. Then one from each pair moved towards the front of the house. The other two vaulted the front fence and moved forward until they were level with the barn. Then they turned inward and moved to face each other. When the manoeuvre was completed there was a black figure standing motionless and scarcely visible at each corner of the rectangle of buildings.

Next, they began to move slowly and silently in a clockwise direction round the perimeter. As each one came to the next corner, they all stopped. They did not speak, but signalled their observations. One pointed to the cows in the far pasture. Another noted the shadowy masses of the vehicles parked against the trees. A third pointed inward to the enclosed courtyard.

Finally, reassured that the outer perimeter was clear, they stepped into the courtyard, two moving towards the back door of the cottage, two towards the kitchen entrance to the house. Before their hands touched the woodwork the lights over both doors came on. There was a sudden billow of flame as the pails of petrol caught fire and all four were cut down by enfilading fire from the barn and the cow-byre.

*

Neylan went into the house to telephone Constable Macmanus. He was with them in ten minutes, but it took an hour and a half to get the Garda and an ambulance out from Cork and another hour to make the appropriate depositions and get rid of them. Murtagh drove the Range Rover down to the boathouse to collect the women. When finally they returned to the house, Britte was chattering with fever. They telephoned the local doctor, who prescribed aspirin and ice-packs and promised to call at nine in the morning. By five she was delirious and screaming with pain. They bundled her into the car and, while Tove nursed her in the back seat, Neylan drove as fast as he dared to the Mercy Hospital in Cork. By the time Britte was admitted, she was in coma. A specialist, summoned in haste, pronounced the verdict.

'Fulminating cerebro-spinal fever. It occurs most frequently in adolescents and adults. Diplegics like your daughter fall easy victims. This form is malignant. The mercy is that it runs a swift course. Already, she is terminal.'

'How long?' asked Matt Neylan.

The doctor looked at his watch.

'I doubt she'll last through midday.' To Tove, standing stricken but tearless at the bedside, he offered a small crumb of comfort. 'In her case there may be a special mercy. She will be spared a great deal of grief.'

Tove seemed not to have heard him. She turned to Matt Neylan and said, with strange detachment:

'Nonno Drexel will be terribly upset.'

Then, mercifully, the tears came, and Matt Neylan held her to him, rocking her and crooning over her. 'There now! There! Cry it out. The little one's fine. She had the best of it. She'll never know the worst.'

Even as he said it the irony hit him. In the old days he would have found a dozen homely words of religious comfort, the standby of grieving folk down the ages. Now they were gone from him and all the love he wanted to pour on Tove Lundberg was the poorer for it. He was finding it much harder than he had expected to come to terms with an indifferent universe.

In the Hall of Consistories, Leo the Pontiff stood to address the assembly. Now the moment was upon him he felt strangely calm. His princes had come to him one by one to offer their ritual homage. They had prayed together for light to see and courage to walk the pilgrim road together. He had read them the admonition of St Paul to the Corinthians: 'It is only through the Holy Spirit that anyone can say Jesus is the Lord. The revelation of the Spirit is made to each in a particular fashion for a good purpose . . .' Then he had announced the appointments in a simple, bald statement.

This was the old Leo speaking, the one who disposed of embarrassing business and embarrassing people in short order. As he laid the text of the allocution before him on the rostrum, he wondered how they would accept the new Leo – and, for one brief frightening moment, whether the new Leo was not, after all, an illusion, the figment of a disordered imagination. He thrust the thought away, breathed a silent prayer and began to speak.

'My brothers . . . I speak to you today in the language of the land where I was born. Indeed, you will hear sometimes in my speech the country accent of my home-place.

'I want to explain to you the man I once was, Ludovico Gadda, whom the older ones among you elected to rule the Church. I need desperately to explain the man I am now and how he is different from the old Ludovico Gadda. It is not an easy story to tell, so please be patient with me.

'I once asked a distinguished biologist to explain to me the genetic imprint, the famous double helix which differentiates one being from another. He called it "the graffito

of God", because it can never be erased. All other imprints
– of memory, environment, experience – he called "human
graffiti". Let me try to decipher for you the marks which I
bear.

'I was born to poor people in a hard land. I was an only child
and, as soon as I could handle a mattock and a hoe, I worked
with my mother and my father. My life was a cycle of labour:
school, farm work, study by lamplight with my mother. My
father dropped dead behind his plough. My mother put herself
into service with a landowner to complete my education and
make me ready for a career in the Church. Understand this: I
make no complaints. I was loved and protected. I was trained
and toughened for a life without concessions. The one thing
I never truly experienced was tenderness, the gentleness of
leisured intercourse. Ambition – which is only another name
for the instinct to survive – was always at my back, hurrying
me forward.

'For me, life in the seminary and in the Church was an
easy experience. I was accustomed both to study and the
harsh disciplines of a peasant farmer's life. Even my adolescent passions were damped down by fatigue and isolation
and the undemonstrative relationship between my parents. So
you see, it was very easy for me to accept without question
– and let me say it frankly, without critical examination –
the maximalist and rigorist interpretations of law, morals and
biblical exegesis which were current in the clerical education
of the day.

'So there you have me, dear brothers, the paradigm of
the perfect cleric, the way open before me to a bishopric,
a Curial appointment, a place in the Sacred College. No
scandal could be breathed about my private life. My teaching was as orthodox as Aquinas, of whom I was the most
diligent copyist. Step by step, I was being initiated into the
political life of the Church, the exercises that prepare a man
for power and authority. Some of you here sponsored me

through that initiation and finally elected me to the office which I now hold.

'But something else was happening to me and I lacked the wit to see it. The small springs of compassion in my nature were drying up. The capacity for affection and tenderness was withering like the last leaves of autumn. Worse still, the desert climate of my own spiritual life was mirrored in the condition of the Church. I do not have to describe to you what has happened, what continued to happen. You read it every day in the reports which come to your desks.

'Let me tell you how I judge my own part in the failure. I was, I thought, a good pastor. I enforced discipline among the clergy. I would not compromise with the libertine spirit of the times. I would not countenance any challenge by scholars or theologians to the traditional doctrines of the Church . . . I was elected to rule. A ruler must be master in his own house. So I thought. So I acted, as you all know. And therein was my great mistake. I had forgotten the words of our Lord: "I have made known to you all that my Father has told me and so I have called you my friends . . ." I had reversed the order of things laid down by Jesus. I had set myself up as a master, instead of a servant. I had tried to make the Church, not a home for the people of God, but an empire for the elect and, like many another empire builder, I had turned the green land into a dusty waste from which I myself could not escape.

'What happened next, you all know. I was admitted to hospital for bypass surgery. This intervention, which is now very common, with a very high success rate, is known to have a profound psychological effect on the patient. This is the experience I wish and need to share with you. It reaches far back into my childhood and is connected with St John's narrative of Jesus raising Lazarus from the dead. You all know the story by heart. Think, if you can, of the effect

357

of that narrative on a small boy, brought up on the fireside ghost stories of country folk.

'As I grew up, it raised more and more questions in my mind, all of them couched in the terms of the scholastic theology in which I had been trained. I asked myself had Lazarus been judged, as we should all be judged by God at the moment of death? Did he have to risk another life and another judgement? Had he seen God? How could he bear to be torn back from that beatific vision? How was the rest of his life coloured by the death experience?

'You see where we are, my brothers? In all but the fact of dying, I went through the Lazarus experience. I want to explain it to you. Bear with me now, I beg you. If our minds and our hearts cannot meet on a matter of life and death, then we are truly lost and wandering.

'I do not propose to weary you with sick-room reminiscences. I want to tell you simply that there comes a moment when you are aware that you are about to step out of light into darkness, out of knowing into unknowing, without guarantee of return. It is a moment of clearness and stillness, in which you know, with strange certainty, that whatever is waiting to receive you is good, beneficent, loving. You are aware that you have been prepared for this moment, not by any action of your own, but by the gift of life itself, by the nature of life itself.

'Some in this room will remember the long process against the distinguished Jesuit, Father Telhard de Chardin, suspected of heresy and for a long time silenced within the Church. In my zeal as a young cleric, I approved what was done to him. But – here is the strange thing – in that still clear moment before the dark, I remembered a sentence de Chardin hand written: "God makes things make themselves."

'When, like Lazarus, I was recalled from the darkness, when I stood blinded by the light of a new day, I knew that my life could never be the same again.

'Understand me, dear brothers, I am not talking miracles or private revelations or mystical experiences. I am talking about *metanoia*, that change in the self which takes place, not in contradiction to, but precisely because of, its genetic imprint, the graffito of God. We are born to die; therefore, in some mysterious way, we are being prepared for dying. In the same fashion, we grow towards an accommodation with the greatest mysteries of our existence. Whatever I am, I know that I am not an envelope of flesh with a soul inside it. I am not Pascal's thinking reed with a ghostly wind whistling through me.

'After the change I have described, I was still myself, whole and entire, but self renewed and changed, as the desert is changed by irrigation, as a seed is changed into a green plant in the dark earth. I had forgotten what it was like to weep. I had forgotten what it was like to surrender oneself into caring hands, to rejoice at the sight of a child, to be grateful for the shared experience of age, for the comforting voice of a woman in the dark, painful hours.

'It was then – so late in life! – I began to understand what the people need from us, their pastors, and what I, who am the Shepherd over all, had so rigidly denied them. They do not need more laws, more prohibitions, more caveats. They act most normally and most morally by the reasons of the heart. They are already imprinted with the graffito of God. They need a climate of love and compassion and understanding in which they can grow to their full promise – which, my dear brothers, is the true meaning of salvation.

'Let me tell you, without rancour, the sad reproach addressed to me by a priest who is fighting a lonely battle to remain in the ministry. "You're the Supreme Shepherd, but you don't see the sheep – only a vast carpet of woolly backs stretching to the horizon!"

'I laughed, as you are laughing now. He was and is a very amusing man; but he was telling me a bitter truth. I was not a shepherd. I was an overseer, a herder, a judge of meat or wool, anything but what I was called to be. One night before I went to sleep I read again the first letter of St Peter, in whose shoes I stand today:

"'Be shepherds to the flock God has given you. Do it, as God wishes it to be done, not by constraint, but willingly, not for sordid gain, but generously, not as a tyrant, but setting an example to the flock."

'The lesson was clear, but how I should apply it was not clear at all. Look at me! I sit here, a prisoner in one square mile of territory, shackled by history, barred by protocol, hedged by cautionary counsellors, surrounded by all the creaking machinery of government which we have constructed over the centuries. I cannot escape. So, I must work from inside my prison-house.

'After much prayer and searching of conscience, I have decided to embark on a programme to reform the Curia itself. I want to make it an instrument truly serviceable to the people of God. The appointments I announced today are the first step in that programme. The next is to set the norms by which we shall be guided. I will state them for you now. The Church is the family of believers. In a more profound symbolism, it is a body of which we are all members and of which our Lord Jesus Christ is head. Our care must be for one another in the Lord. Whatever does not contribute to that care, whatever inhibits it, must be and will be abolished.

'I propose to begin with the Congregation for the Doctrine of the Faith, whose high and holy charge is to keep pure the teaching transmitted to us from Apostolic times. The Congregation has been reformed and renamed several times by recent pontiffs. However, I am forced to conclude that it is tainted beyond remedy by its own history. It is perceived still as an inquisition, an instrument of repression, a tribunal of denunciation within the Church. Its procedures are seen to be secretive and some of them are fundamentally unjust. So long as that image exists, the Congregation does more harm than good. We have been given, all of us at baptism, the liberty of the children of God. In this family, therefore, there should be no question which it is forbidden to ask, no debate which it is forbidden to hold so be it with love and respect, because in the end we all bow ourselves under the outstretched hand of the same Lord who bade the raging seas be still, and they became quiet.

'There have been too many occasions in our history, dear brothers – too many in mine! – when we have claimed to establish a certainty where no certainty existed or indeed exists now. The last word has not been spoken by our venerable predecessor on birth control. We cannot contemplate with equanimity the explosion of human population on the earth and man's ravaging of the limited resources of the planet. It is idle and hypocritical to urge sexual control as a remedy on people living at the farthest edge of survival. We must not attempt to fabricate revelations which we do not have. We must not impose, for the sake of expediency or seeming moral order, solutions to human problems which raise more questions than they answer.

'Especially we must be deeply respectful and careful of our entry into that sacrament from which we have – for good or ill – disqualified ourselves, the sacrament of matrimony and all that pertains to it in the commerce of men and women. Often it seems to me we should rather seek counsel than give it in human sexual relations.

'These are only a few of the reasons why I wish to begin our reforms with the Congregation for the Doctrine of the Faith, because it is there that the necessary debate is inhibited and arguments taken out of the public forum and buried in a private one.

'Let me tell you, in this meeting of brothers, I hold with an iron grip to the ancient symbols of faith, those credal truths for which our martyrs died. I hold also to another certainty – the certainty of doubt, the certainty of not knowing, because

361

the most insidious of all heresies was that of the gnostics who claimed a special pathway into the mind of God. We do not have that knowledge. We seek it in the life and teachings of the Lord, in the traditions of the Fathers and – let us be very clear on this – in our own expanding experience which we, please God, will hand down to other generations.

'We are not a fortress Church. We are a Church of witness. What we do and say must be done in the light. I know what you will tell me: that life today is lived under the scrutiny of television cameras and enquiring journalists and commentators eager for sensation. We are therefore vulnerable to misquotation and misinterpretation. So, I remind you, was our Lord and Master. It is in this spirit of openness and charity and with prudent care, that I propose to examine all the functions of the dicasteries. The process will be set in motion by *motu proprio*, which will be issued before the end of the year.

'However, there is one matter which must be settled now. It is not mentioned specifically in the *Ordo*, but time has been allowed for it. You will remember that the day before I left for the hospital, I told you that my abdication was already written and that you, the members of the Sacred College, would be free to judge whether I were competent to serve any longer as Pontiff. You have seen me. You have heard me. What I offer you is not a challenge, but a choice which you must make in good conscience. If you believe I am unfit, then you must accept my abdication. There will be no drama. I will step down at the time and in the manner you deem appropriate.'

He held above his head a folded document, so that everyone could see the large pendant seal attached to it.

'This, written in my own hand, is the instrument of abdication. *Placetne fratres?* Do you accept it?'

There was a long moment of dead silence, then Cardinal Agostini gave the first answer: '*Non placet*. I do not accept.'

After that there were no voices, only a long, continuous clapping; but in so large a room and so mixed a gathering, it was hard to know who was applauding and who was consenting to the inevitable.

The applause was still going on when the door opened and a prelate from the Secretariat of State summoned Agostini to the telephone.

Anton, Cardinal Drexel was calling from Castelli. His message was curt.

'Neylan called me from Ireland. In the small hours of this morning there was a terrorist attack on his farmhouse. Two men, two women, believed to be Japanese. Neylan and his manager killed them. He believes that there may be an attempt today on the Holy Father's life.'

'Thank you, Anton. I'll talk immediately with the Holy Father and the Vigilanza. Anything else?'

'Yes. My Britte is dying. I've been trying to contact Professor Salviati. I'm told he's attending the Pontiff's Mass.'

'I'll try to get a message to him. Also I'll tell His Holiness. Where can Neylan be contacted?'

'At the Mercy Hospital, Cork. I'll give you the number . . .'

But there was no time left for courtesy calls. The Vigilanza had to be put on red alert and the Pontiff informed. The chief of security shrugged helplessly and pointed to the swelling crowd in the Basilica.

'What do you expect me to do, Eminence? We've got fifty men here; twenty down the nave, ten in the transept, fifteen around the high altar, five on the walkway around the dome.'

'There are four camera teams on scaffolding, all aiming their cameras at the High Altar. What about them?'

'All their papers are in order. They've been cleared by Social Communications. The Japanese have also been cleared by your people at the Secretariat of State. We've checked all the equipment. What more can we do?'

'Pray,' said the Secretary of State. 'But if anything happens don't, for God's sake, close the doors. Let 'em out; let 'em run free, otherwise this place will become a slaughter yard. Meantime, call your colleagues at the Intelligence centre and tell them the news.'

'What about the Israelis?'

'They're out of the picture. The Ambassador will be here this morning as a personal guest of the Pontiff. For the rest, they'll be no help any more. Their number one Mossad man here has been shipped home.'

'In that case, the Vigilanza will do its best; but you should pray very hard, Eminence! And we'd better have an ambulance standing by.'

The Pontiff himself was rather more relaxed.

'At Mass I am the perfect target. Most of the time I am in the centre of the altar. But before we begin I shall tell the Master of Ceremonies that my deacons and sub-deacons must stand as far from me as possible. We can literally conduct the ceremony at two arms' length from each other. No one will notice.'

'We could cancel, Holiness. There is still thirty minutes before Mass. We could begin now to clear the Basilica.'

'To what purpose, Matteo? *Ut Deus vult*. It is as God wills. By the way, I have not thanked you for your vote of confidence at the Consistory.'

'It was a vote for the man, Holiness; not necessarily for the policies. They still have to be tested.'

'And you think they will not be? My friend, we shall be ground like wheat between the millstones; but it will be as God wills it to be.'

It was only then that Agostini remembered to deliver the second part of Drexel's message.

'The child, Britte Lundberg, Anton's adopted grand daughter, is dying. We are told she will not last the day.'

The Pontiff was visibly shaken. His eyes filled with tears. He reached out to Agostini and held his arm to steady himself.

'All of this, all of it, comes back to me. My life was bought with all these other lives. It's too much Matteo! Too much!'

It was mid-morning on the Feast of All Saints when Britte Lundberg died in the Mercy Hospital in Cork. Her mother's outburst of grief was terrible to see. All her controls seemed to snap at once, and she threw herself on the bed, sobbing and weeping and babbling endearments to coax the child back to life. When the nurse and one of the Sisters came in and tried to calm her, Matt Neylan waved them away.

'Leave her be! She'll work through it. I'll look after her.'

Then, quite suddenly, it seemed all her grief was spent. She kissed Britte on the lips, arranged the body decently on the bed and drew the covers over it. Then she went into the bathroom. A long time later she came out, pale but composed, with her hair combed and her make-up repaired. Only her eyes betrayed her. They were unfocused, staring into desert distances. Matt Neylan held her for a long time and she seemed to be glad of the comfort, but there was no passion left in her. She asked vaguely: 'What do we do now?'

'We call an undertaker,' said Matt Neylan. 'If you like we can bury her in the cemetery at Clonakilty. We have a family plot there. She would lie next to my mother.'

'That would be nice. I think she'd like that. She loved you, Matt.'

'I loved her.'

'I know. Could we go for a walk?'

'Sure. I'll just stop by the desk and make a couple of phone calls. Then we'll stroll in the town.'

'Another thing, Matt.'

'Anything.'

'Could we have a priest to bury her? Not for me, not for you, of course; but I think Nonno Drexel would like it.'

'It'll be done. Let's go now. She doesn't need us any more.' Their walk took them past the post office, where they sent separate telegrams to Cardinal Drexel. Tove's read: 'Dearest Nonno Drexel. Your beloved granddaughter died this morning. Her illness was mercifully short, her passing peaceful. Do not grieve too much. She would not want it. I will write later. Much, much love, Tove.'

Matt Neylan's message was more formal.

'Your Eminence will wish to know that Tove is working through her grief. Britte had a happy life and her last conscious words were of her Nonno. She will be buried according to the rites of the Roman Church in my family plot at Clonakilty. If I have any problems with the parish priest, which I doubt, I shall invoke the name and rank of Your Eminence. If you would like to propose an epitaph for her headstone, I shall commission a good carver to execute it. My deepest sympathies in your sad loss. Matt Neylan.'

When he had written the telegram, he turned to Tove and said: 'I called the Vatican and asked them to pass on a message to Salviati, who is attending the Pope's Mass. Don't you think you should send him a personal message?'

'I should, yes.'

She pulled a new form towards her and wrote swiftly.

'Dear Sergio. Britte died peacefully this morning. I am sad, confused and happy for her all at once. It is too early to say what will happen now, or where I shall go. Meantime, Matt Neylan is looking after me. He's a good man and we are comfortable together. Love, Tove.'

If Matt Neylan was disappointed at such passionless praise, he gave no sign of it. The girl who accepted the telegrams pointed out that, because of the difference in time zones, they would not be delivered in Italy until the following day, which would be the Feast of All Souls, the Day of the Dead.

The Basilica was packed to the doors. The diplomats and their wives were all seated. The clergy were assembled, row on row, in their appointed places. The security men were at their posts. The camera teams were perched on their platforms, aiming and focusing on the Altar of the Confession, under the great baldacchino where the Pontiff and his senior cardinals would concelebrate the Mass of All Saints.

The air vibrated with the murmur of thousands, against which the organ tones reverberated in a thunderous counterpoint. In the sacristy the celebrants were vesting, while the Master of Ceremonies moved discreetly in the background, murmuring his last directions to the acolytes. The Pontiff himself was already clothed. They had brought him a chair and he sat, eyes closed in meditation, waiting for the ceremonies to begin.

Now, truly, he was afraid. There was no comfort against a violent death, no merciful anaesthesia, no solace of human kinship, no dignity at all. He was being stalked now, as in olden times his rivals had stalked the King of the Woods, to kill him and take possession of the shrine. The fear was not in the dying, but in the manner of it, the unknown 'how', the unguessable 'when', the nameless 'who'. He had a sudden, heart-stopping vision of his assassin standing, veiled like Lazarus, against one of the pillars of the baldacchino, waiting to offer a final greeting.

He tried to dispose himself for the encounter, and the only way he could do it was by an act of abasement to the will of the unseen Creator in whose cosmos both killer and victim had their place and purpose. He forced himself to frame the words, silently, with his lips: *'Fiat voluntas tua . . .* Let thy will be done. No matter how randomly, no matter with what seeming horror and inequity, let it be done. I surrender, because I have no other recourse.'

Then, by some trick of association – or by some small mercy of distraction – he thought of Tove Lundberg, keeping the deathwatch over her child in that far, misty land which the Romans called Hibernia. Hers was another kind of agony and there were refinements to it at which he could only guess.

Neylan would probably understand them better. He had found the universe so irrational a place that he had abandoned all belief in an intelligent creator. Yet he of all people was behaving with courage and dignity and compassion.

What he could not ask for himself, he could beg for them. He prayed for Drexel, too, caught in the last sad irony of age. He had opened his heart to love and now, in the twilight years, he was to be robbed of it.

There was a touch on his shoulder and the voice of the Master of Ceremonies whispered: 'It is time to begin, Holiness.'

From his post near the Diplomatic Corps, the Chief of Security watched every move of the Pontiff and his concelebrants at the altar and listened to the laconic reports that were radioed every minute from the strategic watch points round the Basilica. From the dome, everything looked normal; down the nave, normal; the transept, normal . . .

They were at the Preface now, the prayer that introduced the central Eucharistic acts. The choir, in full voice, chanted the doxology: 'Holy, holy, holy Lord God of Hosts, heaven and earth are full of Your glory . . .'

The radio reports continued: baldacchino, normal. Transept normal . . . But the big danger points in the ceremony were yet to come: the Elevation, when the Pontiff stood in the centre of the altar and raised the consecrated elements high above his head for the adoration of the faithful, and the moment just before the Communion when he raised the host again and pronounced the final words of praise.

The Master of Ceremonies was following his orders precisely, isolating the Pontiff whenever possible so that, even if he were stricken, casualties would be minimal. It was a terrible irony. Just as the ritual victim was being offered on the altar, the living, breathing target was offering himself to the assassin.

Installed among the members of the Papal Household,

Sergio Salviati and Menachem Avriel managed to carry on a whispered conversation under the sound of the chanting. The Secretary of State had made contact with them both and given a hurried version of the news from Ireland. Avriel wanted to know: 'What will you do about Tove now?'

'Write to her, call her.'

'I thought . . .'

'So did I once. But it was over before she left. Nobody's fault. Too many ghosts in our beds, that's all.'

'So take my advice. Give yourself a break. Come to Israel.'

'I know the rest of it. "We'll find you a nice, bright Jewish girl and . . ." So I'll try it. My junior surgeons are doing good work. Morrison will come down and hold their hands. Where are we now in the service?'

Menachem Avriel pointed to the place in the text and explained in a whisper.

'This is their Passover narrative.'

'How do you know?'

'I read. I study the native customs, which is what diplomats are trained to do. Be quiet now. This part is very sacred.'

The Pontiff was reciting the first formula of consecration: 'While they were at supper, He took bread, blessed it, broke it and gave it to His disciples, saying: "Take this, all of you, and eat it; this is my body which will be given up for you."'

In the murmurous hush that followed, the Pontiff raised the white wafer above his head while the vast congregation bowed their heads in homage. The Chief of Security held his breath. With his arms raised high above his head, the Pontiff was a perfect target. When he lowered them, the Chief gave a long exhalation of relief. The first danger point was passed. Then the Pontiff bowed over the altar, took the gold chalice in his hands and recited the words that consecrate the wine:

'In like manner, He took the cup of wine. He gave thanks,

offered the cup to His disciples and said: "Take this, all of you, and drink from it. This is the cup of my blood, the blood of the new and everlasting covenant which will be shed for you and for all men, so that sins may be forgiven. Do this in memory of me.'"

Again he raised his arms, displaying the consecrated element for the adoration of the people.

It was then the bullet hit him, tearing a hole in his chest, toppling him backwards so that the liquid spilled over his face and vestments, mingling with his life blood.

Epilogue

His Eminence, Karl Emil Clemens, Cardinal Camerlengo, was a very busy man. The See of Peter was vacant and until a new pontiff was elected, it was the Camerlengo who administered the office under the trusteeship of the Sacred College. This time there would be no confusions, no mistakes. He ordered a post-mortem examination and requested that it be performed by the Chief Medical Officer of the Roman Comune in the presence of three medical witnesses, among them Professor Sergio Salviati, surgeon to the Pontiff.

Their findings were unanimous. Death had been caused by a high velocity, hollow-nosed bullet of large calibre, fired from an elevated position. It had ruptured the heart and gone on to shatter itself against the vertebrae, diffusing fragments through the thoracic cavity. Death was instantaneous. This was consonant with the findings of investigators called in to assist the Vatican Corpo di Vigilanza. They found that the sound boom used by the Japanese film team was in fact an elongated rifle barrel which gave extraordinary accuracy to the projectile. However, by the time his equipment had been examined, the boom operator had disappeared. Evidence was given that he was, in fact, a Korean, born in Japan, who had been hired as a freelance. The other members of the team were held for questioning but finally released into the custody of the Japanese Ambassador, who arranged for their immediate departure.

The Pontiff's body was not exposed during the Lying-in-State. The three coffins – one of lead, which carried his coat of arms and enclosed the certificate of death, one of cypress and one of elm – were already sealed and the obsequies were abridged for fear, the newspapers said, of further episodes of violence. After the first waves of shock-and-horror stories, the memorials that were published about Leo XIV were muted, too. They spoke of him as a stern man, unbending in discipline, a model of rectitude in his private life, of zeal in his care of the pure tradition of the Faith. Even Nicol Peters noted coolly: 'There were public demonstrations of reverence, but none of affection. This was a kind of Cromwell in papal history – a man of the people who failed to reach their hearts . . . There were strong rumours that after his illness he was a changed man, preparing a major shift in policy; but since, according to custom, all his papers are taken into the hands of the Camerlengo, we shall probably never know the whole truth.'

Two medals were struck. One for the Camerlengo and one for the Governor of the forthcoming conclave at which the new pontiff would be elected. New Vatican coinage was minted and new stamps printed, bearing the words 'sede vacante'. The front page of *Osservatore Romano* carried the same words and a big black border.

Meantime, the Cardinal Camerlengo had taken possession of the papal apartments, the keys thereof and all their contents, including the Pontiff's diary, his will, his personal papers and effects, as well as the contents of his office files. Monsignor Gerard Hopgood assisted the Camerlengo in these mournful duties and, because he seemed a sensible, discreet and scholarly fellow, the Camerlengo suggested that he remain where he was until the new pontiff was elected, when he could help to induct the new staff. Meantime, he should think about another appointment, for which he could count on a very good recommendation. Which was why, on a cold and blustery Sunday in November, he took himself off to Castelli to visit Cardinal Drexel.

The old man was stooping a little now. The spring had gone out of his walk and when he made his rounds of the garden and the farmlands he carried a walking stick. Yet he still maintained his robust view of men and affairs. When Hopgood mentioned the suggestion made by the late Pontiff that he might work at the villa, Drexel brushed it aside: 'Don't waste your life on it. It was a short-term affair anyway – a personal indulgence of mine, going nowhere. We did some good things, helped a single small group, but it is clear to me now that to make this into a viable enterprise one would need huge money, much public support – which is hard to come by in Italy – and a nucleus of trained staff, even harder to find. You want to use your heart and your head and your muscles? Go out to the emerging countries – Africa, South America . . . Europe is too fat and too prosperous. You will stifle here – or turn into a Vatican mouse, which would be a pity.'

'I'll think about it, Eminence. Meantime, may I ask some advice?'

'On what?'

'An opinion I have: that small justice is being done to the memory of his late Holiness. Everything that is being published emphasises the reactionary period of his reign. Nobody mentions that he was on the verge of making great and historic changes, as you must have known.'

'I knew it, yes.' Drexel was giving nothing away.

'I should like to write a tribute to his memory, a portrait of the new man he had become. I should like' – he approached the subject very gingerly – 'to publish and, indeed, interpret some of his last papers, including his address to the Consistory.'

'Unfortunately,' said Drexel with tart humour, 'you do not have title to them.'

'I believe I do.' Hopgood was quite firm. 'Look!'

He fished in his briefcase and brought out two volumes

bound in leather. The first and larger one consisted of hand-written notes and typescripts scrawled with corrections. The second was the text of the Pontiff's address to the Consistory. Both carried the same inscription:

To
my beloved Son in Christ
Gerard Hopgood
who lent me these words
to interpret my hopes and my plans.

Leo XIV, Pont. Max.

'As I understand it,' said Hopgood cheerfully, 'copyright inheres in the author of the words and in the form of the words. And, lest it should be claimed that I wrote them as an employee or donated them as a gift, His Holiness was very careful to use the word lent.'

Drexel thought for a moment, then laughed with genuine enjoyment.

'I do like a thorough man. Very well! Here is my advice. Get your appointment settled. If you're prepared to go to Brazil, I can recommend you to my friend Kaltenborn, who is Cardinal Archbishop of Rio. Then when you're far from Rome and your bishop is pleased with your work, publish your piece – and give the money to your mission, so no one can accuse you of base motives.'

'Thank you, Eminence. I shall do as you say, and I should be most grateful for a recommendation to Cardinal Kaltenborn.'

'Good. I'll write it before you leave. Strange how God arranges things! His Holiness gained a son. I lost a grand-daughter. I'm running out of time. He had years of useful work ahead of him. I'm still here. He's dead.'

'I keep asking myself' – Hopgood's tone was sombre – 'how much the Church has lost by his death.'

'It has lost nothing!' Drexel's voice rang, loud and startling, through the vaulted chamber. 'On Vatican Hill, pontiffs have come and gone through the centuries, saints and sinners, wise men and fools, ruffians, rogues, reformers, and even an occasional madman! When they are gone, they are added to the list which began with Peter the Fisherman. The good are venerated; the bad are ignored. But the Church goes on, not because of them, but because the Holy Spirit still breathes over the dark waters of human existence as it did on the first days of Creation. That is what sustains us, that is what holds us together in faith and love and hope. Remember St Paul! "No man can say Jesus is Lord unless the Spirit moves him." He broke off as if suddenly embarrassed by his own vehemence. 'Come now, you must try a glass of my own wine. I call it Fontamore. You'll stay to supper, I hope? Good friends of mine are coming in on the evening flight from Ireland. They tell me they have a pleasant surprise for me.'

A List of Morris West Titles Available from Mandarin

While every effort is made to keep prices low, it is sometimes necessary to increase prices at short notice. Mandarin Paperbacks reserves the right to show new retail prices on covers which may differ from those previously advertised in the text or elsewhere.

The prices shown below were correct at the time of going to press.

☐	7493 1771 X	**The Ambassador**	£4.99
☐	7493 1772 8	**The Big Story**	£4.99
☐	7493 1835 X	**Children of the Sun**	£5.99
☐	7493 1840 6	**Daughter of Silence**	£5.99
☐	7493 1071 5	**Harlequin**	£3.99
☐	7493 0495 2	**Lazarus**	£5.99
☐	7493 1384 6	**The Lovers**	£4.99
☐	7493 0699 8	**McCreary Moves In**	£3.99
☐	7493 0700 5	**The Naked Country**	£3.99
☐	7493 1074 X	**The Navigator**	£5.99
☐	7493 1072 3	**Proteus**	£3.99
☐	7493 2073 7	**The Ringmaster**	£5.99
☐	7493 2068 0	**The Salamander**	£5.99
☐	7493 1770 1	**The Second Victory**	£4.99
☐	7493 1769 8	**The Shoes of the Fisherman**	£4.99
☐	7493 1773 6	**Summer of the Red Wolf**	£4.99
☐	7493 1768 X	**The Tower of Babel** ·	£4.99

All these books are available at your bookshop or newsagent, or can be ordered direct from the address below. Just tick the titles you want and fill in the form below.

Cash Sales Department, PO Box 5, Rushden, Northants NN10 6YX.
Fax: 01933 414047 : Phone 01933 414000.

Please send cheque, payable to Reed Book Services Ltd., or postal order for purchase price quoted and allow the following for postage and packing:

£1.00 for the first book, 50p for the second; **FREE POSTAGE AND PACKING FOR THREE BOOKS OR MORE PER ORDER.**

NAME (Block letters) ....

ADDRESS ....

....

☐ I enclose my remittance for ....

☐ I wish to pay by Access/Visa Card Number

Expiry Date

Signature ....

Please quote our reference: MAND